ALL THAT WE HAVE LOST

SUZANNE FORTIN

HEAD
ZEUS

An Aria Book

ALSO BY SUZANNE FORTIN

The Forgotten Life of Arthur Pettinger

First published in the UK in 2021 by Head of Zeus Ltd
This paperback edition first published in 2022 by Head of Zeus Ltd,
part of Bloomsbury Publishing Plc

9 7 5 3 1 2 4 6 8

A CIP catalogue record for this book is available from the British Library.

ISBN (PB) 9781800243781
ISBN (E) 9781800243774

Head of Zeus
5–8 Hardwick Street
London EC1R 4RG
www.headofzeus.com

Printed and bound by CPI Group (UK) Ltd, Croydon, CR0 4YY

*To the village of Lizio and the many untold acts of everyday defiance,
bravery and sacrifice.*

ONE

1944

Papa always told us that to be brave doesn't mean you have no fear, it just means you can move forwards in spite of that fear. I never truly understood what he meant when I was younger. It wasn't the sort of fear of being told off for arguing with my younger brother, Pierre, or for being late getting up, or for daydreaming of playing my flute in an orchestra when I should be concentrating on my schoolwork. No, that's not the sort of fear Papa meant. He was talking about the fear that makes the heart race, that quickens the pulse, makes sweat gather in the armpits and the hairs prickle on the back of the neck. The fear that bunches up the stomach, tightens itself, so there is a constant feeling of sickness, almost a pain.

It was four years ago, when I was fifteen years old, that the fear came and took root. I was at my friend Monique's house and we were practising our flutes for school summer concert. The sun was shining, a gentle breeze lapped at the net curtain of the open window and the birds were singing in the garden as if harmonising with our music. We were both so excited, not to mention proud, to be playing a duet in the concert. Although Monique was two years older than me, we had bonded over our love for music and both dreamed of one day playing before an audience in places like Paris, London, Vienna, in fact, all over the world.

'*Bravo! Bravo!*' Monique's mother clapped her hands as we finished our piece. 'Excellent!'

In that moment, that second in time, all was well in our small little world of living in rural Brittany where the threat of war was something the grown-ups spoke about without much conviction and where life went on at its usual sedate pace. In the next moment, the next second, our world collapsed and the fear took up residency. A fear that would stay with us for the next five years.

Monique's father burst into the dining room, his face ashen. 'Paris has fallen!' He strode across the dining room and turned on the radio.

Monique's mother gasped, her hand going to her chest, as she sank into the chair.

I lowered my flute as I looked from one adult to another. That was when the fear became real.

Two days later, the town of Rennes, less than eighty kilometres away, was bombed and after that the German Wehrmacht marched through Brittany. As a region, we became the occupied part of France and life was to become harsher than we could ever have imagined.

That fear became a constant and unwanted companion, never leaving. Always sitting there on our shoulders, whispering in our ears, invading our thoughts and breaking our hearts. Every action and every decision made with a nod to the fear in our aim to survive.

I was reminded of that moment again, four years on, as I wheeled my bike out of the back gate with my flute case sitting in my basket. I had been granted a permit allowing me the use of a bicycle, as I needed to collect eggs from the

Devereaux farm for Maman to sell in the shop and to deliver food, mainly to the elderly residents of the village who were housebound. My bike had once been in pristine condition but with spare parts so scarce, it was impossible to maintain it. The chain regularly slipped off and the tyres were bald, but I had no intention of giving up this small privilege.

It was a Sunday afternoon and Maman was resting on her only day off from running the family grocery shop. Although these days, it wasn't much of a shop, with more empty spaces than there was produce as France balanced precariously on the cliff edge of famine.

I liked to get out of the apartment as often as I could and on Sundays usually went to see my dear friend, Monique, where we would play our flutes and let our imaginations take us away to filled concert halls, standing ovations and freedom.

The alleyway from the back of the shop led out to the main road and as I reached the junction, I noticed a new poster had been pasted to the wall. The Germans were fond of plastering the village walls and shop windows with propaganda images, depicting German soldiers mixing happily with the French. The worst ones though, were calls for neighbours to spy on each other and report any suspicious activity of flouting of the rules, with the offer of extra rations as a tempting reward.

This new poster by the Reich to try to win over the trust of my fellow countrymen was of a German soldier standing with some children – all smiling at each other. I could feel the anger stir within me. This was such a lie. It was an absolute distortion of the truth. The soldiers were no friends to us; in fact, they seemed to relish their disdain for us, almost as much as we despised them.

I checked all around to make sure no one was watching and slowly slid my hand up the wall. My fingers picked at the top edge. Another quick check to make sure there were no witnesses to the crime I was about to commit. With one swift movement I tore my finger down the poster, slashing right through the middle, letting the ripped paper flutter to the ground. It was then I heard a car engine rev up and across the road a German car pulled out from its parking space, with two German officers in the front.

My heart thundered against my breastbone as I hopped on my bike, trying to casually ride away from the crime scene. How had I not spotted them in the car?!

I had pedalled no more than a few metres when a voice shouted out. 'Hey! Stop! Hey, you on the bike!'

My heart almost leaped out of my chest there and then. I daren't ignore the order to stop. What little brake pads were left ground and squealed against the rim of the bicycle wheel before I came to a halt. On the other side of the road was a café, which the German soldiers liked to frequent and, on this bright sunny morning, several were already enjoying the somewhat reluctant hospitality of the owner. I stared straight ahead, trying to keep my breathing under control, gripping the handlebars tightly to stop my hands from shaking.

Footsteps approached and as I feared, a German officer appeared at my side. 'Didn't you hear me calling you?' he asked. His French was good despite the German accent.

'I'm sorry,' I replied, avoiding eye contact.

There was a small silence, which confused me. I was expecting him to demand to know what I had been doing or say he'd seen me tear the poster but there was nothing. Slowly, I turned my head to look at him and was surprised to see a softness in his features. I hesitated, transfixed by his rich blue eyes. He was several inches taller than me and his hair so blond, it was almost white. I could see he wasn't as old as I expected, maybe in his mid-twenties.

'You dropped this.' He held out a piece of paper and for a moment I thought it was the poster but what I saw was a sheet of music. My music. It must have blown out of my basket without me realising. He gave a small smile. 'Vivaldi. *Le Quattro Stagioni*. A very nice choice, if I may say so.' He offered the music again.

'*Merci*,' I replied taking it from him and pushing it back into the basket of my bike.

'Spring is my favourite one. I take it you play?' He nodded towards the flute case.

'*Oui*.' I looked at the case with my treasured flute. It had been given to me as a gift from my beloved father. It had been his as a child and he'd passed it on to me, teaching me to play as he had himself. As I became more accomplished and greedier to learn more, my parents had paid for me to go to Madame Brun, the local music teacher, for more advanced tuition. I had walked so proudly through the village on my way to the lessons with the flute case in my hand every Saturday afternoon. Tragically, Papa had died several years ago from a heart attack and I missed him every day but his passion for music lived on within me and every time I played, I thought of him and how pleased he'd be. I suddenly felt protective towards my flute.

'Is that where you're off to now? To play your flute?' the German Officer asked.

'*Oui*,' I replied again. I'd had it drummed into me over the years of the occupation never to offer any more information than what was asked.

I don't know whether he sensed the reluctance on my part but he went to say something and then stopped, before giving a small nod. 'Well, then I won't detain you any longer. *Au revoir, mademoiselle*.'

And with that he went back to his car and drove off, leaving me a trembling wreck. The audience of soldiers across the road went back to their drinks as they realised there was no sideshow to entertain them.

With as much composure as I could muster, I climbed back on my bike and cycled past the café and on past the *mairie* – the town hall – where the swastika flags flew in place of the French tricolore and where a framed picture of Hitler, hanging in the centre of the foyer, could be seen through the open doorway. I wanted to spit at it but knew better. There was a difference between bravery and stupidity.

As I rounded the corner, Trédion Château came into view. It was once regarded as the jewel in the village, the sixteenth century building much admired by everyone who saw it. Now, however, since the Germans had requisitioned it, the magic had disappeared. No longer a jewel but an ugly piece of architecture adorned with Nazi flags, abused and disrespected by the officers who now occupied it.

TWO
2019

Four-forty-five on a Friday afternoon was the time of week Imogen Wren dreaded the most. Hated it some weeks. It was when the rest of the team at the interior designers where she worked, would begin winding up their projects for the week. Web browsers closed, work saved, swatches of fabric tidied away, whiteboard cleared of the week's completed tasks, desk lights switched off and email out-of-office automated replies activated. Everyone would be chatting about their weekend plans, what takeaway they were having, who they were meeting up with, where they were going and, of course, the question Imogen dreaded most. It came most weeks and she braced herself for it.

And there it was. Cally, who sat on the other side of the office and was the unofficial social secretary, called out her name. 'Imogen!' Reluctantly, Imogen looked up and, with a rehearsed questioning look, waited for Cally to continue. 'Are you coming over to The Duke for a quick drink?'

'Not tonight, thanks. I've got a couple of things I need to get finished,' replied Imogen. It was handy being a team leader as it meant no one asked too many details about what exactly she had to do, for fear of being given extra work themselves, nor could they tell her to leave it until Monday or to delegate her workload.

'You sure? Not even just for one?'

'I'll see how I get on.' Imogen smiled at her colleague, hoping that was the end of the conversation. She returned to her computer screen where she was mocking up a 3D image of a newly fitted out family room for one of her clients. It wasn't that Imogen disliked her colleagues, but more to do with just not feeling like socialising. It was easier to avoid awkward conversations where she scratched around for any noteworthy input and the need to appear life was just wonderful in a world where she had moved on from the loss of her husband four years earlier.

Her mobile phone bleeped and went into low-power mode. There was a text message from her sister, Meg, asking if she wanted to pop in for supper that evening. Going to Meg's was easier than going out with her work colleagues and she tapped a quick reply saying she'd be there at around seven. It also meant she had a legitimate excuse now for not calling in for that late drink with Cally and the others.

Imogen realised she'd left her phone charger in her locker and thought she'd best charge up her phone while she had the chance.

The office was quiet now, with most staff leaving before the official five o'clock finish, having come in early, worked their lunch or calling to see a client on the way home. The latter code for: 'I'm knocking off early, it's Friday!'

As she opened the door to her locker, she could hear the voices of Cally and a couple of the other women from the office filter through the open window. Imogen didn't pay much attention until she heard her name mentioned. Suddenly, she was on high alert.

Cally was talking. 'Yes, I asked Imogen, as I always do and, as always, she said no.'

'She never comes. I don't know why you bother.' It was Marcie, one of the other designers.

'Why's that?' This time it was Daisy, the new receptionist who started working there last week.

'Because she's all work and no play. She's always first to arrive in the office and last one to leave. Barely takes a lunch break,' said Marcie. 'I don't think she's ever been on a social in all the three years I've worked here. She's like a robot. Devoid of any ability to socialise outside of the work setting. We call her The Android.'

Imogen straightened up at this revelation. The Android? She had no idea she had a nickname.

'I had noticed she was a bit… erm… starchy,' said Daisy.

'Yeah, she's not the type to let her hair down and have a good belly laugh. Bit of a killjoy,' Marcie replied.

'She never used to be like that,' said Cally.

Imogen felt a disproportionate amount of gratitude for Cally's small defence of her. She could smell cigarette smoke waft in through the window as the three women carried on their conversation, oblivious to her eavesdropping. She really should just go. It didn't pay to hear what other people said about you, but for some reason, Imogen found herself rooted to the spot.

Cally continued. 'Her husband died suddenly. Must be about four years ago now. Dropped dead on the spot with an undetected heart condition.'

'Bloody hell,' muttered Daisy.

Imogen's throat constricted and a pain shot through her heart as the turn in conversation startled her. It wasn't that she never thought about James; she thought about him every day but mostly of him in life, rarely in death, as that was just too painful. So to hear someone else say it so… so matter of fact, it was like picking the scab off a barely healed wound.

'I had heard that,' said Marcie. 'She doesn't ever talk about it though, does she?'

'No. I like Imogen, but she's not been the same since James died,' said Cally. 'Plus she's had a couple of miscarriages.'

Imogen winced at the second matter-of-fact comment made about her personal life. She was surprised at how much it hurt. She also hated being the topic of office gossip.

'Oh, no. She's really been through it,' said Daisy. 'My sister had a miscarriage and it took her ages to get over it.'

'Imogen used to be really good fun. We both started working here within a few months of each other,' said Cally. 'She was a good laugh then. Poor thing. Can't imagine what I'd do if all that happened to me. Oh, look there's Babs.'

'Come on, Babs, the pub will be shut at this rate!' called out Marcie.

The conversation changed to what drinks they were going to have and their voices faded away as they picked up their straggler and headed on to the pub.

Imogen gazed without focus into the depths of her locker. So, now she knew why there was a saying about eavesdroppers never hearing any good of themselves. She had no idea the other women in the office felt that way about her. Sure, she kept herself to herself but she was always polite and friendly – just not overly friendly. She didn't realise she was thought of as a killjoy. What was it, Marcie said? The Android.

Imogen took her phone charger from the locker and went back to her desk, unexpectedly hurt at the tag. It was true she did come in early and leave late, but she loved her job and during the week, she didn't have anything else to stay home for or rush home to. Work was a safe place where she could immerse herself in a project and not have to come up for air unless she wanted to. Most days, she didn't want to.

Try as she might to push the overheard conversation from her head and concentrate on her work instead, it was no use. In the end Imogen gave up and left work earlier than intended. She made sure she walked the long way around to the car park so she'd avoid having to pass The Duke where Cally *et al* would be. The last thing she wanted right now was to be hauled in for a drink. Although, she was pretty sure none of them really wanted The Android cramping their style at the bar.

Imogen pulled up outside her sister's house over thirty minutes early, but she knew it wouldn't be a problem. Meg, although graced with the family superpower of being organised, was also exceptionally laid-back. A superpower that Imogen appeared to have lost somewhere in the past four years.

'Hiya!' said Meg brightly when she answered the door. She gave her watch a quick glance. 'Come on in. All OK?'

'Yes, fine. I finished what I was doing and didn't want to start something else,' replied Imogen, trying to sound casual.

Meg's small raise of her eyebrows told Imogen she wasn't fooling her older sister. Before she could be interrogated, however, the thundering of feet on the stairs as her nephew and niece raced down saved her.

After some excited hugging and squealing, with five-year-old Noah and seven-year-old Leah, Imogen managed to extract herself and follow Meg down the hallway to the kitchen cum family room at the back of the house.

Supper with the Saunders family was always an enjoyable occasion and Imogen's brother-in-law, Howard, was such a good sport and always seemed genuinely happy to see her. Never once did she feel she was in the way or had outstayed her welcome.

After they'd eaten, Imogen helped Meg bath the children and get them ready for bed.

'Can you read us a story tonight, Aunty Immy?' asked Leah.

'Of course, it would be my pleasure. What's it tonight? *The Lost Bear*?' Imogen went over to the bookshelf. She loved spending time with her nephew and niece and for the most part revelled in being aunty to them. Sometimes, though, it was bittersweet. How many times had she envisaged a scene like this for herself and children of her own? Something she'd taken for granted once upon a time but not anymore. Not after losing two babies. The second miscarriage coming just weeks after James's death when she was four months pregnant had been particularly difficult to come back from. Her only consolation was imagining their babies were wherever James was now and he had them cradled in his arms. She shook the thought away.

'I can read them a story tonight if you don't fancy it,' said Meg.

'No. I'll do it. I want to.' Imogen smiled at her sister. 'Go downstairs and finish that wine off with Howard. I'll be down once these two are settled.'

Meg gave her sister a hug. 'OK, sweetie.'

Three stories later and an impromptu singsong, Imogen finally managed to settle the two children and went downstairs to join her sister.

'Noah is already asleep and Leah can barely keep her eyes open,' she said, flopping down in the chair.

'Ah, thanks. You're like the child whisperer,' said Howard. He got up and stretched, following it up with a yawn. 'Think I'll just have a quick look at something for work and then I'll have an early night. Leave you two to put the world to rights.' He leaned down and gave Meg a kiss. 'Night, babe.' As he walked behind Imogen's chair on his way out of the room, he reached over and squeezed Imogen's extended hand. 'Night, Immy. Nice to see you.'

'Night, Howard.' Imogen smiled at him fondly as he disappeared out the room. She turned to Meg. 'He's so sweet but a rubbish actor.'

Meg laughed. 'He did his best. Bless him.'

'He might just as well have held up a neon sign saying, "I'm leaving the room so my wife can grill you."'

'Not grill you,' said Meg. 'Just check in with you to make sure you're OK. You don't seem quite yourself tonight. You're not a very good actor yourself.'

Imogen let out a sigh and put her head back, closing her eyes for a few moments, before sitting up again. 'Am I boring?'

'What?!' Meg put her glass of wine on the coffee table. 'What sort of question is that?'

'A genuine question, as it happens.'

'No. No, you're not boring. Genuine answer.'

'Workaholic?'

'A little. What's brought all this on?'

Imogen looked over at her sister. 'Apparently, my secret nickname at work is The Android… No. Don't laugh. It's true.'

'I guess it could be worse,' said Meg, giving her sister a sympathetic smile.

'True. But it's also true I do nothing other than work. I don't go on any of their nights out. I'm not part of their Friday Afternoon Pub Club.' She inwardly winced again as she recalled the conversation.

'Do you want to do all that?' asked Meg.

'Not especially.'

'What's the problem then?'

'I think once upon a time I would have done. I would have been right in there, amongst it all, having fun, being fun.' Imogen picked at the cuff of her jumper. 'I think I've forgotten how to do and be all of those things.'

Meg moved across the room and sat on the arm of the chair. She took Imogen's hand in her own. 'There's nothing to stop you doing all that but only if you want to. If it's not what you really want to do, then it will be fake and it won't make you happy. Having said that, there's also no harm in trying.'

'I'm scared,' admitted Imogen. 'What if I can't find that person I used to be?'

'You'll never be that person because so much has happened and events change us but the thing that makes us unique, makes you unique, is still in there. It's part of your DNA. What fundamentally makes you you, it hasn't gone anywhere. It's just buried under a load of shit.'

Imogen squeezed her sister's hand. 'It's a big heap of shit.'

When Imogen arrived home, she was still brooding over the evening and what had happened at work. For some reason, she just couldn't shake off the feeling of disappointment. She was disappointed with herself. How had she let herself get to this point where the only places she went were work, her sister's, her parents' and to see James's mother, Denise? She didn't have any particularly close friends, not local anyway. She kept in touch with her two uni mates but even that contact had dwindled to Christmas cards, birthday cards and Imogen liking their Facebook posts. That was, of course, one-way traffic as Imogen didn't post on Facebook and her Instagram account was really an advertisement for her work. There wasn't anything personal on there. There was nothing for others to interact with. She didn't do anything – that was why.

She made herself a hot chocolate and sat down on the sofa, switching on the TV more for background noise, just so she didn't sit in silence. With no conscious decision, she found herself tapping the Facebook app on her phone.

As if taunting her, Facebook chose that moment to throw up some memories. Great. Just what she needed. She could cut her life into two distinct parts. Before James's death and after. Here she was on Facebook in full technicolour living her before life.

This particular memory was of her and James taking a selfie standing at the edge of Lac de Guerlédan in Brittany. It had been a wonderfully hot summer's day and they had congratulated themselves every day of their holiday on picking the right week to visit France.

Imogen got up and went over to the bookcase and, tilting her head, looked at the spines of the several scrapbooking journals lined up. She'd been big on scrapbooking in her before life, never in life after James though. No one needed to record the utter grief and heartbreak so they could look back at it in years to come, just to relive those days when life couldn't possibly be any darker and the future looked an impossible fantasy. Locating the right one, she sat back down on the sofa and began to flick through the pages.

Oh, she missed him so much. She missed herself too. Just looking at the photographs, her little annotations, sometimes just a few words, other times several lines or even paragraphs, describing the day and what they'd done. The joy of their life jumped right out of the pages. They'd always had fun, or at least that's how she remembered it.

As Imogen turned another page, two loose postcards slipped down onto her lap. One was of the castle at Josselin and the other a cartoon map of the Morbihan region in Brittany. She didn't remember putting them there and when she turned them over, Imogen was surprised to see James's handwriting on the back.

Life is on the other side of fear, read one and the other: *Follow your dreams; they know the way.*

Unexpected tears swamped her eyes as she thought of the dream she and James had. One of those whimsical conversations where they imagined buying a place in France, moving there permanently and running their own B&B or vineyard. They'd fallen in love with the region and even spent their honeymoon there.

What if they had moved to France? Would things have been different? Would someone have picked up on James's heart condition? Would he have got medical treatment? Would he still be alive today? Would she have kept the second baby had she not fallen to pieces in the wake of losing James?

She indulged herself in the lost hopes and dreams. And then as it often did, the anger came. The outrage at the injustice on James's part. He didn't deserve to die aged just twenty-nine. That wasn't supposed to happen.

The tears dried, as they always did, but Imogen felt something else settle within her. A sense of purpose she hadn't felt before. A defiance towards herself, the person she'd allowed herself to become. James would hate to see her now; she knew that and she felt embarrassed. Why hadn't she noticed Imogen Wren had morphed into The Android?

She stood up, for no other reason than she felt suddenly energised. She went over to the mantelpiece and ran her finger over a framed photograph of her and James, taken on a beach in the Vendée – another one of their French adventures. They promised themselves many more adventures in France. Imogen realised she was still holding the two postcards from the scrapbook. She reread James's words. If she was the romantic, spiritual type, she'd swear James was sending her a message.

Message or no message, she wasn't going to let him down. Imogen Wren needed rescuing and only Imogen Wren could save her.

THREE

1944

After the poster incident, I knew I had to be even more careful and I kept a low profile, not venturing out much. It wasn't until the end of the week Maman finally confronted me. It had been a busy day in the shop, the queue had been long and the food was becoming more and more scarce, which caused the customers to be even more disgruntled than usual. Although they knew it was not our fault, as shopkeeper poor Maman had to deal with some of the more unpleasant women who took out their frustrations on her.

'Surely you have some flour somewhere?' asked Madame Oray, a villager who had five children to feed and whose husband was a prisoner of war in Germany. 'How can I feed my children if I can't even make bread?'

'I'm sorry, Celine, but I really haven't got any more until next week.' Maman had tried to console her.

'I don't suppose you ever go hungry,' retorted Madame Oray. She looked over at me. 'She's not exactly a bag of bones.' There were a few murmurings of agreement and sympathy from the other women waiting in line.

'Now, Celine, that's not fair,' Maman replied. 'I have just

the same rations as everyone else.'

Later that day, after we had closed, Maman gave me a brown paper bag. 'Take this to Madame Oray,' she said. 'But don't let anyone know.'

I looked in the bag and there were several ounces of white flour. 'Where did you get this?' I asked, my eyes wide open.

'It doesn't matter.' I looked at Maman and knew instinctively that it must be her ration. I went to protest but she held up her hand. 'Don't question me, please, Simone. Just hurry over to Madame Oray and make sure you're back before curfew.'

'Yes, Maman.'

'I would go myself but your brother isn't feeling very well.'

'What's wrong with Pierre?' I asked as we went through to the back of the shop. 'Is it his asthma?'

'No. He just says he feels tired and has a headache. He felt a little hot earlier, so I want to check on him.' She took off her apron and hung it on the back of the door. 'Now hurry along.'

I left my apron on the peg also and slipped my cardigan on, before picking up my bag and making sure I had all my papers with me.

The Oray family lived on the other side of the village and it took only a few minutes to reach their house. Madame Oray came to the door. 'Simone? What are you doing here?'

'My mother has sent me. Could I come in for a moment, please?' I knew better than to give Madame Oray the flour in full view of anyone who might be watching. It pained me to know that some villagers were so desperate for food, they would report their own neighbours to the German authorities.

Madame Oray eyed me suspiciously for a moment,

before opening the door wide and waving me in. The Oray children were delighted with the unexpected house guest and swamped me, with excited squeals and tugging of my hand to come and play with them.

I hugged the children and laughed at their over-the-top greeting.

'Come along, children. Leave Simone alone now,' urged their mother and then to me, 'Come into the kitchen.'

Once I'd extracted myself from the clutches of the children and was in the kitchen, I took the package from my bag and placed it on the table. 'From Maman.'

'What is this?' Madame Oray, opened the paper bag and let out small gasp. She looked at me with a frown. 'I knew your mother had a secret supply.'

'Oh no! No, she hasn't.' I felt indignant on Maman's behalf. 'That is from her own personal ration. My mother wouldn't do something so underhand as keep a secret supply. She's given this to you because she knows you have small children to feed.'

Madame Oray's shoulders dropped and she lowered her gaze. 'I am sorry. Please thank your mother for me.' She wiped away a tear from her eye, pulled out the chair and sat down. She let out a long sigh. 'It's just so hard. So very hard.'

I rested my hand on her shoulder, not really knowing what to say but wanting to offer some form of comfort and solidarity. I also felt a surge of anger. The injustice and the inhumane way we were being forced to live by the German occupation. We were powerless to do anything about it and that is what fuelled my anger the most.

The door opened and one of the children came in. '*J'ai faim, Mama. J'ai faim.*'

Madame Oray quickly got to her feet. 'They are always hungry. They go to bed hungry. They wake up hungry.

There is never enough food for them. They are wasting away.' She bent down and kissed the top of her daughter's head. 'I will make some bread to go with our soup tonight.'

The child's eyes lit up. 'Bread!' She clapped her hands together in excitement.

'Please thank your mother for me,' said Madame Oray. 'When I next see her, I shall apologise for my outburst in the shop today.'

As I left the Oray family and began cycling back towards the centre of the village, I was pleased to see my dear friend Monique hurrying along the street. Monique worked at the *mairie* and had been lucky enough to be offered a position there last year working for *le maire* – our village mayor. Of course, this was all under the watchful eye and instruction of the German regime. General Werner of the German army now had overall control. I called out and waved, coming to a stop.

'*Salut, Monique. Ça-va?*'

'*Ça-va. Et toi?*' She kissed me on each of my cheeks.

I couldn't help noticing Monique seemed on edge. 'Is everything all right?' I asked, wondering if work had been particularly difficult that day. I knew from what Monique had told me in confidence in the past that sometimes the administration work was mentally gruelling, especially when detailing any perceived crimes or punishments to the local people for breaking even the smallest of rules laid down by the Germans.

'Yes, everything is fine,' she replied. 'I'm just tired.'

I wasn't sure if I believed her but I knew it would be wrong to question her too much. I was sure there were things she was forbidden to talk about.

'I'm sorry, Simone, but I need to get home,' she said. '*A toute l'heure.*'

'Are we still meeting tomorrow?' I called after her.

She turned around. 'Tomorrow?'

'Flute. It's Wednesday – flute practice.' I was surprised I had to even mention it.

'Oh, yes. See you tomorrow.'

I watched her hurry off down the road for a moment, concerned that she seemed so distracted and not her usual cheerful self and especially her apparent lack of enthusiasm for flute practice. That was most unlike her.

I shrugged off the concern, reassuring myself it was simply the tiredness.

The following day, I made my way on foot to Monique's as planned. Even though the sun was out and there were hardly any clouds in the sky, the village seemed dour. It saddened me to remember how it used to be before the occupation. In those days when life was so carefree, there was always a sense of happiness. People would stop and chat to each other; you would see them smiling and laughing as they exchanged news and gossip. Children would play happily in the street or the park. Their squeals of laughter and shouts of excitement would echo down the street, mingling in with the general burr of daily life passing by. Customers would come into Maman's shop with a smile and an enthusiastic greeting, and more conversations would be had.

Now, there was none of that. It had all been replaced by a tension that wound its way along the main street, crawling into the alleyways and side roads, seeping into the houses, and settling on everyone's shoulders like a heavy blanket. There was fear and mistrust amongst people who were once friends. The only laughter these days came from the soldiers as they used Brittany as a playground, where they spent days on rest and relaxation. It was like they taunted us with their freedom, their enjoyment and sometimes their sadistic pleasure at our expense. Every time I saw a German soldier, my despise for them grew. Some days I struggled not to let the expression on my face betray me.

As I rounded the corner, I saw four soldiers walking towards me, taking up the whole of the pavement. My first thought was to step off the path to avoid them, but something inside of me rebelled and I continued on my trajectory, looking straight ahead.

Three of the soldiers moved into the road but the fourth one continued walking straight towards me. We were on a collision course. It was a game of brinkmanship and at the very last moment, one of the other men pulled his comrade to one side. He made some sort of protest in German. I didn't falter as I passed by and then at the very last moment, I felt my own arm being grabbed and I was spun around to face the soldier.

I swallowed hard but looked him directly in the eye. He returned the look and tightened his grip on my arm. 'Watch where you are going next time,' he hissed in French. I winced as the pressure increased on my arm.

'Apologies,' I said, trying not to let my voice tremble.

He looked down at the case in my hand and before I realised what he was doing, he snatched it from me. Instinctively, I went to grab it but he pulled away. 'What is this?' He flipped open the case. 'A flute.' He showed it to the other soldiers who made appropriately impressed noises.

One of the other men said something to the soldier and I felt he was trying to encourage him away and to leave me alone. The other two joined in and although I couldn't understand what they were saying, they were all definitely attempting to cajole him into going into the village.

The soldier shrugged off his comrade and slowly proceeded to remove the mouthpiece. He said something over his shoulder to the others. Two of them sniggered along with him, but the other gave a sigh and shook his head. Then without warning, the soldier casually threw the mouthpiece towards me.

I let out a gasp and launched myself forwards to catch it. If it landed on the ground, it would surely be damaged. Somehow, my fingertips manged to grasp the mouthpiece but I couldn't stop myself being propelled forwards and landing on the ground, my shoulder taking the brunt of the fall.

The soldier tucked the case under his arm and clapped his hands together. '*Bravo! Bravo!*'

I scrambled to my feet, feeling utterly humiliated but my pride would not let me stay on the ground. He laughed out loud and taking the main body of the flute from the case, he threw it up into the air, roaring with laughter as I scrambled to catch it.

I could feel tears of humiliation, fear and desperation sting the backs of my eyes. This was my father's flute. If it was damaged, it could never be replaced. I wanted to scream and punch the soldier.

At that moment, a car came around the corner and had to brake hard to avoid hitting me as I jumped out of the way. The soldiers immediately stood to attention and saluted towards the vehicle. As I swiped the tears from my face, I realised this was the same officer who had stopped me with the sheet of music.

The officer remained in his car and I could feel the weight of his gaze as he looked at me and then at his men.

Then, without a word being exchanged, the soldier thrust the flute case back at me. I gathered it close to my body. I wasn't entirely sure what was going on and now I had my flute, I just wanted to go, but I daren't.

The officer in the car gave a brisk nod to the soldiers

who saluted as one and then turned and walked swiftly away towards the village.

The officer then tipped the brim of his hat in my direction before carrying on his journey.

I was left standing in the middle of the street, rather bemused, not to mention grateful, by what had just happened.

~

'Are you all right?' Monique asked as she opened the door to me.

I must have looked more upset than I thought. 'Yes. No.' I was on the brink of tears and yet at the same time furious, not just with what had happened but with my reaction. I hated to feel so weak and powerless.

'Come and sit down. Tell me what happened. Papa is at work and Maman is in the garden, so no one will hear.' Monique sat me down on the sofa and fetched a glass of water. Monique's home was a much more glamorous affair than the apartment I lived in. Her parents were financially comfortable, although I didn't really know what her father did before the war but it was to do with banking. Since the occupation, he had been called to work for the Germans but, again, I wasn't privy to exactly what.

I relayed to my friend what had happened in the street and as I did so, the tears dried up and the indignation and outrage took hold. By the time I had finished, I was on my feet pacing the length of the room. 'If it had not been for the officer, I'm sure my flute would have been damaged,' I said, not for the first time. 'I hate them so much.' I stamped my foot to underline how much I despised them. 'HATE THEM!'

'Simone, shush,' said Monique, jumping to her feet and

resting her hand on my arm to placate me. She nodded towards the open window that overlooked the street. 'Someone might hear you.'

'I don't care.'

'You say that now, but when the Gestapo come knocking on your door, because someone has left them one of those poisonous letters telling them what you said, you'll care then.'

She was right, of course, but it didn't help my mood. In fact, it just made me more angry. 'Maybe I should just go home,' I said. 'I'm not in the right frame of mind today.'

'Don't be silly. We should play. It will help you. We can take ourselves away from all this.' She picked up her flute from the side table. 'Where shall we go today? London?' She put the instrument to her mouth and played a few notes. 'Vienna?' She began reeling off all the cities we'd dreamed about, punctuating between each one with a flurry of notes, while she twirled around the living room.

I couldn't help giving in to her infectious moment of fun and light-heartedness. A smile stretched across my face, which turned into a huge grin and before I knew it, I was joining in with her. After several minutes of twirling, playing our flutes and calling out city names, we fell onto the sofa in a heap of laughter.

'There, isn't that much better?' said Monique.

'It is, indeed,' I agreed. 'Let's play some more.'

We spent the next forty minutes or so playing our favourite tunes and luxuriating in our imaginations of a world without war.

'I'll walk back with you,' said Monique as I was packing away my flute.

'There's no need to do that,' I replied. I didn't want Monique to feel she had to babysit me and it never troubled me before walking home on my own.

At that moment her mother walked in. 'Mind how you go, Simone. It was lovely to listen to you both. It made working in the garden so much more enjoyable. Monsieur Aubert next door said he always likes hearing you.'

'I'm going to walk back with Simone some of the way,' said Monique, putting her flute away. 'Won't be long.'

I was about to protest when Monique shot me a look that I interpreted as not to say anything.

'But it's getting dark,' said her mother.

'I'll be back before curfew,' said Monique as she hustled me out of the door.

Once we were out of sight of the house, I came to a stop. 'So, are you going to tell me what's going on or not?'

'It doesn't matter,' replied Monique. 'I just wanted to get out of the house.' She continued walking.

I caught up with her. 'You never walk me home. You're up to something and as my best friend, you are obliged to tell me.'

'I just needed an excuse to get out.'

'I don't believe you. You're meeting someone, aren't you? A boy? Are you meeting a boy? Oh no, it's not a soldier is it?' I caught Monique's arm to make her stop walking. 'Please tell me it's not a German soldier.' A feeling of sickness swept over me as I stared at my friend.

Monique shook her head in exasperation. 'Of course it's not a German soldier. Why would I betray my country like that?'

'Then where are you going?'

Monique looked all around before speaking again, her voice low. 'If you must know, I'm going to meet some people from the village.'

I frowned, clearly not following what she was trying to tell me. 'Some people? Who? And why haven't you told me before?'

'I don't have to tell you everything.' Monique raised her eyebrows at me.

I couldn't help feeling a little offended. We were supposed to be best friends. We didn't have secrets from each other. Maybe I'd misjudged it over all these years? I let go of her arm. 'You don't have to tell me – you're right. I need to get home. I'll see you again.'

'Simone! Wait!' It was Monique's turn to catch me up. She slipped her arm through mine. 'If I tell you, you must promise on the life of your little brother that you won't breathe a word.'

'Of course I won't. I've never broken a promise to you before.'

'Say it. Say, you promise not to tell another living soul.'

'I promise.' Still she hesitated. 'I promise I won't tell another living soul where you are going or have been.'

'You hate the Germans, don't you?' she whispered.

I looked at her in bewilderment. 'Of course I do. You know that.' I felt compelled to whisper too.

She looked hesitant again and was clearly considering her next words. Finally, she spoke. 'I am going to people who are like-minded and want to make a contribution to the effort to oppose our visitors.'

It took me a moment to understand what she was telling me. I looked at her in amazement. Of all the things I thought about Monique, I never imagined she'd be directly involved with the resistance. She always obeyed the rules. At school Monique never got into trouble for anything. She was one of the brightest pupils in the class; she was the model student and the model daughter. I'm sure her parents would have been horrified if they knew what she was doing. 'You're actually… I mean, you're helping them?'

'Yes. I am,' said Monique with a smile. 'But I can't tell you how. It's strictly forbidden to talk about it. The fewer people who know, the less likely there is to be any compromise.'

'But I won't say anything!'

'I know you won't but if you're ever asked questions, if you don't know anything, then you don't have to tell lies. They will know if you're lying and the methods they use to get you to talk does not bear thinking about.'

Monique didn't need to elaborate. Everyone knew the punishments and torture our fellow countrymen suffered at the hands of the Germans.

'Let me come with you,' I said, surprising myself at the suggestion.

'I can't just turn up with you in tow,' said Monique. 'Besides, it's not something you just decide to do on the spur of the moment.'

'But I want to do something tangible. I hate having to comply with their rules and watch my country be torn apart. Take me, please. Or at least tell them I want to help.' I felt desperate to become involved. I had always felt there was something more to be done but had never known who to ask. It wasn't something you could just casually drop into a conversation and ask if they could point the way to the local resistance. Now I had my way in.

'*D'accord*. I will tell them that you might be open to an approach. I can't say we have spoken directly about this, otherwise they will think I go around talking to everyone about it. I've only been doing this for a few weeks so I still need to earn their trust.' Monique linked arms with me again and we continued on towards the centre of the village. 'Now you must be patient.'

We parted company at the front of the store and I watched Monique hurry on down the street to her secret meeting. I felt frustrated I couldn't go with her and can't say I wasn't immensely jealous.

FOUR

2019

'Have you actually thought this through properly?' Angela, Imogen's mother, asked not for the first time. She looked to Imogen's father, Larry, to back her up.

Imogen saved him the trouble. It was excruciatingly painful to see her father caught in the middle of her disagreement with her mother. 'Of course I've thought it through. Honestly, Mum, it's what I really want to do.' She paused before adding. 'It's what James and I both wanted to do.'

Her mother sighed and moved to sit next to her on the sofa, taking Imogen's hand in hers, while her father tried, unsuccessfully, to disguise the look of sadness on his face. Her father was such a dear and it was his guarded feelings of concern that touched Imogen more than her mother's outright objection to her idea, albeit both came from the same place of love and concern.

'Look, darling,' said her mother. 'I don't mean to sound harsh but moving to France was yours and James's idea. It doesn't mean it has to be yours. It's one thing moving abroad when you're a couple but a completely different thing as a single woman.'

'I need to do something, Mum. I'm not happy here.' Imogen couldn't look at her mother. She knew she'd be hurt by that sentence. 'I don't mean you're making me unhappy. What I mean is, I don't feel like I'm living life. I'm sitting here watching it pass me by. James wouldn't have wanted that.'

'But would he have wanted you to move abroad?' Her mother was persistent but Imogen had always known it wasn't going to be an easy conversation. Over the last two weeks the idea of fulfilling her and James's dream had taken hold and had grown and grown. It occupied her every thought and, if she were honest, Imogen would have to admit, she'd become slightly obsessed with the idea.

Imogen looked up at the photograph of her and James on their wedding day, taken six years ago. They were so happy, having run away, as James' mother, Denise, had described it, to Las Vegas to get married. They had done things their way, much to the disappointment of their mothers. Imogen's dad had taken it in his stride and Imogen's sister, Meg, had high-fived her and confessed she wished she'd done the same and avoided all the hassle and stress of a traditional church wedding.

More recently, Meg's advice to Imogen about France was that she should follow her heart because God knows she'd had it broken enough in the last few years; she deserved some happiness. Meg had also added that comment was strictly off the record if their mother ever cross-examined them.

Imogen had hugged Meg so tight, grateful for the sisterly support. Imogen was aware the emotional strain of losing James and two babies had been so heavy, she'd been blindly groping her way through each day, making little headway.

She was tired of existing – she knew she needed to live. Meg was probably the only person who understood her and, although confessing she'd miss her little sister terribly, she had been so supportive of Imogen's decision.

'I was hoping Meg would talk some sense into you,' said her mother as if tuning in to Imogen's thoughts. 'When you mentioned it last week, I didn't think you were that serious. I asked Meg to have a chat with you.'

'Well, Meg has spoken to me in her official capacity as older and wiser sister,' replied Imogen.

'So you're ignoring her too?' Angela was now using her schoolteacher voice, one perfected during thirty years educating primary school children. 'What will you do for work? You can't exactly commute as an interior designer,' she persisted.

'James made sure I wouldn't have any money worries and once I sell this place, I'll have enough to buy somewhere and live off my savings for a good eighteen to twenty-four months if I'm careful. And in that time, not only can I work on the property I buy but I can also build up a client base there. It will give me time to build up my garden design and maintenance work too.'

Imogen had gone through her finances several times and even enlisted the help of Meg's husband, Howard, to make sure she'd got her sums right. The fact that Howard worked in the finance department of a pension company was all the reassurance Imogen needed that her own maths and financial projections were realistic.

'That's another thing, who's going to do our garden?' asked Angela, clearly clutching at straws. Imogen had been their unofficial gardener for several years now. It was one of the few things she genuinely found pleasure in. There was something enriching and comforting being in physical contact with the ground, nurturing and tending the plants.

'I'm sure you can find someone to help out,' said Imogen gently. She glanced towards her father who gave a small nod.

'When are we all going to see you, though? It's not like now when you're just a ten-minute drive away.' Angela was not letting up.

'It's France not Australia,' said Imogen, her patience being thoroughly tested now. 'It's close enough for a long weekend visit.'

'But we'll miss you. We all will. And what about Leah and Noah?'

'Now, now, Angela,' warned Larry, somehow managing to sound both stern and gentle at the same time.

Imogen shot her dad a grateful look. They'd always been good at unspoken communication; it was a much-needed skill when navigating life under her mother's watchful eye. 'I'll make us all a fresh cup of tea.' Imogen needed to put a little bit of space between her and her mother for a moment. That last remark was below the belt – designed to wound. It was unfair of her mother to bring Meg's children into it.

By the time Imogen returned to the living room, her mother had beat the retreat, no doubt aided by advice from her father.

'I don't mean to upset you,' said Angela. 'I'm just going to miss you terribly and you know I'll worry about you.' She held up a hand. 'And before you say I don't have to and you're a grown woman et cetera, but as your mother, it's my job to worry.'

'I know,' said Imogen, placing the tray with the cups down onto the coffee table. 'And I wouldn't want you any other way. Well, most of the time anyway.' She winked at her father and her mother tutted and eye-rolled good-humouredly.

'Have you spoken to Denise about this yet?' asked Larry.

Imogen pulled a pained expression. Telling her parents

and family was one thing but telling James's mother was a different ball game altogether. 'Not yet. I'll tell her this week when I go for dinner.'

'How do you think she'll take the news?' Larry reached for his cup of tea.

Imogen glanced at her mother. 'Much the same, I expect.'

'I think she's relied far too heavily on you the last few years,' said Angela. 'Don't get me wrong, I know she's as grief-stricken as you. I can't even begin to imagine what the poor woman's gone through, still going through, but I do think sometimes she forgot you were grieving too.'

Imogen didn't correct her mother. Grieving just didn't stop and come to an end. It was always there, just not so raw, not so painful and not so dominant. She'd always miss and grieve for James, for what they had and for what they didn't have the chance to have.

'To be fair, I've leaned on Denise too,' admitted Imogen. 'It's a shared grief.' She felt her heart tug a little harder as she spoke. She hadn't always seen eye to eye with her rather conservative mother-in-law over the years, but she liked to think they had a mutual respect and fondness for one another, and in the very darkest of days following James's death, they had found solace in each other. Grieving with Denise had been easier than accepting comfort from others. They had loved the same man, albeit in different ways, so sharing their grief had been natural and they didn't have to pretend to well-meaning friends and family that they were comforted or feeling any better.

A silence fell in the room as it so often did when the subject of James's dying came up.

It was her father who spoke first. 'So, have you started looking for a property yet, or are you going to rent some-where first?'

'This place is going on the market next week. I had the guy from the estate agent's around last week to take photos. I'm going for a realistic price with the hope of selling quite quickly and then I'll start looking at houses in France.'

'Have you decided on a region?' Larry asked.

'Brittany. Southern Brittany. It was mine and James's favourite place to holiday and it's close enough for weekend visits.'

'Shouldn't you try living out there first before making the move permanent?' asked Angela.

'Nope. It would be too easy to come home. I fully anticipate being homesick, lonely and to have some tough days but what's the point in going to all that trouble if it's so easy to back out.' Imogen could tell her mother was fighting the urge to disagree with her, but to her credit Angela managed to tamp down the temptation.

It wasn't without some relief, when her parents left to return home an hour later.

Imogen loved them dearly and she knew her mother's fussing came from a good place, but sometimes Imogen found it all a bit intense. However, she was pleased she'd finally had the discussion with them that she was definitely going. All she needed to do now was to break the news to Denise.

After her parents had left, Imogen didn't know why, but she couldn't settle down to anything. Sunday afternoons were always a strange time of the week, she found. Days when people spent time with their families. Time when she felt the loneliness and loss most acutely. It was a time that was a stark reminder of all the things she didn't have in her life that she had expected to. No partner and no children. The pain was very real on those occasions, sometimes too much to bear. She'd tried various hobbies over the years to keep herself busy, such as knitting, crochet, bread making.

Some becoming more long-term interests, others less so. Reading had always been her go-to pastime though. She'd been a bookworm for as long as she could remember and had gathered a rather large collection of books over the years. Scrapbooking had always been another favourite activity in her before life, but since James's death, she realised she had nothing to fill those pages with. Her days and weeks just rolled into one with no distinct differences.

This realisation and the android comment she'd overheard had been the catalysts for her decision to start living instead of existing. James wouldn't recognise her as the woman he'd married.

And now, here she was, actually making the decision to move to France. She was going to do what she and James had dreamed of doing.

Imogen picked up their wedding photo. 'I'm really going to do it, James. I'm going to live our dream.'

She replaced the photograph, pressing her finger to her lips and then touching James's lips. Despite the difficulty of her parents' visit and the conversation she was yet to have with Denise, Imogen still felt the same sense of purpose and enthusiasm she had two weeks ago. This was the right thing to do. She couldn't explain it, but deep in her bones, she knew James would be cheering her on.

She could hear his voice and see the sparkle of adventure in his eyes. 'The world is out there waiting for us. Let's go meet it with open arms!' She smiled at the memory.

He was right, of course, and soon she'd be living the life he never had the chance to. She owed it to him and to herself.

FIVE
1944

'Now, Simone, on your way to Monique's this afternoon, I need you to take a detour to Madame Oray. I've got a small food parcel for her,' said Maman. It had been two weeks since I'd asked Monique to tell the resistance that I wanted to become an active member. I had been on tenterhooks waiting for someone from the resistance to make contact with me and as each day came and went, my impatience grew and my hopes of becoming involved faded. 'Are you listening to me?'

'What? Sorry,' I said hastily. I took the basket from Maman where she'd placed a small wedge of cheese and four eggs, together with a small pouch of flour. I had done the same last week and although Madame Oray had been reluctant to accept it again, she did so eventually, not because she was happy to receive charity but, as a mother, she couldn't let her children starve.

'Off you go,' said Maman. 'Take your bike.'

A few minutes later I was heading towards Madame Oray's on the edge of the village. It was in the opposite direction to Monique's but it would only cost me an extra ten minutes. As I rounded the corner, I was alarmed to see a roadblock in place that hadn't been there last week. I slowed a little as I assessed the situation. Technically I wasn't doing anything wrong. I was after all just paying a visit to another villager and there was nothing wrong with taking some provisions. As long as I wasn't making some sort of black-market transaction, it was all right. Still, I was nervous.

A car overtook me and stopped at the roadblock. I recognised the German officer who got out as the one who had given my music sheets back and stopped when the soldiers had my flute. I was a little unnerved that I was crossing paths with him quite often. Getting myself noticed by a German officer wasn't a great thing, especially if I wanted to join the resistance.

He motioned with his hand for me to hurry up. I fought to remain calm and tried not to look guilty as I approached, coming to a halt in front of him.

'Mademoiselle.' He glanced towards the basket of my bike. 'Flute practice today?'

'*Oui*,' I replied.

He looked confused. 'Not at your friend's house?'

I was surprised he knew about Monique and this set my stomach churning with anxiety. Did he know Monique was part of the resistance? Did he suspect I was too?

'I'm going to see someone else first,' I said when I realised he was waiting for an explanation.

The officer moved closer and looked into the basket, moving the cloth that was covering the food supply a fraction. 'Shop delivery, I see,' he said, pulling the cloth back into place. 'Very good.' He gave a small smile and then moved to the side of the road, whilst giving an instruction in German to the soldier who immediately lifted the road barrier.

After dropping the food at Madame Oray's, I was

allowed back through the roadblock into the village without any questioning.

By the time I'd reached Monique's I was certain the officer was suspicious of either Monique or myself or possibly both of us.

'It may just be a coincidence,' said Monique after I relayed to her what had happened. 'But I will be more careful, just in case. I will mention it to the group.'

'Has anyone said anything to you about me joining?' I asked as I had been doing for the last couple of weeks every time I saw my friend.

'I've heard nothing but then why would I? They only tell people what they need to know. It's safer that way. Now, please, Simone, stop asking me.'

I could tell Monique was becoming as exasperated as I was, but for different reasons. 'I'm sorry. I will try to be more patient.'

We had just finished our flute practice and, not for the first time, Monique suggested she walk home with me. Her mother didn't object, thinking her daughter was going to spend time at my apartment. Although we never told an outright lie, we never told the truth either, allowing her mother to believe this.

As we stepped out of the house, I noticed the German officer again leaning against the wall on the other side of the street. I gave a small gasp. He was clearly following me. 'That's him,' I hissed under my breath to Monique. He saw me looking but I quickly looked away.

'Just keep walking,' whispered Monique.

We reached the end of the road and turned the corner. 'I think he's following us,' I hissed, catching a glimpse of his reflection in a window. 'You'll have to come to my house. You can't risk going to the meeting.'

The main street wasn't very busy, most of the villagers

having already spent the day queueing for what little food there was. The food shortage was getting worse by the day and having a ration book didn't guarantee you any food, not if there was none to be had. That was another injustice that fuelled my hatred for what was happening. The soldiers never went without food; they were never hungry. Food wasn't a luxury for them. I was reminded of this as I saw a group standing around the water pump, with tankards of ale or cider in one hand and passing around batons of bread with the other, one even having the audacity to throw the crusty end on the ground.

Beyond them, I could see Madame Lafitte, an elderly villager, crossing the road. I knew her from her visits to the shop. She was widowed and was a very kindly lady. I put my hand up to wave to her, but as I did so a lorry came rumbling around the corner at speed. Madame Lafitte was already halfway across the road now, directly in its path.

'*Attention! Madame Lafitte!*' I yelled and then, breaking free from Monique, I went to run out into the road to try to get the driver's attention.

I was aware of Monique screaming out my name and then suddenly I was grabbed by the arm and pulled backwards. The truck's horn blasted out, long and loud. The brakes squealed and somehow the driver of the truck managed to avoid hitting Madame Lafitte by inches as it swerved to the side.

I spun around to see who had hauled me out of the way and was shocked to see it was the German officer who had helped me several times now. However, my mind wasn't on thanking him. I was more concerned to make sure Madame Lafitte was all right but before I could get to her, the driver of the truck, a German soldier, was out of the cab and shouting in German at her.

The officer caught my arm again. 'No,' he said firmly.

I tried to shrug off his hand but he held on to me tightly. I looked back towards Monique who was frozen to the spot, watching the events as they unfolded. The whole street had come to a stop and no one dared intervene.

I could hear Madame Lafitte apologising profusely, her voice trembling. And then, to my absolute horror, the driver raised a hand and slapped her across the face.

There was a gasp from the onlookers.

'Stop him!' I cried, turning to look at the German officer. 'He can't do that to an old woman.'

The driver struck Madame Lafitte again and then a third time.

At this point, the officer let go of my arm and as he marched over towards the soldier, he shouted something in German. Reaching the soldier, he caught his arm as he went to raise it a fourth time. The soldier stopped immediately, acknowledging his superior's rank, and returned to the truck. The officer ushered Madame Lafitte across the road to me. Her face was red and already swollen.

From nowhere Maman appeared and put her arm around Madame Lafitte's shoulder and the other under her arm to support her. 'Come to the shop. Let me clean you up,' said Maman. She glared at the departing truck as she helped Madame Lafitte back across the road.

It was then I noticed Monique had gone. She must have used the commotion as a diversion and slipped away to her meeting. Maman called me to hurry up.

The officer was standing in front of me and I thought he was going to say something, but I was not in the mood to talk to him. He may have stopped Madame Lafitte being beaten any further, but he should have stopped it before it even started as far as I was concerned. Not only that, but the soldier should have been punished, not just allowed to drive away.

I went to walk around the officer, but he stepped in front of me. 'I hope Madame will be all right. I'll arrange for some dressings to be delivered.' He called out an order to one of the soldiers sitting outside the café, who scurried off.

I was rather taken aback by this. It was most unusual.

'*Merci*,' I said. I wanted to hate him as much as I hated all the German soldiers, but there was something about him that stood him apart.

'Not all the men are like that,' he said, as if reading my mind. He stepped aside and with one last look at him, I hurried to catch up with Maman and Madame Lafitte. As I reached the door of the shop, a soldier appeared with some cotton wool and a small bottle of what I assumed was anti-septic. Taking it from him, I turned to look back at the German officer but he was already engaged in conversation with another officer.

Inside the shop Madame Lafitte was sitting on the stool Maman had brought out from behind the counter.

'I saw what happened,' explained Maman. 'I heard the commotion from the apartment. Those bastards! How dare they do that to an elderly lady. Simone, fetch some water in a dish.'

As Maman bathed Madame Lafitte's face, the elderly lady began to cry. It was heart-breaking to see. I crouched down and held her hands. 'It's a good job that officer came along when he did,' I said trying to console her.

'Don't be taken in by that act,' snapped Maman. 'He doesn't care about what happens to us, he just cares about having to make a report or discipline his men if it gets too out of control.'

I went to protest but Madame Lafitte spoke. 'They are all the same. They are subhuman. All of them. Look what they did to Monsieur Rutter.'

I looked blankly from one woman to the other. 'What happened?'

'Yesterday, he was arrested, beaten and sent away to a work camp,' said Maman.

'Whatever for? You never said.' I was alarmed to hear this. M. Rutter was in his sixties and used to work as a tailor.

'He was caught collecting firewood from the forest. As it now all belongs to the Germans, it was considered theft,' explained Maman. 'I only heard this afternoon when he was taken away.'

'That's terrible.' I wanted to cry at the thought.

'So, don't go thanking the officer for anything or thinking some of them aren't as bad as the others,' said Maman. 'They are all pigs and I hope they spend eternity burning in hell.'

'Now, now,' said Madame Lafitte. 'You best keep thoughts like that to yourself.'

SIX
2019

'You haven't told her yet?' Meg stopped pushing her daughter on the swing.

Imogen winced at the amazement in her sister's voice. 'Not yet. I chickened out at the last minute,' she confessed.

'Oh, Immy, that's not good. You can't just spring it on her. It's going to be upsetting enough for Denise as it is. What are you going to do, send her a postcard? *Wish you were here. By the way, I've moved to France permanently.*' She resumed the rhythmic pushing of the swing.

'If only it were that easy. I keep thinking about the time James and I told her we'd got married in Vegas. She didn't take it too well that we'd gone off without telling anyone,' said Imogen, as she stood alongside her sister pushing little Noah on the other swing. To onlookers they probably looked like two mums who had met up for a natter while their children played together. It was a scenario Imogen had expected would be a reality in the early years of her marriage when getting pregnant and having children was something she had naïvely taken as a given. 'I did drop a few hints though. I said I was thinking of spending more time in France.'

'How did that go?'

'She just said, "That will be nice," and then started telling me about a new boutique that has opened in town and how all the clothes have come from a store in Paris.'

'Was she avoiding the conversation, do you think?'

'Possibly. It's hard to say with Denise sometimes.'

'Does she know you're off to France tomorrow?'

'Yes. I said I was going over and might have a look at a few houses.'

'Might?' Her sister eyed her sceptically as her daughter jumped from the moving swing. 'Time to go home, kids.'

Once they managed to get the children out of the park without too many protests, Meg continued the conversation.

'You have a week of viewings booked. There's no might about it.'

'I feel bad not telling her, but I just couldn't bring myself to say it was definite.' Imogen held Noah's hand as they made their way along the path, hopping over the cracks and joints in the paving slabs. Noah laughed as Imogen pretended it was far more difficult than it really was.

'Well, if you want my opinion, which you probably don't, but are going to get it anyway,' began Meg.

Imogen stopped her. 'I know. I've got to be honest and tell her.'

'Yes. She'll feel hurt if she finds out you didn't tell her the truth.'

Imogen knew her sister was right and felt a pang of guilt that she'd put off the difficult task. 'I'll tell her next week when I see her. She's at Tom's for a few days now as his wife's had a small op.'

'I suppose that's one saving grace that she has Tom and his family,' commented Meg. Tom was James's brother and lived just a few miles away. He'd done his best to step into the gap his brother had left, but as Tom pointed out, James had left big shoes to fill.

'Tom finds it hard to live up to Denise's expectations but he's very patient with her and, of course, the children give her some focus.' Whether it was the thread of anxiety of what she was intending to do that was making Imogen feel particularly sensitive that day she didn't know, but the childless void in her life seemed even more pronounced. She knew it didn't do any good to dwell on what might have been, but every now and then it crept out from those dark corners of her mind. 'Right, who wants an ice-cream? We'll get one from the shop up here,' said Imogen, using a technique she'd read about in one of those mindfulness magazines her sister had not so subtly dropped over to her one day – turn a negative thought into a positive one. Instead of grieving for the babies she'd lost, she was going to make the most of the children she had in her life. She looked over at Meg who her gave her a faux look of disapproval. 'Aunt's prerogative exercised,' declared Imogen.

With promises of bringing the children back a present from France, Imogen left Meg later that afternoon to head for the ferry terminal in Portsmouth – a journey she and James had made many a time.

She'd been back to France a couple of times since then, but both times accompanying Meg and her family on holiday. It had made the return so much easier but she was still surprised at the feeling of loss that welled up in her as she staged her first solo journey. It was comforting that she knew the routine and after eating in the café, she retired to her cabin and got her head down. The ferry would dock in St Malo the following morning at around eight-thirty, so she wanted to get up early and have some breakfast before disembarking.

Imogen was surprised and relieved at how well she slept in the end and was pleased when she cleared customs and was on the road to Sérent where she'd prebooked a *chambre d'hotes*, run by an English couple one of Meg's friends had recommended.

Three hours later, Imogen had arrived at the renovated Breton cottage and was sitting in the kitchen drinking a much-welcomed cup of tea.

'Just what I needed,' Imogen said, smiling at Lisa, the business owner.

'So you're house-hunting?'

'Yes. I've got some viewings already lined up. I did some research before I came as I didn't want to waste any time waiting for appointments to be made.'

'Very wise,' replied Lisa. 'The French can be laid-back at times, which is a good thing but not when you're in a hurry to get things done.'

'Exactly.'

'I take it you've visited the area before?'

'Yes. I used to come with my husband. We loved it here,' replied Imogen, knowing she would have to expand on where James was now. From past experience, she knew people would assume she was separated or divorced and she hated that idea. It felt like a slight on their marriage, a disservice to James, more than that – a betrayal. So, despite knowing it would be awkward for Lisa, she elaborated. 'My husband passed away four years ago. We'd always dreamed of buying a place out here so now I'm doing it.'

'Oh, I'm so sorry,' said Lisa.

'It's OK. Honest.' Imogen offered a reassuring smile and swiftly moved the conversation on. 'So, how long have you been out here?'

And so the next thirty minutes or so passed with Imogen asking Lisa lots of questions about the expat life and getting plenty of tips too.

After finishing her second cup of tea, Imogen looked at her watch. 'I'd better get myself sorted out. My first viewing is this afternoon, over at Malestroit.'

'Very nice. Hope it goes well,' said Lisa.

Malestroit was less than an hour's drive and Imogen arrived with plenty of time to spare. At first glance the property – a two-bedroom cottage set at the end of a long drive – looked idyllic but as she approached on foot, she could see that the building needed rather more than minor repairs as the property details had indicated. Even with her own experience of interior design and advising clients on property development, she could see it was rather more than a DIY project. The roof had a worrying dip in the middle and as she reached the front door, she could see it was ajar. She knew from the *immobilier* – estate agent – that the property had been empty for some time, but even so she hadn't been expecting the door to be open.

There was no sign of a car parked anywhere so she didn't think the *immobilier* would be waiting inside. Tentatively she pushed open the door.

Imogen was expecting it to be quite dark inside but was surprised by how light it was. The first thing she saw was a pile of debris, timber, bricks and roof tiles all in a big heap in the middle of the room. As she looked up, she saw the reason. There was a huge hole in the roof where it had collapsed.

She didn't bother going in any further. It should have been described as derelict by the *immobilier* rather than in need of repair. Mentally, she crossed the property off her list and returned to her car to wait for the *immobilier*. She could tell him straight away not to even bother getting out of his car. She'd also check with him to make sure the other two properties she was viewing that afternoon weren't in an equal state of disrepair.

Imogen returned to the *chambre d'hotes* that evening a little deflated. None of the properties she's seen that afternoon would even make it onto a shortlist. Two had been derelict, their redeeming features being the large size of land that came with them which, had the properties not been practically falling down, she might have been tempted by. The final one she'd seen that afternoon had looked promising until she was informed the garden wasn't actually within the grounds of the property but fifty metres down the road.

'Don't be too despondent,' said Meg when Imogen had phoned her that night. 'It's just the first day.'

'Yeah, I know. I was just excited. I thought I'd find that dream home straight away. Not very realistic, I appreciate.' Imogen was lying on her bed, having just had the evening meal Lisa had prepared. 'I've got appointments tomorrow with a different estate agent and I've double-checked the details. They look a bit more promising but it seems French estate agents are equally creative with their descriptions as their UK counterparts.'

'Just don't rush into anything or feel you have to find your dream property this visit,' said Meg and then added more softly, 'It's about you finding the right place and trying something new, not just doing it to fulfil a promise or a dream you shared with James.'

Imogen knew her sister was right. 'It's OK. I'm not going to sign on the dotted line just because I feel I need to. James would hate that.'

∽

The next three days followed pretty much the same pattern for Imogen. She turned up at the properties, which for one reason or another weren't right for her. Too much work needed, too modern, not enough outdoor space, no running water, no electricity, no septic tank or mains drains and the list went on. She wasn't afraid of bringing a house up to scratch but she needed to feel the house would be right for her in its finished condition.

'*Je suis désolé, monsieur*,' she said after she had declined the last property that day. 'It's a lovely house, but not really what I'm looking for.'

M. Henry, the *immobilier*, had looked at her thoughtfully. '*C'est bon*. I understand. Forgive me for being too forward, but I sense you don't really know what you're looking for. I mean that in a kind way. You're looking for something on a deeper level.'

Imogen was startled by his words. She considered them before answering. 'I think, maybe, you're right. I hadn't looked at it like that.'

'You will know it when you find it or, rather, your heart will know,' said M. Henry. 'Now, it's late in the day and I must go home. If I think of anything in the next twelve hours or so, I'll contact you.'

'Yes, please do,' said Imogen. She was really quite tired now from all the driving around and viewings she'd undertaken. That coupled with a despondency at not having found somewhere yet and the comforting words from M. Henry made her suddenly feel exhausted.

It was something of a surprise later that evening when she checked her emails and found one from M. Henry.

It may not be what you had in mind but if you could indulge me for an hour or so tomorrow, I would very much like to show you the attached property. It hasn't been lived in for many years and is in need of plenty of love but I feel it might just be something you will be interested in.

Imogen had scanned the rest of M. Henry's email and then burst out laughing when she opened the attachment and the picture of a beautiful château popped up on the screen. It was a small château by French standards, situated in the nearby village of Trédion with amazing-looking grounds and its own moat! Imogen reread the description. Yes, it definitely said a moat. As she read on and now being something of an expert in interpreting *immobilier* jargon, she learned the property was in need of renovation throughout, including a whole wing that had suffered fire damage. Somehow this didn't faze her as it might have done earlier in the week. Perhaps now she was immune to the condition of some of the old French properties. The more she read and the more she gazed at the photographs, the more intrigued she became by it.

The château was everything she had been turning down all week, it ticked all the wrong boxes and yet it was everything she'd ever wished for. Was this what M. Henry had meant when he said it would ultimately be her heart that decided?

SEVEN

1944

I didn't sleep well over the next few nights and I wasn't entirely sure why. The scene in the village with Madame Lafitte being beaten played heavily on my mind. Of course I had witnessed and heard of such brutality, and much worse, over the years of occupation but the look of pleasure on the driver's face haunted me. How could a man beat a defence-less old woman? Had he no mother or grandmother of his own? How could he be so... subhuman? That's what Madame Lafitte had said and she was right. I shuddered at what might have happened to her if the officer had not intervened.

My nights had also been punctuated by Pierre coughing. It was something I was used to when his asthma flared up but last night especially, it seemed worse. Maman had taken his nebuliser in to him. A horrible thing and Pierre always complained that the powder we had to put in the tube that he then had to inhale tasted disgusting.

'Is Pierre all right?' I asked Maman who was in the kitchen making a pot of coffee. Her eyes looked heavy and there were dark circles underneath.

'I think he may have a cold coming,' said Maman. 'You know what Pierre is like – he catches everything going.'

It was true, Pierre had been born early and had always been a sickly baby, something Papa would say he'd grow out of, but alas that didn't appear to be the case. 'Is there anything I can do?'

'Perhaps you can stay up here with your brother and make him some breakfast. Come down to help me in the shop afterwards.'

After Maman had gone downstairs to open up, I warmed some bread in the oven and made a warm lemon drink for him.

'Hello,' I said, going into his room where he was lying in bed but already awake. '*Ça-va?*' I placed the plate and cup on the bedside table and went over to the window to open the curtains. As I looked down to the street, I could see the queues already forming outside the butcher's and our shop below. A line of women that would only grow and snake its way down the street, for several hours. Those unfortunate enough to be near the back not even knowing if there would be any food left for them once they reached the front of the queue.

'Did I wake you in the night?' asked Pierre.

'No, not at all,' I lied, coming over to the bed. 'Now, there's your breakfast.'

'I'm not hungry.'

'But you need to eat, so no arguing.'

I sat with him while he nibbled on the bread and sipped half-heartedly at the lemon water. His complexion was pale and even just the act of eating appeared to tire him. It was concerning but perhaps Maman was right and he was just getting a cold.

'I can't eat any more,' he said, dropping the bread back down onto the plate. 'You eat it.'

'Try to get some rest,' I said, tucking the blanket up around him. 'You need to get your energy back up.'

I finished the bread Pierre had left, but despite knowing wasting food was an absolute sin, I still felt guilty having extra.

I joined Maman in the shop to help move the queue along quicker. We worked well together and I liked the sense of purpose it gave me. Eventually, the queue was cleared and we were able to relax for a moment. I took the opportunity to voice my concerns about Pierre, and Maman said she'd check on him at lunchtime. I could tell she was a little more worried than she would normally be, even though she was attempting to hide it from me.

The bell above the shop door jingled and Madame Oray came into the shop.

'*Bonjour,* Celine,' Maman greeted her friend. '*Ça-va?*'

They exchanged pleasantries and Madame Oray smiled in my direction before checking over her shoulder that the shop was empty and then turning back to Maman. 'I wanted to thank you,' she said in a low voice.

'To thank me?' Maman gave a shrug.

'For the chickens?' continued Madame Oray.

'I'm sorry, Celine, I don't know what you mean.'

Madame Oray looked towards me as if I could explain what she meant but I was equally in the dark. 'You don't know, do you? Either of you.'

Maman shook her head. 'No. I'm afraid we don't.'

Madame Oray bit her bottom lip. 'The day after Simone visited me, I had a visit from a German soldier and an officer. They brought two chickens. The officer said my request had been approved and as long as I handed over six eggs each week to them, I could keep the rest for my own use.'

'Had you requested to keep the chickens?' asked Maman, the surprise evident in her voice.

'No. That's just it. I went to say as much but the officer wouldn't let me speak. He said I wasn't to argue and it had all been approved.'

'Well, I should do as he says, in that case,' said Maman. 'Besides, you need it with your little ones to feed.'

'I know. It's like my prayers have been answered,' said Madame Oray.

Before the conversation could continue, we were interrupted by the bell jingling again. This time, however, it wasn't one of our regular customers, but a German officer.

We all stopped talking and tension immediately filled the shop.

'Thank you, Madame,' said Maman, trying to sound normal. *'Au revoir.'*

Madame Oray nodded at us both and, keeping her gaze to the floor, left the shop.

The German officer was casually strolling around the shop, looking at the shelves. *'Bonjour, Madame, Mademoiselle.'*

'Bonjour, Monsieur,' replied Maman.

'Monsieur,' I said in acknowledgement.

The German officer fixed his gaze upon us from the other side of the shop counter. There was amusement in his eyes and I countered it with one of defiance – it was all I could do. The door opened again and in walked another officer. I managed to catch my breath when I saw it was the officer who had stepped in to stop Madame Lafitte being beaten further. He said bonjour to us and then browsed the shelves in an uninterested manner. The first officer's gaze rested on me for a long moment and I was repulsed by his attention.

Maman's hand found mine and she squeezed it, not in a reassuring way, but one which clearly said, 'Simone, bite your tongue.' I returned the squeeze, acknowledging the request. I knew better than to speak out of turn to the *Boche.*

The German officer at the counter smiled. 'I would like some cheese,' he said in heavily accented French. He moved his hand to his pocket and to my dismay, I felt myself flinch. His gun was holstered to his side. He paused. 'My pocket. I'm getting something from my pocket. Something for you.'

'We don't have any cheese left today,' replied Maman. There was a nervous twang to her voice, which I was unaccustomed to hearing. In fact, I had never heard nerves in her voice before the Germans were here. She had always been a very strong woman who had raised me and my brother single-handedly since dear Papa died.

'I was told I could get cheese here,' the disgruntled officer replied. He slid his hand from his pocket and turned his hand, palm up so we could see the bar of chocolate he was holding. I couldn't help a small gasp escaping, which earned me a scowl from Maman and a grin from the officer. He placed it on the counter. 'For you.'

I desperately wanted to take the chocolate bar. I couldn't remember the last time I'd seen one. Pierre would have loved the treat and so would I, in fact, but I knew better than to take anything from the soldiers. Another of my mother's warnings – if I was to take the chocolate, then I would have to pay for it, one way or another. And seeing as Maman didn't have any spare money, I was not naïve enough to think the chocolate was merely a gift.

The officer nodded encouragingly at the confectionary.

'*Non. Merci*,' replied Maman politely but firmly.

The second officer turned and said something in his native tongue to the first and the latter didn't seem very happy. His brow knitted and his thick dark eyebrows darted together like angry tadpoles. He spoke in French for our benefit. 'Ungrateful bitch.'

The second officer stepped towards the counter. 'No, my friend, not ungrateful, just cautious.' He turned to us.

'Madame, mademoiselle, I apologise for my comrade. He is from the west of Germany and, as such, not so graced with manners as myself from the east.' He held up his hand to abate the protestations from his colleague. 'We will leave the chocolate there. No strings attached. It would make us very happy for you to enjoy it.'

Maman didn't move. I was willing her to take the chocolate or at least not make a fuss in protest and insist the Germans take their disgusting bribes with them – because that was, of course, how she would see it. Maman took a deep breath while I withheld my own, unsure what she was going to say. 'I'm very sorry, we don't have any cheese.'

The scowling German made a huffing noise and slammed his hand down on the counter, millimetres from the chocolate bar. 'You don't have any cheese? Are you sure about that? What about out the back?' He went to lift the counter but the other officer placed a hand on his arm.

'Hey, Claus, leave it. I don't want the cheese now anyway. We have plenty back at the château.' He cast his gaze across the shelves behind us. 'I'll have some of the sugar, *s'il vous plaît.*'

The one named Claus made another huffing noise and shrugged off the hand on his arm but said nothing and watched as Maman moved around me and took a bag of sugar from the shelf and placed it on the counter. The heightened tension in the air was like an explosive charge waiting for the touch paper to be lit. 'Is there anything else?' she asked stiffly.

Claus looked me up and down. I wanted to dip my head, but again I wouldn't allow myself to surrender. 'Now you mention it—' he began but the other officer cut him off.

'No. We have everything we want, *merci*. How much do I owe you for the sugar?' He deftly manoeuvred himself between Claus and the counter.

Maman rang up the amount on the till and the German handed over the money.

'You're too soft on them,' said Claus, giving me another look that made me swallow down a ball of unease.

'And you are far too miserable and bad-tempered, my friend!' He slapped Claus on the back, picked up the small bag of sugar and ushered his comrade towards the door where he paused and nodded in our direction before leaving.

No sooner had the door closed than Maman snatched up the bar of chocolate. 'We cannot keep this.'

'But, Maman!' I watched as she strode through to the room at the back of the store, across the courtyard and opened the gate, before throwing the bar of chocolate into the gutter.

'The rats can have it,' she declared. 'It's not fit for my children to eat after it has been touched by those filthy German hands.'

I knew what Maman meant, but the chocolate – oh to taste such luxury.

For the rest of the morning, I helped in the shop, which did indeed include serving a small sliver of cheese to some of the families. Maman had it hidden in the back room in the depths of a cupboard and I was grateful the soldiers didn't insist on searching the room. Besides, they were not short of food; they had what they needed and more. They didn't suffer with hunger pangs or go to bed with their stomachs rumbling and wake up with an empty burning sensation in their gut. No, they just took what we had without a thought to us.

'Time to close for lunch,' announced Maman at twelve-thirty. 'Lock the door and I'll go up and get lunch ready.'

I waited for Maman to ascend the wooden staircase up to our accommodation on the first and second floors. Once I was certain she was out of the way, I quickly closed the shop as per usual and then hurried out to the alleyway. The bar of chocolate was still where Maman had thrown it. I would share it with my brother later – in secret so Maman didn't know. She wouldn't have been very happy to know her daughter was picking food out of the gutter.

As I bent to pick it up, two booted feet presented themselves in front of me. My heart thumped wildly as I instantly recognised the German soldier's footwear. As I slowly straightened up, a bead of sweat trickled its way down my spine.

I swallowed, trying to counter the dryness in my mouth as I looked up into the eyes of the officer who had been in the shop earlier and heaved a sigh of relief that it wasn't Claus but the other one – the kind one.

He reached out and took the chocolate bar from my hands. 'It won't be very nice now it has been in the puddle.' He produced another bar from his pocket. 'Here, take this one.'

'I… er… I…' I struggled to find the right words, suddenly conscious that Maman or one of the neighbours could be watching from their windows. What would they think of me openly accepting a gift from a German soldier? I knew it was wrong and, yet, to say no seemed impolite. And when I thought of how much Pierre would love the chocolate, how *could* I refuse?

He smiled at me again. 'I won't tell if you don't.'

Whether it was the warmth of his smile or the kindness in his eyes I wasn't sure, but I found myself reaching out and taking the bar from him. '*Merci*,' I managed to say in a relatively calm voice. In reality, my stomach was flip flapping like crazy and I wasn't sure if it was the thought of the chocolate or the thought of the man in front of me. 'I'm going to give it to my little brother.'

'He's a very lucky young man to have a sister so thoughtful.'

'He's not very well and I'm sure the chocolate will help him feel better,' I replied.

'I could get you some more chocolate,' said the soldier. 'If you'd like me to, that is.'

'*Je n'ai sais pas.* I don't know…' I stopped myself. 'That would be very kind of you but I'm afraid I cannot pay for it, money or otherwise.' I looked him straight in the eye as I spoke, wanting it to be clear that I was not about to offer him any favours. I'd heard some of the women had made themselves available, as Maman put it, to the soldiers and those women were scorned by the others in the village.

'I'm not asking for payment… of any kind.' His smile dropped and he looked serious. 'My name is Max Becker.' He held out his hand.

I was rather taken aback at this formal introduction, especially as we were at war and since we had crossed paths several times now. It was most unlike any introduction I had expected but I felt compelled to respond in kind. With a confidence I didn't necessarily feel, I shook hands with him. 'Simone Varon.'

'*Enchanté*,' Max replied, dipping his head a fraction.

I glanced up and down the alleyway, feeling nervous that we might be spotted. 'I need to go,' I said, pushing the chocolate bar deep into my pocket. '*Merci. Merci, beaucoup.*'

'You are more than welcome, Simone Varon,' he said with a smile. He went to turn but paused. 'Oh, I hope Madame Oray's chickens are happy in their new home.' I looked at him in surprise, wondering how he knew about the chickens. 'Now, I must go,' he continued. 'I hope to see you again soon.'

EIGHT

2019

Imogen sat on the edge of her bed in the *chamber d'hôtes* and picked up her phone to take another look at the property details the *immobilier* had sent through to her yesterday evening.

She was definitely excited, even though the idea of buying a château had never entered her head. However, this one seemed to have put a spell on her already and she hadn't even seen it in the flesh yet. It had somehow seduced her the moment she'd opened the attachment, stealing her heart almost instantly. The fact that it was within her price range was amazing.

She would, of course, be crazy to sink all her money into a run-down sixteenth-century château that hadn't been lived in since the late 90s but she'd be equally crazy to let such an opportunity pass her by. Wouldn't she?

Imogen looked at the price tag again, just to convince herself she hadn't misread. It was ridiculously cheap and the *immobilier* had warned her that the whole building needed renovating, especially one wing that had been badly damaged in a fire many years ago and had never been restored.

If she'd done her sums right, Imogen had the funds to buy it outright, leaving her enough money to live on and to carry out the repairs – make that renovation – for approximately twelve months. She would need to see it first, of course.

The grounds were vast and it was the thought of the gardens and the moat that really tipped the scales. The whole project was practically irresistible.

Before she could talk herself out of it, she phoned M. Henry who didn't seem at all surprised to hear from her and they agreed a time for Imogen to view the château that morning.

From her room, Imogen could hear the soft murmurings of Lisa and her husband, accompanied by the clink and chink of the breakfast table being laid. There was the faint burr of music filtering up the wooden staircase, too quiet for her to make out the words, but the upbeat tempo matched the brightness of the day streaming in through the muslin curtain at the window. The muffled notes of the wind chime hanging from the beech tree in the garden found their way in through the open window, adding to the magical sensation of the new day.

'Good morning, Imogen. How are you today?' asked Lisa, as Imogen went into the breakfast room. Lisa's husband, Ben, was setting the open fire ready for the evening. The old stone cottage with its metre-thick walls was great for keeping out the warmth of the Breton spring day, but by the evening, it could still be a bit nippy.

'I slept very well, thank you. I've got an early viewing today.' Imogen took her seat at the breakfast table. Lisa had made a fresh Breton butter cake and the smell of the sweet sponge filled the kitchen/diner acting as a counterbalance to the smell of the rich coffee brewing in the cafetière.

'I hope it's a bit better than the ones you've seen so far,' commented Ben, going over to the sink to wash his hands.

'It needs some work,' admitted Imogen. 'But I'm taking heart that the estate agent is accompanying me on this visit.' If nothing else, she had learned that when the local estate agents sent a purchaser off on their own to look at a property, where no key was necessary, then basically they were looking at no more than a loose description of a barn, in so much as there were four walls and a roof, albeit a tin roof. 'He emailed to say it had come on the market recently but no one has lived in it for years and it needs some love apparently.'

'Do you think it's another non-starter?' Lisa set a pot of tea on the table for Imogen's benefit.

'It's actually a château,' said Imogen. 'A small one though. It's run-down and needs renovating.'

Ben looked up and raised his eyebrows at her. 'A château? Wow. Whereabouts is it?'

'Trédion? Do you know it?'

'Trédion. That's about fifteen to twenty minutes away by car.'

'Well, if it's at Trédion and I'm pretty sure there's only one château there,' said Lisa placing the breakfast on the table, 'then it was commandeered by the Germans in the war.'

'Do you know anything else about it?' asked Imogen.

'No. Sorry. I expect the estate agent will have more details. I think it's been in the same family so I'm not sure why it wasn't lived in for so long.' Lisa put some toast on a plate for Imogen. 'I just remember one of the ladies from my art group telling me about it last year when we were trying to decide on what subject to paint.'

'Did you paint the château in the end?' asked Imogen.

'No. One of the local women was dead set against it. She said it was considered unlucky by the locals. I think the conversation moved on after that, so I didn't get to the bottom of it.'

'Unlucky? Ooh, now I'm intrigued.' Imogen made a mental note to quiz M. Henry further when she went to view the property.

The drive out to Trédion was very straightforward. The quiet rural roads took Imogen through woodland, typical of the area, passing through a couple of small villages before arriving in Trédion centre. As the road dipped down past a church, Imogen found herself at a T-junction. Looking straight ahead she could see the château standing proudly amongst a variety of equally majestic-looking trees, with its two imposing circular turrets shouldering the front of the building. The stone was a pale grey, but filthy from years of grime that had never been cleaned. Imogen could see the west turret was boarded up and was particularly blackened from what must have been the fire. The roof on the turret had been decimated and was open to the elements with exposed rotting timbers.

The grounds were a mass of bushes and brambles that looked like they had been tended to at some point but, in more recent times, left to grow wild. Imogen could see white conical hydrangeas and silver birch trees lining the gravel driveway that swept its way over the stone bridge and up to the front of the château.

Imogen felt a rush of excitement at the time capsule before her. She had sudden images of what the château must have looked like in its prime and the potential it had if its splendour was restored. It would make an absolutely ideal place for a wedding venue.

The driveway led straight up to the front of the château where Imogen found another car parked and M. Henry waiting by the door.

'*Bonjour!*' he called as Imogen got out of the car. 'I'm so glad you came.' He went over to the entrance and used several keys to unlock the old oak door. As Imogen followed M. Henry, she felt something brush against her leg and, jumping back, she gave a small yelp of surprise.

'It's a cat,' she gasped as a grey striped feline mewed and wound its way around her legs. Imogen gave the animal a stroke. 'Silly cat. I nearly squashed you.'

Rather nonchalantly, the cat stretched and sauntered off across the grass, disappearing through a gap in the hedge.

M. Henry had opened the door by now and waited patiently for Imogen to join him on the stone step. 'Please come in.' He moved to the side to allow Imogen to enter the property first. 'Now, you have to remember nobody has lived here for such a long time. The whole building is rather run-down.'

'Why has it been empty for so long?' asked Imogen.

'The owner passed away. There were no children or family to inherit and the owner specified that it wasn't to be sold until now.'

Imogen stepped over the threshold and into a large reception hall. The musty smell of damp and dust hit her first, together with the coolness of the building. The air temperature inside was noticeably lower than that outside.

M. Henry walked across the hall to open a set of double doors before entering the room, where he then proceeded to open the windows and then the shutters beyond, allowing the space to be swamped with light. A huge fireplace dominated one wall with an oak beam and stone hearth. Beyond that was another set of double doors that led into another reception room.

'This is where the guests would have been entertained,' said M. Henry.

Imogen seized her chance to ask about the history. 'I understand the château was commandeered by the Germans during the war.'

M. Henry hesitated briefly before continuing to walk around the room and open more windows and shutters. 'Yes. That's right. Now, look at this view – you can see the gardens and the moat from here.'

Imogen wasn't going to be deterred that easily. 'What did the Germans do here exactly?'

The estate agent turned and looked at her over the top of his glasses. 'What did they do? Who knows? It was a long time ago. Logistics, maybe.' He gave a shrug. 'Now, if we go back out into the hallway, we can look at the kitchen.' Imogen followed M. Henry out as he gave a running commentary of their tour. 'On the left here is a small reception room, probably once a study or a library and further along, here's the third room.'

By the time Imogen had looked around the final reception room, she knew her heart was well and truly won over. 'This would make a lovely snug,' she said as she followed her guide out and along the hallway again.

'This is the kitchen. As you can see it needs thoroughly bringing up to date. There's an oven here in the fireplace but I can't imagine that it still works. Or that you'd want it to work. Try to imagine this room as fully renovated. Such a large space with a view of the rear gardens.'

And so he went on with his job of highlighting the

features and potential of the property. Imogen wanted to tell him that he really didn't need to bother – she was already working out when she could move in and where she'd put her furniture and how much it would cost.

They moved back through the rooms to the entrance hall where a sweeping stone staircase curled its way up the turret to the floors above. There were five bedrooms on the first floor and three more in the attic. The rooms were large and airy and Imogen was captured by the beauty and mystery of the château. She stood at the window of the master bedroom overlooking the rear gardens and with her fingertip rubbed at least thirty years of dust and grime from the pane of glass, creating a porthole to look out. From that vantage point she could see the grounds had been formally laid out. There was a privet running along the side of the garden and although it was very much overgrown, Imogen could imagine strolling through the hedged tunnel with the dappled light filtering through the foliage. Overall, the grounds were in much better shape than the château itself.

'The gardens,' she said as she looked on. 'They look like they've been upkept more than the house.'

'Yes, that was Marcel. He always tended the gardens. He used to be employed as the gardener here and when the owner died, he just carried on tending to the grounds. Sadly, he passed away last year and I'm afraid no one has done anything since then.'

As Imogen peered to her right, she could see the other side of the château as it dog-legged out into the garden, a perfect symmetry of the other side, forming three sides of a quadrant. 'I need to look at the other turret,' she said.

'Oh, I don't think that's a good idea,' said M. Henry. 'There's nothing to see. You do know there was a fire there and it has been closed for many years.'

'I still need to see it,' insisted Imogen.

'Very well,' said the estate agent. 'We can get to it by going along this passageway, which links the east and west wings. The rooms to the front are on our right and the rooms to the left overlook the rear. Come.'

At the end of the passageway, which effectively cut the château in two, there was a door that M. Henry unlocked with one of the keys he had brought with him.

As he pushed open the door, the smell of damp wafted out. They were on the stone staircase of the west turret, which had a corridor leading off to the left and the rooms beyond. Imogen looked up and could see the sky above them through the remains of the rafters.

'This part of the property is safe,' said M. Henry, 'but needs totally rebuilding.'

Imogen gave a small shiver as they proceeded along the hall, where again most of the roof of the wing had either been brought down in the fire, or by the elements over the years.

It certainly needed more work than she had expected. A scuttling noise made her jump and M. Henry gave a small laugh as he explained it was probably mice. 'And this hasn't been touched since the fire?' she asked.

'No. The blaze was put out and the wing shut up. As far as I know anyway.'

They were only able to walk a few feet down the corridor before a gaping hole in the floorboards prevented them from going any further. A rope had been tied across the hallway in a rather rudimental but typical French style; it did the job. 'Such a shame nothing was done to it,' mused Imogen.

'It is, but the owner insisted it should be left. Now, would you like to view the gardens?'

M. Henry was already walking away. Imogen stood at the edge of the void for a little longer, feeling almost hypnotised by the building as she tried to imagine what it looked like in its glory days before the Germans took it over.

A small breeze lifted a wisp of hair and tickled the back of her neck. She shivered again, not from the wind but the sensation of a history to the house that needed to be discovered. Why had it been shut up all this time? What had happened here on the night of the fire? Goose bumps pricked her skin and a shot of adrenalin skittered through her.

Outside, the gardens stole her heart just as the interior had. A beautiful rose garden in one corner, another garden with boxed hedging and a now overgrown vegetable patch, the privet and a sunken walled garden. Imogen could visualise how it must have looked once and the thought of bringing the gardens back to life excited her the most.

They walked the whole circuit of the grounds, arriving back at the front door.

'I just want to take one more look inside,' said Imogen.

'*Bien sûr*. I shall wait here,' said M. Henry.

As Imogen went back inside, she could see the estate agent taking out a cigarette. She spent a few minutes walking back through the ground-floor rooms and then did a quick tour of the first floor and the attic above. The château had been stripped of every shred of furniture but it didn't matter, Imogen could see in her mind's eye exactly how she thought it should look.

Standing at the top of the staircase, looking out of the small slit window in the turret, she asked herself could she really do this? Did she have the courage to take on such a vast project? Equally, did she dare walk away from something that could be the saving of her?

'What do you think, James?' she said out loud, a habit she'd developed from her early days of grief when it comforted her and she wasn't ready to give up that connection with her husband. Now, she did it simply because she missed him and it gave her a moment to steady herself before making any rash decisions in life.

As she stepped out of the château and onto the driveway, M. Henry was just answering his phone. To allow him some privacy, she wandered along the front of the château, inspecting the now overgrown flower beds. However, his voice carried across the drive.

'*Non,*' he was speaking quite insistently. '*Non. Pas possible.* That's impossible. I have someone here right now looking at the château.'

Imogen's ears pricked up and she listened harder to the fast-flowing French.

'I will have to call you back after this client has finished their viewing… I cannot take your offer over the phone… Of course, if this purchaser doesn't proceed, I will call you… *non*… Please, sir…' He let out a sigh. 'Very well, I shall ask.'

By now Imogen wasn't even pretending she wasn't listening. From what she could make out M. Henry had another client on the phone who was very keen to buy the château.

Surprisingly, her heart rate picked up at the thought and a sense of panic settled in her. She didn't want anyone else to buy the château. She wanted it herself. She didn't know that for certain until that moment but, yes, she absolutely wanted the château and the thought of someone else buying it filled her with dread. She couldn't lose out. Not now.

'I want to buy it,' she blurted out to M. Henry. '*Je veux acheter le château. Je vais signer les papiers aujourd'hui. Je peux payer la caution aujourd'hui.*' Her French was rusty and she hoped she was making sense. She wanted to buy the château. To sign the papers and pay the deposit today. Right now.

The estate agent looked at her, uncertainty etched on his

face. 'You want to buy it?' he repeated as if he needed the clarity.

'*Oui. Absolutement.*' Imogen felt the panic rising higher. The palms of her hands were sweating. She just wanted him to say yes to her. 'Monsieur Henry, *s'il vous plaît…*'

NINE

1944

After accepting the chocolate from the German officer, I went back into the house, closing the door softly behind me.

'What are you doing?' It was Maman.

I nearly jumped out of my skin and made a concerted effort to dislodge the smile from my face before turning around. 'Nothing. I was just looking out at the weather and wondering if it was going to rain and should I bring the washing in.'

Maman didn't look convinced by my story. She came over to the door and, pulling back the curtain, she looked up at the sky. 'Rain? The sky is blue. What are you talking about? Now come and have your lunch.' She hustled me upstairs and into the small kitchenette, before she began dishing up the food. It was potato soup again. It was what we had most days for lunch. Just enough to fill a cup with a small lump of bread, torn from yesterday's loaf. Having fresh bread was no longer a daily occurrence as it used to be. Papa loved the fresh baguette he used to buy from the *boulangerie*. I don't know what he would think of the meagre rations we had to survive on today but I was glad he was not here to witness our suffering. It was bad enough having to cope with Maman's guilt when she saw we were still hungry after making us the best possible meal she could with so few ingredients at her disposal.

I walked over to the sofa where Pierre was lying. His eyes were half closed and he looked very pale. If only he were strong enough to come outside, then I was sure, he'd feel better but Maman was adamant he couldn't as she was worried the pollen in the air would set off his coughing. I stroked the hair from his brow and his eyes fluttered as he tried to look up at me. 'You're very hot.'

'I feel cold.'

'Simone, stop fussing. Leave the boy alone,' scolded Maman. 'What is wrong with you today? Worrying about the weather and if it is going to rain and now if your brother is too hot. It's beautiful out there; of course he's bound to be hot.'

'No, hot as in he has a temperature.'

Maman came over and felt Pierre's brow. 'Hmm, he does seem a little hot. Let me get a cold compress.' She ran a cloth under the tap and squeezed it out, before folding it into a pad and placing it on Pierre's brow.

She returned her attention to the pot on the stove. I leaned down and whispered in Pierre's ear. 'I have a treat for you later, if you promise to eat all your soup.'

'*Qu'est que ce?*' What is it?

'You have to eat your soup to find out.'

'Simone, what are you doing now? Don't crowd your brother like that. I don't want you two exchanging germs. I can't have two sick children on my hands.'

'I'm eighteen. I'm hardly a child,' I retorted, indignant at the reference. I stood up and looked at my reflection in the mirror, smoothing down my hair that had escaped from the hair band.

'You'll always be my child,' replied Maman and the fondness that I had once been so used to reappeared for a moment. I missed those times before the war when Maman wasn't weighed down with the worry of where our next meal would come from, if we had enough food to sell others and to make a small profit for ourselves. I missed the days when working alongside Maman in the shop was a pleasure, when customers passed the time of day and their biggest concern was the fresh bread or exchanging gossip in the street. When the days just passed gently. Those days were long gone and I had no idea if they would ever return and, even then, if they did, whether they would be the same. The village had been stained by the Germans.

My thoughts were interrupted by a bout of coughing from Pierre. I rubbed his back and finally he stopped. Maman brought over his soup.

'I'm not hungry,' said Pierre.

'You must eat,' encouraged Maman. 'It is good food and you cannot waste it, not to mention it will keep your strength up. Pierre, please.'

In the end, Pierre did eat his soup, together with the bread from Maman. He broke the second piece in half and offered it back to me. 'I can't eat any more.'

I wanted to say no and insist he ate it, but I understood he didn't want to feel he was a burden and by this small gesture, he would feel he was making an equal sacrifice. For nothing else, other than his pride, I took the bread.

'Thank you. That's very kind.'

Pierre laid his head back against the pillow. He coughed again, but fortunately this did not lead to another prolonged episode and Maman helped him back to his bedroom while I took the bowls over to the kitchenette.

'Do you think he needs the doctor?' I whispered to Maman when she returned.

'I don't know and we don't have the money to call the doctor out unless it's an emergency.' Maman picked up Pierre's nebuliser and the small packet of powder that was used to relieve his asthma. She looked inside, sighed and put it away in the cupboard. 'We will have to get some more of that soon.'

I could see her eyes glistening with tears but she hurriedly blinked them away. I knew that was another worry too – trying to find the money to buy the medication for the nebuliser. I felt powerless to offer any words of comfort. I knew Maman well enough to appreciate a sympathetic hug would probably unlock the floodgates and she would hate to break down in front of her children. Instead, I turned my attention to scrubbing the pot.

When I had finished in the kitchen, I checked on Pierre again. He was awake and idly looking at a book I had given him for his birthday the year before. It had belonged to one of my friends who had given it to me in exchange for some tomatoes. Maman hadn't been particularly impressed by the barter but, at the same time, had appreciated my gesture.

'How are you feeling?' I asked sitting down on the end of the sofa.

Pierre shrugged. 'My throat's sore and my chest hurts.'

'You poor thing.' I ruffled his dark curls, so much like Papa's, and held the back of my hand to his forehead, which didn't seem so hot now.

'What about my surprise?' Pierre whispered, casting a furtive glance towards the door.

I put my finger to my lips. 'Patience.'

'I'm going to open the shop now,' Maman called from the living room doorway. 'Sit with your brother for a while. If I need you, I'll call you.' She kissed the tops of our heads before leaving.

I grinned at Pierre and went over to the top of the stairs,

listening for her footsteps as she descended and for the door of the shop to open and close.

Back in Pierre's room, I produced the chocolate from my pocket rather like a magician would produce a bunch of flowers from his top hat.

Pierre gasped. He sat up straighter. 'Where did you get that from? Is it real?'

'It doesn't matter where it came from,' I said, as I unpeeled the wrapper. 'And, of course, it's real – can't you just smell the cocoa and sugar?!' I held it close to my face and took a deep breath, which made my mouth water in anticipation of such luxury. I broke off the first square and gave it to Pierre, enjoying the excitement on his face. He shoved it into his mouth without hesitating.

I broke off a chunk for myself and with rather less haste than my brother, because I wanted to savour the moment, I popped it into my mouth. It was heaven.

'Can we eat it all?' asked Pierre eagerly.

'Not in one day. Just one more piece today. I don't want you being sick. And don't say anything to Maman. She'll tell me off.'

I went up to my room in the attic and hid the remaining three blocks of the chocolate in its wrapper at the back of my dressing table drawer. I could hear Pierre begin another bout of coughing and hoped it wasn't the richness of the chocolate giving him indigestion or heartburn. He groaned between breaths and I felt so sorry for him.

I went back down to the kitchen and looked in the larder. There was the tiniest drop of honey left so I boiled the kettle on the stove and made him a warm honey drink.

'Here, try sipping this.' I passed him the cup. 'It will help soothe your throat and stop you coughing.'

Pierre sipped the drink. It wasn't much but he looked like he was enjoying it, the warming fluid helping him to relax. When he was finished, I pulled the blanket higher up his shoulders and sitting on the floor next to him, I took his book and began to read aloud from it.

When I next looked up at Pierre a few minutes later, he was asleep.

TEN
2019

Imogen had stood there waiting for what seemed an eternity for M. Henry to say if she could buy the château. It had mattered so much to her that he said yes. She was determined to buy the building out of sheer bloody-mindedness, if nothing else. She wasn't about to have it snatched from her grasp at the last moment. M. Henry had had quite a job on his hands placating the man on the other end of the line but eventually managed to do so by promising to contact him should the sale not go through.

Imogen wasn't sure what James would have thought of her approach and she smiled as she envisaged him shaking his head and rolling his eyes in resigned amusement.

It was with much relief and a sense of triumph when M. Henry had nodded at her and said if she signed the paperwork that afternoon and transferred the deposit, then the château was hers.

There had been some tense minutes but ultimately, she'd won the battle of the purchase. To be honest, Imogen wasn't sure if she would have offered the asking price so readily had she not felt under pressure but the agent had accepted her offer, taking the moral high ground that she had seen it first. Fortunately, the man didn't appear to have the money to outbid her and kick off a bidding war, for Imogen was sure she would have ended up dipping into the funds she'd mentally put aside for the renovations.

Imogen had gone straight to the *immobilier's* office and signed the agreement form, transferring her deposit at the same time. No going back now. Time to hold her nerve.

So, here she was again, a few days later, to have a final look around the château before she went back to the UK. It was exciting to think that in just a few weeks, all going well, she'd be back again to sign the final contracts and move in. She had already warned work of her plans and, amazingly, they had offered her some part-time remote freelance work, which she gratefully accepted. It would be a handy top-up to her finances while she restored the château.

M. Henry was already there when she arrived, his car parked outside the main entrance. She pulled up next to him and as she got out, she noticed a black Mercedes tucked under the car port in the corner. She could just see the nose and the badge poking out. 'Oh! Whose car is that?' she asked M. Henry.

'There shouldn't be anyone here.' He frowned. 'That's very odd.'

'*Ah, bonjour, monsieur et madame,*' came a voice.

Imogen and M. Henry spun around at the same time to see a man walking from the far corner of the building. He held up his hand in greeting. '*Désolé.* I didn't mean to startle you.'

Imogen could tell from the look on M. Henry's face that he didn't know who the man was any more than she did. Her instinct was to step back and let the estate agent deal with it.

'Can I help you?' asked M. Henry as the man came to a halt in front of them.

'Laurent Roussell,' he announced holding out his hand, which M. Henry shook and then introduced himself.

'You shouldn't be here without an appointment. Besides, the château is sold now. This is Madame Wren who is to be the new owner.'

'I do apologise,' said the man. He offered his hand to Imogen. 'Pleased to meet you.'

'So, what are you doing here?' M. Henry pressed.

'I'm in the construction industry and I heard the château had come back on the market. I was wondering if I could tender for any works that need to be carried out. It's such a beautiful building. I was intrigued and couldn't help having a look around. I remember it from when I was a boy. It's been closed up for so long. We used to play in the grounds when we were children – that's if the gardener didn't catch us and shoo us away.'

'You're from the village?' asked Imogen, wondering if this was her first encounter with a local. She really wanted to try to integrate as much as possible.

'I moved away but my grandmother lived here, so I would visit often,' explained Laurent.

'You're not the man who phoned yesterday about the château?' asked M. Henry.

Laurent gave M. Henry a blank look. 'As I said, I would love to work on the château.'

'*Alors*, that is for Madame Wren to decide,' said M. Henry. He looked at Imogen.

'I haven't got as far as that yet,' said Imogen, slightly sceptical of the man. He didn't look like he was in the construction industry, not hands-on anyway, if his immaculately manicured fingernails were anything to go by. 'If you have a business card, maybe you could leave that with me and I might get in touch.'

'*Bien sûr*,' he replied, taking his wallet from his pocket and withdrawing a card.

Laurent Roussell

Architecte

Roussell & Martel

There was a Paris address and telephone number on the card.

Imogen raised her eyebrows. 'Paris? You're a long way from home.'

Laurent Roussell gave an incline of his head. 'I'm looking for some projects further afield.'

Imogen dropped the card into her handbag. 'Thank you. I'll bear you in mind.' She had absolutely no intention of bearing him in mind at all. A Parisian architect would cost an arm and a leg. There was no way she'd be able to afford his prices.

'*Merci*. Now, I will leave you to your viewing and I hope to hear from you in the near future.' He shook hands again and then headed over to his car.

From the safety of the château, Imogen watched through the sitting room window as the car made its way down the drive, across the bridge and headed into the village.

'What do you make of that?' She turned to ask M. Henry but he was already moving into the next room, seemingly not interested in Laurent Roussell now.

Imogen spent the next thirty minutes or so wandering around the château, taking pictures with her tablet, making notes of what, if any, structural work may need doing in each room or whether it was just aesthetics, in which case she jotted down ideas, such as colours, fabrics, what direction the room faced, what original features remained and so on. There was, of course, the rather onerous, not to mention terrifying prospect of restoring the fire-damaged wing, but she batted that away, allowing herself the luxury of rose-tinted glasses where that was concerned.

She was keen to start work on planning the refurbishments as soon as she could. There would, of course, have to be a full survey. She gulped at the thought. Anyone in their right mind would have instructed a structural survey to be carried out before agreeing to buy the place. She was definitely out of her comfort zone on that front and a practice she would never advise any of her clients to follow. However, here she was, about to renovate a château. A château! Not a cute little cottage or barn, but a sixteenth-century French château! The thought of James saying 'go large or go home' sprang to mind. Well, she certainly wasn't going home for good now.

Once she was happy with the notes she'd made on the interior, Imogen took herself out to the gardens. Almost at once she felt a sense of calm, not dissimilar to that when she was tending her parents' garden. There was something about being in touch with the ground itself, to feel the soil beneath her fingers, that gave her such a sense of wellbeing. It was really hard to describe, but it filled her with a sense of tranquillity.

There was definitely a charged atmosphere within the building that wasn't present outside.

She appreciated the mature shrubs and trees in the grounds and the deep flower beds which, although now unruly, she could definitely imagine in their former glory.

M. Henry was waiting at the front of the property for her, leaning against his car, smoking a cigarette, which he hurriedly scrubbed out under his foot when he saw her coming. 'Have you seen all you wanted to?' he asked.

'Yes, thank you.' Imogen turned back to look at the château. 'I tried to find out some of the history of the building last night but there's not much online. Is there anyone local who I could talk to? I'd really like to restore the château in keeping with its former self – I want to recreate the atmosphere and sense of such a wonderful structure. To know the history would really help me achieve that.'

'I don't know much about the château, but I don't think it's had a happy past. Maybe you should create a new future for it instead.'

'You mean because of the fire?'

He shrugged. 'And maybe because the Germans occupied it during the war. I don't know. I'm just guessing. Not being from around here I don't know the details and as agents, we were just told to sell it.'

'*D'accord. Merci,*' replied Imogen realising she wasn't going to get any more information out of him. Something in her peripheral vision caught her attention. She looked over to the hydrangea – it was the cat from before. It sauntered its way across the gravel path as if it were a member of royalty on a walkabout and, as before, wound itself around Imogen's ankles.

'I think the cat likes you,' said M. Henry. 'That must be a good sign.'

After allowing Imogen to pet it for a while, the cat then continued on its way across the drive and around the corner of the château.

'Funny old thing,' said Imogen. 'I wonder who it belongs to.'

'Maybe it will be you. Cats choose their owners, you know.'

Imogen smiled at the thought. She'd always wanted a pet but she and James had worked full-time and living on the top floor of a converted Edwardian house in the middle of

London, didn't lend itself to having pets, unless you were thinking of a goldfish or a hamster and the latter just reminded Imogen of mice. If the cat wanted to adopt her, then she was more than happy to oblige.

After leaving M. Henry and the château, Imogen drove into the village. She wanted to take time to soak up what was to be her new home. As she sat at a table in a café overlooking the street, she had visions of walking down to the local *boulangerie* in the mornings to get her bread and croissants, saying good morning to the villagers who would become her new friends, taking lunch in the cafés and restaurants, shopping at the market and then going back to the château to work on the renovations. It was something many people would only dream of, she and James included, and now she was about to make it her reality. Gosh, she wished James was here. The pang struck her hard and sharp. It did that every so often and she knew it would pass; she just had to absorb the emotion.

As she drank her coffee, Imogen took out her mobile and searched for some local builders in a bid to distract herself and cushion the emotional blow. She needed to arrange a survey on the château so she could begin to put together a schedule of works. She wanted to source local builders to do the work and a quick search on the internet gave her three leads.

She didn't want to wait, because what was the point in that? The sooner she got a quote, the sooner she'd know exactly what she was dealing with. The call was answered promptly and Imogen explained her situation.

'And where is the property?' asked the builder.

'It's in Trédion. It's actually the château. I expect you're familiar with it as I see from your website you're based in the village.'

'The château?'

'Yes, that's right.'

'No. Sorry. You will need to find someone else. I can't help you. *Au revoir.*'

With that the call ended. Imogen frowned at the phone. How odd. Oh well, she'd just have to try the next one on the list. To her surprise, she got a similar response.

'I would like to help you but we're a family-run business and my father has his reasons, but we cannot help you with the château.'

'Why not exactly, if you don't mind me asking?'

'I'm sorry. We just can't. You'll be better off finding someone outside of the village or, if I may say, not buying the château at all.'

'But why?' asked Imogen, feeling totally in the dark as to why everyone was against it being renovated.

'It is tainted. Very bad things happened there. It's unlucky. That's all I can say.'

Feeling deflated and confused, Imogen rang the third and final building company on her list. She wasn't at all surprised when they too declined to even conduct a survey, never mind carrying out any work.

Honestly, what was wrong with everyone?

After leaving a five euro note on the table for her drink, Imogen left the café in rather a huff feeling extremely frustrated at the whole situation. She walked down the road, turned the corner and looking down the hill could see the château.

It looked glorious in the sunshine and was crying out to be brought back to life but why was everyone so against it?

On the other side of the road stood the village church and although not a religious person, Imogen thought she might see if it was open so she could have a look inside. She wanted to get a feel for the village and an understanding of it in order to help her with the renovation. Although, at this point, if she didn't source a builder from somewhere, that wasn't going to happen any time soon.

As she crossed over the road and walked around to the main entrance, her attention was caught by a small garden of remembrance and war memorial.

The garden was enclosed by a low stone wall, with an entrance directly in front of it with flower beds lining the gravel path. The flower beds looked like they could do with some tender loving care, Imogen noted as she walked up to the monument. The soil needed a good digging over, weeding and some fresh plants brought in.

The monument itself was a granite column with a cross at the top and two smaller ones, each about a metre high, standing at either side. Carved into the stone itself was the French resistance symbol of *le croix de Lorraine* – a small crucifix sitting on top of a bigger one.

It was dedicated to those from the village lost during the war, fighting for the liberation of France. In gold lettering, the main stone listed the local resistance fighters. The stone on the left was the French Forces of the Interior, the official name for the resistance fighters in the latter stages of the war, and the stone to the right the parachutists. Despite being near the centre of the village, there was a certain stillness about the memorial garden that Imogen couldn't quite determine.

'It's a very moving place, isn't it?'

Imogen startled at the voice behind her and spun around, surprised to see Laurent Roussell standing there. 'Oh, you made me jump!'

'Sorry. I didn't mean to frighten you. I was just walking past and saw you.'

She turned back to look at the monument. 'Yes, it is very moving. I can't help wondering what happened to these men and women. What did they do? What was their part in the resistance?'

'People don't like to talk about it,' replied Laurent coming to stand beside her. 'What the resistance did as a collective is very well documented but nobody wants to talk about individual stories. Not here.'

'Why is that? I mean, I can't find anything out about the château either, other than very vague information about it being commandeered during the war and the fact that there was a fire.'

'Some things are best left in the past. It opens up too many wounds.'

'You sound like one of the locals.'

'I sincerely hope not,' said Laurent with conviction. There was no amusement in his voice. 'Look, this is a small village in rural Brittany. People here are not so worldly. I don't mean that in a derogatory way, but they lead simple lives and many here are third-, fourth- or even fifth-generation locals. They have long memories and deep wounds.'

'From the war?'

Laurent nodded. 'They don't like outsiders.'

'You?'

'*Oui*,' he replied slowly.

'And me. I guess they like me even less, being from the UK.'

'You have to win them over in some way.'

'Not sure I'm up for a battle like that,' said Imogen, wondering even more what on earth she had been thinking of, signing for the château. It wasn't the building that was bringing her down, it was the villagers. This wasn't how living the dream was supposed to start out.

'*Alors*, I really must go,' said Laurent. 'Please do get in touch if I can be of any help.'

'Thank you. I might just do that,' Imogen found herself

replying. As she watched Laurent walk away, she wondered if she really had any choice in it, seeing as none of the local artisans wanted to come anywhere near the château. She gave a sigh and looked from the memorial over to the château and couldn't help wondering what dark secrets the château held and if the names of the men and women on this monument were in any way connected.

ELEVEN

1944

Despite our efforts, Pierre did not show any signs of improvement over the coming days – if anything he appeared to be getting worse. His cough continued but more concerning was his lack of energy and he'd started complaining his throat was becoming particularly sore.

'Please try to eat your bread,' Maman encouraged him. 'I've put the last of the honey on it.'

Pierre was lying listlessly on the sofa, where he'd been for the past two days. He turned his head away from the food. 'Sorry, Maman, but I'm not hungry,' he croaked. I stood in the doorway as Maman whispered soothing words to him, telling him he was going to be all right. When Maman looked up at me, I could see the concern in her eyes.

She got to her feet and ushered me into the kitchen. 'We should get the doctor. I'll find something to sell or offer him.'

'I have my flute.' It pained me to say this. I absolutely didn't want to part with it, but I couldn't think of anything else of value in the apartment.

'You can't sell that,' said Maman, with genuine shock in

her voice. 'No. I won't allow you to do that. I'll think of something.'

'But what, Maman? We have only enough money in the till to buy in new provisions. We don't have any spare money.'

'There must be a way.'

I didn't want to argue and to be perfectly honest, I was relieved Maman had refused to allow me to sell the flute but at the same time, I couldn't help feeling a small surge of guilt about Pierre. 'Is there anything we can give the doctor that he can keep so that one day, when the Germans have left and the war is over, he can sell it?' It was the only solution I could think of.

Maman shook her head. 'Nothing.' She paced up and down the room before slumping into the chair, clasping her hands together on the table. 'I'll find a way.'

She didn't meet my eyes and I wasn't sure I liked the look on her face. One of resignation, with an odd mix of determination.

'Please don't do anything you'll regret,' I said, sitting down opposite her and reaching across to cover her hands with mine. 'If you give them too much, they will keep coming back for more. There will be no end.'

'This is not for you to decide.' Maman pulled her hands away.

'Please, Maman, this is not the right thing to do.' Was my mother really going to offer herself? 'I cannot allow you to do this.'

Maman rose to her feet and gave a snort. 'What has become of us, that I am now taking orders from my own daughter who is barely over eighteen years of age?'

'I'll sell the flute,' I said with determination. 'I know you don't agree, but it is better than the alternative. If Papa were here, then he wouldn't object. He would understand. I'll ask the doctor if we can swap if for medication and then when we have money again, we can buy it back.'

Maman let out a sigh. 'You are a very sweet child. You make it sound so easy.'

Once again, I ignored the child reference; I certainly didn't feel like one but that wasn't the point to take issue with. 'It sounds easy because it is. Now, I'll go and see the doctor.'

As if to remind us what was at stake, Pierre made a groaning noise from the sofa and rolled his head from one side to the other. Sweat beaded on his forehead.

Maman went over and knelt beside Pierre. Tenderly she wiped his brow and moved his hair from his eyes. She looked up at me. 'He's not well at all,' she said. 'Go to the doctor now. Ask him to come. Tell him how we will pay.'

I grabbed my jacket from the back of the door and with my flute case in the other hand, rushed outside. After hopping on my bike, I pedalled furiously down the alleyway, barely slowing down as I exited onto the main street.

I was so concerned with getting to the doctor, I didn't look to see if there were any vehicles coming. There was an almighty honk of a car horn as it swerved to miss me. I heard shouting. German voices, but I didn't look back. I wanted to get to the doctor and that was all that mattered.

'Halt!' The voice boomed loud and a shot was fired into the air. Someone in the street screamed and there was a collective gasp of a group of villagers who crouched down, while others ran for cover.

Suddenly, I realised the warning shot had been fired to catch my attention. I pulled hard on the brakes of the bicycle, almost sending myself over the handlebars, but I managed to put my feet down and stop myself from tumbling over. My heart was pounding furiously from both the effort and the fear.

I could hear to sharp clip of boot heels on the cobbles. 'You there!' he shouted in French.

Slowly, I turned around hardly daring to breathe. When I saw who it was, a wave of sickness came over me. *Merde*. It was the soldier from the shop last week. What was his name? Claus, that's right. I wished it was Max, the nice one who had given me the chocolate bar for Pierre and who had stopped Madame Lafitte from being beaten any further – I wouldn't be so frightened of him. The German officer was standing in front of me now, flanked by two other soldiers who moved to block my path. 'What do you think you're doing?' he demanded. 'You nearly got yourself killed, riding out into the road like that.'

I kept my head down and my gaze fixed on his black leather boots. 'Sorry,' I said with deference. The quicker I got this over with, the quicker I could get to the doctor.

'I should think so,' continued Claus. 'Where are you going in such a hurry?'

'The doctor. My brother is sick.'

'He's that ill that you need to cycle like that?'

I nodded. 'Yes, he is.' I looked up at him. 'I really need to get the doctor.'

Claus began a slow walk around me and I could feel his eyes raking up and down my body, so much so, I could imagine the touch. I quelled an internal shiver of disgust that accompanied the thought. 'I suppose you want me to let you go,' he said.

'Please.'

'How ill is your brother?'

'Very.'

'How much is the doctor worth to you?'

'Sorry. I don't understand.' It wasn't true. I had an awful sinking feeling; I knew where this conversation was going.

He was close to me now and I could feel his breath on

my cheek, his mouth so near to my ear, if I moved even an inch, he would be touching me.

'I think you know what I mean.' He leaned in a fraction and when he spoke his voice was a whisper. 'Virgins are my favourite.'

I swallowed hard, refusing to let this pig of a man intimidate me even though I wanted to cry out in fear. I looked straight ahead at the two other soldiers who were with the pig. One had the decency to look away while the other met my gaze, a smirk on his mouth.

'What's this?' Claus asked, picking the flute case from the basket of my bike.

'It's my flute.'

He opened the case. 'You play it?'

'Yes.'

'You know we have instructions to seize musical instruments?' said Claus. Of course I knew. Early on in the occupation, several Jewish families in the village had been ordered to hand over their instruments. 'Looks expensive.'

'It's not worth anything.'

'I'll be the judge of that.' He took the mouthpiece from the blue velvet lining. 'I think I'd like to see you play this.'

The urge to snatch it from his hand and tell him not to touch it was strong but somehow I managed to control myself. I didn't want to get arrested or held up any longer than necessary. I had the feeling he was enjoying teasing me and I didn't want to give him the satisfaction.

'Oh, a flute! That looks a nice one.' The voice of another man sounded out and as I looked beyond the smirking German, I almost gasped in relief. It was Max. He strolled over to stand next to Claus and casually took the case from him, clearly pretending he'd never seen it before. 'I'm a piano man myself but I do love the sound of the flute.

May I?' He managed to ease the mouthpiece from Claus in the most natural of manners.

'I was actually in the middle of negotiations,' said Claus tersely.

'Negotiations?' Max pushed the mouthpiece into the folds of the blue velvet lining and closed the case.

'Yes. So if you want to… you know… go, I have unfinished business.'

Max looked at me and although his face was unsmiling, the was a sense of reassurance about him. He flicked the clips locked on the case. 'You might have to close negotiations for now,' he said. 'We're needed. The general has called a meeting. An on-the-spot inspection, actually.' He passed the case over to me, which I grabbed and held close to my body.

Claus let out a long sigh as once again he openly ran his gaze up and down my body. 'Well, today is your lucky day. You get to go on your way, but as my comrade rightly says, negotiations will have to take place another day. You owe me.' He ran his finger down my arm and I couldn't help myself from flinching and turning my head away. Claus gave a mirthless laugh. 'I shall have to remedy your shyness. I like a challenge.'

From somewhere deep within me, although I was scared, I decided I wasn't going to let him know that and I forged my best glare in his direction. As the two officers strode off to the car, Max gave his comrade a slap on the back, said something to him and they both laughed. I wanted to believe Max was different, but maybe they were all the same. Pigs.

TWELVE

2019

'Wow! That's brilliant news,' said Imogen. She had just taken a phone call from the estate agent who was selling her property as she pulled up outside Denise's house. There had been an open day yesterday with six viewings that had resulted in two offers for under the asking price and one just in that moment for the full asking price. She spent the next few minutes discussing the formalities before the call ended. Things were certainly moving fast now. She looked up at Denise's house where her mother-in-law would be in the throes of preparing supper for them both. Imogen called in two or three times a month for supper, a routine they'd fallen into after James's death.

Denise had lived in the three-bedroom 1930s semi for over thirty years, as she proudly pointed out on a regular basis. She and Peter, definitely not Pete, had bought it when they first married and had paid off their mortgage by the time they'd hit their mid-fifties. It was a badge of honour to Denise. James had often teased his mother about his parents' lack of adventure – their fear of doing anything that might rock their plans for the future. And then Peter had died suddenly of a heart attack and Denise was left all alone in the house, which James had always felt cruelly proved his point. Imogen couldn't help agreeing.

Denise opened the front door wide for Imogen to enter, pausing to exchange a customary kiss on each cheek before heading into the living room. Imogen always admired her mother-in-law for looking so elegant no matter what she was doing, whether she was attending a party or a function or, like tonight, cooking a meal. Her blonde hair was cut neatly into a bob, her make-up perfect, never a broken nail in sight and today she was wearing a simple shift dress with a cardigan. She was classical and effortless when it came to style.

Denise made Imogen a drink before going back to the kitchen to 'finish off the tea'. It was a comfortable and familiar routine.

Tonight, however, Imogen on was on edge. She was going to have to tell Denise about her plans to move to France and she knew it was going to be every bit as difficult as she expected. Worse than telling her own parents, in fact. At least they still had each other, but Denise was a widow herself and Imogen couldn't help feeling she was abandoning her mother-in-law.

'Dinner's ready!' called Denise from the kitchen a short while later.

Imogen went into the dining room where, as always, the table was laid to Denise's high standards. Imogen had long ago given up offering to help. Denise liked things done a certain way and always said she liked cooking for Imogen. It gave her something to do, if nothing else.

'Here we are,' said Denise, coming in with two roast dinners. It was chicken this week. She placed the plates on the table and then opened the wine and poured them each a glass.

'This looks very nice,' said Imogen. Denise was a very

proficient cook and a mid-week roast dinner was not to be sniffed at.

'Is that a new dress you've got on?' asked Denise, nodding to the floral wrap-around dress that had been hanging in Imogen's wardrobe for the past four years at least.

'No. Just something I dug out. I had a meeting with the bank today.' Imogen took a sip of wine as she laid down the opener for her news.

'The bank? Is everything OK?' asked Denise. 'I can always help you out if you need anything. James wouldn't want you to be down to your last pennies that you have to go cap in hand to the bank.'

'No, it's nothing like that. But thank you, anyway.' Imogen smiled at Denise. She needed to tell her now. There was no point prolonging the agony for either of them. 'It's to do with the property I saw last week. I've fallen in love with it and… and I've put a deposit down.'

'Oh. A deposit? I didn't realise you were that serious about buying somewhere.'

'I've had an offer on my house here,' continued Imogen, the need to blurt everything out as quickly as possible taking over. 'The full asking price to be exact.'

'That was quick,' said Denise. 'I suppose you'll have to find somewhere quickly to move to. You mustn't rush into buying anything though,' she continued, not giving Imogen a chance to say anything. 'You can always stay with me until you find somewhere. It will actually be nice to have the company.'

'That's a lovely offer, Denise, and I really appreciate it,' said Imogen, grabbing the opportunity to speak as Denise picked at her dinner. 'But I'm not looking to buy anywhere in the UK. The property in France is for me to live in permanently. I did mention it before.'

Denise put down her fork and took a sip of her wine. 'I didn't think you meant it. I thought it was a holiday home you were looking for.' Her voice was small and Imogen couldn't help feeling even more guilty.

They finished their meal in silence and Denise insisted on clearing the table herself while Imogen sat in the living room.

Denise came in a short while later with two cups of tea. 'I'm trying to be gracious about this,' she said, 'but it's not easy.'

'I know it's difficult,' replied Imogen. 'Would you like to see the property details?' Imogen fished the sheet out of her bag and passed it over to her mother-in-law.

Denise's eyes widen. 'A château, no less. Just as well James left you well provided for.'

There was an edge to Denise's voice and Imogen wasn't sure if she liked the tone but she let it slide. 'I fell in love with it the moment I saw it. I know it needs renovating but it will look wonderful when it's done.'

Denise put the property details on the coffee table. 'Tell me, Imogen, have you met someone else? Only doing this on your own seems... I don't know... so bizarre. I mean, how are you actually going to do it?'

'To answer your first question, no I haven't met anyone else,' replied Imogen patiently. 'I have a little experience in this. Granted it's mostly to do with interiors but I'll get experts in to do the structural work.' Imogen went on to explain about getting quotes and carrying the work out in stages, together with her freelance work for the design company.

'I see. You've got it all worked out, haven't you?' said Denise as Imogen finished explaining.

'I hope I have.'

'What do your parents think about it? I can't imagine your mother's very happy.'

'She wasn't at first, but she's getting used to the idea.'

'And I suppose you're hoping I will too,' said Denise. 'Although, it doesn't seem I have any choice in it.' She let out a long sigh. 'I'll miss you. I'm not sure what I'm going to do with myself every other Thursday evening. Sorry, I don't mean to make you feel guilty and I know I'm being selfish, but I'll be lonely without you popping in.'

This was even harder than Imogen imagined it would be. 'You've got Tom and Kelly. They're not that far away.'

'It's not the same.'

'No, it's not. It's better. They've got Lizzie and Beth.' Imogen felt she was stating the obvious reminding Denise of her own granddaughters.

'Tom's always very busy,' said Denise. 'I've always felt like an inconvenience to them. You know, I get in their way. He and Kelly are always running the girls to ballet, or swimming or a playdate. There never seems a good time to call, let alone visit. It was always different with you and James. You always made me feel welcome. After their father died, the boys reacted so differently. Tom withdrew from me whereas James just drew me closer.'

'I know. He was very good like that,' said Imogen, smiling fondly as she remembered how James was always checking in on his mum, either phoning her or calling in several times a week.

Denise rose and pulled her cardigan together, wrapping her arms around herself as she stood in front of the window. 'You're moving on, aren't you? I don't just mean in a physical sense but in an emotional sense too.'

'James will always be with me,' Imogen said softly. 'I'm not leaving him behind but I can't spend the rest of my life in mourning. He'll always be in my heart but I do need some purpose in my life.'

Denise's shoulders stiffened and she tipped her head up a fraction. 'See that wheelbarrow in the garden? When James was a boy, he used to pretend it was a ship and he was sailing across the oceans, through uncharted waters and discovering new lands.' She turned to face Imogen. 'I always knew I wouldn't have him for long, especially after Peter died. I just thought I'd have him a bit longer and now, you're my only link to him.'

Imogen gave a small smile. 'You'll always have a link to him, wherever he is. All the time he's in your heart and mind, he's with you.' She rubbed Denise's arm. 'You don't need me for that.'

Tears filled Denise's eyes and Imogen had to fight to keep a check on her own as the emotion, the grief and the memory of the one human they had both so loved charged the room.

Denise drew a deep breath. 'I know what it's like to lose a husband. I understand what you're feeling but you cannot comprehend my own feelings since you've never lost a child.'

Imogen felt the words like a punch to her stomach. 'That's so unfair and hurtful,' Imogen said. 'You know what happened.'

'I'm sorry. I didn't mean it like that,' said Denise, wiping a tear from her eye.

'It's still a loss,' said Imogen, feeling the rawness of that loss as if it were yesterday. 'It may not be quite the same. It may be different but it's no less.'

'I shouldn't have said anything,' said Denise. 'I apologise. I'm being clumsy. And James would tell me off.'

Imogen was very aware they were both battling with the grief that united them as much as it divided them. And Denise was right, James wouldn't be happy to see them warring. She forced a brighter tone into her voice. 'We'll stay in touch. You can come and visit. I'll still be coming back to the UK when I visit my own family.'

Denise sighed. 'I hope so.'

They sat back down and finished their drinks whilst watching a TV programme that Imogen was sure neither of them was really concentrating on; it was just easier than having to talk.

Usually, Imogen stayed at Denise's until nine o'clock but the atmosphere was so awkward, Imogen wished she could think of a plausible reason to leave early. Denise saved her the trouble. 'You know, I have a bit of a headache. I think I'll go to bed early tonight.'

'Yes, I could do with an early night too,' replied Imogen, gathering up the cups and taking them out to the kitchen. Denise came out into the hall as Imogen was getting her jacket on.

'I'll see you before you go to France, won't I?'

'Of course, you will. I'm not just going to disappear and not tell you.' Imogen hugged her mother-in-law. 'And even then, I'll be phoning and emailing to keep you up to date with everything. You'll be sick of hearing from me.' She tried to make light of it.

Denise attempted a smile but didn't quite manage it. 'I'm sure you'll be far too busy dealing with all that red tape the French are so fond of to worry about me.'

Imogen gave Denise a peck on the cheek. 'Not a chance.'

As Imogen went down the path, she paused at the gate and turned to wave to Denise and felt another wave of guilt at the sight of Denise looking so forlorn.

Imogen climbed into her car and moved the sun visor up out of the way from where she'd needed it earlier. She paused at James's photograph poking out of the pocket. She slipped it out and smiled despite the grief that battered her heart. It was one of her favourite photos of him, taken by a friend of theirs, when he was mid-laughter with her at a festival, his arm draped over her shoulder, a beer bottle in his hand. She couldn't remember what they were laughing at but it was clearly hilarious at the time.

'Oh, James, I hope your mum will forgive me.' Imogen ran her finger across the photograph as an unexpected wave of doubt washed over her. 'I am doing the right thing, aren't I?'

THIRTEEN

1944

For a moment I was rooted to the spot, as I watched the two German officers get in their car and drive off. Max gave a glance in my direction but I looked away, avoiding eye contact. I didn't know what had happened this time, whether the intervention was a coincidence or not, although I was certainly grateful. I could feel my knees begin to shake from relief.

One of the villagers, an elderly woman who worked in the café, came over to ask if I was all right. After promising her I was, I hopped back on my bike and cycled as fast as I could to the doctor's house.

Despite my reassurances, I had to admit I was unnerved by what had happened but had a strange and somewhat guilty feeling of gratitude to Max for all the help he'd given me. I pushed away those emotions. He was a German officer; he was the enemy. He couldn't possibly be any different to the rest of them. Or could he? The notion tortured me as it didn't sit right with my conscience and loyalty to my country.

Twenty minutes later, with the doctor trailing behind me, I burst back into the shop.

'Oh, thank you for coming,' said Maman with relief as the doctor greeted her. She took off her apron and smoothed her hair. 'This way.'

I stayed in the shop as the two of them went up to the apartment. The doctor had refused my offer of the flute, stating he'd visit Pierre and we could sort out payment later. I didn't know how we were going to do that, but quite frankly, I didn't care; I just wanted medical help for my brother.

An agonising fifteen minutes dragged by before I heard footsteps on the wooden staircase and the doctor and Maman appeared in the shop.

'Call me again if there's no improvement,' he was saying.

'Have you given him any medication?' I asked.

'Please, Simone, not now,' said Maman.

The doctor looked uncomfortable standing between the two of us. 'Have you given him any medication?' I asked again.

'If he gets worse, then I'll prescribe something,' said the doctor.

'But that's not what you really think he needs, is it?'

'Simone! Enough.' Maman's voice was firm and I knew I'd overstepped the mark.

'I'm sorry,' said the doctor, moving past me.

'Sorry! Sorry for what?' I demanded, not being able to help myself. 'Sorry Pierre is ill? Sorry you can't help him? Sorry we can't afford to pay for the medication?'

'Simone, it really is not your place to speak to the doctor like that. Apologise this instant,' Maman snapped at me.

I folded my arms, not being able to bring myself to apologise even though I knew I should.

'*C'est bon*,' said the doctor with a distracted wave of his hand in my direction. 'I understand and I wish I could do more but it's the way things are in the circumstances.'

I looked on, the mix of anger and despair raging inside me. How could the doctor be so cold-hearted? I watched him climb on his bicycle and ride away.

'That was very embarrassing. I did not bring you up to speak to someone like that.'

'I just want Pierre to get better.'

'I know. We both do. Come on, Simone,' coaxed Maman, taking on a more sympathetic tone. 'Now, Doctor Tasse thinks Pierre has pneumonia. He has to stay in his room in isolation. You mustn't go in there in case you get ill too.'

'Pneumonia?' I knew the illness caused breathing difficulties and with Pierre's existing asthma condition, it was worrying.

'I need to take everything from his room and clean it with carbolic acid. We're to leave a bath of carbolic acid outside the door so I can put all his bed linen in when I change it,' explained Maman.

'What about medication?' I asked.

Maman dropped her gaze for a moment. 'If it worsens then we might need some but whether it will be medication for his asthma or for the pneumonia, I don't know. It depends which one is worse. The harsh reality is, we cannot afford both.'

'It's so unfair,' was all I could think to say. What an awful position to be put in.

'I know but we must be brave and weather the storm,' said Maman. 'Now while I clean down Pierre's room, I want you to go and serve in the shop.'

The next hour or so passed with a steady flow of customers. It was hard to concentrate and once I weighed out too much sugar for the ration coupon. It was only because it was Madame Oray and she was so honest that she pointed it out to me, that I was aware of my mistake. I could have got in serious trouble if that had happened and the Germans found out. Maman could have her shop shut down or given away to someone else to run.

As I finished serving another customer, the sound of Maman's footsteps hastily navigating the staircase alerted me to something being wrong. I rushed out to the foot of the stairs.

Maman looked ashen with worry. 'Pierre isn't good at all. The pneumonia is setting off his coughing. I've had to use the last of the powder.'

I could hear Pierre cough again. 'I'll go to the doctor now. I'll take my flute.' I rushed past her before she could protest and was back downstairs almost immediately.

'I'm so sorry,' said Maman. 'I didn't want it to come to this. I know how much the flute means to you.' She kissed me on each cheek and then from the fridge in the back of the shop, she took a small slab of cheese and wrapped it in some wax paper. 'Take this as well. Madame Tasse likes her cheese. Now go quickly.'

I didn't need telling twice and was shrugging on my jacket as I sped out of the door. This time, however, I was rather more cautious when exiting from the alleyway onto the main road – the last thing I wanted was a repeat encounter with Claus.

Soon I was outside the doctor's house, banging on the front door.

'I'm coming. I'm coming,' came the voice of his wife. 'Oh, my goodness it's you, Simone Varon. What are you doing here?'

'I want the doctor. He saw my brother earlier today.'

'He's out. Madame Armoir is having her baby. He won't be back for a long time, I wouldn't have thought.'

'Oh no. But this is important!'

'And so is a new baby.'

'Can you help me? I need some medicine for Pierre's nebuliser.' I looked at both the flute and the cheese in my basket and made a snap decision. I held my flute case up to her. 'I can pay with this. It's very valuable. You could keep it and if we need more medicine, the proceeds from that will cover it.'

Madame Tasse eyed the case for a moment. 'Hmm. And where are we going to sell this? Who has the money for such a valuable item?'

'What about this?' I asked desperately, taking the small slab of cheese Maman had given me.

Madame Tasse looked decidedly more impressed with this offering. 'Very well. Wait here.' She took the cheese from my hand and walked back into the house.

I could have cried with relief. Much as it pained me to pass on precious provisions, I knew we didn't have a choice. Besides, we could manage without cheese for the next few weeks. Life and the living were far more important.

The doctor's wife returned a few minutes later with the nebuliser powder and a brown bottle with a cork stopper. 'This is for the pneumonia. My husband had put this aside in case you needed it. It's only a small drop so use it sparingly.'

'Thank you so much,' I said, slipping them into my pocket. The glass was sticky and I wondered if Madame Tasse had syphoned off some of the medication to an amount she felt was a fair exchange for the meagre piece of cheese I had given her.

'I hope your brother recovers soon.'

I hopped on my bike and pedalled furiously back towards the village. It was getting dark and I was sure I was going to miss the curfew if I didn't get a move on. I almost skidded around the corner of the church as I took the turn in the road with speed, only slowing a fraction to navigate my way. On the other side of the road I could see a group of soldiers sitting outside the *tabac*, smoking, drinking wine and laughing heartily. How could they have such a clear conscience with everything that was going on?

One of the men caught me looking and as I took a second glance, I realised it was Max. I was surprised to see him back in the village that evening. He continued to watch me as I cycled by and raised his glass in my direction. I wanted to smile because for some reason it felt a natural response, but I stopped myself. *Les Boches*, no matter how nice they appeared, were no friend of mine or my country.

A few minutes later, I was standing in the doorway of Pierre's room watching my mother pour a dose of the medication onto a spoon and feed it to him, before setting up his nebuliser, where she mixed the powder with some liquid from one vial into another. A length of tubing ran from the vial and Pierre held the end of this to his mouth. A rubber ball, which acted like a pair of bellows, was connected to the other side of the vial and Maman gently squeezed the ball, forcing the air to push the vaporised powder along the tube and into Pierre's mouth. I said a silent prayer both medications would work.

After a few minutes, Maman settled Pierre and he was asleep before she'd even closed the bedroom door.

As we went back to the living room, Maman saw the flute case on the table. 'You didn't have to give it to Madame Tasse?'

'No, she was happy with the cheese.'

'That is good news, although I'm afraid we will have to go without for the rest of the month.'

I shrugged. 'It's all right. I don't mind at all. It's a small sacrifice.'

Maman smiled at me and, stepping towards me, she put her arms around me and held me tight. I hugged her back. We didn't speak. We didn't need to. I could feel all her love, gratitude, hopes, fears and worries all in that one embrace.

'Now, I'm going to bed,' she said, breaking away after a few moments. 'I'm very tired and I may need to get up to Pierre in the night.' She kissed the top of my head. 'Thank you. Goodnight, my darling.'

After Maman had gone to bed, I went around the apartment, closing the shutters and windows. From the balcony window in the living room, which overlooked the street below, I had a clear view of the *tabac* where Max was sitting. At that moment he looked up towards the apartment. I ducked away from the window, mortified that I had been caught spying on him. Very slowly I sneaked another look but the table was empty and the soldiers were standing to leave. I couldn't see Max amongst the group and didn't dare risk trying to see more clearly in case I was spotted again.

It was too early to go to bed and with nothing else to do, I picked up my flute and began to play a lullaby very softly. It was one of the first tunes Papa had taught me to play and the gentle tune was so soothing. The memories of Papa always appeared the strongest when I was playing the flute and that evening, I wished for him to be here more than I had ever before.

Tears found their way to my eyes and eased themselves down my face but I carried on playing. In some strange way the pain of wishing he was here also made me feel closer to him. The years of occupation had been so brutal, they'd almost numbed me of my emotions. Always having to be strong and not let our guard down was tiring and that night I didn't want to fight it anymore. Feeling those emotions made me feel alive again. It was in some small way an act of defiance and resistance to what was happening around me.

I played for a little longer before putting the flute away. I don't know how long I sat on the sofa for, thinking about the past, the present and the future, fantasising what might become of us and also fearing the prospect, but it had grown dark outside and the room had chilled. I got up to go to bed and as I passed the staircase to the ground floor, I couldn't remember if I'd locked the back door or not, such was my haste earlier, so I nipped down and rattled the door handle to make sure. As I was about to climb the stairs, I heard a noise outside. I stopped still in the darkness of the stairwell with only the faint glow of the moon filtering through the glass in the back door.

Footsteps. There were definitely footsteps approaching the door. I recognised the sharp clip of the heels on the flagstones. The same footsteps I'd heard when Claus was walking across the square earlier that day. I held my breath and, not daring to move, I strained to hear where they were going.

The footsteps paused and there was the sound of something being placed on the step. Still I didn't move but pressed myself back against the wall, trying to disappear into the shadows as much as possible in case whoever it was tried to look through the window.

For a few moments there was silence and I was beginning to wonder if the person had crept away without me hearing but then there was a scuffing noise and the familiar sound of heeled boots, this time receding. The tell-tale click of the gate latch being lifted and then dropped and the gate closing could just about be heard from my hiding spot. I waited until the footsteps faded away and I was sure that whoever it was had gone.

I took great care to unlock the door and open it, making

as little sound as possible so as not to alert Maman. To my surprise there was a small brown glass bottle and a box of the nebuliser powder. I read the label on the bottle. It was the exact same medicine that the doctor's wife had given me, only this bottle was full.

Who would leave those things for us?

I ran to the gate and leaned over, scanning the alleyway in both directions, trying to look for the person who'd left the medicines there but I couldn't see anyone – the alleyway was empty.

Bemused by this generous donation, I went back inside and locked the door. The logical explanation was the doctor himself had left it – maybe he had realised his wife had only given us a small amount and was making up for her mean-spiritedness. The only flaw in my rationing was the booted feet on the cobbled yard outside. I was certain I wasn't mistaken when I had marked them as German boots.

Whoever it was didn't want to be known to us or anyone else and if I ever found out who it was, I would thank them profusely.

FOURTEEN
2019

Imogen stood on the driveway looking up at the château, the keys weighing gently in her hand. She had signed the papers at the *notaire's* office that morning and had wasted no time in coming straight over.

She let her gaze wander the height of the east turret and back down, following the wisteria as it draped its way along the building and over the main entrance, making its way to the west turret.

It had rained that morning but it hadn't dampened her spirits and she drew in a deep breath, appreciating that crisp after-rain smell in the air. A few translucent clouds drifted across the sky, causing a hazy veil in front of the sun every so often.

Imogen smiled to herself and savoured the moment. This was home. Hers and hers alone. This was her new start.

Opening the exterior doors and then the interior doors to the main entrance, Imogen performed a 360-degree turn, her arms outstretched.

'*Bonjour*, house,' she said out loud. 'I've come to rescue you.'

The rumbling of a lorry pulling up outside made Imogen turn. It was the removal firm from the UK. They had diligently packed and loaded the few possessions she was bringing with her and transported them across the Channel on the overnight ferry.

'How was the crossing?' asked Imogen, as Mick, the one who seemed in charge, got down from the cab. His colleague followed suit from the passenger seat.

'Not too bad at all. You made it over then?'

'Yes. I was waiting outside the *notaire's* office at ten o'clock on the dot,' said Imogen. 'Although, I've only just got here. There was so much paperwork to sign.'

'We're just going to have a quick cuppa and a smoke, then we'll get a shifty on.' Mick looked up at the building and then back at the lorry. 'Do you know where you want everything to go? You're going to rattle around in it, aren't you?'

'I'm just going to live in two rooms for now,' replied Imogen. She'd worked this all out in the four weeks she'd spent back in the UK waiting to complete on the sale. 'I've got a plan to give you. All the boxes are numbered and I've marked on the floor plan the corresponding room numbers so just follow that and I'll sort it all out afterwards.'

'That's what I like – someone who's organised,' said Mick.

While the removal men had their drinks, Imogen went back into the house and began opening the windows and shutters, letting the Breton sun seep into the rooms. Dust motes danced in the beams of light and a faint waft of the untamed lavender plants in the flower beds drifted in.

The removal men worked steadily for the next couple of hours, unloading the possessions Imogen had brought with her, which looked totally lost in the reception room at the rear of the property. Her four-seater dining table and chairs, her large comfy sofa and one armchair, two bookcases, together with a coffee table and accessories, like table lamps, mirror and ornaments. It looked quite pathetic really. The sum total of her life was in this room.

'Well, that's the last of it,' said Mick as he came in with two boxes on a sack trolley. 'I don't think I've seen anyone bring so many books over with them. Have you pinched all the books from the Bodleian Library or something?'

'Sorry, I'm a bit of a bookworm,' said Imogen. 'I managed to streamline everything, apart from the books.'

'Just as well,' said Mick. 'You'll need something to keep yourself occupied with. It ain't exactly Piccadilly Circus round here is it?'

'I don't mind. I'm looking forward to a bit of peace and quiet.'

'That's what they all say. I've seen plenty of expats move back to the UK because they found it too boring. Come over here, looking for the good life and realise the bills and problems don't go away. Same hassle, just a different country, made even worse by the lack of language.'

'I speak French, so I'm one step ahead already,' said Imogen, feeling a little miffed that Mick was so readily spouting doom and gloom prophecies. 'It doesn't suit everyone, I'm sure, but I'm equally sure it will suit me.'

'OK, so I won't be seeing you again in about eighteen months going in the opposite direction?'

'No, actually, you won't,' said Imogen. She tagged on a smile, which she didn't mean. 'Anyway, thanks for all your help.'

She wasn't sorry to wave the removal lorry and the doom merchants off down the road a few minutes later.

Imogen checked her watch. It was one-thirty and she

could murder a cup of tea. The shops in the village would all be shut for lunch so buying some milk would have to wait too. She may have had the foresight to buy a French kettle last time she was here but grabbing some milk had passed her by.

A loud bang on the front door made her jump. At least that's what it sounded like. She stood very still, listening and waiting. There it was again. It was definitely someone knocking on the front door. She left the kitchen and glanced out of the tall windows as she hurried along the parquet floored hallway that ran parallel with the front windows but couldn't see the removal van, so it wasn't Mick back having forgotten something.

Opening the door, she was greeted by a bouquet of flowers. Laurent Roussell popped his head out from behind them.

'*Bonjour!* Happy new home,' he said. In his other hand he held a shopping bag. 'I have brought supplies.'

Imogen was taken aback. Laurent Roussell was the last person she'd expected to turn up on her doorstep today.

'*Bonjour,*' she said after regaining her composure and inviting him in. It seemed rude not to and she had checked him out on the internet when she was back in England so was confident he was who he said he was and not some murdering axeman.

They went through to the sitting room where the removal men had placed all Imogen's belongings. 'Sorry about the mess,' she said. 'I've not had time to sort anything out yet.'

'*Pas de problem,*' replied Laurent, handing the flowers to her. 'It's one of those bags with water in so you don't have to put them in a vase. I guessed unpacking a vase wouldn't be high on your list of things to do right now.'

'Thank you so much. They're beautiful,' Imogen said,

admiring the arrangement of sunflowers, blue delphiniums, blue veronica and cerise roses.

Laurent lifted a box from the table. 'Ouf! That's heavy.'

'Books,' said Imogen with an apologetic expression. 'There's rather a lot of them, I'm afraid.'

Laurent placed the box on the floor and lifted a second one from the table. He took the flowers from her and stood them on the space he had made. 'Table decoration,' he said. Then fishing in the carrier bag pulled out a bottle of champagne and a box of chocolates.

'That's so generous!' Imogen was certainly hungry and for a moment mulled over the idea of tucking into the champagne and chocolates right there and then. However, she had company so probably not the best idea. Her stomach gave a small rumble, betraying her thoughts. 'Sorry,' she said clutching at her tummy and felt the burn of embarrassment hit her face.

'Aha, much as all this is very appealing, it's not very practical,' said Laurent as he delved once more into the bag. He produced a flask and two small baguettes stuffed with ham and cheese. 'This, however, is,' he said as he laid out a checked napkin on the table and placed the food and flask down. Then grabbing two dining chairs, he put them at an angle next to each other at the table.

'Oh, wow,' said Imogen. 'I never expected this.'

'*Mademoiselle*,' said Laurent with a flourish and waved his hand in a grand gesture towards the seat.

Imogen took the seat offered. 'This is so thoughtful of you.'

'I thought you might appreciate it. No point going to the local restaurant in the village – they close all day on a Monday. If it's quiet, which it often is, ironically, they shut for lunch too.'

'So very French,' said Imogen with a laugh.

They sat at the table and began to eat the lunch, mainly chatting about the day and how the move had gone so far.'

Laurent looked around the room. 'These smaller boxes, they are all books?'

'Mostly. I didn't bring much with me, just the essentials.'

'And books are essential?'

'Of course!' exclaimed Imogen, entertained by his look of disbelief.

'What about the internet or an e-reader? I understand they are very popular in the UK.'

'They are, but it's not the same. I like to be able to feel the pages, to smell the newness and the oldness of a book. You can't do that on the internet.'

'True, but you can carry a device with you without dislocating your shoulder.'

'Sorry, you won't convert me,' said Imogen.

'You won't have much time to read if you are planning on having all this work done,' said Laurent.

Imogen resisted the urge to roll her eyes. Why did everyone always feel the need to mention how much work needed doing to the château – it wasn't like she hadn't noticed! 'No, but when I want to relax in the evening, I'll have something totally different to occupy myself with.'

'And these books, are any of them reference books, guides to renovating your property?' There was a small look of amusement on Laurent's face.

Imogen wondered for a moment if he was teasing her or mocking her. She looked over at the boxes and her gaze rested on the one marked 'CARE'. The books inside were all from James. He'd always indulged her passion for books, often buying her limited-edition hardback copies and, whenever possible, had somehow managed to get some of them signed by the author. After he'd died, when Imogen had been sorting through some of his things, she'd come across a box stuffed at the back of his wardrobe. When she'd opened it there was a note on top of a sheet of wrapping paper. The note had been from James.

Bugger, you've found this box.

It's for your 30th.

Please indulge me and pretend you know nothing of this. x

Underneath the paper was the start of a collection of early edition books by Daphne du Maurier.

In the weeks and months after James's death, Imogen had sought comfort in reading and rereading the books. It somehow made her feel closer to him and she relished that connection but, of course, it also hurt like hell. And that was the thing about losing someone, the pain and grief suffocated the love and memories. However, in a conscious bid of self-therapy, when the other pastimes she'd indulged in didn't relieve the pain, she had continued to reread the books, willing the happiness of their time together to rise to the surface and overpower the heartache. For the most part it had worked... was still working.

Imogen realised Laurent was looking at her and forced thoughts of James away. 'There might be one or two reference books amongst them,' she replied. 'Just for your information, it is actually my job. I'm a designer.'

Laurent gave a nod of acknowledgement. 'Yes but designing and dressing a room or a house is very different to renovating, especially if you are working on something as old as this.'

Imogen wasn't quite sure she liked what he was implying. He sounded very dismissive of her career. She had looked at his website while she was in England and Laurent Roussell was all about modern buildings, sleek designs and minimalism. She couldn't help herself retorting, 'And what qualifies you to be such an expert on old buildings?'

There was that amused look on his face again. He lifted his glass. 'Touché.'

They ate the rest of the meal in silence and Imogen wondered if she'd made a mistake inviting him in. On the one hand he was easy company but on the other there was a spike there and she wasn't sure she liked the spiky version very much.

'That was just what I needed,' said Imogen as she finished eating.

Laurent smiled and dabbed the napkin to his mouth. He looked around the room. 'If most of these boxes are books, then you didn't bring much with you.'

'I thought it would be easier to get the work done to the house, if I didn't have much to keep moving around.'

'That sounds like a very sensible decision.'

Hooray, they were agreeing with each other. 'To be honest, it will be nice to start afresh.'

'No bad memories to bring with you,' said Laurent, looking at her.

'Something like that.' She dropped her gaze, suddenly feeling self-conscious.

'The end of a relationship?' There was a softness in his voice, no accusation, more of an understanding.

'A marriage,' she replied taking a sip of her water.

'It still hurts you.' It was a statement rather than a question.

Imogen let out a small sigh. 'Not hurts in the way you're thinking. My husband died.'

'Oh, I am so sorry. Please forgive me.'

'It's fine. Honestly, don't apologise,' reassured Imogen, trying to push away the pain that always accompanied the explanation. 'It was four years ago now.'

'He was young, no?'

'Yes. Twenty-nine. Heart attack.' Imogen ran the tip of

her finger around the rim of the cup. 'There was a family history of heart disease; it's just no one knew until it was too late.'

'That must have been a shock for you.'

'It was, yes.' And for no reason she could possibly think of, she said, 'I lost a baby shortly afterwards. I was four months pregnant. I'd already miscarried eight months earlier.'

Laurent reached out and covered her hand with his. 'I can only imagine your pain. I'm so very sorry.'

'Sorry, I didn't mean to…' She found it hard to finish her sentence, but Laurent's gaze, full of concern and understanding, gave her the resilience to carry on. 'I didn't mean to say all that. I'm usually very private about what happened.'

'I'm glad you told me. You obviously felt you needed to say it.' He moved his hand away.

Imogen offered a weak smile. 'I'm not sure why though.'

'It doesn't matter. I guess it's all part of your reason for coming here and buying this place.'

She nodded. 'I was looking for something a lot smaller but then I saw this and my heart was stolen.' She smiled at him, attempting to recover the light mood of earlier. 'We – me and James – had a crazy idea of doing something like this one day. We never got to do that together but I'm doing it now for us both.'

'Chasing away the demons,' said Laurent softly.

'Maybe not demons. Maybe more of a cathartic thing. No, that's not right either. Perhaps holistic is more appropriate.' She dipped her gaze. 'Crazy idea, right?'

'Not if it makes sense to you.' His voice was soft and they sat quietly for a few moments until Laurent sat back, wiped his hands on the napkin before dropping it onto the table and standing up. 'Now, is there anything I can help you with?'

She took his lead and stood too, relieved he hadn't pursued the conversation further. 'I need to sort out an electrician and, in the meantime, a generator.'

'Leave it with me,' replied Laurent. 'I can get you a generator this afternoon. May take a little longer for an electrician but I'll arrange it.'

'Thanks, so much.' Imogen picked up the plates and headed out to the kitchen with them.

Laurent followed on but stopped at the door to the west turret. 'Have you had chance to decide what you're going to do with this side of the building?'

'I want to restore it, eventually, but I need to make sure it's structurally sound and do the essentials to make it weatherproof.'

'Good idea. It's not going to be cheap, whatever you decide to do.'

'Hmm, tell me about it.' Imogen stepped through into the kitchen and placed the dishes on the counter. 'I'm glad you're here, actually.'

'Oh yes, why's that?'

'I'd like to take you up on your offer of an estimate for the works, please.'

A fleeting look of surprise, and possibly relief, whisked across Laurent's face. 'Great,' he said, almost immediately composed again. 'Do you want me to look now?'

'Don't worry about it today. I'm not in a huge rush. Come back another day, when you have more time.'

Laurent paused and glanced back at the turret door. 'Sure.' He went into the kitchen where Imogen was rinsing the plates.

'I had the water reconnected and, so far, there don't

appear to be any leaks. I might be able to manage without electricity for a few days, but I needed running water.'

~

After Laurent had headed out on his generator quest, Imogen wiped down and cleaned the kitchen cupboards so she could at least unpack some of the crockery and kitchen utensils she'd brought with her.

Imogen took some empty boxes out to the front of the house. She would go in search of the communal bins later. She would have to get used to not having door-to-door refuse collection.

As she walked back up the path, she noticed the cat ambling its way towards her. It gave a small mew and Imogen waited for it to approach, before stooping down to give it a stroke.

'Hello, Kitty,' she said. 'We meet again.' The cat rubbed itself against her leg and then with a majestic tip of its nose into the air, it curled away from her and slid between the metal gates and disappeared into the bushes.

As Imogen made her second trip to the gate with flattened cardboard boxes, an elderly gentleman was waiting for her. A big black Labrador with grey whiskers was standing at his side. The man introduced himself as Claude Picard, who lived in the cottage opposite the château.

Imogen explained about the cat. 'Do you know whose it is? It's not yours, is it?'

The man shook his head. '*Non*. I have a dog,' he said needlessly as he patted the big Lab's head. 'Why would I want a cat?'

'It's probably a stray. Might have belonged to Marcel, the old gardener. He's no longer with us.' Claude made the sign of the cross. 'Is everything all right with the château?' he asked, the cat conversation now dismissed.

'Everything is fine.'

Claude nodded. 'I don't wish to alarm you, but the other night, I had got up to let my dog out and I thought I saw someone lurking around. I came around with Bruno and sent him on ahead. I'm a bit old to be confronting anyone in the middle of the night. Next thing, I could hear Bruno barking but I didn't see anyone.'

At that moment, Laurent's car turned in from the road and over the bridge. He stopped at the gates where Imogen and Claude were standing and lowered his window. Imogen introduced the two men to each other.

Laurent nodded towards Claude. '*Monsieur.*'

Claude returned the acknowledgment. 'I've got the generator,' Laurent said to Imogen, who couldn't help thinking he was being rather offhand with the older man. Claude hadn't said anything but Imogen was aware he'd been looking keenly at Laurent. 'I'll take it inside for you,' said Laurent as he gave Claude another nod before putting his car into gear and driving on through the gates.

He couldn't have got away from Claude any quicker if he had tried, thought Imogen.

Imogen gave an apologetic shrug before thanking Claude and making her excuses to get on. As she went back inside, she couldn't help wondering what the tight exchange between the two men was all about. Perhaps the locals really were as bad as Laurent had suggested.

FIFTEEN
1944

'It must have been the doctor,' Maman declared the following morning as we sat in the kitchen, the bottle of medicine and box of powder on the table. 'He must have taken pity on us. I'm not sure I like that idea.'

I knew my mother was a proud woman and that it would trouble her to think others thought we were of charitable status, but at the same time, how could we refuse the offer? 'Whoever it was, they didn't want you to know and they wanted to do it discreetly,' I said. 'I think it would be an insult not to accept it. Besides, can we really refuse it?'

As if on demand, Pierre's hacking cough sounded out. Maman looked towards the living room door. 'I don't want people to feel sorry for us.'

'They're not. They are just helping in the same way you would help another. Just like you helped Madame Oray. I know for you it's a dilemma but we have to put Pierre first.'

Maman rose from her chair and picked up the bottle. 'You don't have to remind me of my duties as a mother.'

'I'm sorry. I didn't mean to.' I was stung by Maman's words but at the same time, I knew she didn't mean it. I rose from the table too. 'I'll get off to the farm and see if we can buy some eggs for the shop.'

'Thank you. There's a small bag of coffee under the till to take with you.'

I enjoyed the ride up to the Devereaux farm on the outskirts of the village and it was especially pleasant that day with the sun warming my face as I cycled along the lane. It was the same lane I had raced down the previous evening to fetch the doctor and as I rounded the bend, his house came into sight.

The doctor's wife was sweeping her front doorstep and I wondered briefly whether to stop or not and ask her about the medicine, but as I slowed and called out a '*bonjour*', the old woman – who had clearly seen me – hurried back indoors.

She was a funny woman at times, I decided, and carried on towards the farm.

'*Ah, bonjour, Simone,*' Monsieur Devereaux greeted me. He was in his early eighties. '*Ça-va?*'

'*Bonjour, Monsieur Devereaux.*' I hopped off my bike and rested it against the fence as we exchanged pleasantries. 'How is Madame Devereaux today?'

'*Pas trop mal, pas trop mal.*' It was his standard response that his wife wasn't too bad. Old age had not been a friend to Madame Devereaux and she struggled to walk these days. Unsteady on her feet, her confidence had left her. 'She's in the kitchen if you want to say hello while I get your eggs.'

I knocked on the door of the farmhouse and let myself into the kitchen, where Madame Devereaux was sitting in an armchair beside the aga. Her eyesight was failing her too but she said she always knew when it was me as I smelled so sweetly of rose water.

I greeted Madame Devereaux with a kiss on each cheek before going over to the aga and taking the coffee pot from the hot plate. I opened the lid and sniffed the roasted acorns, which Madame Devereaux used due to coffee being in such short supply, before pouring her a cup. 'There you go.' I placed the cup on the table and then taking the pouch of coffee beans from my pocket, I opened the pouch and held it up towards the old lady. 'Here, I have something special for you today.'

Madame Devereaux held my hand and sniffed deeply. 'Oh, la, la. That smells good.'

'It was fresh in this week.'

Madame Devereaux took another sniff, a smile forming on her mouth. 'Put it in the tin. You know which one. And thank your mother for me.'

I went over to the shelf and, moving the jars of home-made jam, I found a metal tin and placed the pouch of coffee inside, before replacing it at the back of the shelf. Although the barter system wasn't entirely banned, the Germans didn't encourage it either.

'The soldiers were here,' said Madame Devereaux switching the topic of conversation without any preamble.

'Oh no, when was that? Is everything all right?'

'Earlier today. They took some eggs and milk.'

'Was that their only reason?' I knew the soldiers some-times raided the farm for food, not that they didn't have enough of their own, but they just liked to do it because they could – another way of repressing the villagers and reminding us who was in charge.

'They were looking for some airmen.' Madame Devereaux gave me a long look through her watery eyes.

'And did they find any?' I asked carefully, my voice lowering.

Madame Devereaux spread her hands out wide. 'I am still here so that is your answer.'

There was a secret chain across Brittany that worked to

get Allied troops either up to the north coast and back to the UK or a more circuitous route via Spain, although both pipelines, as they were known, were becoming increasingly dangerous.

Something in my peripheral vision made me look out of the window. I couldn't be sure but I thought I'd seen a figure dash between two of the outbuildings. I leaned on the worktop and peered through the glass. There was nothing and no one there.

I turned to look questioningly at Madame Devereaux and motioned with my hand back towards the outbuildings. 'I thought I saw…'

Madame Devereaux interrupted me. 'No. No you didn't.'

'Are you part of the…?'

Again, I wasn't allowed to finish my sentence. 'We don't speak of it unless it's absolutely necessary. It's bad luck.'

'Bad luck?' I wasn't a superstitious person but I respected Madame Devereaux's wishes.

'You must not breathe a word. Not even to your mother.'

'I won't. I promise,' I replied solemnly. The fewer people who knew about things, the safer it was for everyone.

As I looked out of the window once again, I saw M. Devereaux trudging across the yard with a basket of eggs. I said my goodbyes to Madame Devereaux and went to collect the basket.

'I can only let you have ten eggs today,' he said. 'The Germans came earlier. Took what they could. Thieving bastards.'

'I heard they had been.'

'Really?'

'Yes, Madame Devereaux mentioned it.' The farmer raised his eyebrows in surprise, making me quickly explain further. 'Oh, it was only because I happened to be looking out of the window and thought I saw something… someone.'

'And did you see anything or anyone?' He passed the basket over.

'No. Nothing and no one.' We looked at each other for a moment as an unspoken understanding passed between us.

'That's good,' said M. Devereaux eventually. 'Wouldn't want to start rumours in the village.'

'No. Not at all.' I placed the eggs into the basket of my bike. 'If you ever need any help, you can always ask me.'

'I'll remember that.'

I cycled away from the farm with a sense of excitement and if I was honest, a thread of fear. Even suspecting the Devereauxs were hiding Allied airmen and not telling the Germans could at the very least get me deported to a German workcamp and at worst shot.

I felt honoured that M. Devereaux had even hinted at the possibility to me. It must mean that he felt he could trust me or was perhaps testing me. Maybe now I was finally going to be contacted by someone in the resistance. I'd given up asking Monique if her group were going to contact me as I knew it was out of her hands. I hadn't seen much of her this week. She'd been busy with work and I wasn't sure if she meant her official work at the *mairie* or otherwise.

Lost in thought about the conversation with M. Devereaux and what I could do to help, I didn't hear the rumble of a car engine until it was right behind me.

Despite being confident I wasn't doing anything wrong, the fear of being stopped and questioned was strong, especially so after my run-in with Claus the day before.

The car slowed but I kept pedalling and was relieved as the car overtook me and then disappeared around the corner. As I followed the road, I was dismayed to see the car had stopped a little way ahead.

The driver's door opened and out stepped a German soldier. '*Bonjour*,' he said.

I pulled on the brakes hard, relieved to see it was Max. He tipped his hat at me. 'I thought it was you.'

'*Bonjour*,' I replied, glancing towards the car, wondering if anyone else was with him.

'I'm alone,' he said, as if reading my mind. 'Where are you off to?'

'I'm just on my way back to the shop. I've been to the farm to stock up on some eggs. We buy them and sell them in the shop.'

'Is that the Devereaux farm you've been to?' asked Max, in such a casual way, I almost felt as if we were embarking on an everyday conversation.

However, that one question shifted the ground between us and immediately I was reminded I was talking to a German soldier who could quite possibly have been involved in the search of the farm today. My body stiffened involuntarily and I was sure he had noticed the change in my demeanour.

'Monsieur Devereaux said you were there today,' I said, feeling offended on behalf of the elderly couple.

'That's right. We were,' replied Max. 'We had reports of some enemy pilots in the area.' There was a tightness to his voice and his tone had dropped a level. 'You wouldn't know anything about that, would you?'

'No.'

'I have to ask. It's my job.' He studied me for a long moment. 'I've heard you playing your flute,' he said, surprising me with the turn in conversation. 'I heard you and your friend playing. It was beautiful and I couldn't help stopping to listen. I wanted to compliment you on your playing, but you and your friend scurried away.'

I remembered that day. It made sense now why he was

outside. 'That was the day Madame Lafitte was attacked,' I said stiffly as I recalled the events that followed.

'Yes. It was unfortunate.'

'Unfortunate?' I made a huffing noise as I quelled my anger. 'I'm glad I don't have to do your job,' I couldn't help snapping.

'You know this isn't my choice of profession,' he said, looking across the fields. 'Back home in Hamburg, I was a music teacher. Young kids, ten-year-olds.'

Immediately, I felt the tension inside me evaporate as I drew a mental picture of Max standing in front of a classroom teaching children roughly my brother's age. I remembered him looking at the flute yesterday. 'What instruments do you play?'

'Piano mostly. Classically trained. I also play the guitar and I can hold a note on a trumpet.'

'Impressive.'

'My parents were musicians. I suppose it was only natural I'd inherit their love of music.'

'It's the same for me. My father played the flute. He taught me.'

'And your flute, was that his?'

'Yes. It was.' The was a pause in the conversation and rather than making eye contact, I looked down and noticed his hands. He certainly had long, elegant fingers and I could imagine them caressing the keys of a piano. I glanced up and saw him looking at me. I felt flustered as if he had read my thoughts. 'Do you miss teaching?' I blurted out to cover my embarrassment.

'I do. I certainly won't miss this...' he cast his hand across the landscape '...what's going on here.' He let out a big sigh. 'What about you? Have you always worked in the shop with your mother?'

'I wanted to be a musician, to play in an orchestra,' I

confessed. 'But I can't do that until the war is over. At least I hope I can but who knows what the future holds.' I realised I was being a bit tetchy but I hated the thought of the occupation and what it was doing to my country.

'How is your brother? He is not well as I understand.'

I was taken aback by the question as once again the turn in conversation caught me off-guard. 'How do you know about Pierre?'

'I heard him coughing when we were in the shop and from the doctor's ledger, which he has to provide us with, I saw he had paid a visit.'

'He has some medicine. I hope it works.'

'You should keep your flute out of sight,' said Max, taking the conversation back again. 'It's too precious to lose.'

I studied the man in front of me. It was hard to see beyond the uniform and not see the German soldier, part of the occupying force, but if I looked closer there was a man, a person, someone with compassion and empathy standing there. 'Did you come by the shop last night?'

'What makes you ask that?'

'Someone was outside the back of my house. I heard them. I heard their footsteps – boots. They were wearing boots.' I glanced down at Max's feet. 'Military boots.'

Max raised his eyebrows. 'You can tell what sort of boots by their sound?' The corners of his mouth tipped upwards a fraction.

'I can, actually. I've heard enough German soldier boots marching through the village to know what they sound like.' I gave him a defiant look, suddenly angry that he was finding it all rather funny and trivial.

'I'm sorry,' he said, a look of sincerity now settling on his face.

Begrudgingly, I found myself accepting his apology. 'So, was it you? At my house last night?'

'Would it matter if it was?'

'You're doing a very good job of avoiding answering my questions.' Once again, I had to remind myself not to be so bold in my responses to Max. I stopped dead in my thoughts at my own subconscious labelling of him. I was calling him Max, as if he were a friend. When did I stop thinking of him as a German officer?

Before Max could respond, the sound of a horse clipping along the road pulling a cart interrupted us. It was the doctor and his wife.

'*Bonjour*,' said the doctor as the horse plodded past.

'*Bonjour, Doctor. Madame Tasse*,' I said. The doctor's wife fixed me with a hard glare but did not reply.

'*Bonjour*,' said Max to which he received a nod of acknowledgement from the doctor and another stony silence from the wife. I watched the cart travel along the road and out of sight.

'I don't think your doctor's wife approves of you speaking to me.'

'Actually, what she doesn't approve of is me speaking to a German soldier.'

'Ah, I see,' said Max. 'Am I a German soldier to you or just a man?'

I took my time to consider the question and further time to consider my reply. 'I'm not sure,' I confessed 'Maybe at this point, you're somewhere between the two.'

'And I suspect the German soldier is not your preference.'

'I don't like speaking to the uniform.' I was treading a fine line between polite conversation and insulting a German officer, but I couldn't help myself.

Max nodded an understanding. 'Maybe if you got to know the person, then the uniform would be less important.'

My heart threw in an extra beat as I took a moment to

wonder whether I was understanding him correctly. Although he spoke excellent French, had I missed something in the translation? 'I... er... I...' I stopped myself from answering. What was I thinking? How could I consider even befriending the enemy? What would the villagers say anyway? I would be branded one of those whores who collaborated with the enemy. 'I think it takes more than just a uniform to make a good man,' I said haughtily, wishing the tremor in my voice wasn't so apparent. 'Now, if that's all, I'll be on my way.' I swallowed hard at my rather brash response.

Max pursed his lips and after taking a long look at me, he gave a slight bow and stretched his arm out to the side. 'Please don't let me hold you up any longer.'

I couldn't decipher the expression on his face nor the tone in his voice and I briefly regretted dismissing him so offhandedly but it was done. I hopped on my bicycle and pedalled away. By the time I reached the bend in the road, I regretted being so hasty in dismissing the olive branch of friendship he had offered. I glanced over my shoulder and was surprised to see him still standing in the road, his hat in his hands, watching me.

SIXTEEN

2019

Imogen admitted she had been rather more gung-ho about the whole idea of moving into a deserted château when she was back in England, than the reality she now faced.

The bedroom she'd designated as hers was passable, once she'd cleaned it. That had been no mean task. The decades of dirt, grime and cobwebs had taken some serious elbow grease. She'd learned from the *notaire* that although most of the château hadn't been lived in since the fire of 1944, several of the rooms had been in use up until 1999 when the owner had passed away. Since then, the château had remained in trust with the *notaire* on the condition that it wasn't sold until 2019 at the earliest. Imogen had asked about the significance of 2019 but the *notaire* was uncertain and thought it was a date when the owner believed no one would be able to make a claim on the estate.

'The proceeds of the sale are to go to a war veteran's charity,' the *notaire* had explained. 'The owner had no direct descendants to pass the property or the sale proceeds on to.'

Imogen put on a thick jumper and a pair of socks. It may be heading towards summertime in Brittany but there was still a chill in the air first thing in the mornings and with the château lacking any kind of working heating system, she was resorting to layering up her clothing.

The stone steps of the turret staircase harboured enough cold from the night to seep through her woolly socks and although never one for slippers, Imogen decided that now might be the time to invest in some.

The kitchen and the living room were the other two rooms in serviceable condition, which she anticipated using while she could. She'd brought with her a camping stove and planned to live off a basic diet of tinned food for the time being until she sorted out an electrician.

In the kitchen, Imogen filled the kettle and placed it on the camping stove to boil before rummaging around in the box of tins she'd brought over from the UK, looking for something she could have for breakfast. 'Baked beans it is,' she said, taking the tin from the box.

As she ate her beans and drank her instant latte, she grinned to herself. She was actually doing this. It was no longer a fanciful idea or a daydream; she was actually living her and James's dream – after a fashion.

Imogen had phoned her parents the night before, to let them know she'd arrived safely and everything was OK.

She smiled at the thought of the conversation – her dad calling out in the background while she was on the phone to her mum.

'I'm just looking at ferry crossings now. I'm actually quite handy when it comes to DIY, despite what your mother says!'

Imogen looked around her at the peeling paint, the damp on the walls and rotting window frame. Her dad was being optimistic if he thought a bit of DIY was all that was needed.

Meg had been on the phone a couple of times too,

making sure Imogen had arrived safely and settled in. When Imogen mentioned Laurent Roussell, her sister showed far more interest than was necessary, teasing Imogen that she'd be going on a date with him next.

'I shall be doing no such thing,' replied Imogen. 'I suspect he's just being kind because he wants the work. I'm not stupid, you know.'

'I know you're not. I'm only teasing you,' Meg had replied and then laughed like she wasn't really teasing at all.

'Honestly, you're terrible,' scolded Imogen fondly. After she'd ended the call, Imogen realised that it was probably the first time since James had died that she and Meg had joked about Imogen going on a date. Prior to that, their conversations about Imogen meeting someone again had always been drowned by the sadness the subject evoked and although wasn't a taboo topic, it was one they tiptoed around with care.

Imogen wondered about phoning Denise but decided against it. She and Denise had seen each other a few times before Imogen had left for France but each time had become more difficult than the last. Denise had tried to put on a brave face but Imogen knew her well enough to know she was desperately struggling with her imminent departure. Imogen decided to email instead and quickly tapped out a message from her phone.

To: D Wren
  From: Imogen Wren
  Subject: Just saying hi

Hi Denise

Hope you are OK. Just a quick note to say I've arrived in France. I've found a builder who is going to give me a quote and I've met my elderly neighbour across the road who seems nice. I'm surrounded by packing boxes but looking forward to settling in as much as I can before the work on the château begins. I'll send you some photos when I'm a bit more organised.

Take care,

Love Imogen
  x

Imogen took her latte over to the window and looked out across the gardens. She wanted to create a pond. It was something James had always said he'd love in a garden and the task was high up on the list of things Imogen wanted to do. A tranquil space she could escape to and feel close to James. She also wanted to do something in the garden in acknowledgement of the babies they'd lost but hadn't yet come up with the right idea. Whatever she decided on, she knew it would have to be something positive. She didn't want it to be a place of negativity, the kind that ate away at you from the inside. No, she wanted it to be something beautiful, just as her babies would have been.

Not wishing to get melancholy, Imogen finished her drink and picked up her handbag. Today she was going to embrace French life as much as she could and walk into the village to collect her bread from the *boulangerie*. The sun was already breaking through the clouds and the warm air, coupled with the sound of birdsong coming from the garden bushes, gave a lightness to her heart and her step.

The moat around the château was particularly beautiful that morning, with the sun's sparkly reflection making the water look like a glitter ball.

Turning the corner, she climbed the gentle hill that led

up to the village centre, exchanging several '*bonjours*' along the way as she passed some locals and an elderly man coming the other way, already having been to the *boulangerie* judging by the French stick resting in his arm like a baby.

As she neared the church at the foot of the hill, she went over to have another look at the memorial garden. For some inexplicable reason, she felt drawn to it and wondered, once again, what personal stories lay behind the names engraved into the marble.

'Ah, I must apologise for the garden,' came a voice behind her.

She turned to see a man, roughly in his fifties, dressed smartly in a suit with a briefcase in his hand. '*Bonjour, monsieur*,' she said. 'I was wondering about it. Such a pretty space.'

'Unfortunately, Marcel who used to tend to it passed away last year and we haven't been able to get someone to volunteer for the upkeep. Well, not someone who knows what they are doing,' said the man.

'Oh, that is a shame,' said Imogen. She remembered her neighbour talking about Marcel and the now orphaned cat who seemed to be in the process of adopting her. The man in front of her had an official air about him and, hoping he'd oblige with an introduction, she held out her hand. 'I'm Imogen Wren. I've recently moved to the village.'

'Yes. I know.' The man smiled and shook her hand. 'Bernard Le Roux, Maire of Trédion.'

Imogen gulped. She was speaking to the most powerful man of the village. 'Pleased to meet you,' she said. 'Actually, I'd be more than happy to tend to the memorial garden.' She'd said the words before she'd even had time to think about it but it was too late to consider the wisdom of her offer.

The maire looked a little startled. 'You would? I don't mean to be rude, but do you know much about gardening?'

'Sorry, I should have explained. I'm an interior designer – not just of homes, or in my case, abandoned châteaux, but I've helped on some garden designs too. I used to look after my parents' garden. It's a bit of a passion of mine.' She forced herself to stop talking, aware she was on the point of rambling a little, not dissimilar to the untamed garden before them.

Bernard Le Roux appeared to be considering her offer. 'In that case,' he said finally, 'I think I would very much like to consider your offer further. If you call at the office and arrange a time to meet, we can discuss it in more detail.'

'I'd like that. Thank you, so much.' Imogen knew she was beaming with happiness.

They said their farewells and Monsieur Le Roux headed into the *mairie*, leaving Imogen feeling slightly dazed but excited too.

She was still grinning to herself when she reached the centre of the village, which was breaking into life as the weekly market was being set up. Mostly local produce of fruit and veg, with a mobile fish van and a rotisserie van where whole chickens were turning on a spit. The smell of the roasting chickens combined with the aroma of potatoes, garlic and onions gently frying in the tray beneath filled the air.

Locating the *boulangerie*, which also doubled as a patis-serie, Imogen entered the shop. '*Bonjour, messieurs, dames*,' she said and in return was greeted with a murmur of replies. She liked the way French people acknowledged the whole shop and hoped adopting the local customs would help her be accepted more readily into the community.

The smell of freshly baked bread and croissants filled the shop and Imogen watched as the baker brought out another batch of golden-coloured *pains au chocolat*, which he placed on a cooling rack behind the shop assistant. A young child in the queue with her mother looked longingly at the chocolate-filled pastries. Imogen couldn't blame her; in fact, she thought she'd probably treat herself to one to celebrate being here in Trédion.

As she waited to be served, Imogen eyed the cold counter. It was full of the most beautiful cakes and pastries she'd ever seen. It looked like something out of a glossy travel magazine. Fresh cream eclairs with a selection of toppings. Sweet pastries and tartlets filled with exotic fruit in a set custard-like crème, individual cakes, whole cakes, all crafted expertly.

Having made her purchases and managing to restrain herself from buying nearly every cake on display, Imogen headed back along the road, idly looking up at the apartments above the shop fronts. She wondered which one Laurent Roussell lived in but couldn't remember if he had specified exactly where. A quick scan of the overlooking balconies told her no one was sitting out – OK when she said no one, she actually meant Laurent.

'*Bonjour, Imogen,*' came a voice.

Imogen's gaze returned to ground level. '*Oh, bonjour, Claude.*'

Her neighbour was standing with a woman about Imogen's own age and she wondered if it was his daughter. She smiled at the woman.

'This is Elodie Bonnay.' He turned to the young woman. 'This is my new neighbour Imogen. She is renovating the château.'

'The château! So, you're the mad Englishwoman who's bought it, then.' There was a look of surprise and amusement on Elodie's face.

'*Oui, c'est-ça,*' replied Claude.

'Yes, that's me,' replied Imogen smiling in an attempt to strike up some rapport with someone her own age. 'Do you live in Trédion? Are you familiar with the château?'

'Everyone knows about the château,' said Elodie. 'You have a lot of work to do there.'

'Yes, it needs more than just painting and decorating.'

'And you are going to do it on your own? I admire your enthusiasm.'

Imogen gave a small laugh. 'I'm getting some professional help with it. I met a builder, well, architect really, Laurent Roussell. He's going to help me. He's recently moved here from Paris.' She stopped speaking as she registered the look on Elodie's face, which had gone from mild interest to one that Imogen could only describe as hardened.

'Who did you say?' asked Elodie, her tone reflecting her expression.

Claude replied quickly. 'Yes, you heard right. Laurent Roussell. I was just about to tell you.'

Imogen looked from one local to the other. What was going on here? What was she missing?

'You know him?' she ventured, hoping to have some light shed on what was clearly a surprising development on Elodie's part.

Elodie hesitated for a moment, exchanged a glance with Claude, and then turned back to Imogen. 'Yes, I know him, but I haven't seen him for a long time. He used to stay with his grandmother, Simone, during the holidays.'

'Oh, wow, as we say in England, it's a small world.' A thought then struck her and she frowned, recalling the day before when Claude and Laurent had met at the gates. 'So, Claude, do you know Laurent?'

He had the courtesy to look a little uncomfortable. 'I wasn't sure when I saw him yesterday but afterwards, yes, I remembered him.'

She waited for either of them to expand on their knowledge of Laurent, but nothing was forthcoming. 'You remember him from when he used to visit his grandmother too?' she probed, hoping to encourage a conversation.

'*Oui*,' was the only response she got from Claude.

'Is everything OK? You look concerned. You certainly don't look happy about meeting Laurent again.'

'Imogen,' began Claude. 'You seem to me a very nice young woman. I'm not sure if having Laurent Roussell help you is a good thing.' He shifted on his feet and exchanged another look with Elodie.

'What do you mean?' asked Imogen. Talk about getting blood out of a stone, she was having to wrench every word from her neighbour.

'What Claude means,' interjected Elodie, 'is that Laurent isn't really a local; maybe it would be better to use a local artisan. Especially if you want to be part of the community. It's a small gesture but would go a long way to helping you settle into village life.'

'If any other locals wanted to help, that is,' replied Imogen. She wasn't keen on being told what do. 'I'm sure at least a Frenchman carrying out the work will go down better than maybe a British expat.'

'That's a shame,' said Elodie.

Imogen decided to steer the conversation in a different direction. 'Do you live in the village or nearby?' she asked the Frenchwoman.

'In the village,' Elodie replied as if it was a stupid question. 'Near to the school.' She gestured with her hand further up the street.

'And you've always lived here?' It was certainly hard work getting a conversation out of Elodie. Maybe she should give up?

'Always.'

'I'll have to tell Laurent I bumped into you,' said Imogen, now wanting to draw the conversation to a close, if you could call it a conversation – it was more like an interrogation with a reluctant informer. Elodie certainly wouldn't get a job on a welcoming committee. 'Nice to meet you.'

'I'd sooner you didn't,' Elodie said. 'Tell Laurent, that is. Now, I'm late so I must go. *A bientôt, Claude. Au revoir.*' She gave Claude a kiss on each side of the face and nodded towards Imogen, before hurrying away.

'I'm not sure that went so well,' commented Imogen. She gave a sigh. This fitting into the community lark was perhaps going to be harder than she'd imagined.

'Elodie is a very nice young woman,' replied Claude. 'But there's a reason for her frostiness.'

'There is? Perhaps you'd care to tell me, as I wasn't exactly getting the "let's have coffee one day" vibe.'

Claude gave a smile but then his face turned serious again. 'She and Laurent… they were a couple.'

'What?! As in boyfriend and girlfriend?' Imogen hadn't been expecting that.

'Yes. It was a long time ago when they were very young.'

'How young?'

'About ten years ago. Elodie would have been eighteen and Laurent twenty.'

'If it was so long ago, why the frostiness?'

'People here have long memories,' said Claude. 'I don't want to gossip but the Varon-Roussell family are not very well thought of in Trédion and it would be better for you if you kept your distance.'

Imogen looked at Claude in disbelief. 'What exactly do you mean?'

'It's complicated.' And with that he went on his way, leaving Imogen staring after him.

SEVENTEEN

1944

The moment of satisfaction at telling Max I wasn't interested in being friends was short-lived and by the time I reached the village, I was already feeling churlish about my behaviour. I was not naïve enough to believe that every single German soldier was exactly the same, although sometimes it did feel like it, but something deep inside me, some belief in the human race that not everyone was bad stirred within me. It was something Papa had tried to instil in me and Pierre as we grew up – that we were to judge everyone on their individual merits, not to make assumptions and not to be prejudiced against a fellow human just because they were different.

It was a philosophy that Papa deeply believed in and often showed, not in grand gestures, political protests or speeches, but in the tiny ways he tried to make a difference. Like the time when he brought home a man who was drifting from town to town, village to village, someone Maman might have called a vagrant, but Papa had seen beyond that and the man had eaten at our table that evening, bathed in the bathroom and slept on the sofa before leaving the following morning. Or the time Papa had come home starving one evening from work, having given his lunch to the Hindberg family because the children had nothing to eat after their father had been injured falling from the back of a lorry and unable to work for ten days.

Papa led by example and although Maman used to roll her eyes at his latest quest to help someone, we all knew deep down she was very proud of his principles.

So, because of this, I found myself questioning my attitude towards Max and wondering if I had judged him far too sweepingly. It continued to bother me all week, so much so, I had taken to going out into the street in the hope of bumping into him so I could apologise for my behaviour.

'What's got into you the last few days?' Maman asked as I came back from another fruitless walk. 'You're in and out of this shop every day. What's going on?'

'Nothing. I'm just bored, that's all.' It wasn't a lie – I was really bored. There wasn't much for a young woman my age to do at the best of times, but with the German occupation, there was even less.

'*Alors*, I can soon remedy that.' Maman put her hands on her hips. 'You can clean out the cellar if you're bored.'

Fortunately, the sound of Pierre calling out brought the conversation to a halt and I eagerly offered to go to see what he wanted.

The doctor had warned us that the pneumonia could be spread in the air and Maman had sewn two face masks to cover our noses and mouths, which we were to wear when we went into Pierre's room. The window was open, again as instructed by the doctor, to help circulate fresh air but lately the German soldiers who frequented the bar and *tabac* had become particularly raucous in the evenings as the nights grew warmer and lighter and they made the most of their downtime. Often their late-night rowdiness disturbed Pierre.

'*J'ai soif*,' said Pierre as I entered his room and crouched beside him.

I reached for the water and tilting his head with one hand, I brought the glass to his dried and cracked lips. 'Take little sips,' I coaxed.

Pierre managed a few sips before closing his eyes and rolling his head to one side. 'Am I going to die?' he wheezed.

My heart wanted to break at this. 'No! No, you're not,' I insisted. 'You're just unwell. You'll get better. I promise.' I was shocked by his question but also aware of the unwelcome thought had started to creep out from the dark corners of my mind. 'You're going to get better very soon.'

Before I had even finished my sentence, Pierre had drifted back to sleep. I looked at the bottle of medicine we had been donated and could see there wasn't much left at all.

I crept out of the room so as not to disturb him and after taking off my mask, I laid it on the stool outside Pierre's room where Maman often sat listening out for Pierre. I washed my hands with the carbolic soap Maman had managed to get from the hardware shop in exchange for some flour.

Returning to the shop, I reassured Maman that Pierre was all right but I avoided telling her what he said about dying. She didn't need to know that; she had enough on her plate. I set about cleaning and tidying the shelves, a task that had once taken an hour or so before the war when the shelves were stacked fully and an abundance of supplies available. However, now the food was rationed it was becoming too difficult to get enough stock and the shelves housed just a few tins of essential items. I knew the people in the cities were suffering worse than those of us in the rural areas who were able to benefit from homegrown produce but even so, the Germans were greedy and although they paid for food from the shop, I'd heard plenty of stories of them helping themselves from the local farms – the Devereaux farm was not an isolated incident.

The bell tinkled the arrival of a customer. I glanced over my shoulder to see it was Christine Arnold, the mother of one of the boys from the village with whom I was friends.

'*Bonjour, Christine,*' greeted Maman.

'Marianne,' replied Christine, she glanced in my direction and there was a hardness in her eyes.

'How can I help you?' asked Maman, who I was sure hadn't missed the look.

Christine Arnold drummed her fingers against the edge of her wicker basket. She cleared her throat. 'I'm not here to buy anything today.' Her voice was tight as if the act of speaking was painful. 'I was hoping to speak to you in private but perhaps it's better if I say what I need to say to you both.'

I climbed down from the stepladder I'd been using to reach the higher shelf and went to stand beside Maman. I had no idea what was going on, but it didn't sound good.

'Perhaps you'd like to get to the point,' said Maman. She nodded towards the army vehicle pulling up in the road outside. 'Before we have any other customers.'

'*D'accord*. As you wish. It has been noticed that Simone has been fraternising with the German soldiers,' said Christine, certainly getting straight to the point.

'What?' I cried. 'That's not true.'

Maman held my hand. 'Simone… please let Madame Arnold finish.' Switching to formally addressing her friend was the only clue that Maman was not impressed with Christine's observation.

'Last week, you were seen talking to a German soldier in the lane that leads to the Devereaux farm,' said Christine, looking directly at me.

'He was questioning me,' I protested.

'Questioning or talking? They are two different things,' continued Christine. 'You were alone and so was he. By all accounts, it looked an amicable conversation.'

'And who exactly saw this?' asked Maman, giving no indication of what she was thinking.

'I'm not at liberty to say but it wasn't the only occasion. Simone was also seen talking to another or possibly the same soldier in the street.'

'Again, I was being questioned,' I snapped exasperated. 'He nearly knocked me off my bike. Anyone else will tell you.'

'I think my daughter has explained herself and I believe her. Whether you do or not is of no concern to me,' said Maman, her back poker straight. 'I'd thank you not to come accusing my daughter of any sort of collaboration before you have some hard evidence.' She locked eyes with her contemporary.

'I'm merely passing on the concerns of the villagers.'

'You mean the doctor's wife, Madame Tasse,' I said, which earned me a look of disapproval from Maman.

'I don't think there's any need for this conversation to continue. Now, if you're not buying anything, perhaps you'd like to leave. I have other customers.'

Christine gave a quick look over her shoulder at the German soldiers heading towards the shop. She turned back to Maman. 'Look, Marianne, you're a good woman, well respected in the community and you've brought your children up very well in difficult circumstances. I'm just looking out for you and letting you know what's being said so you can prove them wrong.'

With that Christine turned and left the shop, passing the German officer in the doorway. Before I had time to consider what Christine Arnold had said and the implications, I realised too late the officer in the doorway was Claus the Pig, as I had begun to think of him.

'Nice to see you're still in one piece,' said Claus as he strode into the shop.

I ignored both Claus and the look Maman sent my way. This didn't deter Claus as he walked around the room, as if looking for something in particular. 'I want something special. A treat.' His eyes rested on me. 'Something sweet.'

'I'm afraid we don't have anything like that,' said Maman.

'Pity,' replied Claus. 'I'm hosting a party at the château this weekend and I wanted something for my guests.' He paused, his finger held aloft as if an idea had just struck him. 'I know! If I can't offer my guests anything special foodwise, maybe I can offer them something a little different.'

I exchanged a glance with Maman, feeling decidedly uncomfortable, and I hated myself for this. I hated to feel defenceless and weak, knowing there was nothing I could do.

Claus walked over to the counter and smiled. 'Madame…?'

'Varon,' replied Maman, realising he was waiting for an answer.

'Madame Varon, I had the misfortune to nearly run your daughter over the other day, but thankfully, we avoided such an incident. However, when I spoke to her, I noticed she had a flute in her basket. She tells me she plays.'

Maman looked as uneasy as I felt. '*Oui. C'est vrai.* That's right,' replied Maman.

'Plays it well, does she?'

'Very well.' There was a note of pride in Maman's voice.

'Excellent. Then my special treat shall be your daughter playing to my guests at the weekend.' Claus looked very pleased with himself.

Inwardly, I was shrieking no. I wouldn't play for the

German soldiers, especially not when they had commandeered the château, throwing out the family who had lived there for generations and practically abusing the beautiful property, tainting it with merely their presence; never mind what else went on in there. I'd heard stories of wild parties lasting several days and how many of the paintings and pieces of art had either been shipped away to Germany or destroyed. It was abhorrent what they were doing to the place.

'Oh, I don't know if she's up to that standard,' replied Maman, uneasy but obviously trying to dissuade Claus from persisting with this.

'But you just said how well she played. Come now, Madame Varon, I'm sure with a little practice, your daughter will perform beautifully for me.'

'I don't know,' said Maman hesitantly.

Claus held up his hand to silence her. 'Madame Varon, there is just one other thing I should mention. There have been cases of counterfeit ration coupons being used in the area. You know how serious an offence that is and I'm sure you would not accept these.'

Maman shook her head. 'No, of course not.'

'Good, I wouldn't want to have to search these premises.' The threat was loud and clear. 'I know, from your daughter, that your son is very unwell and needs medication for his condition. It would be tragic if that supply was to dry up, wouldn't it?' He looked from Maman, to me and back to her again.

There was absolutely no misunderstanding and I saw Maman pale at the implications. Papa's words of bravery came back to me as they so often had since the occupation and I knew what I had to do.

I stepped forwards and smiled at the officer. 'That is fine. I would be honoured to perform at the château,' I said, even though every fibre in my body was screaming the opposite. I would indeed detest and loathe every single second but I could not let Maman's shop be searched because even though she would never accept counterfeit coupons, I was sure Claus would fix it so some were found. Not only that, but if withholding medication for Pierre was also a possibility, I would give my life not to let that happen.

A flurry of activity out in the street caught Claus's attention. 'Aha, here we are. This is what I came into the village for.' He tipped the peak of his cap with his fingers. 'Be at the château at six p.m. Saturday evening. And make sure you have something decent to wear.' He made the 'Heil Hitler' salute and marched out of the shop. The bell jingled violently above the door, matched only by the shaking of my legs as the fear tore through me.

EIGHTEEN

2019

Imogen was grateful for Laurent sourcing a generator for her. It certainly made life a bit easier now. She had brought several sets of festoon lights with her from the UK and had strung them up in the kitchen, along the main hallway and the living room. For the stairwell, the upstairs landing, her bedroom and the one bathroom that was useable, she had placed battery-powered motion sensor lights. Not ideal but it worked for the time being until she could get an electrician in.

Laurent was coming over that morning in his official capacity of advisor to take a thorough look at what essential building works needed doing. He was bringing with him a surveyor to conduct a full structural report on the west wing and what was needed to make it at least safe.

Imogen made herself a cup of tea and sat down to check her emails. She was pleased to see one from Denise.

To: Imogen Wren
From: D Wren
Subject: France

Dear Imogen

Thank you for your email and I trust you are well.

Glad you are settling in and I hope the work involved isn't too onerous in terms of time, effort and/or pocket.

I am well, thank you. A little lonely if I'm honest, but that's to be expected.

Please do send some photographs. I'm going to visit Tom and Kelly at the weekend and it will be nice to show them. Apparently, Lizzie and Beth wanted to know if you could see the Eiffel Tower from your castle!

Best wishes,

Denise

Imogen took heart that Denise's reply had a light-hearted note at the end when she spoke of the children. It was also encouraging that Denise was going to visit Tom – maybe things would work out well after all.

As she reread the email, Imogen became aware of a scratching sort of noise somewhere in the room. She paused, her cup halfway to her mouth, as she listened more intently. Mice? Please don't let it be mice, although, to be fair, she could hardly complain. It had probably been their play-ground for the past twenty years or so. As long as it wasn't rats, she could cope.

There it was again, near the back door. She put her cup down and went over to the other side of the kitchen. Imogen peered through the glass of the back door. Two luminous amber eyes stared up at her – it was the cat.

'Hello, Kitty,' she said opening the door. 'I haven't got any food for you but you're welcome to some milk.'

Taking the milk from the camping fridge she had set up on the worktop, Imogen poured some into a saucer for the animal, which lapped it up appreciatively. Imogen crouched and gave the silvery fur coat a stroke.

'I know I'm not your owner but maybe we can look after each other.' Oddly, she was comforted by the thought. It was a fanciful notion but she liked it all the same.

Laurent arrived with the surveyor and after formal introductions, Imogen led her two visitors around the château, discussing which rooms needed what work doing to them and what sort of budget she was looking at.

'The kitchen, bathroom, living room and bedrooms are my priorities,' explained Imogen. 'But from what I can tell it's interior design that's needed rather than anything structural in here.'

'*Oui, c'est ça,*' replied the surveyor, agreeing with her. 'The whole château is very sound structurally. There's a little bit of woodworm in the attic rooms but nothing that can't be treated.'

'There's the west wing too,' said Laurent. 'That needs to be dealt with urgently.'

'Maybe not urgently but it's something I'd like to make sure is safe and dry,' said Imogen, not entirely sure she liked Laurent speaking for her.

'We should look at it today, though,' continued Laurent. He gestured towards the west turret and the two men headed out the door.

Imogen was a little put out. Sure, she'd asked Laurent to have a look at the château and give her a quote for the works, but he was acting as if he owned the place and was instructing the surveyor himself.

Laurent turned and paused, as if realising his mistake. 'Err, that is of course, if you want us to look now.'

Imogen resisted the urge to put her hands on her hips by way of reprimand like an old-fashioned schoolteacher; instead she took the keys from her bag to open the door to the west wing.

'Oh, it certainly needs making dry,' commented the surveyor looking up through the joists to the open sky. He spent some time walking around the ground floor, picking his way over the debris that had fallen through the floors above. 'There doesn't seem to be too much damage at ground level. But up there, where the fire took hold... that needs completely rebuilding.'

Imogen followed his gaze up through the gaps and couldn't help wondering how the fire had started. 'I don't suppose we'll ever know the details of the blaze,' she mused.

'That really doesn't matter,' said Laurent quickly.

Imogen gave him a look. 'No, it doesn't matter after all this time, but even so, it's my house now, and I'd quite like to know the history.'

Laurent gave a shrug of indifference. 'There's so much more to know about this house than how a fire started.'

Imogen didn't know what he was being so prickly about but it annoyed her. Before she could say anything else, the surveyor spoke.

'It could have been from an open fire. See here.' He pointed to the fireplace. 'There would have been fireplaces in each of the rooms. The chimney stack is still standing after all these years; it's a testament to the building work.' He walked over to the side of the mantelpiece to a small cupboard-like door in the wall, which Imogen hadn't noticed before. It took a bit of force but he managed to pull the door open and peered inside.

Laurent went over. 'What's this? Some sort of shaft?'

'Yes, a dumb waiter. Obviously not an original feature and probably installed in the 1920s – used to send trays of food or linen up to the next floor. Although this isn't in the kitchen where I'd expect to find it.'

Both Laurent and Imogen were standing at his side now, looking at the shaft. 'Does it go down at all?' asked Laurent as Imogen looked inside.

'I think so. I assume there's a basement or a cellar,' she replied. 'I didn't realise. I'm not sure the estate agent mentioned it.'

'You've not seen a door? What about in the turret?'

'I haven't explored this side much,' admitted Imogen. 'I wanted it made safe first.'

'Let's see if we can find how to get down there.' Laurent was already leaving the room and heading for the door to the turret.

'It's locked,' said Imogen, jangling the bunch of keys in her hand. 'I'm not sure what there is to see down there though.'

'It might have been where they did the laundry and stored things to keep them cool,' said the surveyor. 'I suspect the staircase is in the kitchen somewhere.'

'Let's just check here first,' said Laurent.

Imogen unlocked the door, aware Laurent was eager to explore the turret. As soon as she unlocked the door and stepped aside, he went through.

The stone staircase was an exact replica of the one on the other side of the house and wound its way up to the first and second floors. 'There's no door to go down,' said Imogen. 'It must be in the kitchen then.'

The initial search of the kitchen was fruitless, even though they looked behind every cupboard door and tapped on the walls in a bid to discover the mysterious doorway.

'Ah, it might be behind this,' said the surveyor, inspecting a full-height cupboard at the end of the worktop. 'This actually is freestanding.'

Between the surveyor and Laurent, they managed to shift the cupboard forwards and, much to Imogen's surprise, a doorway was revealed. It was bolted at the top and bottom with a lock in the centre. Laurent pulled the bolts out of their holders and tried the handle but it was definitely locked.

Imogen inspected her bunch of keys, looking to see if one would match with the lock. 'I don't think I've got a key for it,' she said at last.

'You'll need to get a locksmith in,' replied the surveyor. 'Anyway, going by what I've seen, I don't think this ground floor has any structural issues. A couple of the floorboards need replacing but if you're planning on a new floor, which I think you said you were, then it doesn't really matter. Whatever is below is structurally sound.'

'Are you sure there's no key?' asked Laurent. 'It might be wise to look down there anyway.'

Imogen eyed the door and every scary film she'd ever watched that involved a basement skipped through her mind. 'I'm in no rush to go poking around down there right now,' she said.

'But you should just look,' persisted Laurent.

'No. I'm happy not to for now. When we start the renovations in the kitchen, I'll look then. Not today.'

The surveyor spent another twenty minutes or so inspecting the upstairs of the west wing and the turret before coming back into the kitchen where Imogen had been taking a call from her parents.

'Sorry about that,' she said as she ended the call. 'My mum and dad were just checking up on me. Making sure I'm OK.'

'I've seen everything now,' said the surveyor. 'I'll get my report to you by the end of next week.'

Imogen saw the surveyor out and returned to the kitchen. Laurent was inspecting the hidden door. He glanced up as she came in. 'Shame we can't get in there now.'

'You're desperate to look in there, aren't you? What are you hoping to find – long-lost treasure?' She gave a laugh and for a moment Laurent just stared back at her. 'I was only joking,' she added hurriedly, wondering if her sense of humour had got lost in translation.

'Oh, yes, of course,' said Laurent.

He laughed but Imogen wasn't convinced. There was something she couldn't quite put her finger on, but it definitely felt out of kilter.

NINETEEN

1944

Maman and I watched from behind the counter at the commotion in the street that had drawn Claus from the shop. Two army trucks had pulled up outside and numerous soldiers disembarked from the back, lining the main street on both sides, their weapons drawn as a warning to anyone who thought they might intervene.

From a third truck, the back was flipped down and a German soldier angrily shouted and gesticulated with his rifle for the occupants to get out. I watched as four men and two women were herded to the top of the street, outside *le mairie*. I couldn't see clearly who they were as the trees at the top of the road were partially obscuring my view. Another group of soldiers appeared with more villagers, who were jostled into a huddle with the others. The soldiers shouted commands at them in a mixture of German and French.

'Go upstairs with your brother,' ordered Maman.

I ran up the stairs and checked in on Pierre. He was fast asleep in his room, so moving to the living room, I looked out from the full-length window at the scene below.

An uneasy silence had fallen across the street, as

everyone waited, fearing what was about to happen. Even the breeze from that morning had fallen, leaving the red Nazi flag on the wall of *le mairie* hanging limp, shouldered on each side by two long Nazi banners, also static, hanging from the upstairs windows. It was then I noticed a black saloon car draw into the street and come to a stop where the villagers had been lined up. The door opened and General Werner climbed out. The officer accompanying the general barked an order at his men.

Immediately the soldiers lining the street began banging on the doors of the shops and houses, ordering everyone out.

Maman's feet pounded the wooden staircase and I charged out to meet her on the landing, just as the bell above the shop door jangled frantically followed by the stampede of boots on the wooden floor and a hail of German followed by French.

'*Raus! Raus! Sortez! SORTEZ!*'

We stood shoulder to shoulder in front of Pierre's bedroom door as a German soldier stomped up the stairs.

'SORTEZ!' he commanded, waving his gun at us.

'My son is sick,' said Maman. 'He's too ill to be moved.'

The soldier brandished his rifle again. 'Move out of the way.'

Maman and I clung to each other as we had to step aside and let the soldier into the room.

'Please…' I began.

'Hush,' said Maman. 'Do not beg.'

I closed my mouth tight to stop a whimper from escaping and drew a deep breath. I must be brave. I must not be intimidated.

The soldier came out of the room. 'Leave him. Both of you, downstairs. Now.'

There was not a sound from Pierre and I hoped he

would stay oblivious to what was going on. We had no choice but to leave him and be escorted out of the shop. I noticed one of the soldiers grab an apple and stuff it in his pocket. Greedy bastard. He probably didn't even need it. He caught me looking at him, laughed and then picked up another apple and, calling to his friend, he chucked the piece of fruit to him.

I turned my head away in disgust, frightened my expression would betray my feelings. I'd heard some Germans be particularly nasty and spiteful to the locals who dared stand up to them, even if it was with just a look.

We were ordered to the top of the street, rounded up like sheep and penned in by a circle of soldiers.

I stood on tiptoe to try to see who the prisoners were. There were murmurings of who had been hauled up and at first I didn't recognise the names being touted but then the man in front of me spoke and one name jumped out at me. I tapped him on the shoulder. 'Who was that? What was the name you just said?'

He glanced back at me. 'Monique Caron. The secretary from the town hall.'

I gasped, somehow managing to quell a cry. Not Monique! Not my friend. I pushed my way to the front of the crowd, desperate to see for myself and praying that it was a case of mistaken identity. But my hopes were shattered as I saw my friend standing in the line. *Dear God, please let there be some mistake.*

All I could do was to stand and watch. I fixed my gaze on my friend, hoping she would look over and see I was there, supporting her and witnessing her bravery, but Monique's eyes remained staring straight ahead, never wavering.

Someone knocked into me, trying to get nearer to the front, and as I moved to one side to make room, something made me look to my left. I did a double take as I saw Max standing at the kerb with some other officers. His eyes moved and connected with mine but he was impassive, not even acknowledging me.

Was he angry with me after the way I'd spoken to him when I last saw him or was it because he didn't want anyone to realise we knew each other?

I told myself it didn't matter either way. He was the enemy and right now he was part of what was happening to my fellow countrymen.

By now the Germans had hauled everyone out of the shops and houses in the village. The general stood on the steps of *le mairie* and addressed the people.

'Last night there was an act of sabotage and the communications line between here and Ploërmel was cut. I may have tolerated minor things that were happening before and not been so hard on you all, but this I cannot leave unpunished. I had hoped to foster good relations here in Brittany and I believe my men have behaved impeccably towards you all so I now feel angry and betrayed. I also feel you need reminding who is in charge. Now these people you see before you, they have all been involved in treacherous activities against my men and, as such, they must pay the ultimate price.'

He withdrew a sheet of paper from his pocket and began to read their apparent crimes of being involved with the destroying of the communications last night. Once he had finished, he nodded to his officer who gave the order. A group of nine soldiers jogged over and lined up in front of the row of the detainees. The soldiers raised their rifles to their shoulders. There were audible gasps and a woman's cry rang out across the stillness of the village.

The sun clouded over as if Mother Nature herself was protesting and a dark shadow swept across the crowd. Goose bumps prickled my arms. A dog barked somewhere in the distance.

The silence descended like a blanket of snow, absorbing all the sound. All I could hear was my own breathing and the blood pumping through my ears.

The cry of one of the prisoners broke the silence.

'*VIVE LE FRANCE!*'

Almost simultaneously, the officer gave the order to fire and the rapid shots from the firing squad splintered the air.

The prisoners fell. Some crumpled under the weight of their bodies; one spun around, forced backwards by the velocity of the bullets pumped into him; another fell forwards landing with a thud. I saw Monique stagger forwards, drop to her knees, and a bloom of red seeped across her blouse as, for a few seconds she gently rocked one way and then the other, reminding me of a poppy swaying in the fields, before she slumped to the ground, her eyes staring wide open at the grey sky overhead.

I clasped my hand to my mouth, quelling my desire to gag at the awful sight before me. An arm reached around my shoulders and pulled me in to a warm, living and comforting body. I knew it was Maman without having to look. I clung to her, wanting to feel her breathe in and out, feel the warmth of another human being, one with compassion and love.

'Don't cry,' Maman whispered. 'Stand up. Hold you head high. Do not let the bastards see what they have done to you.' She peeled me from her and, standing upright, she took my hand and squeezed it, not with love but with defiance.

I squared my shoulders and lifted my chin. I wanted to look at Max and was sure I could feel his gaze upon me, but I resisted the urge and, taking Maman's lead, I looked straight ahead as the general addressed the villagers.

'Now let this be a lesson to you all.' His voice penetrated the silence. 'I do not want to have to repeat this but I shall if necessary. Anyone coming to me or one of my officers with information of any resistance fighters will be treated most favourably.'

With one hard glare out across the crowd, he turned and strode into the *mairie* building without so much as a glance at the dead bodies at the foot of the steps. Some of the villagers, those related and those not, broke away from the crowd, rushing to their dead. Cries, wails and moans of distress now filled the street as friends and family grieved for their loss.

'Come,' said Maman. 'We need to get back to make sure Pierre is all right.'

As Maman threaded her way through the dispersing crowd, I found myself seeking out Max. I tried to read the expression in his eyes but to no avail. He looked away and then was swallowed up in the throng of soldiers.

Pierre was still sleeping and Maman closed the shop as a mark of respect to the events of earlier. Behind closed doors, she allowed the facade of a defiant and strong woman to disappear as she slumped down on the sofa. 'I just want to sit awhile,' she said, putting her head in her hands. 'I want to appreciate what I have. Everything can change in an instant and there is nothing we can do about it.'

I made Maman a coffee, using a few beans she had saved for a day when they were needed. Today was certainly one of those days. 'I need some fresh air,' I said, taking my jacket from the peg.

'Where are you going?'

'Just out. Don't worry, I'll be careful.'

'I'd sooner you didn't.'

'I need to get out. Please don't worry.'

It was probably a useless request – I knew Maman would

indeed worry but at the same time, I knew I had to get out of the house. Away from the village. The constant presence of the German soldiers was stifling.

I went out the back door and after taking my bike, cycled down the alleyway away from the village, stopping only at the checkpoint. My regular trips to the Devereaux farm meant only a cursory glance at my papers.

I breathed in deep gratifying breaths of air that smelt sweeter and clearer out here in the lanes than in the village. I could hear the birds chirping in the hedgerow as I cycled past and the sun even came out for me, warming my face as I freewheeled down the lane. I was heading for the lake and the woodland surrounding it, a place where Papa used to take me and Pierre when we were younger. He'd sit and fish in the lake while my brother and I played hide and seek in the woods and Maman would lay out a picnic blanket and set up a whole feast of treats. Oh, such glorious happy days.

The spot was deserted as I expected it to be. No one came down here for pleasure anymore. Times were tragically sad and bleak now and as I rested my bike against a tree and lay down on the grass, I wondered again if there would ever be beautiful days like those I'd experienced as a child.

A tear worked its way from the corner of my eye and down my hairline, trickling into my ear as I mourned for the loss of happiness, the loss of freedom and the loss of life.

The noise of feet scuffing through the grass had me bolting upright and spinning around. My heart thundered at the unexpected person before me and I let out a small cry of fright.

TWENTY

2019

Imogen was grateful for the generator. It made moving around the château far easier in the evenings and at night-time being able to see where she was going. It wasn't powerful on an industrial scale, which meant the light wasn't quite strong enough to reach into the darkest corners of the rooms and length of the hallways or corridors, but for the most part it didn't bother her. She wasn't one to let her imagination run away with her. She liked nothing more in the evenings than being curled up on the sofa with Kitty, enjoying their newly formed alliance.

Imogen had taken to going into the village first thing in the morning to buy fresh bread and whatever else she needed for the day. With only a small camping fridge, she didn't have the luxury of a big shopping expedition – not that she wanted to anyway. Even though she was still in holiday mode and the novelty of living in the village had not yet taken on a permanent feel, she appreciated the laid-back pace of rural French life.

As she stepped out onto the street from the boulangerie, she was surprised to see Laurent waiting for her.

'*Bonjour*,' he said with a smile.

'Laurent, nice to see you,' she replied. He hadn't stayed long the other day after discovering the secret door in the kitchen and, for some reason, his demeanour had played on her mind.

'I was just going to call you,' he said. 'I've been working on the plans for the château and thought you would like to see them. I saw you from across the road.' He indicated to a town house on the other side of the street. 'I was just sitting out on my balcony with a coffee.'

Imogen looked at the house. It was three storeys high with a small balcony at one of the full-length windows. The ground floor had a centre door and two large windows each side. 'You have a nice spot,' she commented.

'It belonged to my grandmother and her mother before that. After my grandfather died in the early 60s, my grand-mother came back to live here,' explained Laurent. 'It used to be a shop at one point if you're wondering about the windows.'

'It looks… very traditional.' Imogen stopped herself saying old-fashioned, not wishing to offend Laurent.

He laughed. 'That's very subtle of you. By traditional what you really mean is old and run-down.'

'I didn't actually say that.'

'But you were thinking it.' He grinned at her. 'It's OK. It is old and run-down but I just haven't been here for some time.'

There was a look on his face that told Imogen there was more to that than he was letting on but she didn't want to push him into talking about it. Not here in the street, anyway.

'Do you want to come over to the château? We can look at the plans.'

'Exactly what I was thinking.' Laurent held up a folder in his hand, which Imogen hadn't noticed before.

As they walked back towards the château, Imogen saw the *maire* and smiled as she said good morning.

'*Bonjour, Madame Wren,*' Bernard Le Roux called back. 'Will I be seeing you soon?'

'Yes, I'll call into your office and make an appointment.'

'I shall look forward to that. *Au revoir.*'

'You have a meeting with *le maire*?' asked Laurent.

'Yes, about the memorial garden. I've offered to look after it seeing as there's no one to do it anymore.'

Laurent gave a low whistle. 'And you don't think the château is going to keep you busy?'

'It might be nice to do something different from time to time. It won't really take up much time once I've got it under control.'

'I admire your enthusiasm and optimism. I'm sure the locals will be there to give you lots of advice.'

Imogen gave Laurent a sideways look, unsure how to take that comment. 'I always get the impression you're not very fond of the villagers.'

'I think you'll find it's them who don't like me.'

'Really? Why?' They were at the bottom of the hill now, about to cross the junction.

'You'll have to ask them that.'

Before she could probe any further, Laurent was shepherding her across the road, out of the way of a car, which came around the bend rather too fast. Laurent murmured some insult at the driver and then let out a sigh as he looked up and saw Claude standing at the moat bridge.

'*Bonjour, Claude!*' greeted Imogen enthusiastically as they approached him.

'*Bonjour.*' He nodded and held up a punnet of strawberries. '*Pour vous.*'

'Oh, thank you, Claude, that's very kind of you.' Imogen was touched by this gesture, hoping it was the start to being accepted within the community. 'Laurent is just coming over to discuss the plans for the château, perhaps later on you'd like to call in for a coffee?' Imogen thought it might be a good opportunity to try to glean some local information about the château as well as strengthen her relationship with her neighbour.

Claude looked at Laurent and gave a small grunt and Imogen was unsure if the older man was accepting or declining her invitation. Laurent just stood there with his hands in his pockets, looking back at Claude, and Imogen could once again feel the awkwardness between the two men. She didn't want to say hostility, but there was certainly an atmosphere.

Claude mumbled something more indistinct than before, in which Imogen could only make out a goodbye before he turned and walked across the road to his cottage.

'Am I missing something?' she asked Laurent as she watched Claude disappear through his garden gate. She thought back to her conversation with Claude and Elodie last week. 'Is there a problem between you two?'

'No. He's just another small-minded villager.'

Their feet crunched on the pea shingle driveway as they walked up towards the château. 'What's that supposed to mean?' asked Imogen.

'Nothing. Ignore me.' Laurent gave her a broad smile. 'Those strawberries look nice.' He picked one from the punnet and bit into it. 'They taste good too.'

'I thought I might have a vegetable patch,' replied Imogen, aware Laurent was trying to steer the conversation away from Claude. She'd let him do so for now but logged the avoidance for a later date. 'I like the idea of growing my own fruit and vegetables.'

Laurent looked sceptical. 'It's a lot of hard work. I remember my grandparents spent hours tending to their garden. Wouldn't you prefer the easy life and just be able to buy them from the supermarket or the market?'

'Where's the fun in that?' she replied. Although she knew it would take up a lot of her time it was something she and James had fantasied about and she was happy to keep that ideal alive. 'I'd like to grow herbs too for natural remedies, herbal teas, that sort of thing. I love the idea of a sensory garden or throwing part of it back to nature, with meadow flowers, a small pond, not cutting the grass too short – a mini nature reserve, if you like.'

Laurent chuckled. 'I'm not sure what the locals will think of that. Haven't you noticed how manicured their gardens are?'

It was true. The gardens were extremely neat and tidy. The lawns were mowed into neat stripes, edges practically at right angles, and a strict pattern of marigold, geranium, marigold, geranium was adhered to in some unspoken agreement of conformity. Hedges were trimmed to within an inch of a secret specified height and hydrangea bushes cultivated into an almost perfect dome.

'I can get away with it though,' replied Imogen.

'Is that so?'

'Yep. I'm the crazy Englishwoman who not only bought the château that needed totally renovating but also gave the garden back to nature.'

'Ah, yes, I can hear them now,' said Laurent, taking another strawberry from the punnet. 'Shall we go to *le maire* and demand she is served with a notice to conform to village regulations?' He mimicked an old woman's voice, which had Imogen laughing. 'Or they might even hold a secret meeting in the hall and call you up for interrogation. They'll want to know what your real motives are.'

'Oh, stop – they're not that bad.' She paused. 'Or are they?'

Laurent gave a very unconvincing innocent look and shrugged. 'Maybe I'm only half-joking.'

'You're teasing me,' she said, flicking his arm with her fingertips. 'Now, stop eating all my strawberries or there'll be none left!'

They spent a good couple of hours going through the plans and the costs involved, the different options available. It wasn't until Imogen's stomach rumbled rather loudly, much to her mortification, that she even realised it was nearly lunchtime.

'Sorry about that,' she said clutching her stomach. 'It's becoming a rather embarrassing habit of mine.'

'It sounds to me like you need a good meal inside you,' said Laurent.

'I've got some soup. Would you like to stay for lunch?' Imogen hadn't been planning to ask him that but she suddenly didn't want him to leave.

'Why don't you let me take you to lunch?' he said.

'Oh, you don't have to do that. I'm very happy with soup.'

'I'm sure you are, but I'd like to take you for something to eat.'

Imogen couldn't deny the flutter of excitement her stomach gave. She couldn't remember the last time someone asked her out for lunch. Meg would be smitten with her prediction too. Imogen reined herself in as a pang of guilt attached itself to the thought. She wasn't going on a date. Laurent was simply suggesting they eat out. She wasn't doing anything wrong by accepting either. 'In that case, I accept but on the condition, we split the bill fifty-fifty.'

Laurent raised his eyebrows. 'It's not exactly what I had in mind.'

'Then I'll stay here with my soup.'

He let out a sigh. 'Are you always this independent?'

'Most of the time.'

'Hmm. I get the feeling arguing would be pointless.'

'Yep.' She folded her arms and smiled.

'*D'accord*. Fifty-fifty it is.'

They walked back into the village, which was very much quieter now as everyone was taking their long French lunch. 'So, where would you recommend?' asked Imogen as they turned onto the main street.

'We are in luck, the restaurants are open for lunch today,' said Laurent. 'We have two choices. There's St Michael's on this side of the road. It's a little old-fashioned but they do very good food or so I assume – they always seem busy. Or over on the other side you have the more casual restaurant where they do pizza and burgers.'

'Let's go for traditional.'

As they entered, Imogen noticed the other diners turn to look at them and the hum of conversation die out. Laurent glanced at her with uncertainty on his face. '*Ça-va?*' she asked.

'If you are,' came the steady reply.

The woman serving behind the bar at the rear of the restaurant looked over at them. 'We are fully booked,' she said, drying a glass with a tea towel. Her face was unsmiling and there was a hard line to her mouth.

'You don't have a table for two?' asked Imogen, looking around her. There were certainly tables free.

'*Non*.' The reply was bluff.

Before either of them could say any more, the door opened and in walked two men dressed in shirts and ties who Imogen assumed were office workers on their lunch break. '*Nous sommes deux,*' said one of the men. '*Vouz-avez un table?*'

'*Oui*. Wherever you want – they're all free,' replied the woman.

At first Imogen wasn't sure if she'd translated correctly but as the men quickly discussed which table they preferred and took one near the window, she realised she hadn't misunderstood anything. She went to protest but Laurent put his hand on her arm.

'Don't,' he said. 'We'll eat across the road.'

Rather bemused at the exchange, Imogen allowed herself to be guided out of the restaurant. 'What went on there?' she asked. 'I don't think I've ever experienced such unwelcoming behaviour.' She stopped outside the other restaurant. 'Is it because I'm English, do you think? Or because I've bought the château? Or both?' It was an uncomfortable thought that she was already being ostracised by the locals.

'I'm sorry,' said Laurent. 'I promise you, it is not your fault. It's me.'

'But I don't understand.'

'Come, let's eat and I'll explain.'

This time they had no problems at all and were soon seated and having placed their orders were waiting for their food to arrive. Imogen was somehow keeping a check on her patience, waiting for Laurent to choose the right moment to explain.

He took a long swallow of his drink and blew out a breath. 'People around here have long memories,' he began. 'As you know, I used to go out with a local girl – Elodie. I believe you met her recently. Anyway, we broke up and everyone in the village felt sorrier for her.'

Imogen eyed him sceptically, unsure whether this was the truth or some excuse he was reeling off. 'How old were you?'

'Twenty.'

'And people like that old woman hold a grudge? That seems a bit extreme. What else happened?' She wasn't buying what he was telling her.

'It was a long time ago. There's nothing really to tell other than that old woman happens to be Elodie's great-aunt.'

Imogen still wasn't convinced. 'I'm not that gullible. You're going to have to come up with a better excuse than that. Actually, the truth would be best.'

Another sigh escaped Laurent. Whatever he was hiding it had a far greater weight than Imogen had imagined but she remained silent, waiting for him to answer.

'*Alors*, if you must know… It goes back to my grand-mother. She fell out with some of the locals. They didn't like her and by default didn't… don't… like me. When I broke up with Elodie it was an excuse to hurt my grandmother more by rejecting me.'

'Wow! That all sounds very bitter, not to mention extreme.'

'Believe me, these old women can hold a grudge like no other. It gets passed down the generations.'

'What exactly happened with your grandmother to make them hate you so much?' It didn't make sense in Imogen's eyes. She really couldn't make the leap from grandmother to grandson so easily.

'I'll give you the abridged version,' conceded Laurent somewhat reluctantly.

It was obvious to Imogen that whatever happened with his grandmother caused him a great deal of angst but she was also aware he was confiding in her, something she suspected he didn't do very often with anyone.

'*Alors*. There is no easy way to say this but my grandmother had a friendship with a German officer during the war when the region was under occupation. That is the rumour anyway.'

'And what do you think about that?' asked Imogen, aware she was sounding like a therapist.

Laurent gave a small smile as if the idea had crossed his mind too. 'I like to think it's not true but my grandmother would never talk about it. She never confirmed the rumours but neither did she deny them.'

'So, apart from having this friendship, was there anything else? It's a long time for a grudge to be held.'

Laurent fiddled with the cutlery in front of him. 'There was talk of collaboration but I don't know. Something else obviously happened that she would never talk about.'

'And no one in the village will tell you?'

'No. As you just witnessed, I'm not exactly very popular around here either.'

Imogen steeled herself. If there was ever a time to probe Laurent further about his relationship with Elodie, then it was now. 'What else happened between you and Elodie?'

Laurent looked sharply up at her. 'I thought we were talking about my grandmother?'

'You can talk to me,' said Imogen gently. 'I don't hold any preconceptions.'

Laurent shook his head. 'We all do. We just don't always know it.'

Imogen knew when to back off. She could read the signs. Whatever it was Laurent was holding back, he wasn't ready to tell her yet. She suspected he never opened up to anyone about his past, or even his grandmother's past, so for now she'd have to be content with what he'd told her and hope he could tell her more in time.

The arrival of their food was a timely interruption, which broke the intensity of the moment, allowing them to fall back into their easy way of before. Imogen was, however, aware that they had both now put a toe across the line separating professional and personal relationship.

TWENTY-ONE
1944

I shielded my eyes against the sun to see who had crept up behind me and let out a sigh of relief. '*Oh, Doctor Tasse, c'est vous.*'

I rose to my feet, looking around to see if his wife was about. The last thing I wanted was a run-in with Madame Tasse, especially as she was the likely candidate to have spread rumours about me talking to Max, which Christine Arnold had believed.

'*Bonjour, Simone,*' he replied, tipping his head in acknowledgement and propped his bicycle against the tree. 'I'm sorry, I didn't mean to frighten you.'

'No, it's all right. I just needed some time away from it all.' I smoothed down my dress. 'You were in the village this morning?'

The doctor nodded gravely. '*Oui. C'est barbarique.* It's a terrible business.'

'It's just awful. I keep seeing Monique's face. The Germans are devils. I hope they rot in hell.' I stopped myself from saying anything else. Although I didn't think the doctor was a collaborator, I didn't want to take any chances.

'Hush now, Simone. We must be careful what we say.' The doctor put his finger to his lips and looked around. 'You mustn't talk so freely. You don't know who you can trust.'

I looked intently at the doctor for a moment before speaking. 'And can I trust you?'

'I was about to ask you the same question.'

A heartbeat thumped between us. Followed by another. 'I'm not a collaborator,' I said finally. 'Christine Arnold came to the shop and warned me off talking to the Germans. She was told I had been seen.'

The doctor stroked his beard, once dark but now peppered with grey. 'Not everything is as it seems on the surface.'

'Indeed.' I tried to sound confident, wanting to give Papa's memory the justice it deserved. Be brave. Be scared but always be brave. 'Is there anything else? Only, I should be getting home before Maman starts to worry.'

'There is just one thing. I've known you since you were a child, since you were born, and I've seen you grow into the fine young woman you are now. You are very much like your mother and, indeed, your father – strong and principled.'

'I try to be. It's a lot to live up to.'

'*Bien sur. Alors…*' He hesitated, looked thoughtful and then as if coming to a decision continued. 'I hear you're to play at the château at the weekend.'

I raised my eyebrows in surprise at the speed the news had travelled. 'How do you know?'

'I had to attend one of the officers at the château this morning and I heard them talking. The shopkeeper's daughter who plays the flute. It could only be you.'

'The officer asked me. I didn't have any choice.' I wanted to make that point clear.

'I know. I know,' reassured the doctor. 'I understand what you're saying to me.'

'You do?'

'Of course.' He paused for a few moments before continuing. 'You could help your country. You could use your... let us say... your popularity with the German officers.'

I drew in a sharp breath. 'What do you mean?'

'It's not as bad as it sounds,' replied the doctor. 'No one is expecting you to...' he waved his hand as if trying to pluck the word from the air '...to sleep with the Germans, although if you did it would make your position more authentic.'

'Stop! Enough.' The words burst out before I could prevent them. I paced back and forth at the idea of having sex with someone like Claus. Frankly, the idea repulsed me. It wasn't because I was a virgin – that wasn't the issue – but I couldn't imagine having sex with someone I didn't have feelings for. My mind turned to Max and I had to admit I found the idea more appealing.

Appalled at myself for even letting the image enter my head, I pushed it away and came to a halt from my pacing in front of the doctor. 'I'll do whatever it takes,' I said solemnly.

He nodded his understanding, placing a hand on my shoulder. 'You must speak of this to no one, not even your mother.'

'Don't worry, I have absolutely no intention of speaking to her.' I could imagine Maman's anger, only because she wanted to protect me, but I knew I could not sit around doing nothing. I thought again of Monique and what a wasted life hers had been and what a cruel end. 'I want to do this. I want to fight for my country. To be part of the resistance. I can't sit around and let all these terrible things happen without retaliating in some way.'

'You're sure about this?'

'Positive. In fact, if you hadn't come to me, then I think I probably would have gone to you or at least to Monsieur Devereaux.'

The doctor looked surprised. 'You know about him?'

'I guessed. I thought I saw someone on his farm the other day.'

'I'll shall speak to him and tell him he must be more careful. After today, I fear the Germans have upped their cruelty, if that is possible. They are sparing no one they feel is involved: man, woman or child. You do understand what you're letting yourself in for, don't you?'

'Absolutely and I couldn't be more sure of my decision.'

'Good. Then, I want you to make yourself more available to the Germans. That one you were speaking to – he's an officer – you could befriend him properly. And try to be more friendly towards the one called Claus Gossman – the one who invited you. I overheard him saying how cold you were to him. He's made it his personal mission to change that.'

I swallowed hard at the thought. Befriending Max was easy and natural but behaving like that towards Claus went against every fibre in my body. I could see the doctor studying me for any sign of weakness or doubt. I pushed my shoulders back and lifted my head a little higher. 'I understand.'

'No one is forcing you to agree to this. It is, of course, highly dangerous. If you're found out, you could face deportation or even death. There is no point dressing this up. Your life depends on how convincing your deception is. If you're not up to it or are not fully committed, then now is the time to say no.'

I bristled at the thought of not being brave enough. Of course I had the nerve to do this. 'I know what I'm doing,' I replied stiffly.

'Good. Now, I need you to do something this week.

Every Friday, a red case is delivered to the château for Goss-man's attention. In the case is a list of the movements of troops, supplies and munitions in and out of the region. Gossman has to sign them off and usually does that Friday nights. Anyway, there will be an extra copy of this document in the case. A yellow duplicate copy. You need to obtain the copy and bring it to me.'

I nodded but swallowed down a lump of fear in my throat at the same time. 'How... I mean...'

'After your performance, go up to the room directly above you. It is the last room at the end of the corridor. If anyone stops you, you say you are going to wait for Ober-leutnant Claus Gossman.' He paused. 'Do you understand what I'm saying?'

'Yes.' I understood perfectly.

'Good. Go into the room. It will be left unlocked by one of the servants. Get the duplicate paper, which will be underneath the original. That way if anyone finds it first, it will just look like a genuine mistake that it has been attached to the original. Hide it in your flute case. How you do that is up to you. Maybe inside the flute.'

'And then what?' I could feel my hands already shaking just at the prospect.

'You leave the château, go home and use the outside toilet in your back garden, leave the document on top of the toilet cistern. Then go to bed. Do nothing else. By morning, it will have gone.' He eyed me speculatively. 'Do you think you can do that? If not, you need to speak now.'

I felt indignant at the suggestion. I thought of Papa and my heart swelled with courage. 'I can do that. It is not a problem.'

The doctor nodded and spent the next few minutes going over the instructions in more detail. 'You understand everything? Any questions?'

'I understand.'

'Don't let me down.'

'I won't. I promise.'

I watched as the doctor pushed his bike across the grass and out onto the road, before he cycled away and I thought of the task that lay ahead with a mix of fear and excitement. Finally, I was doing something tangible to help my country.

TWENTY-TWO

2019

As the days in France turned into weeks, Imogen felt she was definitely moving from holiday mode to home mode and it felt good.

She had exchanged several emails with Denise and she could sense her mother-in-law thawing with each email that passed between them.

Since Laurent's partial opening up to her about his grandmother's story, there had definitely been a shift in the ground of the relationship and although still very much professional, she could sense a friendship building too.

'And it is just a friendship,' she said to Meg on the phone that morning after her sister had quizzed her when Imogen happened to mention they'd had a picnic lunch together the previous day by the moat.

'I'm sure it is,' said Meg. 'But lunch on the grass by the moat in the grounds of a French château – you can't get much more romantic than that.'

'You can if there's no romance,' retorted Imogen.

It wasn't until she'd finished the call and was tidying up the kitchen from breakfast that she had her first thought of

James. She stopped mid-rinse of her bowl as she went back over the conversation and her feelings. Surely she'd thought of James or at least had some feeling of guilt? Had she really only thought of him now? 'Oh, James, I'm so sorry,' she said out loud.

Bloody hell, grief and guilt were so complicated. She rallied herself with the notion that Laurent was just a friend and there was nothing wrong with that. She certainly wouldn't be standing there worrying about it if she'd made friends with, say, Elodie.

To distract herself from going around in circles with it all, Imogen turned her thoughts to the château.

She had seen Laurent regularly over the past few weeks to discuss the renovations to the property and she was waiting to hear whether planning permission from *le maire* would be granted for the renovation works on the west turret.

Imogen was confident this would be approved, having met with *le maire* a couple of weeks earlier to discuss the remembrance garden. M. Le Roux had been very encouraging, telling her not to worry, that it was just a formality and he would make sure it went through.

M. Le Roux had also arranged a small float of money for Imogen to use as she saw fit to give the remembrance garden a makeover. He was keen for it to look good well in advance of Bastille Day where he gave an annual speech to the villagers before the celebrations of the day ensued.

~

It was another glorious day in Brittany and Imogen took her cup of tea out into the garden, wandering down to what she guessed was once an orchard. The trees had long since died and only their twisted and gnarled framework remained. She swept her hand down the bark of what would have been an apple tree, thinking how back in the 1940s the fruit would have been healthy supplements to diets during the war. She had an overwhelming sense of time as she stood there, imagining how someone before her during those occupied years might have done the exact same thing with an earlier tree. How they could have stood in the same spot she was right now. She'd like to recreate the orchard, she decided, bringing in new fruit trees – apples, plum and pear would be nice.

She moved on around the garden, picturing in her mind how it might have been in years gone by, how it would have changed as horticultural fashions came and went. Reaching the far corner of the garden, where a large walnut tree stood, Imogen knew straight away this was where she was going to have the pond that James would have so loved. With the surrounding shrubs and bushes, this would make an ideal woodland area around the pond, which would in turn lead on to the wild meadow garden she also wanted and then lead to the hedged privet.

She would have poppies as one of the main flowers, she decided. They symbolised so much and would be especially poignant here as a tribute to those who lost their lives during the occupation. It would also be a living memory of her two lost babies who she would never forget. Maybe she'd find a local artisan who could create three identical poppy sculptures. Nothing big, just modest ones she could stand overlooking the pond and be the link to the wildflower meadow. James most definitely would approve of that.

When she went back indoors, she emailed Denise to tell her about her plans and the memorial garden. She finished the email by saying she hoped Denise could come and visit soon and perhaps help with the pond and wildflower gardens. It was a genuine wish and she hoped it would help Denise as much as it would her.

~

Imogen spent the rest of the morning, sketching out and planning what she was going to do with the orchard, woodland area and wild part of the garden. She knew this wasn't really a priority but it was nice to think about the outside area for a change. She couldn't put anything in motion with the interior until she'd received planning permission.

She had managed to find her watercolours from the depth of a box marked 'Office box 1' congratulating herself on writing the contents on the side of each container.

It had been a while since she'd used her watercolours and once she was happy with the château plan, she turned her attention to the memorial garden. She was so lost in her planning that she jumped when there was a robust knock at the front door.

She was surprised, but equally pleased, to see Laurent standing there.

He held up a picnic hamper in one hand and a bottle of champagne in the other. 'I've brought lunch,' he announced.

'Well, this is a nice surprise and that's some lunch.' Imogen looked at the bottle in his hand. 'You'd better come in.'

'I have good news,' declared Laurent placing the hamper on the kitchen table.

Imogen hurried forward to move her artwork. 'Here, let me clear a space.'

'What are you working on?' asked Laurent, nodding at the pad.

'Just some ideas for the memorial garden.'

'May I?' Laurent gestured towards the sketch pad and Imogen, flattered he was interested, passed it over to him.

On one side of the double page she had prepared a small mood board, with notes and pictures of the type of plants that would suit the garden. On the adjacent page, she had sketched and painted an overhead impression of the garden, showing the planting. 'Obviously, this is once it's all had time to establish itself, but this is the look I'm going for. A flagstone path here, a bench at the entrance of the garden and one further up on this side, plus an area in front of the memorial itself so *le maire*, or whoever, can stand in front and pay their respects or make an address to the village.'

'I have no doubt *le maire* will like that idea,' said Laurent dryly and then rather more cheerfully: 'What about the flower beds?'

'Tall plants at the back and smaller spreading ones near the front. Lots of lavender too and poppies.' She looked at Laurent who had remained silent. 'Do you like it?'

'It's very… charming,' he said carefully.

'You don't like it.' She felt more deflated than she thought she should.

'I didn't say that,' he replied, turning the page around to face him. 'It's traditional and the villagers will like that.'

'You like modern?'

'I like modern too but I'm not really into gardening,' he admitted. 'I'm more about the buildings and indoor space.'

'You're more of a minimalistic modern type of person, aren't you?'

Laurent didn't answer immediately as he considered his reply. 'I wouldn't describe it as such. My apartment in Paris, for example, is very eclectic. I don't think it has a particular style. It has things in it I like to look at or that are comfortable. If I'm honest, it's not really an advert for my line of work.' He flashed her an apologetic grin.

'Old meets new?'

'Maybe,' he replied. 'And maybe you'd like to see it?'

'You're inviting me to your apartment?' Imogen laughed, suddenly feeling self-conscious. 'I'm not sure what to make of that.' She inwardly winced at her attempt at humour to cover an awkward moment.

'Make nothing of it,' said Laurent. He held her gaze with those hazel-brown eyes of his.

Make nothing of it, she thought. Well, that was a put-down if ever she'd heard one. She looked away and closed her sketch pad but, sensing his eyes still on her, she looked back up at him. 'What?'

'Make nothing of it,' he repeated. 'Or make something of it. You decide.'

Imogen could feel her breathing quicken. Had he just propositioned her? He was teasing her, surely. God, she felt like such an idiot. Her scrambled brain tried to think of a witty comeback. 'That sounds like a challenge to me,' she said, thinking what another lame reply that was.

'Not a challenge, just a suggestion.'

'Well, any more suggestions like that and I might just take you up on them.' She feigned a laugh to hide her nerves. Flirting! She was definitely flirting with him. To hide her embarrassment, she made a big deal of putting her sketch pad and watercolours away in a cupboard, keeping her back turned to him until she was sure she wasn't blushing anymore.

'Anyway, I have good news,' said Laurent, apparently unfazed by their exchange.

'You do?' Imogen finally extracted herself from the cupboard and turned to look at him.

Laurent gave her a mischievous smile, before pulling out a chair and waving his hand towards the seat. 'Would madame care to sit down?'

Imogen played along, intrigued to see what the good news was and took her seat at the table, inspecting the food before her. It was a chicken pasta mix with salad. 'Did you make this yourself?'

'If I said yes, how high in your estimation would I be?'

'Very but, of course, if that turned out to be a lie, then you'd slide right down to the bottom of the scale where, possibly, there'd be no chance of recovery. There's a saying in the UK of honesty being the best policy.'

'*Alors*, in that case, I confess to buying it from the super-market this morning.'

'And for that honesty, you are high up in my estimation.'

'So, the good news,' said Laurent, popping open the champagne and filling two glasses then passing one to her, 'I had official confirmation from *le maire* today that approval of the restoration work on the château has been granted. Everything we've asked for has been agreed.' He held up his glass.

'Oh, wow! That is good news!' cried Imogen, clinking her glass against his. 'I'm so pleased and relieved. Not that I doubted you, but it's always nice to get it officially confirmed.'

'There is some bad news, though,' continued Laurent.

'How bad? On a scale of ten, where are we?'

'About a six.'

'Six is OK. It means it's not totally shit. Wait, before you tell me, I need to savour the moment of celebration,' said Imogen. She took a gulp of her champagne. 'Come on then, what's the bad news?'

'Ideally, it would be easier if the château was empty when all this work is being carried out – or at least the struc-tural work when there's always the possibility something might go wrong. Not that I'm expecting it to, but you can't tell with old buildings and especially those that have been damaged by fire.'

'Empty? But I need to live here. I can't move out.'

'There are certain rules and regulations I would have to ensure were implemented. I am slightly concerned about the risks involved in you living on a building site if you chose to stay while the work is carried out. I'm not sure you want to spend all day in one room wearing a hard hat. I'd have to look at the insurance side of things. It could push up the costs.' He didn't quite meet her eyes as he continued. 'It wouldn't be the first time clients have moved out while major works are carried out.'

Imogen grimaced. 'Move out completely?'

He nodded and looked quite regretful. 'Ideally.'

'I don't know if I can. I mean, where would I go? I haven't got anywhere to stay. I know the place I was staying in before – The Retreat in Sérent – that's booked up now the summer season is in full swing. Besides, I can't really afford anywhere.'

'And you couldn't go back to England for a few weeks?' he suggested.

'Back to England? You must be joking. I can't go back. Actually, that's not true, I can but I don't want to and I abso- lutely won't.' She let out a big sigh and slugged a large gulp of champagne, which somehow didn't taste so sweet now. This had thrown her completely off course. There must be a way around this. 'So, how much extra will the insurance cost to have me in situ?'

Laurent made a huffing noise and gave a typical Gallic shrug. 'I don't know. It could be a lot. I can check and shop around for the best price…'

'Just when I thought everything was going so well. I should have known it was too good to be true.'

'There is another solution,' he said after a moment. She

sat up straight in her seat. He hesitated and frowned before finally speaking. 'No, it's a stupid idea. Ignore me.'

'No! You've got to tell me now.' Imogen leaned forward, her arms resting on the table. She was desperate for a solution that didn't involve going back to the UK.

'No. Really…'

'No. *Really*, you have to tell me.'

He looked embarrassed and tapped the table with his forefinger before speaking. 'You could stay at my apartment in the village. There is a spare room.'

'Your apartment? I… I don't know. I mean… I don't know if it's a good idea.' She shook her head. 'Not that there's anything wrong with you. I'm not saying I don't trust you. It is very generous of you but I couldn't possibly intrude like that…' Her voice trailed off.

He had totally surprised her with that suggestion. Stay at his apartment? That was so out of left-field and yet, if they were friends as she liked to think they were, then it was a perfectly natural idea.

'I'm sorry. I've put you in a difficult position and made you feel awkward,' said Laurent sincerely. 'I told you it wasn't a good idea.'

'Aren't you worried about what people will say?'

Laurent gave a snort of laughter. 'Do I look like I care what they say? But… I appreciate you might. Please pretend I never said it.'

'It's a very good suggestion,' said Imogen hastily. 'It just threw me a bit, that's all.' She looked across the table at Laurent who appeared to be having some sort internal struggle. He clearly felt guilty he was having to be the bearer of bad news about her staying at the château, but her response to his offer had embarrassed him and made him feel awkward. And now, she felt embarrassed and awkward. She should have been more gracious.

She cleared her throat. 'Laurent,' she began. 'It's a very generous offer of yours and if there was any way I could stay here or somewhere else, I absolutely would. I understand what you're saying about the risks. God, you should live in the UK – you can't do anything for fear of breaking some health and safety law.'

'I'm sorry, I…' He went to interrupt but she held up her hand to stop him.

'I really appreciate your offer and I'm only being hesitant because it is such a lovely gesture. My reluctance is in no way a reflection on you.' God she was waffling and making it sound like some formal acceptance speech. She should just cut to the chase. 'What I'm trying to say is that I'd be delighted, not to mention grateful, to stay at your apartment.'

There! She'd said it. She studied his face for a response. He looked shell-shocked. Shit, maybe she'd totally misread the situation after all. Then he broke into a broad smile.

'I'm delighted you're delighted,' he said. He held out his hand and she shook it solemnly.

'It's a deal.' A momentary stab of guilt assaulted her as she thought of James but she put the thought to one side. She had nothing to feel guilty about. Laurent was merely offering a solution to a problem and Imogen was all for that.

Before they could discuss it further, Laurent's mobile phone bleeped in his pocket. 'Excuse me,' he said, taking out the device. He read the message and a frown crossed his face but he popped his phone back in his pocket without explanation.

Imogen took a surreptitious peek at Laurent while she ate. He was looking intently into his pasta, moving it around the plate but not actually eating it. Sensing the weight of her gaze, he looked up and plastered on a smile.

'Is everything OK?' she asked.

'Yes. Absolutely.'

'Are you sure?'

Laurent sighed and placed his cutlery down. 'I had a message from my father's cleaner. She's just been in at my father's house and was a little concerned so called the doctor. It's not serious, just a water infection and the doctor has given him antibiotics.'

'Oh, I am sorry,' said Imogen. 'That's a worry for you. Are you the only family he has?'

'I don't have any siblings. My mother is away in the UK visiting her sister. My father is a lot older than my mother though and didn't want to travel, but he's impossibly stubborn and independent and wouldn't agree to a carer. Fortunately, Silvie, their cleaner, is very good and keeps a discreet eye on him.'

'Where is your father?'

'In Paris.' Laurent took a sip of his drink. 'I'm sorry, I didn't mean to dampen the day, not when we have such good news.'

'But it's nothing, my news. Your father's far more important.'

'And he is fine.' He reached over and squeezed her hand. 'Honestly, I'll speak to him later. I appreciate your concern.'

Imogen smiled sympathetically, understanding Laurent didn't want to talk about it anymore but she was glad he had opened up to her. It was a vulnerable side to him that she was beginning to realise he didn't like to expose.

'So, the château,' said Imogen, turning the conversation back to safer ground. 'We've got all the permissions to start work. This is so exciting. I really can't wait.'

'As we discussed, we need to get the west wing cleared, made structurally sound and weatherproofed,' said Laurent. 'I'll give the contractors a call tomorrow and see when they can start but there is, of course, the matter of the cellar.'

'Ah, yes, the cellar.' She got up from the table and went over to her bag. 'Ta-dah!' She held a brass key up in her hand. 'I have a key!'

'A key!' Laurent jumped up from his seat and then checked himself, walking over to her in a controlled manner.

'Turns out the *notaire* had another set of keys he forgot to give me. He dropped them off the other day.'

'Have you tried it in the lock?'

'I have but I didn't fancy going down there on my own,' she admitted.

Laurent laughed. 'I thought the modern woman didn't need a man.'

'It's not necessarily a man I need, I just need someone to go with me. Don't go getting all alpha male on me now.'

Laurent gave her a wink. 'I wouldn't dream of it.'

'As soon as we've finished eating, we'll explore.'

Imogen couldn't help noticing Laurent ate his lunch as quickly as his manners would allow. He was certainly keen to investigate the cellar.

'Right, you ready?' he asked, sliding his plate away from him.

'You don't want a coffee first?' She was teasing him and it was amusing to see the look he gave her, as if to question was she in her right mind.

'No. I'm perfectly fine,' he replied.

'A dessert?'

'No. Again, I'm perfectly fine.'

'Maybe we should leave the cellar for another day.' She couldn't help herself.

Laurent cursed under his breath in French. '*Merde.*' And then looked up at her with his best patient face. 'I don't want coffee, tea, water, dessert, a rest, a walk; in fact I don't want anything.' He looked at her and then swore again. 'You are teasing me, *non?*'

Imogen laughed out loud. 'Of course I am. Come on, let's go down there before you burst.'

The cellar turned out to be a complete anti-climax and Imogen wasn't sure who was more disappointed, her or Laurent.

A stone staircase led directly into a large space, which was the footprint of the kitchen above and the west wing of the house. There were a few empty crates and fruit boxes stacked to one wall and a collapsed wooden rack, which was probably a wine rack once upon a time. Underneath the ground floor of the west wing, there was a pile of bricks and rubble heaped up against the wall.

'It looks like the chimney down here has collapsed,' said Laurent. 'I'm surprised the whole chimney stack hasn't caved in.'

Imogen held up the flashlight she'd brought down with her. 'I assume the chute for the dumb waiter is around here too.'

Laurent inspected the bricks and rubble. 'Yes, the bottom of it must be buried under all this debris. Don't worry, I'll get it cleared for you.'

Imogen was ready to go back upstairs. She didn't particularly like it down there – the air was musty and stale with a distinct smell of damp. It was hardly surprising though, given the age of the place and how long the cellar had been shut up for. She toured the walls with the beam of light from the torch.

'Hey, look, Laurent!' On the opposite wall, there was an opening but Imogen couldn't see into it as the torch wasn't powerful enough.

They crossed the room, Laurent shining his torch too. 'It's a passageway,' he said.

'A secret passageway?'

'I'm not sure about secret, but it probably leads to

another part of the house and was used by the servants to move around unnoticed. By my reckoning, it should come out in the east wing, where the main reception room is perhaps.'

'Shall we see?'

'Why not?'

Laurent led the way through the archway and into the corridor, which did indeed go all the way to the other side of the château, ending at the foot of another stone staircase.

'I don't remember seeing any door in the main reception room,' said Imogen.

'Neither do I.'

They climbed the steps but their path was blocked at the top by a wooden door. 'We're definitely at the main room,' said Imogen. 'Perhaps the doorway is hidden in the panelling. Discreetly, so the servants could slip in and out.'

'There's one way to find out.' The handle offered a certain amount of resistance to Laurent's initial attempt to release the catch but eventually, brute force won and the lock released itself with a squeak and a click.

'Yay!' said Imogen as the hinges protested at being requested to move but the door opened and, as predicted, they found themselves standing in the corner of the main reception room.

'How amazing is that?' enthused Imogen. 'I have my very own secret passage!'

'This is such a fantastic room,' remarked Laurent. 'Perfect for entertaining.'

'I know! It has that feel to it, doesn't it?' Imogen had previously made copious notes as to how she'd like the room to look after the refurbishment, but today, she felt, she was seeing it again for the first time – not just seeing it, but feeling it too as she imagined this room being used to entertain guests.

There were long red velvet curtains with gold trims, clinging by mere threads to the pelmets above the full-length windows that lined two sides of the room. Now faded, moth-eaten, full of dust and no doubt dust mites, they weren't salvageable but definitely ideal for inspiration.

The plaster cornices around the room and on the ceiling were yellowed with years of dust, crumbling in one corner where the damp had seeped in through a broken window, which had once been boarded up but over time the chip-board had rotted away.

A dome-shaped chandelier hung from the ceiling, the glass pendants – like everything else in the room – coated in dust, but it must have looked spectacular in its day. Imogen was definitely going to get that refurbished.

She imagined guests in evening gowns and dinner suits standing around quaffing champagne, whipping glasses from the passing trays of waitresses, a quartet playing in the corner, perhaps a grand piano occupying the space? She had an inexplicable sense of time and place as if she were catching a glimpse of the room's history and it sent shivers down her spine.

TWENTY-THREE
1944

'You look very nice,' said Maman, standing back and looking me up and down. 'Very professional.' She adjusted the neck on my blouse where she had sewn a dart to stop the fabric from gaping. I was wearing one of her dresses for my performance at the château that night. It was a simple black dress with buttons up the front but I wasn't as curvy as Maman and it gaped around the bust without her handiwork.

'I don't care what I look like,' I remarked. 'I just want to go, play for them and then come home. I'm sure they won't even look at me.'

Maman's lips tightened together before she spoke. 'Simone, they are all young men and they will indeed look at you, which is exactly why I've sewn up the neckline.'

'Don't worry. I'll be all right,' I said. I wasn't sure who was trying to comfort whom at this point. Neither of us wanted this to happen but we both knew we had absolutely no choice in the matter. 'I'd better go.' I slipped on my coat and picked up my flute case, before kissing Maman on each cheek and leaving.

Dusk was beginning to fall and I hurried along the street with the pass in my pocket that had been delivered to the shop that morning, allowing me to be out after curfew.

My heels clipped on the path as I made my way down the hill and when the château came into sight, it took my breath away. All the windows on the ground floor were glowing brightly from inside and garland lights were strung across the hydrangea bushes and trees that lined the drive-way. Music drifted across the moat as a string quartet enter-tained the guests. There were several cars parked in the driveway and I had to wait to cross the road as two more rounded the bend and turned into the entrance of the château.

The guard on the gate looked at my pass and waved me through. My hand gripped my flute case, my palms sweating as I approached the château. I'd heard so many rumours about these parties – not just the outrageous evenings but the glamour of these events – the dresses the women wore, the jewels and the food. Apparently, there was so much food.

I wanted to see for myself if these were just exaggera-tions and had been wondering for the past couple of days if there was any way I could smuggle some food out. If Pierre could have something more nutritious to eat, then maybe it would help him get better.

I hadn't seen Max for nearly a week now, not since the executions, and I had to admit I was disappointed but also relieved. I didn't know what I would say to him. My heart was so full of confusion about how I felt and what I should be feeling towards him and what he represented. It was too muddled to try to untangle.

I was extremely nervous, not just the thought of playing my flute to an audience but what I needed to do for the doctor. I had been waiting for this call to action and I was determined to see it through, it was the least I could do to honour Monique's memory.

There was a member of staff waiting at the entrance to the château, guiding visitors to where they needed to be. He looked me up and down with a certain amount of contempt.

'I take it you're here as waiting staff,' he said in French. 'Round the back to the kitchen door.'

He was a French national but I didn't recognise him from the village. 'I'm the entertainment,' I said, not caring for his manner.

He made a scoffing noise and smirked. 'Entertainment. Aren't you a bit young?'

Before I had time to protest and explain that I was not that sort of entertainment, a voice from behind interrupted us. 'Thank you, Jacques.' I looked up as Claus appeared in the doorway. 'Mademoiselle Varon is one of the musicians. A guest of mine.'

'Pardon,' said Jacques, bowing his head. 'I apologise.'

'Please come this way,' said Claus. He was dressed in his uniform, which looked particularly smart. He was clean-shaven and smelt of sandalwood and pine. I wasn't charmed by him though even if I was more than happy Jacques had been made to look an idiot. 'Let me take your coat.' Claus stood behind me and slipped the garment from my shoulders, lingering slightly with his face far too close to the back of my neck.

I looked around the entrance hall at the wide spiral staircase that glided up and out of sight in the turret. The stone steps were covered in a bright red carpet, held in place with gold rods and brass caps at each end. I didn't think I'd ever seen such luxury. The walls of the entrance hall were lined with oil paintings, mostly of landscapes although I had noticed several gaps on the walls where artwork had once hung. An oil painting of a beautiful woman with her hair piled on her head had suffered at the hands of the Germans – the woman now had a black painted beard and her eyes had been poked out with a sharp object.

I turned to face Claus. 'Where will I be playing?'

He smiled as he took my coat over to the corner where a cloakroom attendant hung it up in return for a ticket, which he gave to me. 'You do look very nice,' he said. 'Very nice indeed.'

It was then from over Claus's shoulder I saw Max coming down the stairs from the east turret. There was the slightest of hesitations as he saw both myself and Claus, but he smiled as he joined us. 'Good evening. How are you?'

'Good evening. I'm very well, thank you.'

'Ah yes, I forgot you two know each other,' said Claus. 'Mademoiselle Varon is playing her flute for us tonight.'

'I shall look forward to that,' replied Max.

Several more guests had arrived now and Claus's attention was caught elsewhere. I was relieved as he excused himself, asking Max to show me where I could get ready.

'You'll be performing in the main room here on the left,' said Max. 'Have a quick look.' He opened the doors and guided me in, his hand resting between my shoulder blades.

I stood to one side, close to Max as I looked around the room. It was painted a beautiful duck egg blue with full-length arched windows along two sides overlooking the moat and the rear gardens. At the far end was a small raised stage where currently the string quartet was playing. A grand piano was to the left of the stage. I suddenly felt extremely nervous. 'It's been so long since I played in front of anybody. It's all a bit intimidating,' I said.

Max lowered his head next to mine. 'You'll be absolutely fine. I'll be standing right here watching. Look at me if you need reassurance. Think of me as the conductor.'

'Thank you.'

'See that corner over there, next to the flower display?' I followed his gaze as he continued speak. 'There's a door in the panelling. See where that waitress with the empty tray is going? There… well that is a passageway that takes you under the house and through to the kitchen. That's the way you'll come when it's time for you to play. Come, I'll show you to the dressing room.'

'A dressing room?'

Max smiled. 'It's really just another reception room in the other wing, but for the purposes of parties, we call it the dressing room' He took me across the main hall. 'You look very beautiful tonight,' he said softly.

Claus's compliment had made my skin crawl but Max's made me blush. 'Thank you,' I said trying not to sound too shy.

'This is the kitchen,' he said, opening the door for me. The kitchen staff all looked up as he came in and I noticed the wary glances directed his way. Max politely nodded at the head cook. 'I'm just showing mademoiselle the door to the basement passageway. Please don't let me interrupt you.' He opened a wooden door on the right. He pulled a cord and the staircase lit up. 'You can't go wrong. Left at the bottom of the stairs.'

Next Max showed me to the dressing room. He stopped outside the door. 'I'll come and let you know when it's time.' He looked at his watch. 'In about thirty-five minutes.'

As I looked up, I noticed a rectangular patch on the wall by the side of the door, the tell-tale sign that a piece of artwork or photograph had once been in place, and my conscience was immediately jolted, reminding me the Germans had taken this beautiful building from its owners.

'Is everything all right?' Max was asking.

'Sorry. I was just thinking about the château.' I looked down at the ground, not wanting to meet his gaze.

'It's a very beautiful building.'

I was angry with myself for temporarily forgetting how the house had been violated by the Germans. Angry that I had momentarily been swept up in the glamour of their party culture. Angry I was, to all intents and purposes, being forced to perform for their pleasure. I snapped my head up. 'Do you have a room here?'

If Max was taken aback by my forthright manner, he didn't show it. 'I do,' he replied with care. 'Just above here as it happens. Claus has the room next to me. The other two officers are on the other side of the building.'

'You're very lucky to be sleeping in such comfort when it's not yours. When it's been forcibly taken.'

'Ah… I see,' said Max. 'If it was down to me, then I wouldn't be here.'

'But you are.'

'That is true. And all the time I am here, I intend to treat the château and all its contents, and all its guests, with respect and care. I can do no more.'

'It's stealing,' I said.

Max gave a long sigh. 'Look, Simone,' he said in hushed tones. 'I know you don't want to be here. And believe me, I don't want you to be either. I'd sooner you were at your house where you are safe and out of sight from men like Claus, but the fact of the matter is you're here. Now, I suggest you do what you need to do without making a fuss, without any display of petulance or defiance, and when you've finished, I shall personally escort you home.'

'I'm perfectly capable…' I began but stopped as he rolled his eyes in frustration.

'Yes. In normal circumstances I have no doubt you are but please, for me, don't do anything to draw attention to yourself.'

'I'm not that stupid.'

He raised his eyebrows as if to say he didn't believe me and before he could say as much, I slipped into the dressing room and closed the door behind me.

I had twenty minutes to get upstairs to Claus's room and get the document from the case. My heart was pounding with fear and adrenalin at the thought. My palms were sweating profusely.

I waited until I was sure Max had gone back to the party and opened the door a fraction to check before slipping out into the hallway. The doctor had said there was a servants' staircase at the end of the corridor, which I was to use. I hurried along, trying to avoid the heels of my shoes making too much noise on the tiled floor.

The wooden staircase was narrow and, fortunately, was empty. At the top, I hesitated again to listen for anyone walking around on the landing but it was silent, all I could hear was the distant sound of the musicians playing. All the time they were performing, I was safe but I had to get back to the dressing room before they finished.

The carpet on the first floor was thick enough to muffle my footsteps. I approached the door that was Claus's and rested my hand on the handle, taking a deep breath. I wondered if I should knock, just in case he was there. I tapped gently.

Max's room was the next one along. All being well, he should be downstairs in the main reception room. There was no answer from inside Claus's room and with a trembling hand, I opened the door and stepped inside, softly closing it behind me.

The curtains to the room were open and fortunately the evening wasn't dark enough that I couldn't see what I was doing without having to put on a light.

There was a large four-poster bed in the centre of the room and an ornate armoire on the opposite wall. A beautiful dressing table sat underneath the window and I could see a men's grooming set laid out on the glass top.

Where on earth was the briefcase? My heart was pounding even harder now as I prowled the room looking for it.

It was then I heard voices approaching from the hallway. I froze on the spot, next to the bed, momentarily blinded by fear. The voices grew louder. They were outside the door. They were speaking German and I had no idea what they were saying.

Suddenly, my survival instincts kicked in and I sprang into action, running around the side of the bed and scrabbling underneath it, hoping the long valance sheet would offer me some protection. If I was caught now, there was no way I could explain what I was doing in here and get away with it.

It was then I heard a French voice.

'Herr Gossman! You're wanted downstairs immediately, sir. The general's special guests have arrived.' I didn't know who it was but I thanked God he had come, even if it was at the eleventh hour. I willed Claus not to come into the room. It had been left unlocked as planned but I knew Claus would immediately become suspicious.

'I was just going to get my case,' came Claus's reply. He spoke in French to the man who I could only assume was a member of staff. 'I was going to get my paperwork done early so I don't miss the flautist.'

I cringed at the laugh he tagged on the end of his sentence.

His companion said something in German and then the voices began to recede. I heaved a sigh of relief, resting my forehead on top of my hands for a few moments. As I lifted my head and looked across the floor of the bedroom, I spotted it!

The red briefcase was sitting on the floor at the side of a writing table in the opposite corner. I was just about to scramble out from under the bed when the door opened. I looked to my left and saw someone in black trousers and a black pair of shoes come into the room.

'Psst!' hissed the voice of a man. 'Where are you?'

I held my breath. Who was this? Was it a trick? I clasped my hand over my mouth as a nervous whimper threaten to bubble up in my throat. The feet moved towards the bed and then the man knelt down and whipped up the cover.

I rolled over out of reach and scrambled out from under the bed. Me on one side and a waiter, judging by his uniform, on the other.

'Who are you?' I demanded.

'Keep your voice down and don't be so stupid,' he said. 'You nearly got yourself caught. Have you done whatever it is you need to?'

I shook my head, not daring to speak. He must be the one who unlocked the door for me. 'Not yet.'

'Hurry up. I'll wait outside.'

He nipped out through the door and immediately I rushed over to the writing desk. Kneeling down I flicked open the case and looked for the document the doctor had instructed me to find. It was third on the pile and underneath, as predicted, was a yellow carbon copy. I snatched the copy and put the briefcase back before opening my flute case and carefully picked at the edge of the lining in the lid. Earlier I had managed to detach the lining enough to slip a piece of paper into. I slid the carbon copy into the secret pocket of the blue velvet cloth and then pushed the fabric back into place.

I could have cried as I exited the room. Relief flooded through me. I had to remind myself this was only the first part. I still had to perform for the guests and get out of the château. As I fled along the hallway to the staircase, I glanced back and saw the waiter lock the door to Claus's room and then calmly walk away. I didn't have the luxury of time. Any minute now, Max would be back to collect me.

I had just sat down on one of the chairs in the dressing room when there was a knock at the door and Max was calling my name.

I opened the door and attempted a smile.

'Don't look so nervous, you'll be fine. Remember, I'll be there,' he said misreading my nervous state for stage fright. He reached out for my flute case.

I snatched my hand back, holding the case to my body. 'I'll carry it,' I said. He gave me a strange look but said no more and accompanied me down to the cellar and along the passageway. He stopped at the door to the reception room.

'Good luck,' he said. 'Remember, where I am if you need me.'

'Thank you,' I replied, grateful for his moral support.

He hesitated with his hand on the door handle. I looked at him, the dim light casting half his face in shadow, and I felt transfixed by his eyes. I thought for a moment he was going to lean forwards and kiss me. I saw him swallow and then take a deep breath. 'I'm reminding myself that I am not just an officer but a gentleman also,' he whispered and before I could reply, the door was opened from the other side and the space flooded with light as the string quartet exited the stage.

The next hour went in a blur as I gave the performance of my life, concentrating hard on the music in front of me, thankful I had spent the past week practising every day. I may not have liked performing to the German army officers and their guests, but I had my pride and in my mind I was performing in a packed concert hall with Papa standing in the wings watching.

As I finished and left the stage through the passageway, he was already there, waiting for me.

'You were marvellous!' he declared. 'Wonderful!' He hugged me in delight and spun me around at the top of the stairwell. 'Bravo! Bravo!'

I was exhilarated from the performance and I laughed out loud, delighting in his enthusiasm. 'I so enjoyed playing,' I admitted.

'You looked to be in a world of your own at times,' said Max as we almost skipped along the corridor.

I came to a halt, my mood dipping. 'And if I confessed that's exactly where I was?' I asked.

'I would have done the same thing,' he replied gently. 'Now, come. Let me take you home before Claus insists you stay for the after-party. I'm sure you don't want to do that.'

TWENTY-FOUR

2019

Imogen looked at the packed case on her bed. She didn't need to take a great deal of things over to Laurent's, she reasoned with herself. To all intents and purposes, she was just going to be using his spare room as a place to sleep. During the day while the works were going on to make the west wing sound, she'd be busy with the memorial garden or the gardens at the château.

Laurent said she'd be able to check on the progress being made once the contractors had finished for the day and he would take her around and bring her up to date with everything. All this while wearing a high-vis jacket and hard hat – he was taking his responsibilities very seriously and Imogen was reassured by the professionalism he was showing.

'All set?' asked Laurent as she took her case downstairs. He was waiting in the entrance hall for her, with the cat basket containing Kitty. Imogen had been worried about leaving the cat at the château while the work was going on and had persuaded Laurent to let her bring the cat with them, although he was convinced it would just make its way back to the château.

'I think I've got what I need. I can always pop back if I've forgotten anything.'

Laurent's mobile phone started ringing and he took the call as they made their way out to his car.

Imogen wasn't intentionally eavesdropping, but it was hard not to hear what he was saying. In actual fact, Laurent wasn't saying a great deal but as he put the cat basket onto the back seat, his voice took on a grave tone. 'I see… Is it bad…? How is he in himself…? Yes. Of course… I'll go straight away. Don't worry. I'll ring you.' He looked over the top of the car towards Imogen as he ended his call.

'What's wrong?' Imogen could tell from his expression something wasn't right.

'That was my mother. My father's had a fall. The water infection has made him a bit unsteady on his feet. Sylvie found him this morning when she went in to do the cleaning.'

'Oh, no! Is it bad?'

'He's been taken to the local hospital in Paris for an x-ray. They think he's hurt his hip.'

'I'm so sorry.' She moved around the car to stand in front of him and put her arms around his shoulders, drawing her to him. She had to stand on tiptoe and for a moment he resisted the embrace but then she felt his shoulders drop and he rested his head against hers. His hair smelt of coconut and there was a hint of citrus bodywash. For one brief moment, she forgot why she was holding him.

Laurent must have suddenly become aware of himself too, for he stood up and pulled away rather abruptly. 'Thank you.'

'Sometimes we all need a hug, no matter how big and tough we are,' said Imogen softly. 'What are you going to do?'

'My mother wants to come home, but I've told her not to. There's nothing she can do right now. I've told her to stay there and I'll go and see him. I'll get a couple of things together in a bag.' He checked his watch. 'I can be there by this evening.'

'But it must be about a five-hour drive,' said Imogen. 'What about flying? You could get a flight from Rennes and be there in an hour.'

'Good idea. Why didn't I think of that?'

She knew it was a rhetorical question, but she answered all the same. 'Because you're worried about your father and not thinking straight.'

He gave her a grateful smile and then let out a groan. 'What about you?'

'Don't worry about me,' replied Imogen. 'I'll sort something out.'

'No. No, I can't leave you stranded, especially when the work is about to start.' He rubbed his fingers across his forehead.

'Go,' Imogen insisted, taking the cat basket from the car. 'Honestly, Laurent. Go. Just phone or text me so I know you've got there safely. Take your time.' She felt embarrassed as soon as she said it. He was a grown man and quite capable of getting himself to Paris without her fussing over him like a clucking hen.

He smiled giving her a mock salute and went to get in his car.

He stopped, turned around and walked over to her. 'Come with me?'

'What?'

'Come with me to Paris.'

'Er… to Paris?' What was she supposed to say to an offer like that?

He ploughed on. 'The company would be nice – from my point of view that is. You could do a bit of sightseeing while I visit my father.'

'Oh, I wouldn't want to intrude,' said Imogen, although the idea of spending some time with Laurent in Paris was, to say the least, very appealing but to counterbalance that was the thought of his father being unwell. 'Besides, what will I do about Kitty?'

'You wouldn't be intruding. And Claude will look out for the cat.'

She hesitated, biting down on her words of refusal. Maybe he actually wanted her there for moral support? It was one thing staying over at his apartment in the village for a few days while renovation work was being carried out, but it was another going away with him to Paris. Or was it?

Laurent moved in front of her. '*S'il te plaît?*'

The change in the noun to a term of more familiarity wasn't lost on her. Imogen was also aware that she'd been given another glimpse of the Laurent Roussell who wasn't as calm or in control of things as he liked to be. He was worried and anxious and he was asking her along because he needed her. 'OK. If you're sure,' she found herself replying.

'I'm sure.'

'I won't get in your way but I'll be there if you need me.'

'You won't. And I do.'

'I'd better ask Claude to look after Kitty in that case.'

His smile of relief was palpable. '*Merci. Merci beaucoup.*'

∽

They had caught the early evening flight from Rennes out to Paris and just over an hour after taking off, they were touching down at Charles De Gaulle airport.

'I'll go straight to see my father. I can arrange for another taxi to take you to my apartment and I'll meet you there later.' The plane bumped as the wheels made contact with the tarmac.

'I'm happy to come with you,' said Imogen. 'I won't get in the way. I can just wait in the reception area.' She didn't add that she would be close by in case he needed her, if his father was worse than they thought.

'I like that idea,' agreed Laurent.

The plane taxied to a halt and soon they were making their way off the aircraft, through security and into a cab. Imogen looked out of the window as the car drove into the city and from nowhere the thought of James hurtled its way to the fore, making her catch her breath. Laurent was on the phone to the builders and didn't appear to notice, giving Imogen a few moments to face the thought of James.

They'd been here once on a city break and had done all the touristy things, such as the Eiffel Tower, La Louvre, Arc De Triomphe and a boat trip along the Seine. They had talked about going back one day and she felt a small pang of guilt that she was indeed here again but with another man.

'The builders are going to start work tomorrow. Everything is in place so you don't have to worry about a thing,' said Laurent, when he'd finished his call. He gave her a smile. 'Don't worry, it's all under control.'

'I wasn't…' Imogen cut herself off. She didn't need to tell Laurent that wasn't what she was thinking about. 'Thank you,' she opted for instead.

'The hospital is just up ahead.'

She smiled at him and thought it should be her who was offering the reassurance, not Laurent. The taxi pulled up outside what looked like a hotel rather than a hospital and Imogen imagined it must be a private medical centre.

'You OK?' asked Imogen as they walked in through the double doors.

'I will be once I've seen Papa,' he replied. A quick word with the receptionist and he was given directions to his father's room.

'I'll wait here,' said Imogen, not wanting to intrude any further. 'I have my phone on, so call me if you need me or come and find me, whichever you prefer.' She gave him a quick kiss on the cheek for no other reason than it seemed the natural thing to do.

'Thank you,' said Laurent with a depth of sincerity she hadn't heard before. She watched as he entered the lift and the doors closed on him before she settled herself in one of the chairs with their bags at her feet. The reception area was empty apart from her, the receptionist and a security guard.

The receptionist offered her a coffee, which Imogen accepted and then began checking her emails. There was one from Denise and albeit somewhat irrational, Imogen had another small feeling of guilt that she was in Paris with a man. She swept it aside, telling herself she was a grown woman and didn't have to justify herself to anyone, least of all herself.

Denise's openings and closings to her emails were becoming warmer, Imogen noticed as she opened the latest one.

To: Imogen Wren
    From: D Wren
    Re: Gardens

Dear Imogen,

That's a very generous offer of you to do the remembrance garden, but I know how much you enjoy it so I don't expect it will be too much of a hardship. It sounds quite a responsibility and I'm sure the mayor and the villagers will be pleased if you manage to strike the right tone.

I must say, I am very touched that you are going to create a garden with James in mind. Maybe you could send me some photos?

I suppose while it's summer and the weather is good, getting out and doing something in the gardens while you wait to start work on the château means you don't waste any valuable time.

I'm going to tea at Tom and Kelly's today to break up the day. Last time I was there, they took me out for dinner, which was rather nice. One of their friends babysat. It was certainly different being able to concentrate on a conversation without one of the children. The girls are so sweet though. They both made drew me a picture and said they would miss me.

Take care.

I'll tell them you were asking after them.

Love from Denise

It was certainly an improvement and Imogen hoped she was making headway. She was pleased Denise was happy about the garden for James.

'I just hope she likes it when it's done. If you're listening, James, wherever you are, I could do with a little help there.'

Imogen realised she had spoken out loud, but a quick glance towards the receptionist told her either the woman hadn't heard her or was politely pretending otherwise; either way, she was studying her computer screen.

Imogen finished her drink and took out her book. She must have dozed off at some point but the next thing she knew, Laurent was sitting next to her, gently rubbing her arm and calling her name.

'Imogen, *allez*. Wake up. It's late.'

She sat up with a start. 'Laurent. Sorry, I must have nodded off. How is your father?' She scanned his face trying to work out if it was good or bad news.

'He's sleeping. He was awake when I arrived and I was able to sit with him for a while. He's broken his collarbone. His hip is just bruised, thankfully.'

'Oh, what a relief. I mean, it's bad he's broken his collarbone but his hip would have been worse.'

'Yes, exactly.'

His eyes were heavy and there was a tiredness in his face. A shadow of dark stubble grazed his jaw. 'You need some rest,' she said. 'You look shattered.'

'You must be tired too,' he replied. 'I feel guilty dragging you all the way here when it's not as bad as I thought it was – thank God.'

'Hey, don't feel guilty. I'm glad I could come.'

She rose from her seat as Laurent picked up both bags. 'Let's get back to the apartment.'

The second taxi of the evening whizzed them efficiently to the sixteenth *arrondissement* – an area Imogen was fully aware was a very expensive part of Paris. The apartment they pulled up outside served to confirm this. It was a stone building, made up of four floors. Tall windows hugged by black iron balconies ran from top to bottom with an array of flower boxes and blooms.

Laurent tapped in the code on the keypad and pushed open the oak door. They stepped into a large hallway, which oozed Parisian sophistication. An impressive staircase led from the parquet entrance hall up to the floors above, while in the centre was a wrought-iron lift, which looked like an ornate art deco birdcage.

Laurent opened the gate and let Imogen enter first. 'It's perfectly safe,' he reassured her. 'I'm on the top floor and I'm too tired for the stairs.' He slid the gate across, which clattered into place, and then he stabbed at the button to take them to the top.

'Ooh, penthouse suite,' said Imogen with a smile but she was only half-joking. This building oozed money and sophistication. It was very different to any of the houses in Trédion and she was having trouble matching up the Laurent Roussell of Brittany to the Laurent Roussell of Paris.

The apartment was as expensive looking on the inside as it was from the outside, if not more, thought Imogen as she admired the 1920s décor. More parquet flooring covered the entrance hall to the apartment. A kitchen was to the left, which Imogen caught a glimpse of as Laurent ushered her straight down the hallway where he opened a pair of double wood-panelled doors, revealing a large living room that spanned the width of the apartment. Two deep-seated sofas faced each other, separated by a coffee table. An imposing marble fireplace was the centrepiece of the room, with a gilt-edged mirror hanging above. A small TV was pushed into the corner leading Imogen to assume it didn't play a major part in Laurent's life. However, she didn't miss the discreet, no doubt surround-sound speakers nestled in the walls. Music seemed higher up Laurent's preferred mode of entertainment.

As if to confirm this, he picked up a remote control,

pushed a couple of buttons and the soft sounds of jazz filled the room.

'I didn't have you down as a jazz fan,' remarked Imogen.

'I can change it if you don't like it.'

'No, not at all. Your place. Your choice.' She wandered over to one of the four tall windows that graced the living room and moved the floaty muslin fabric to peer out into the city's night sky. 'Wow! What a view.'

He came to stand next to her and opened the floor-to-ceiling windows and stepped out onto the small balcony. 'Here, if you stand here, you can see *la tour Eiffel*.'

The Eiffel Tower rose above the rooftops of the buildings, lighting up the night sky as it towered over the city. The hum of traffic and the occasional beep of a car horn drifted across the urban landscape, punctuated by the occasional sound of footsteps along the pavement, coupled with laughter or people talking, calling their goodnights, and the muted thud of car and front doors opening and closing. Despite the activity of the city, there was a tranquillity being on the top floor of the building.

Imogen hadn't noticed Laurent leave her side but he returned to stand next to her with two glasses of wine. 'I think we both deserve this after today.'

She took the glass and they sipped in a contented silence as they let the stress of the day drain away.

'It's such a beautiful city,' said Imogen eventually. 'I take it you're planning on coming back here to live.'

'What makes you say that?'

'Oh, I don't know. Maybe you seem more suited to the city. You seem very at home here.'

'And I don't in Trédion?'

'Ignore me, it's been a long day,' said Imogen.

'No. I'm intrigued. What did you mean?'

There was no avoiding it. 'Sometimes you seem a bit

tense when you're in Trédion, as if there's something both-ering you. It's just tiny glimpses, but now and again, there's a troubled expression on your face.' She looked at him with his glass in one hand, the other hand in his pocket, gazing out across the night sky. 'A bit like you are now,' she added.

He turned to face her. 'Like now?'

'Yes, you seem pensive. I know you're worried about your father and it's that sort of look I've seen on you.' Inwardly, Imogen could hear a voice in her head telling her to stop talking. She'd said too much and had probably offended him now. He really didn't need this when he was concerned about his father. 'Sorry, I didn't mean to upset you. Like I said, ignore me.'

'No, don't apologise.' He placed the glass on the bistro table. 'I admit, I do sometimes feel… shall we say, uncom-fortable in Trédion but that's not because of you, just in case you were wondering. No, it's because I have mixed feelings about the place and sometimes the not so happy memories resurface, but that is all.'

'So why come back? Why stay there when you clearly have a good lifestyle here?' It was a question that had been percolating for some time in Imogen's mind, a question she hadn't quite been able to reach but she had definitely been aware something wasn't sitting right with Laurent's return to the village.

'It's complicated,' said Laurent. 'I have to decide what to do with my grandmother's apartment. I haven't made up my mind yet. Maybe I'll commute between there and here. I do like living in the city…'

'I sense there's a "but" coming.'

'Very perceptive,' he said, sliding his other hand into his other pocket. 'You know what they say about how being in a city full of people can actually be very lonely.'

Imogen made a scoffing noise. 'You – lonely? I can't

imagine that.' And then she caught sight of the expression on his face, partially shielded by shadow, but not enough that she missed it. One of sadness. She immediately regretted her flippant comment. 'Actually, that's not true. What I mean is, I imagine you as someone with lots of friends and work colleagues and lots of people to socialise with, lots of invites, lots of company and... lots of women only too willing to keep you company.'

'Is that how you see me?' he sounded a little put out. 'A playboy?'

Oh God, now she had really offended him. 'I don't know enough about you.'

'For the record. I'm not a playboy.'

'Good.'

'Up until a few months ago, I was in a long-term relationship. I'm not into one-night stands as a rule.'

She noted the caveat – as a rule – and wondered if she was an exception to the rule. She had after all agreed to come with him to Paris, albeit it as a friend to offer support but she was here in his apartment, standing on the balcony, drinking wine. Was she sending out the wrong message? Did she even know what sort of message she was trying to send out? She was confused herself.

'When you say a long-term relationship, how long are you talking?' she ventured because suddenly it seemed important.

'A little over two years,' replied Laurent. 'And I'm going to pre-empt your next question – why did we split up?'

'Only if you want to tell me.'

Laurent gave a wry smile. 'Apparently, I never her let her get close to me. In the emotional sense,' he added quickly.

It was Imogen's turn to smile, as if there was any doubt in what sense he had and hadn't let her get close. 'I can probably see where she's coming from.'

Laurent looked at her in surprise. 'You can?'

'Mmm. It's like you're carrying a heavy load but won't let anyone help you.'

'I'm not sure if that's strictly true. You're here. You came when I needed you.' Laurent pushed himself up from the railing and leaned back against them. Their shoulders were almost touching.

She took a sip of her drink, fully aware of their close-ness. She looked out across the city of lights and couldn't think of a more beautiful place to be. She was aware Laurent had leaned towards her, his head turned so his mouth was close to her ear.

Then with immaculate timing, his mobile phone rang out. 'Sorry,' he whispered as he checked his phone. 'It might be the hospital.' The moment was broken and the tension disappeared as if caught on the evening's breeze.

Imogen remained where she was on the balcony as Laurent took the call inside, reappearing a few minutes later. 'It was my mother.'

The stubble on his chin even more prominent, his hair ruffled and dark circles weighed under his eyes. 'You need to get some sleep,' she said gently. 'You look exhausted.'

'You should too.'

'Please don't say it's because I look as exhausted as you.' Imogen was aware after the hurried exit from Trédion, the flight and mad dash to the hospital, she probably wasn't looking her best either. She wasn't even sure she'd brushed her hair since she got up that morning and she'd been in the same clothes all day.

Laurent rubbed his chin. 'I have no doubt I look as shit as I feel. You, on the other hand, look as lovely as ever. Come on, I'll show you where the bedroom is.'

The bedroom. Not *her* bedroom. Not bedrooms in the plural. Not even the *spare* bedroom. She followed him back into the apartment. Laurent picked up both holdalls and headed down the hallway. He opened the door on the right. 'Here we go,' he said far too casually.

Imogen hesitated. He was taking both bags into the room. She needed to decide now if she was going ahead with this and sharing a bed with him. She was slightly irked Laurent was being presumptuous that she was going to sleep with him and although she knew she wanted to, she didn't necessarily like to think it was a foregone conclusion.

'Laurent, I think we need—'

He interrupted her. 'This is your room. It's the guest room. You've got your own bathroom.' He plonked the holdall on the bed and went over to the door in the corner, opening it for her. 'Shower room, really. There's a cupboard in there where you'll find fresh towels.' He stopped and looked at her. 'Everything OK?'

God, she felt disappointed now. He didn't want to sleep with her after all that. What was wrong with her! She realised he was expecting a reply. 'Yes, everything is fine,' she forced herself to say. 'It's a lovely room.' And it was – a double bed, white furniture in a fresh simple Scandinavian style.

'I'll be just across the hallway if you need me,' he said.

She wanted to ask what he meant by needing him but didn't trust herself. 'Thank you,' was the best she could manage.

'Thank you again for coming with me. I do appreciate it.' He headed for the door, pausing to kiss her on each side of the face. 'Goodnight, Imogen.'

Did he linger a little too long with the second kiss? Or was that just wishful thinking? 'Goodnight, Laurent,' she finally managed to eke out as he left the room, closing the door behind him. She heard the opening of his door and the gentle click of it closing. Well, that was that. Here she was in one of the most romantic cities in the world, in a room, on her own, with an extremely attractive Frenchman just a few metres away and a couple of doors separating them. She didn't know whether to laugh or cry.

TWENTY-FIVE

1944

It had taken me a long time to get to sleep the night of the performance at the château. Max had walked me home and as he paused outside the back gate of my house, I had for one moment thought he was going to kiss me, but he was the perfect gentleman and had smiled, wishing me a good night's sleep.

I had watched him go with a surprising feeling of disappointment but then been cross with myself for even having such thoughts. I paid a visit to the outside toilet and hid the document as instructed.

The following morning, it had gone and I felt a sense of victory and accomplishment. I had held my nerve and I had outwitted the Germans. I was keen to be given another task and hoped the doctor would be pleased with what I'd done.

I cycled up to the Devereaux farm later that morning to collect the eggs for the shop. My heart was still brimming with pride and I wanted to shout it out to everyone, which of course I couldn't. When I spoke to M. Devereaux I was half expecting him to whisper a congratulations in my ear, but he said nothing and carried on as normal.

On my way back to the village, I heard the sound of a car approaching. It slowed and drew level with me. As I glanced over, I saw Max at the wheel. He waved and then accelerated ahead of me before pulling over on the side of the road.

'*Bonjour,*' I said, bringing my bike to a halt at the driver's side. Today the sky was a clear blue and I noticed again how blue Max's own eyes were; they were almost an exact match.

He got out of the car and lit a cigarette, before leading my bike over to the side of the road. 'How's your brother?' he asked.

'He's not so good,' I replied honestly. 'He's got pneumonia.'

'Is he being seen by the doctor?'

I hesitated before answering. 'Not continually. Just when he's very ill.'

'Money?' Max asked. 'Is that what's stopping the doctor visiting?'

'We're all getting by as best as we can,' I replied stiffly, my pride rearing up. 'If it wasn't…' I stopped myself from finishing the sentence.

'If it wasn't for the war,' supplied Max. 'Or were you thinking more specifically if it wasn't for the Germans?'

I shrugged. 'What does it matter? The fact is my brother is sick and medicine is scarce and expensive.'

Max drew on his cigarette and looked across the fields towards the village. I followed his gaze and thought how pretty and peaceful it looked from up here. The spire of the church was standing proudly in the centre, surrounded by rooftops of the shops and houses. Beyond that I could see the pointed cones of the turrets, which stood at each corner of the Château de Trédion.

'I'm glad I've seen you. There's something that's been playing on my mind. I was going to say something last night, but I didn't want to spoil the evening.' Max looked earnestly at me.

'What did you want to say?' I couldn't even begin to imagine what it was, but Max looked serious. Had I already been found out for what I did last night?

'I want to apologise,' he said.

'For what?'

'For what happened in the village the other day.'

Relief surged through me, quickly followed by anger, which I couldn't tame. 'Oh, for my friend being shot for allegedly being part of the resistance?' I snapped the words out before I had time to check myself.

Max turned his head away and I thought for a moment I saw a look of embarrassment on his face. He dropped his cigarette to the ground and stamped it out. 'Yes. That.'

The raging flames of anger were tempered a little by his honest response and I acknowledged a confusion inside me. I was angry at the uniform, not the man. I knew that but my anger wasn't ready to be so logical yet. 'Why can't you stop it?' An unrealistic question maybe?

'There is only so much I can do,' explained Max. 'I hold very little weight or influence and if I speak too loudly against what is happening, then I am likely to be court-martialled, tried for treason or collaboration and then shot. What good would that do?'

'So you just accept it?'

'I try to make small differences.'

I looked at him for a moment. 'Do you know anything about Madame Oray being allowed to keep chickens?' I asked.

'Does it matter if I do?'

'Yes. It matters a lot.' I needed to know if Max was a man of more than just words and sentiment.

Max nodded. 'I thought it might help.'

Relief filled my heart. 'It has. Thank you.'

'We can all do things to help,' said Max. 'It may not make a difference on a big scale but it can make a big difference on a smaller scale to the individual lives of others. I wish I could have done something to help your friend.'

'She didn't deserve to die,' I said, once again feeling the pain of her loss. 'She was my friend and it's just so unfair. It feels personal now.'

'I understand but you mustn't let the hate eat away at the good person inside you.'

His words sounded so profound and personal. 'You've lost someone too, haven't you?'

'Yes. My best friend, Dirk. We grew up together in the same village. We both trained to be teachers. He was an amazing mathematician. He was like a brother to me.' He smiled at the memory and then his expression darkened. 'We were called up at the same time. The last time I saw him was after we finished training. I always assumed we'd meet again after the war but that wasn't to be.'

'What happened?'

'He was killed in Hamburg last year during the British and American air raids. He was there to inspect the armament production. He didn't choose to be there. He didn't choose war but war came to us both.'

I could hear the pain in Max's voice. 'I'm sorry,' I said softly.

'It's estimated around thirty-seven thousand civilians were killed that day,' said Max. 'Another one hundred and eighty thousand maimed and injured. Innocent people just going about their days.' He let out a sigh. 'That's how it works both ways.'

We lapsed into silence, both lost in our thoughts for a moment.

'If you weren't here, if there was no war, what would you be doing instead?' I asked at last.

'Standing here as a tourist and hoping you'd agree to have dinner with me.'

The anger was snuffed out almost immediately. 'And I would be accepting,' I replied softly. 'But I fear, it is not possible.'

'Why is that?'

'Because of who we are.'

'It's precisely because of who we are that we will be able to make it possible,' replied Max.

'I don't want to be a German's whore and neither do I want to be shunned by my community.'

'You would never be a whore to me.'

'But to others, I would.' I looked down, not being able to meet his gaze.

'Not if they didn't know.' Max reached out his hand and closed it over mine.

I knew I should be feeling anger towards him, that I should be repulsed by what he was suggesting, that I should be putting country before self, but although those emotions were present, they were faint and far away in the distance. What I actually felt was a tingle of excitement at his touch, the desire to respond in kind, the anticipation of what was to come.

I closed my eyes briefly to try to regain a degree of control over my response, reminding myself of what I'd done last night and why.

Max went to withdraw his hand but I caught it in mine. 'I'm scared,' I confessed, which was wholly true. I could feel my knees shaking involuntarily and my breathing deepened.

Max stroked his thumb across my knuckles. 'You can trust me.'

'I believe I can,' I replied. 'I can trust you as a man…'

'But you can't trust me as a soldier?' he finished.

'That scares me too.'

'I'll make this promise to you now,' said Max softly. 'All the time it is just the two of us, I will only ever be Max Becker. Never Oberleutnant Becker. I will also be respectful and caring to you. You have my word.'

'And when you are Oberleutnant Becker and you see me, how will you be then?'

'Courteous. Polite. Respectful. And I will always look out for you.'

I nodded. I believed him; I didn't know why. I barely knew him, but there something about him that made me feel he was sincere. I was usually a good judge of character and went with my gut feeling so despite all the warning reminders that he was a German soldier going off like fireworks in the background, I found myself smiling at him.

'*D'accord*,' I said. 'But don't think I'm one of those women who will roll over and open my legs just because you've said some nice things.'

He looked startled for a moment and then threw his head back and let out a deep laugh. His eyes sparkled bluer and his grin stretched across his face. 'Well, I've never had an answer like that before,' he said as he caught his breath. 'You, Simone Varon, are as unique as you are beautiful.'

'And you, Max Becker, have seen nothing yet.'

'I feel I might just have my hands full with you,' said Max, still smiling.

TWENTY-SIX

2019

Imogen woke first and took a moment to lie there while she listened to sounds of Paris coming alive. She idly wondered what Laurent was doing and then almost immediately she thought of James and for some bizarre reason, Denise. She wasn't sure what Denise would think of her lying here in a Parisian apartment with Laurent just across the hallway.

She reached over for her mobile and searched for the photos and the album she'd dedicated to James. It was where she'd saved all her favourite pictures of him so she could look at them any time she liked. She scrolled through, smiling at the images, her heart filling with both love and sadness. She stopped, mid-scroll, analysing her reactions. Today there were no emotional torrents, causing her heart to white-water raft its way through the rapids of grief and pain. No, it was different today. Still there but a more gentle undercurrent of sadness.

'You don't mind do you, James?' she whispered to the photograph on her phone. She drew it to her lips and kissed the image. 'No, I don't think you do, my darling.' She sat up and swung her feet onto the floor, taking one last look at her phone before putting it back on the side.

From somewhere in the apartment, Imogen could hear a radio playing accompanied by the occasional clink of crockery. The smell of freshly brewed coffee wafted down the hallway to her room.

After a quick wash and then getting dressed, Imogen went in search of Laurent in the kitchen.

'*Bonjour*,' he greeted her with a kiss on each side of her face. He was barefooted and dressed in a pair of jeans and a black crew-neck T-shirt, looking impossibly cool. 'Coffee? I was going to make some breakfast. Scrambled eggs OK with you?'

'Have you heard from the hospital at all?' she asked, wandering over to the window that looked out onto a courtyard. She hadn't investigated this view last night and realised now this side of the apartment formed one side of a courtyard with three other identical buildings. Below was a communal garden. A little bit of paradise hidden in a bustling city.

'I've just spoken to the hospital. Papa had a good night. I'm going to arrange for him to have a few weeks in a convalescent home before he goes home, by which time my mother will be back from her travels. I don't want to rush him back if his shoulder's not too good.'

They sat out on the balcony at the bistro table, the sun warming their faces as they ate their breakfast, and Imogen couldn't imagine doing anything more French than this in Paris.

'You're a very good son. Are you close to your father?'

'I try to be a good son and, yes, I'd say we have a close relationship. I'm going to visit him this morning once I've confirmed the details with the convalescent home. You're welcome to come or you can wait here.'

'I don't know if your father would want a stranger coming up to the hospital. I might do a little bit of exploring of the city instead.'

'Papa won't mind. Come with me. I'd like to take you out this afternoon. A thank you for your kindness.'

'You don't have to thank me. I did it as any friend would.'

Laurent looked over the rim of his coffee cup, his expression hidden, and Imogen had no idea what he was thinking. He put his cup down. 'OK, but I'd still like to treat you to lunch and a visit to the *Jardins des Plantes*.'

'*Jardin des Plantes* – I'd love to go there.' Imogen grinned at the opportunity.

'I knew you would. That's why I suggested it.'

'Yay!' Imogen was well aware she was still grinning and when Laurent returned the expression, she was sure hers just broadened even further. And then, the smile dropped from his face and his eyes darkened.

There was an intensity Imogen hadn't seen before in him and as her own smile dissolved, she realised she couldn't break his gaze even if she wanted to. 'Laurent,' she said his name so softly, she wasn't even sure if she'd said it out loud.

He reached out and hooked the leg of the chair with his hand, pulling it towards him, as he twisted in his chair and moved her closer so her knees were touching the inside of his thighs.

Nerves threw themselves around in her stomach and her heart beat at double speed as she felt her whole body lean in towards him with a hunger she didn't know she still possessed as she kissed him. Tentatively and slowly. His response was immediate as he returned the kisses.

Then he stood up, holding her hand. She stood too, as they punctuated their movements with kisses. 'Bedroom,' said Laurent. His voice was guttural. 'Don't want to give the neighbours a show.'

~

Sex with Laurent had been fantastic, Imogen thought as she lay curled up against him with his arm wrapped around her shoulder, keeping her close to him. The first time had been a passionate and raw affair. One of wanting and need. The second time was just as passionate but they had taken their time, explored each other's bodies and reached some deeper level of emotional connectivity.

Laurent dropped a kiss on top of her head. 'Much as I would love to stay here and make love to you again…' he said, not finishing the sentence.

'I know we can't stay like this forever.'

'Don't think of it as the end, just a pause.'

She was happy with that. It didn't appear he was having second thoughts.

Laurent made fresh coffee and they sat out on the balcony again at Imogen's request.

'It's so beautiful,' she said, as she sipped her drink.

'I have the most beautiful view.'

She laughed when she realised he was looking straight at her as he spoke. 'You're very charming.' She silently wondered how many times he'd used that line on a woman. How many times had a different woman sat here having breakfast with him? She looked away, knowing she should prepare herself for the potential brush-off that might follow – not necessarily now, today or even tomorrow but at some point, it would be time for him to move on. She understood that, but for now, she'd enjoy the time she spent with him.

'You're not very good at accepting compliments, are you?' said Laurent.

'Out of practice, I guess,' she replied, suddenly feeling shy in front of him. It was one thing revealing herself physically to someone but revealing her innermost thoughts and feelings – she wasn't sure she was ready to take that step yet.

He reached over and took her hand and when she still didn't look at him, he gave it a gentle shake to force her attention. 'I meant what I said. You're a beautiful woman. And brave. I'm honoured you trusted me.'

Oh God, and now she wanted to cry. His words were spoken with such tenderness, as if he somehow knew she hadn't slept with anyone in a long time. He lifted her hand and kissed her fingertips, which only served as a trigger for those tears. Imogen swiped them away with her other hand, embarrassed at this show of emotion. 'Sorry,' she said. 'Not sure where they came from.'

He gave a long look. 'You don't have to be sorry,' he said eventually. He let go of her hand and smiled that easy way of his, immediately pegging back her anxiety levels. 'Now, I need to phone the convalescent home and then go to see my father.' He checked his watch. 'Do you think you'll be ready to go in an hour?'

'Yes but I won't actually go in to see your father. I'll wait outside.'

'Why outside? Come in and meet Papa.'

'I'm sure he doesn't want some stranger appearing at his bedside when he's ill.'

'You don't know Papa. He'd love that,' said Laurent. 'It will cheer him up.'

Imogen wasn't sure it was a good idea but decided not to argue. 'Maybe I'll just pop in and say hello but I don't want to outstay my welcome.'

'*Ce n'est pas possible.*' Before she could argue the point any further, Laurent rose and, taking his phone from his pocket, went over to the sofa and began to confirm respite care arrangements for his father.

Imogen went back to the bedroom to get showered and dressed again. Afterwards as she gathered her toothbrush, she realised she'd left her underwear somewhere on Laurent's bedroom floor.

She could hear him still on the phone, so nipped across the hallway and into his room. Locating her underwear, she had an impulsive urge to leave Laurent a note. Something he'd find when he was next here. There was a desk in the corner of the room where there was bound to be paper and a pen. The glass desk had an architect's plan of a house folded in half with a notepad on top of it. Imogen picked up the notebook intending to rip a page from it. As she did so, a photograph slipped from inside the cover. She went to replace it but stopped abruptly. She recognised the image; it was the château in Trédion but it wasn't a recent photograph. It was an old black and white one. She peered closer in case she was mistaken but, no it was definitely her château. She recognised the shutters, the turrets, the moat and the bridge. Something made her look at the folded drawing.

Her hands shook as she opened the plan. Yes, that was the château. It was hard to put an age on it as it was a structural drawing but she was in no doubt what she was looking at. Hearing Laurent begin to wind up his conversation, Imogen hurriedly refolded the drawing and shoved the notebook back on top of it.

She didn't know what to make of it all. Could it relate to the work she wanted Laurent to do on the property? Was it something to do with the French planning application? But that didn't make sense. Why was it here? She was sure Laurent hadn't been back to Paris since she'd been in Trédion and first met him, so why did he have details of the château? She wanted to ask him but winced as she wondered how to without it sounding like she was snooping.

Now he was calling her. It was time to go and the taxi was waiting. She'd think of a way to ask him later.

~

The hospital was just as calm and quiet when Imogen and Laurent arrived as it had been the night before.

'Is this a private hospital?' Imogen whispered as they were led down a corridor by a nurse.

'Yes. I topped up my parents' health insurances a few years ago, just for emergencies like this.'

The nurse left them outside the door of a private room. Laurent knocked gently and opened the door, beckoning Imogen to come too.

'Are you sure?' she asked, hesitating in the doorway. 'Can't you warn him first? I feel awfully intrusive.'

'I'm positive. *Allez.*' He took her hand and trailed her into the room behind him.

The man in the bed had his eyes closed but, even so, Imogen could tell where Laurent had inherited his looks from.

As Laurent leaned over the bed, his father opened his eyes. 'Laurent.' He gave a broad smile and his pale brown eyes twinkled with delight.

'*Ça-va, Papa?*'

'*Bien. Pas trop mal,*' he replied. His eyes then moved to Imogen and he gave a look of surprise. 'You did not tell me you were bringing a guest.'

'A special guest.' Laurent held out his arm, to bring Imogen closer to the bed. 'This is my friend Imogen. She's English.'

M. Roussell shuffled in his bed. 'Help me sit up,' he told Laurent. 'That's better. Pass my glasses.'

Laurent did as he was told and with his spectacles now in place, M. Roussell senior looked up at Imogen. 'Pretty. *Très jolie. Est-elle mariée?*' He spoke in French.

'Yes she is pretty,' agreed Laurent, and then looking back at Imogen. 'And no she isn't married but she does speak excellent French.' He gave his father a teasing look.

'*Oh, merde!*' He muttered, putting his hand to his mouth. '*Pardon.*' Then tapping Laurent's arm with his good hand: 'You could have warned me.'

Laurent laughed and Imogen found herself giggling too. She addressed M. Roussell. 'Thank you for the compliment. I'm actually widowed and speak French and Italian.' She held out her hand. 'Imogen Wren. *Enchanté, monsieur.*'

'*Enchanté. Daniel Roussell.*'

Imogen shook the older man's hand and felt the same warmth she'd felt from Laurent. 'How are you after your fall?'

'Very cross with myself. Very cross.'

'Don't be,' said Laurent. 'Try not to think about it now.'

'Hmmm. I suppose I should be grateful it wasn't worse.' Daniel Roussell fussed with the edge of the bed sheet. 'I don't like being here. Have you come to take me home?'

Laurent exchanged a glance with Imogen. 'Not today,' he replied. 'I've arranged for you to go to a convalescent home for a couple of weeks, just until your shoulder is better and while Maman is away.'

'I don't want to go anywhere. I just want to go home.'

Imogen noticed M. Roussell's eyes had taken on a glassy appearance. 'It will only be for a few weeks,' she said, trying to help Laurent out with the obviously difficult conversation. 'It's very nice there. You'll be well looked after.' She had no idea if she was saying the right thing or even if M. Roussell was listening to her.

But the elderly gentleman turned his head towards Imogen. 'When you get to my age, everyone else thinks they know best and wants to make decisions for you. Your children start treating you like a child. That's not the way it should be.'

Laurent placed his hand on his father's arm. 'We just want to help you, that's all.'

'Then take me home. Not to a convalescent home but to my own home.'

'You know that's not possible, Papa,' said Laurent softly. He tidied the sheet unnecessarily, unfolding it and refolding it across his father's chest.

M. Roussell sighed. 'I hate being told what to do.'

'I know you do, Papa,' replied Laurent.

M. Roussell pointed towards Imogen. 'Could you get me some fresh water please? There's a kitchen down the corridor. You'll find some bottled water in there, I believe.'

'Of course,' said Imogen, grateful for something to do. She felt very awkward and wished she'd been a bit more insistent about waiting outside. She left the room and took her time finding the kitchenette and refilling the jug with the bottled water from the fridge.

As she walked back along the corridor and approached the room, she noticed her shoelace was undone, so stopped to tie it. She could hear Laurent and his father talking.

M. Roussell was speaking. 'Have you looked where she told you to?'

'I haven't been able to yet. It's difficult,' replied Laurent. 'I'm going to be doing some work there, so as soon as I get the chance I will.'

'Maybe you should forget about it.'

'I can't. I made a promise and I can't break it.'

Their voices were low and had a secrecy about them. Imogen stayed crouched, even though her shoelace was tied. It felt wrong to interrupt them but it also felt wrong to be eavesdropping.

'This should all have been sorted out years ago,' M. Roussell was saying. 'I don't know why you had to be involved.'

'Papa, don't go through all that again,' replied Laurent. 'It's something I need to do.'

Imogen frowned to herself as she wondered what they were talking about.

'It will cause more trouble than it's worth.' It was M. Roussell again. 'She seems like a very nice young lady.'

Imogen held her breath as she waited for Laurent's reply. 'Yes, she's very nice.' Imogen felt herself smile at his response as she thought back to that morning being in bed with Laurent. Nice – she'd show him nice. She grinned even wider at the delectable thought.

'You can't tell her the truth though,' Laurent's father went on.

The smile on Imogen's face downgraded itself from broad to meagre. The truth? What truth? She waited for Laurent's reply.

'I know that. I want to but I know I can't. Things have gone too far.'

Imogen felt a tightness in her throat, followed by the heaviness of her heart. How could she go from feeling on top of the world to absolute rock bottom in such a short space of time?

TWENTY-SEVEN

1944

The day after talking with Max in the lane, I was once again cycling back from the farm with my cargo of freshly laid eggs, albeit a slightly depleted batch as some hungry Germans had already been there that morning, to lay claim to a dozen or so, I wondered when I'd see Max again. In my haste to ride off yesterday, I hadn't actually agreed anything with him and there was, of course, no way I could contact him.

I freewheeled down the lane that threaded its way through the fields to the village. The sun was shining and I held my head up to catch the warmth of the rays as the wind whooshed over my face. Impulsively, I pulled out the hairband and shook my head, setting free my hair. It was a simple pleasure and for a moment I felt the same freedom. I could pretend just for those few seconds that all was right in the world. My bike picked up speed and I tugged at the brakes as the bend in the road appeared sooner than I expected. I hurtled around the bend, just about keeping my balance, and it was then I saw the motorbike parked near the gated field where Max had met me before. A man was leaning rather laconically against it.

For a moment the sun blinded me and I couldn't make out who it was, but as I whizzed down the hill and drew nearer, I realised it was Max. He smiled as he saw me coming and pushed himself away from the gate. But I was travelling too fast to stop and my brakes drew little traction against the steel rim of the bicycle wheel.

Max's happy expression turned to one of concern and as he took in the scene before him, he threw his cigarette to the ground and jumped into the road, grabbing my arm and almost comically running alongside the bike, in an attempt to slow me down.

I let out a scream as the bike flanked to the right and although slowing, there was still enough momentum to propel me, the bike and Max who was still valiantly holding on, into the ditch.

'Simone! Simone! Are you all right?' Max jumped to his feet and was pulling the bicycle away, which had landed on top of me. 'Are you hurt?'

I groaned and moved to a sitting position. 'The only thing hurt is my dignity,' I complained, rubbing my shin. 'And perhaps my leg.'

'Let me look.'

'I'd sooner get out of this ditch first.'

'Not until I've checked you over.'

I decided not to argue as Max began a visual examination of my limbs. Then he took the leg I'd been rubbing into one of his hands, and ran his other hand upwards, stopping at my knee. He glanced up and met my gaze.

I swallowed as all thought of the accident left me at once. The only thing I could focus on now was the touch of his hand on the bare skin of my leg. I remained locked with Max's eyes, so blue were his they looked like drops of liquid sapphire. A lock of blond hair had fallen across his forehead and without realising what I was doing, I reached forward and swept it from his face.

Max broke the deadlock first. 'Let me help you to your feet,' he said.

Together we exited the ditch, Max supporting me at the elbow with one hand and his other around my waist. We stood on the side of the road, neither of us moving apart and I realised that I had this unexpected desire to tilt my head up to kiss him.

Max took a step back. 'Are you sure you're all right?'

'Just a physical bruising,' I replied, dejectedly. My heart was bruised too but not from the accident, from the rejection I'd sensed from Max.

He pulled the bike from the ditch. 'A few broken eggs but surprisingly most of them look intact. Your bike looks all right too.' He checked over the bicycle, pulling on the brakes and then trying to move it forwards. He looked at the brake blocks. 'They are worn right down – no wonder you couldn't stop.'

'It's hard to get bicycle parts.'

Max looked thoughtful but said nothing. 'Well, that's one way to make an entrance,' he said, smiling at me.

'I wasn't expecting to see you there, least of all on a motorbike.'

'I don't always have the privilege of a car but I've swapped the use of this for a packet of cigarettes with another officer.'

'I should feel flattered then that you gave up a packet of cigarettes for me. I hope it was a full packet.'

'Of course.' He leaned the bicycle up against the gate. 'I'm glad I caught you.'

'Not as glad as I am.'

'I meant figuratively,' said Max. 'Although actually is good too.'

'I meant both,' I replied. Somehow, I didn't feel shy in front of Max and found it easy to talk to him, to flirt with him. Something I'd never have imagined myself doing. 'It's probably not good for us to be seen talking in the open like this.'

'Of course,' said Max, scanning the road up and down. He lifted the gate open. 'Let's take our bikes into the woods, where they won't be seen.'

I followed him, pushing my bike through the field. Thankfully there hadn't been any rain for a while and the ground was dry and hard. With our modes of transport well hidden, we walked through the woods to a clearing.

'Do you think the war will ever end?' I asked as I gazed out across the valley.

'Everything ends sooner or later.'

'I just want everything to go back to how it used to be.'

'I think it's too late for that now,' replied Max, a frown settling on his face. 'Too many dreadful acts have been committed.'

I let out a long sigh. 'I probably shouldn't say this, seeing as you're a German soldier...'

'Then say it to me as a man.' To reinforce this idea, Max shrugged off his uniform jacket, tugged his tie and removed his shirt, leaving him in a short-sleeved vest. He certainly didn't look like a soldier anymore.

'I wish I could do something meaningful to help France win.'

Max didn't reply immediately but studied the view ahead of him. It was some minutes before he did speak.

'Sometimes, the art of winning is not one big demonstrative action, but many small actions, continuous actions – on their own they seem insignificant, but together they amount to something meaningful. Everyone has a part to play.'

I tugged at a blade of grass and wound it around my finger absentmindedly. 'What if two people met from opposing sides? Is it possible they can play the same part?'

'They would have to thoroughly believe in what they were doing and believe their small act would be worth the danger.'

Max lay back on the grass and tucked his hands behind his head.

'Listen, can you hear that?' I said. I cocked my head to one side. 'It's the sound of birdsong.' I took in a deep breath. 'The air here on the hillside always smells so clean and fresh.'

'It reminds me of home,' said Max fondly. 'I'm from a rural area in Germany. I miss just being able to sit and listen to nature, to breathe in the scent of the trees, the foliage, the water – it all has a different and distinct smell.'

'Especially when the cows come by for milking,' I said, with a laugh.

Max sat up and nudged me with his shoulder. 'You know how to spoil a romantic moment.'

'Romantic?' I gave him a sideways look, the laughter lingering in my voice.

'It can be,' replied Max, his expression now serious. 'If you want it to be.'

My amusement faded as I held his gaze. 'As a man and a woman?'

'Yes. A man and a woman. Not a Frenchwoman and not a German man. Not a resistance member and not an occupying soldier.' He put his finger to my lips to quell my denial at the mention of the resistance. 'Just a man and a woman. That is all.'

'That's what I want it to be,' I replied, uncertainty and excitement making my voice wobble.

Max inclined his head towards me, his mouth now just a breath away from my own. 'With each other we can be safe and just enjoy precious moments.'

I wasn't sure who moved first, but the next thing I was aware of was our lips meeting and our arms around each other, pulling our bodies close and falling backwards onto the grass.

TWENTY-EIGHT

2019

At that moment a nurse chose to walk down the corridor and Imogen knew she could no longer stay in her crouched position outside the room. She rose and with a smile to the member of staff, went through the door into the room.

'Water,' she announced with a false cheer to her voice as she placed the jug on the bedside table. She avoided looking at Laurent even though she could feel his eyes on her.

'*Merci*,' replied M. Roussell.

'We should get going,' said Laurent. 'I'll come back later this afternoon.'

'There's no need,' said his father. 'I need to rest and as much as I like seeing you, it's really not necessary.'

'But they might be moving you to the convalescent home,' protested Laurent.

'In which case there will be even less for you to do and you can visit me there tomorrow instead.'

Laurent let out a sigh. 'You will give me grey hair.'

'Why don't you go and do something a little more fun?' M. Roussell continued.

'It won't be a problem at all for us to come back,' reassured Imogen. To be honest, right now, she'd sooner not be alone with Laurent – it would mean she'd have to confront him about the conversation and she wasn't sure she was ready to just yet. She needed time to think.

'No. I insist you both do something nice together,' carried on M. Roussell.

'I did promise Imogen I'd take her to the *Jardin des Plantes*,' said Laurent.

'*Jardin des Plantes*. What a splendid idea,' said M. Roussell. 'Now, forgive me, I'm very tired and I should rest.' He put his head back on the pillow, folded his hands and closed his eyes. The finality of the conversation clear.

'As you wish, Papa,' said Laurent.

They said their goodbyes and headed out of the hospital where Laurent had already arranged for a taxi to be waiting for them.

'*Jardin des Plantes?*' confirmed the driver.

'*Oui, c'est ça.*' Laurent sat in the back with Imogen. 'Are you OK?' he asked shifting slightly in his seat towards her.

Imogen looked out of the window pretending to be studying the passing scenery. 'Yes. I'm fine.' She felt the light touch of his fingers on her shoulder and the gentle caress of his fingertip on the side of her neck, making her catch her breath.

'Are you sure?'

'Yes.' She continued her observation of the street, knowing she wasn't doing a very good job of hiding her true emotions.

Laurent's hand dropped away and the rest of the journey was completed in silence. Minimal conversation passed between them as they made their way into the botanical gardens, the only sound was their feet crunching over the gritted pathways. It wasn't until they were walking under the rose arches, that Laurent finally broke the deadlock.

Imogen braced herself as he took her arms and faced her towards him. 'Do you want to tell me what's going on?'

The sun was high in the cloudless sky and a gentle breeze carried the delicate scent of roses in the air. She really didn't want to have this conversation but she knew she had to and forced herself to look at him. 'When I came back from getting your father some water, I overheard you talking. I didn't mean to listen in but I couldn't help it.'

'OK. What did you hear?'

His face was expressionless. Imogen took a deep breath before speaking. 'Your father asked if you'd told me the truth and you replied something along the lines that you couldn't because it was too late now. Things had gone too far.'

'And you took that to mean?'

'I don't know. You tell me. What are you hiding from me?' asked Imogen. 'Ever since I first met you, I had this sense there was something troubling you. I haven't been able to pinpoint it, but every now and again, I catch you off-guard. Laurent, please, what is it?'

'Whatever you think it is. You're wrong.' His voice had an air of sadness but his eyes remained steely.

Anger stirred inside her. 'Is that it? Is that all you're going to say?'

He puffed out a sigh. 'I didn't mean it to happen this way.'

'You're not making sense,' she insisted. 'You're still not telling me the truth. I don't even know what it all relates to. I've been so stupid. I let myself become involved with you when I know nothing about you.'

She went to walk away, but Laurent caught up with her. 'Imogen, please. I don't know what to say.'

'Try saying you're sorry. Try telling me the truth.' The words shot from her mouth as her anger bubbled high in her chest. 'Who are you? You told me you were a builder looking for work in Trédion. You're not any sort of builder I know. You're actually an architect who lives in a lavish apartment in the sixteenth *arrondissement* in Paris. You pay for your father to stay in what is clearly a very expensive private hospital and at a moment's notice, you can arrange for him to be moved to an exclusive convalescent home. Then you and your father whisper about you not telling me the truth. What is this all about? What sort of game are you playing?'

God, she couldn't believe she was having this argument. How had she been so stupid? What the hell was wrong with her? How did she possibly think she could get involved with another man?

'Aren't you going to say anything? How about starting with why there is a picture of the château on your desk?' she demanded as Laurent pinched the bridge of his nose between his finger and thumb.

'You saw it?'

'I was looking for a pen,' confessed Imogen. 'I wanted to write you a cheesy love note. More fool me.' She turned away and then turned back again. 'Do you know what? I don't actually want to know. I've had enough. What's the point of all this if I'm having to drag every last drop of truth out of you when you obviously don't want to tell me? It's all pointless.' Her anger began to wane. She was tired of this already. She didn't need this shit. She held out her hand. 'Can I have the key to the apartment? I want to go and pick up my stuff, then I'm going to get the next flight back to Brittany. I'm going back to the château. I don't care what you think about it not being safe. I'll take my chances.'

'Please, Imogen…'

'Oh, and I don't want to see you again. You're fired.' She held out her hand. 'Now can I have the key, please?'

TWENTY-NINE

1944

I raced down the hill towards the château. It was nearly seven o'clock and I was supposed to be there to perform for another party. As I had feared, Claus's request hadn't been for just the one night and when he'd come into the shop earlier in the week, he had voiced his disappointment that I hadn't stayed for the rest of the party.

'The guests were very entertained by your performance,' he'd said. 'So much so, I would like you to come back again this weekend. And this time, don't go running off before I've seen you.' He had placed a small bottle of medication on the counter. 'There's more of this if you keep on my good side.'

I was sure Claus could have sourced a larger bottle if he'd wanted to but I knew it was his way of keeping control. I hated him for it and hated myself even more for having to do what he said.

I hadn't seen Max all week as he'd had to attend a meeting in Paris but was due back that day. I hoped I would have time to speak to him. I'd found myself missing him more than I had expected.

I slowed as I reached the bottom of the hill but my foot slipped on the lose stone chippings and skidded out from underneath me. I landed on my hands and knees in the dust. My knee stung like fury and when I inspected it, I was dismayed to see it was bleeding, but that was the least of my worries. I'd ripped a hole in the knee of the only pair of stockings I possessed.

'*Merde!*' What was I going to do now? There wasn't any time to darn them. Even though a darn wouldn't be particularly attractive, it was better than a hole, which would only get bigger and bigger. There was nothing for it.

Taking refuge behind a tree, I quickly slipped out of my stockings, carefully rolled them up and put them in the pocket of my coat. I looked down at my legs, which did actually have a bit of colour to them from being exposed to the elements. The war had made stockings a luxury and I couldn't remember the last time I'd worn them.

Claus was waiting for me at the main entrance, smoking a cigarette as he leaned against the balustrade. He looked at his watch as I approached. 'Just made it.'

'Sorry,' I muttered, attempting to nip by him, but he stepped in my path. 'I see you have the same dress. Do you not possess anything else?'

'No. We cannot afford to buy new clothes.' I wanted to add *while you pigs are here*, but I kept the thought to myself.

Claus's gaze went to my legs. 'What happened here?' He lifted the hem of my skirt to reveal more of my blooded knee.

'I fell.'

'Hmm. Right, come with me.'

He marched down the hallway to the opposite turret, encouraging me to catch up with him. I was reluctant to go. I knew his bedroom was upstairs and all sorts of thoughts were rampaging through my mind.

As I feared, Claus took me into his bedroom. 'Wait there,' he ordered before disappearing out of the room.

My whole body began to shake and I paced the room nervously, not knowing what was about to happen. Claus returned a few minutes later.

'Here, put these on.' He held out a packet of stockings to me. 'Finest silk all the way from Germany.'

My hand shook as I took them from him, withholding a gasp of amazement at the hosiery. Draping them over one hand, I didn't think I'd ever seen such a beautiful pair of stockings, a pale tan colour with a dark seam running up the back.

Claus gave a laugh, which jarred me from my admiration. 'I thought you might like them.'

'Thank you,' I replied in the most neutral tone I could muster.

'Thank you doesn't seem very adequate for such a beautiful pair of stockings.'

'Thank you... very much.'

He laughed again. 'I'm sure we can do better than that.' He took a step closer and trailed a finger down the silk hanging over my hand. 'But, alas, guests will soon be arriving and you're performing first tonight. Now, be a good girl and put them on. No, don't turn around.'

I hesitated. He wanted to watch me dress. More disgust filled my throat making me want to vomit. Suddenly, the stockings looked like the most horrible thing in the world and I wanted to rip them to shreds.

'Come along. We're in a rush, remember?' He took a seat and sat back as he watched me slip my legs into the stockings. 'Very nice,' he murmured. 'Now, off you go and join the others but don't run straight home tonight, not until I've seen you. Understand?'

I gulped again. Nodded and hurried away as fast as I

could, pushing unimaginable thoughts of what the pig had planned for me later from my mind.

I had a couple of minutes in the dressing room to compose myself and steady my nerves before there was a knock at the door. I was so relieved to see Max standing there. He stepped inside and I threw my arms around him.

'Hey, that's a nice welcome,' he said with a laugh. And then more seriously as he stepped back to look at me, holding me at arm's length: 'Is everything all right?'

'I'm fine,' I said with a smile. 'I'm just happy to see you.'

'And I you.' He pulled me towards him and kissed me. I wanted to sink into him and never let the moment end. Somehow, Max could make everything seem normal and right with no consequences or guilt. 'I will walk you home again tonight,' he said as we finally broke away.

'Claus wants me to stay after the performance,' I explained.

'He does? Well, we will see about that,' said Max. 'Now, come. It's time for you to play but before you go, I have something for you.'

From his pocket he took out a sheet of paper and passed it to me. 'What is it?'

'Open it and see.'

I unfolded the paper and was amazed to see a music score. 'What's this?' I looked at the score and hummed the notes. It was a beautiful melodic tune and I imagined a ballerina serenely moving to the music. 'What's it called?' I asked looking at the title written in German. '*Für immer*'.

'It's called "Forever". Play it on your flute,' encouraged Max.

It sounded even more beautiful as I played the instrument and felt absolutely enchanted by it. At the end I lowered my flute and looked at the sheet of music again, trying to find the name of the composer. I let out a small gasp of amazement as I noticed the name in the bottom corner. 'Maximillian Karl Becker.' I looked up at him. 'You wrote this?'

Max smiled and bowed his head. 'I did indeed. And it's for you.'

Tears sprang to my eyes and Max rushed forwards, apologising if he'd upset me. 'No you've done the complete opposite,' I explained. 'I've never had something so beautiful done for me. Thank you so much.' I hugged and kissed him again. 'I shall play this tonight for you. No one else will know, only us.'

'I'd like that very much. Now, we must hurry. You will be late.'

Max left me at the kitchen doorway of the underground passageway and I scurried along towards the east wing. As I trotted up the stairwell to the door at the other end, I let out a small scream of shock as a figure emerged from the darkness.

'Be quiet,' hissed the voice.

'Oh, Doctor Tasse, you frightened me,' I began.

'Let's not worry about that. Now, I haven't got much time but you need to get another document from Gossman's briefcase again. Just like last time.'

'Again?' My heart plummeted at the thought.

'Yes, again,' insisted the doctor. 'You can't back out now. Not after the trouble I've gone to get you here.'

'What? I don't understand.'

'It was I who suggested to Gossman that you perform here. I needed someone on the inside who wouldn't be suspected.'

'You set this up? I didn't know.' I was trying to compute the information. I hadn't realised the doctor was friendly enough with the Germans to suggest this.

'There's a lot you don't know or need to know,' said the

doctor. 'Now remember. Same as before. Don't let me down.'

With that he slipped past me and disappeared into the shadows of the staircase, the sound of his footsteps receding as he carried on down the passageway.

I didn't have time to think. The door opened and Claus was there, frowning at me for being late. 'Don't ever be late again,' he said, his eyes boring into mine. 'I don't want to have to punish you. I'd rather it was altogether a more rewarding experience.'

I apologised and took my place on the stage. It was only the knowledge of Max being out there in the audience watching me that made me hold my nerve as I took out the sheet of music and played 'Forever'. The music moved me so much, I could feel tears welling up and I wondered what our forever would hold.

THIRTY

2019

Imogen remained with her hand outstretched waiting for the keys for what seemed an age before Laurent spoke. 'I have only the one set. I'll come with you.'

She sighed realising this was probably the truth. 'If you insist,' she said, before striding off down the gravel path, not giving him chance to say anything else. He jogged to catch up with her.

'Will you at least let me explain while we make our way back?'

'Up to you. I'm past caring.'

'It's a long and complicated story that concerns my grandmother on the one hand and you on the other.'

Imogen didn't break stride despite finding her interest piqued, which annoyed her immensely. 'I would cut to the chase if I was you,' she said, her eyes fixed straight ahead. 'It doesn't take that long to get to your apartment. Not by taxi anyway.'

'Can we at least slow the pace a little?' He gave some exaggerated puffs as if trying to catch his breath.

'If you can't keep up, that's your problem.'

'I'll give you the abridged version. If you still think I'm a loser, you can tell me and I won't waste my breath. How does that sound?'

'Sounds fine.'

'As you know, my grandmother used to live in Trédion. The reasons I have a plan of the château and an old photograph of it is because she had a connection to the property.'

This little nugget of information did manage to slow Imogen's pace and cause her to look at him. 'Your grandmother had a connection to the château?'

'*Oui.*'

'Is that what this is all about? You feel you have a claim on it?' She stopped and let out a laugh. 'Oh, wait, don't tell me: you're the guy who tried to buy it when I was viewing it?'

He had the decency to look a little embarrassed. '*Oui.*'

'Bloody hell. Why am I such an idiot?' She shook her head in disbelief at her own stupidity. 'No wonder you've seemed suspicious at times. All along you've had a plan to get your hands on the château. It was nothing to do with me… you know… us sleeping together. No, that was just part of your plan. You must have been really pissed off when I bought it.'

'You are jumping to conclusions. It was not like that,' Laurent snapped back at her and he sounded genuinely angry at the suggestion.

She wasn't letting him off that easy though. 'Why didn't you just tell me the truth in the first place? Why? I don't understand. Is that what you and your father were whispering about? Why would you keep it a secret?' She shook her head.

'Which question would you like me to answer first?'

'None of them. All of them!' She blew out a long breath.

'My grandmother asked me to do something for her. I

didn't know whether I should and I had spoken to my father before for his advice. I didn't plan to deceive you, to become involved with you… That just happened.'

'You're going to have to give me more than that.' Imogen stood facing him, her anger still bubbling just below the surface.

'My grandmother, she was there the night of the fire. She was playing for the Germans – she played the flute. In all the confusion to evacuate the building, her flute was left behind and she wanted me to get it back.'

Imogen eyed Laurent, trying to gauge whether this was the truth – any, some or a fraction of it. She couldn't tell. Part of her wanted to believe him but part of her was reeling from the deceit. 'So you think the flute is still in the château after all these years? Don't you think it would have been found by now?'

'It is in the cellar under the west wing. My grandmother was very specific about what happened to it.'

A few of the puzzle pieces fell into place. 'No wonder you were so interested in the cellar and getting the renovations done. Is that why you were so keen to get on with the works and to get me out of the way? So you could find the flute? What's so important about it? And why didn't you just ask me?'

'Because I didn't know if you would give it to me. You had bought the château and the contents and that included the flute. What if I had told you and you decided it was yours? She said there's something in the case that will change the history of the village. I don't know what, but it was so important to her. I couldn't let my grandmother down.'

'I understand that, but I feel totally cheated and used.' Tears sprang to her eyes. 'I… I confided in you. I slept with you, for God's sake. I thought it was all genuine. I didn't realise you were just using me so you could get the flute.'

She was on the move again. Marching out across the flagstones and onto the street, her eyes scanning the *rue Cuvier* for a taxi.

'Imogen! Wait, please.'

'Go away, Laurent.' She stepped forward to hail a taxi, but it sped by. 'I'm going straight to the airport. I don't even want to go back to the apartment with you anymore. I just want to get back to Trédion.' She flung her hand in the air again as another taxi came down the road. This one did stop. Imogen jumped in and slammed the door shut behind her. She pressed the window down. 'Please bring my bag back with you tomorrow or whenever you fly back. Text me when you want to come and find this flute. I'll get Claude to let you in.'

'But, Imogen, I haven't told you everything. I haven't explained.'

'I've heard enough. Goodbye, Laurent.'

THIRTY-ONE

1944

'That was wonderful,' said Max, coming to stand next to me.

I had not long finished performing and was now standing by the piano, with a drink in one hand and my flute in the other. I was trying to sidle out of the room without being noticed so I could go up to Claus's room and get the document the doctor had ordered.

Unfortunately, I had tried to slip away straight after the performance but Claus had been waiting to pounce. Currently, he was talking to one of the other officers.

'Thank you,' I said to Max. 'It's such a wonderful piece of music. I'm going to play it over and over again until I know it by heart.'

He beamed back at me. 'I'd love you to play it again for me, one day.'

'I will. I promise.'

'Ah, sorry about that.' Claus arrived at my side. 'Max.' The two men nodded at each other in acknowledgement. 'What do you think to our flautist?' He put a hand on my back, making me tense, but there was nowhere to move.

If Max noticed, he didn't say anything. 'She was wonderful. Simone and I were just discussing her musical background. I, myself, was a music teacher.'

'Oh.' Claus almost curled his lip with distaste. 'I see you're on first-name terms. You know each other that well?'

'We do indeed,' said Max, fixing Claus with a stare.

I wasn't sure what power game was playing out in front me right at that moment, but I could feel the tension rising between the two men. I took the break in conversation to make my escape. I put my glass on the table at the side of the piano. 'If you don't mind, I need to go to the bathroom. I won't be long.'

Before Claus could protest or whisk me away somewhere else, I nipped around behind Max, allowing my hand to discreetly brush across his back, before heading out of the room. I was relieved to make it to my dressing room and hoped Claus wouldn't follow me. Or Max for that matter.

Peeking through the door, I made sure no one was about and as I had done the week before, I raced down the hallway to the servants' staircase and in no time was up in Claus's room.

This time I was more prepared for what to do and found the case in the same spot as before. I was in and out of the room in less than a minute and another minute later I was back in the dressing room. I collapsed into the chair and took a moment to catch my breath and try to stop my hands from shaking with adrenalin.

When I finally went back to the party, I was relieved to see Claus was preoccupied with his guests and appeared to have forgotten about me. I wanted to keep an eye on him though, as I decided it was safer to know where he was and what he was doing, rather than let my guard down.

He was sitting at a long dining table with his little gang of friends, who seemed to fawn over him at every opportunity. This evening, an older blonde woman was sitting to his left and was practically draping herself over him like some sort of shawl. I didn't recognise her from the village and assumed she'd been ferried in from somewhere nearby. The woman spoke fluent French with a small hint of a Breton accent.

I was a little put out to see Max sitting at the table, but every now and then he glanced my way and gave me a reassuring look. I suspected he was probably doing the same – keeping an eye on Claus.

I chatted politely with some of the guests who came my way but mostly they ignored me or just congratulated me on my performance. I was happy with the limited passing conversations and to maintain my position at the side of the piano where it seemed natural for a musician to be; besides I was genuinely enjoying the recital the pianist was giving.

As the evening was drawing to a close, the Frenchwoman sitting next to Claus was stroking his hair with one hand while her other hand was finding its way inside his shirt after successfully unfastening the buttons on his jacket. She had one leg over his knee, the long split in her scarlet dress revealing practically all of her flesh up to her thigh. Claus's hand firmly gripped her hip. Another woman had joined them and was snuggled up on the other side, swigging from a bottle of champagne.

This was clearly the prelude to one of the wild after-parties I'd heard talk of.

Claus was revelling in the attention of the two women, going from one to the other, kissing and fondling them. Now was a good time to make my escape, especially as the number of guests was thinning out and I didn't want to draw attention to myself. Hopefully, Claus was far too drunk and had a much better offer for the night to think about me.

I slipped back to the dressing room via the secret passageway so I didn't have to pass the dining table.

I'd had to leave my coat and flute case in the dressing room, much as I loathed to do so. I was fearful that it might be taken or searched but it would look even more suspicious if I'd taken it into the party with me.

I'd also not given my coat to the attendant that evening as I had already decided it would only hinder any quick exit I needed to make.

I was thankful for both decisions and was about to slip on my coat when the door burst open.

I spun around as Claus came bundling in through the doorway. He gripped a nearby chair and swayed slightly, before righting himself, while holding on to a glass of champagne in his other hand, sloshing the contents onto the floor.

'You're not rushing off, are you?' he slurred.

'It's late,' I replied, pushing my arm into my coat.

He lurched forwards and grabbed at my coat. 'Not so fast. There take that off.'

'I really need to go. My mother will be worried about me.'

Claus wagged a finger at me and smirked. 'She'll just have to wait. If she gives you any trouble, I'll deal with her.'

I hardly dared think about what he meant. I let the coat drop onto the chair next to me as I backed away from him.

'That's better,' said Claus. 'I was very impressed by your performance tonight and thought I'd reward you.'

I wanted to scream at him that I wasn't some kind of performing pet that needed rewarding, but I clamped my lips together as I fought to control the urge.

From his pocket he pulled out a small brown glass bottle. Medication. I recognised it straight away. Claus took a few unsteady steps towards me and I wanted to back further away but I was up against the dressing table and had nowhere to go.

His eyes glinted in the light and a hungry look spread across his face. He held the bottle up and waggled it around.

I thought of Pierre and his dreadful cough that the medication helped ease. Every fibre in my body wanted to push Claus away but how could I when he had what I so needed?

By now Claus was right in front of me and I could smell the alcohol and cigarettes on his breath. He ran his forefinger down the side of my cheek, under my jaw, down my neck to my breastbone.

'Not here,' I heard myself saying, wondering if I could somehow make my escape.

He gave a laugh. 'Oh, my, aren't we the fussy one.' He slugged back the last of the champagne from his glass and then threw it to one side, where it shattered on the stone floor.

'Upstairs,' I urged as Claus now began to unbutton the front of my dress. 'Please, upstairs.'

'You're rather demanding. I'm not sure that's a good thing. Perhaps I shouldn't let you dictate. Perhaps, I'll just take what I want now.'

He moved quicker than I anticipated and before I realised what was happening, my skirt had been pushed up and with one of his legs wedged between mine, he was fumbling with the zip on his trousers.

I panicked and pushed him away with both hands, using all the strength I could find. Fortunately, the alcohol consumption wasn't conducive to his sense of balance and the German stumbled backwards, falling over a chair and rolling onto the floor. 'Bitch!' he hissed, getting to his hands and knees.

Before he could stand, the door opened and Max

appeared in the doorway. His eyes flitted around the room as he took in the scene before him.

I clenched my dress together and pulled my skirt down from around my thighs. I knew I was on the verge of tears but I refused to give in, focusing on my anger instead. I went to speak, but Max held up his hand. I thought Max was going to defend me but instead he gave a laugh and went over to Claus, helping him to his feet and dusting his jacket down. 'Oh dear, my friend, it seems the champagne and an eighteen-year-old have got the better of you.'

'Bitch,' said Claus again. 'I haven't finished with her yet. In fact, I haven't even started.'

Max still held Claus by the shoulders. 'And I think you may have to postpone for another day. When you can... how shall I put it?' He lowered his voice. 'Perform better and make the most of it.' He gave a conspiratorial wink to his comrade. Then Max looked at me. 'Get your things and go home.'

I was stunned at what I'd just witnessed. 'But he...'

Max cut me off. 'Don't argue. Do as you're told.' He picked something from the floor. It was the bottle of medicine, which must have fallen out of Claus's pocket. He tossed it towards me. 'I take it that's yours.'

I grabbed my coat and flute case and dashed out of the room while Max, propping up Claus who was cursing me all the way, staggered with him out of the room towards the turret and the staircase.

I tore down the driveway, across the bridge, out onto the road and up the hill, not stopping once until I reached the back of our shop. I almost forgot to leave the document, I'd taken from the château, in the outside toilet in my hurry to get indoors.

Maman was asleep in the chair and I was grateful she didn't stir as she would have known in an instant something was wrong. I didn't want to have to tell her what had happened. I gently laid a blanket over her and placed the bottle of medicine on the table.

Maman had left a jug of water out on my dressing table next to the china washbasin and bowl. Despite the coldness of the water and the lateness of the hour, I scrubbed every inch of my body in a bid to rid even the thought of Claus touching me, before climbing into bed and crying myself to sleep as I thought of what had happened and how I wasn't quite as brave as I thought I was.

THIRTY-TWO
2019

It had turned out to be rather an expensive escape from Paris back to Trédion by the time Imogen had bought a new ticket for her flight and then had to pay for an hour's taxi ride from the airport to the village, but she was home now, safe inside her château.

The builders were surprised to see her and after a somewhat difficult conversation with the foreman, she made it clear that she was going to be staying at the château and would keep well away from the work going on at the west turret.

She was pleasantly surprised to see the west wing had been cleared of all debris and rubbish with the new roof struts already in place.

'What about the cellar?' she asked the foreman. 'Have you done anything with that yet?'

'No, nothing. Monsieur Roussell gave explicit instructions we were not to touch the cellar.'

'Did he, indeed?' She didn't elaborate to the foreman; it wasn't necessary to drag him into the deception. Laurent obviously had plans to clear the cellar himself so he could find the flute.

Returning to the sanctuary of her living room, Imogen wondered if Laurent had been planning on telling her at all about the flute. And once he'd found it, would he then have just hot-footed back to Paris with his prize, leaving her alone, emotionally battered and bruised after taking that leap of faith with him?

She was angry with herself for being such a fool. Angry with Laurent for deceiving her and, quite unreasonably, she was angry with James. He wasn't supposed to have died and left her a widow at such a young age. They were supposed to grow old together. They were supposed to be doing all this together. She wouldn't have to be dealing with all this crap if he was here.

Hot tears burned her eyes and spilled down her cheeks. Imogen curled up on the sofa, wrapping the throw around her and indulged in the anger and tears she could no longer hold back.

It was a relief when a few hours later the workmen finished for the week. Imogen would be grateful for a couple of days' peace and quiet. She needed to be alone to process what had happened and how she'd allowed herself to be drawn in and deceived.

A soft mewing from outside the window had Imogen sitting up, momentarily forgetting her heartache. 'Kitty. Oh, am I pleased to see you,' she said, opening the window.

The cat jumped down onto the floor and sat in the middle of the room, as if patiently waiting for Imogen to close the window, before curling herself around Imogen's legs in its usual fashion.

Imogen scooped the feline up and nuzzled her face into the soft fur. 'I hope Claude isn't worried about you. Perhaps we should let him know you're here.'

Imogen took her mobile and rang Claude's house phone.

'I wasn't expecting you back today,' he said once she'd explained the cat was with her and where she was.

'Change of plan.'

'I hope you're all right.'

'Yes, perfectly,' Imogen reassured her neighbour.

'I hope it's nothing that Laurent Roussell has done.' There was a knowing tone in Claude's voice.

'Nothing at all. Why would he?'

'I wouldn't want to see you get hurt.'

'Claude,' began Imogen, 'is there something you're not telling me? I get the feeling everyone knows more than me, especially where this château and Laurent are concerned.' She avoided mentioning Laurent's grandmother and the flute; she wanted to see if she could get any information from Claude first.

'There's nothing to tell about the château and not much to say about Laurent Roussell either,' replied Claude. 'As I said before, the Varon–Roussell family don't have a very good reputation around here.'

'Oh, come on, Claude, you can't leave it at that.'

'You need to ask Laurent himself,' said Claude. '*Au revoir*, Imogen.'

The line went dead, leaving Imogen staring at the handset. Claude absolutely did know but was refusing to tell her. It was so frustrating! What was wrong with everyone around here? She sat back down on the sofa, deciding she'd have to start asking elsewhere and wondered if she'd get any further with *le maire*, Bernard Le Roux. Or possibly the café owner who had refused to serve Laurent. What was her name? Madame Petit.

Her mobile pinged with a message alert.

Laurent: Just wanted to check you got back all right.

Imogen couldn't deny she appreciated his concern even though he was the last person she wanted to communicate with. However, she tapped out a courteous reply.

Imogen: Yes. I did. Thank you.

Her finger hovered over the send button. She wanted to say she hoped his father would soon settle into the convalescent home but decided against it, as that would have the potential to open up a conversation with him and she didn't have the emotional capacity for that right now. She pressed send without saying anything more.

Laurent, however, appeared to have other ideas.

Laurent: I'm going to be in Paris until Wednesday. Do you need your bag before then? I can arrange for it to be sent.

Imogen: No rush for it.

As she put her phone down again, she decided she might ask Claude to get her bag for her when Laurent returned. That way Laurent wouldn't have to come to the château and she wouldn't have to see him. She knew she wouldn't be able to avoid him forever, but she needed a few days to get over the disappointment and hurt she was feeling. She'd got over worse. She was a survivor and she'd be able to survive this setback, just as she had before.

THIRTY-THREE

1944

For the next couple of days, I made myself as scarce as possible. Maman had queried several times if I was all right and I had reassured her everything was fine. I didn't want to worry her with what had happened as I knew she would feel both guilt and anger when, in actual fact, it was something out of our control. I was sure Maman would feel the need to defend my honour in some way and that would achieve nothing.

Neither Claus nor Max had visited the shop that week and I was relieved. I had received an order from a junior soldier that I was to arrive at the château at seven p.m. the following Saturday for another performance.

On the Thursday, as I was cycling back from the Devereaux farm, having collected a dozen eggs, I saw the familiar figure of Max leaning against the five-bar gate in the same spot he'd waited for me before.

On seeing me, Max stepped out into the road. 'Start slowing down now!' he called.

I was already braking, even though there was hardly any grip on the brake pads. My front wheel squealed as I squeezed the brake lever. As I neared Max, I put my feet down and hopped off the bike, running alongside it for a few strides until I could stop.

'I'm impressed,' said Max, his hand resting on the handlebars. 'I'm also glad you stopped.'

'I must admit, I wasn't sure if I wanted to,' I replied, trying to hold on to at least a fraction of my pride. I wasn't upset about what happened with Claus now, just angry.

'I'm sorry for what happened to you,' said Max. 'Are you all right? Did he hurt you?'

'It's a bit late to worry about that now.'

Max dipped his head with obvious embarrassment. 'I didn't want Claus to know there was anything between me and you; he would have taken great pleasure in trying to sabotage it.' Max looked genuinely remorseful. 'I had to keep up the charade that I was looking out for him when, in fact, it was you who I was concerned about.'

I let out a sigh. 'I'm sorry too. I shouldn't direct my anger at Claus towards you. It's unfair of me.' I rested my hand over his. 'It's good to see you.'

Max smiled and leaned forward to kiss me. 'It's good to see you. Have you got time to walk?' He nodded towards the trees. 'I've already hidden my motorcycle.'

Max hid my pushbike next to his motorbike as he'd done before and took my hand. We walked into the woods, heading for the clearing.

The sun was already beating down from the morning sky, the mini heatwave we were experiencing showing no sign of easing. 'The weather comes straight up from South America,' I explained. 'We have our own climate here in this part of Morbihan.'

'We have very warm summers in Germany too,' replied Max. 'But we also have very cold winters.'

'You sound wistful. Do you miss home?' I settled myself down on the grass.

'I do. I miss the normality of life. I used to think I had a quiet life and sometimes I would wish for more adventure but now I have the adventure, I'm not sure I like it.'

'I wish everything was back to normal too. It scares me to think that might never happen.'

'There is nothing wrong with admitting to fear,' Max said softly.

'I don't want to be frightened though,' I countered. 'And anger. I feel that too. I hold on to that to keep me going. I think of my friend, Monique, and it keeps the anger burning. I cannot forget it and I refuse to forget it, for her sake. I don't know how but I will...' I stopped myself from speaking, worried I'd already said too much in front of Max.

'You will what?'

'Nothing. It doesn't matter.'

'You will get revenge? Is that what you were going to say?'

I got up, wrapped my arms around my body and began to walk back towards the trees. I heard Max scramble to his feet and run to catch up. 'I have to go,' I said, without breaking stride.

He nipped in front of me, walking backwards as he spoke. 'Please don't look for revenge.'

'What does it matter to you?'

Max frowned and gave me a quizzical look. 'What does it matter to me? Are you really asking me that?'

I stopped walking. 'I'm just a young Frenchwoman who has no say in what happens to her or with whom. I am a mere plaything to keep you German soldiers entertained while you have some rest and relaxation out here in rural Brittany.'

'You really think that of me?'

'You're not denying it.'

Max's mouth set in a firm line as his gaze bore into mine. 'Do not judge me as you judge the others. I am NOT like Claus or any of his friends. I thought I'd made that clear. I thought you trusted me and I could trust you to see beyond our nationalities. I thought you had that in you.'

It was Max's turn to stomp off and for a moment I stood rooted to the spot. 'I'm sorry!' I called. 'Max! Please.' I ran after him, apologising again.

We were now amongst the trees where the sun threaded its way through the canopy of branches and foliage, dappling the ground with shimmery silver spots of light.

Max let out a long sigh and stopped walking. His shoulders dropped on his exhalation of breath. 'I don't know if us is a good idea,' he said at last. 'I enjoy spending time with you. I care about you.' He touched the side of my face with his fingertips. 'I've found comfort and friendship, something I never thought was possible. And I think, I could find more… but it's no use if all we are going to do is fight and accuse each other of being something we are not. I thought you felt the same but maybe I was wrong.'

I shook my head and took his hand in mine. 'You weren't wrong. Not at all.'

Max pulled me into his arms and held me tightly. 'The other night, when I came into the dressing room and saw Claus there, I wanted to kill him. I had to do everything I could to stop myself from strangling him. Afterwards, when I lay in bed, I realised it was because I care about you. Care very much.'

I tightened my hold on him. 'I care about you too,' I said into his shirt, embarrassed at admitting my feelings and at the same time acknowledging the pang of guilt that I felt this way about a German soldier. I corrected myself almost immediately. I didn't care about the soldier but I did care about Max.

We kissed, this time more passionately than we had before with an intensity I had never experienced, the hunger for each other shared in a way I hadn't thought possible, and all thoughts of Max as a German officer disappeared as we made love.

Afterwards, much as I wanted to stay in Max's arms, I was very much aware Maman would be once again waiting for me and I could imagine the women lined up in the shop, clicking their tongues with impatience and disapproval when I finally appeared.

'I need to go,' I said, giving Max a peck on the cheek and getting to my feet. I straightened my clothing and Max dusted down the back of my skirt and blouse.

'We need to think of another way to meet,' he said. 'A snatched twenty minutes in the morning is not enough.'

'I know but I don't want anyone to see us. They will think I am a collaborator.'

'I understand.' Max looked away and then back again. 'What if I were the collaborator?'

His voice was so quiet, I wasn't sure if I'd heard him properly. 'You a collaborator? What do you mean?'

'What if I knew something and was to pass that information to you?' Uncertainty rested on his face. 'You'd know what to do with that information, wouldn't you?'

I realised what an enormous gesture this was and how I'd be able to go back to the resistance and not only help with the fight against the Germans but also to establish a greater role within the movement. I was also aware of the possible price. 'If you were found out, you'd be shot.'

'I know but there are certain things my conscience cannot stand by and let happen.'

'Don't do this for me.'

'I'm not. I'm doing it for myself. When this war is over, I want to be able to live with what I have done.'

I looked into his eyes and all I could see was sincerity. I had no reason not to trust him. 'You're a good man.'

'I try to be.' He placed his hands on the tops of my arms. 'Now, listen, this is important. This evening, just before dusk, the Devereaux farm is going to get another visit from General Werner and his men. They are looking for airmen.'

I sucked in a breath. 'I must warn them.'

'Be careful who you tell, Simone. Trust no one.'

THIRTY-FOUR

2019

Tapping the key to the cellar in the palm of her hand, Imogen looked at the locked door, debating whether to go down there in search of the flute. She hadn't slept well the night before, as her mind churned over and over what had happened in the last couple of days. Now, with the benefit of time and distance, she was beginning to wonder whether she had overreacted to Laurent's *deception*. But every time she got that far with her thoughts, she stumbled at the word deception because no matter how she dressed it up or tried to make excuses, she couldn't get past that point. He had intentionally deceived her. It made her wonder if everything about him was just a pretence – namely his true feelings towards her. And if she was honest, that hurt a lot. She'd allowed herself to become involved with him and now she felt humiliated. And in some bizarre way, she also felt she'd let James down.

As she chastised herself, the sound of car tyres crunching over the gravel broke through her thoughts.

'Oh, please don't let it be Laurent,' she said to the cat. Perhaps he'd come back from Paris early for some reason.

She went out to the hall and looked through one of the full-length windows.

A grey VW Golf was parking outside the front of the château. Imogen peered harder. It couldn't be? Surely not.

The door opened and the elegant figure of Denise Wren emerged from the car. She was wearing a linen trouser suit with a white blouse, which somehow didn't appear to have a single crease in it. Imogen had often marvelled at her mother-in-law's ability to look like she'd just stepped out of a photo shoot for a glossy magazine.

Imogen watched as Denise removed her sunglasses and looked up at the château and then around at the grounds.

'We'd better go and let her in,' said Imogen to the cat who had trotted out after her.

'Imogen! Oh, I do have the right address. Thank goodness for that.' Denise strode across the drive and embraced Imogen.

'This is a lovely surprise,' said Imogen, not entirely sure she felt the sentiment completely. 'I didn't know you were coming.'

'No. Sorry to turn up out of the blue but it was the spur-of-the-moment decision. I can quite happily find a hotel in the village if it's not convenient.' She paused to take a breath. 'I know I wasn't very gracious about you coming here and it's been playing on my mind for weeks. I've been thinking about you a lot.'

'Oh, Denise.' Imogen instigated the hugging this time. 'Come on in. I'll make you a coffee. Where have you driven from?'

They chatted about the journey as Imogen made some fresh coffee for Denise and then they settled themselves in the living room.

'I'm just using this room until the rest of the rooms are refurbished,' explained Imogen sitting in the velvet armchair at the side of the fireplace. 'Eventually, I want this to be my office and library.'

'It's… it has a lovely view of the garden,' said Denise.

Imogen inwardly smiled at Denise's struggle to come up with something positive. Bless her, she really was trying. 'I'll show you around in a little while. You can see where I want to create the pond I mentioned in my email.'

'That would be lovely.' Denise looked down at her coffee.

'Is everything OK?' asked Imogen noting the troubled look on her mother-in-law's face.

Denise pushed her lips together and placed her cup on the table. 'I wanted to apologise for not supporting you in your decision to move here. I had no right to expect you to put your life on pause just because James is no longer with us.' She looked away as she mentioned James, never having been able to meet Imogen's gaze when she talked about her son. Imogen understood. Denise found it too difficult to see her own pain reflected in Imogen's eyes.

'You don't need to apologise,' replied Imogen. 'I do understand.'

'Yes, but just because you understand, that doesn't mean it's fine for me to behave like a sulky spoilt child and try to guilt-trip you into staying.'

Imogen nodded and appreciated Denise's honesty. 'How have you been?' she asked after a moment.

'Oh, you know… plodding on. Doing all the usual things. My WI, embroidery club, book club and I've even joined the local walking club. I'm all about the clubs these days!' She gave a self-depreciating laugh. 'Seriously, I've been trying to keep myself busy and to be honest, it's all good fun. As you know, I've seen a bit more of Tom and Kelly. I've sort of had to shoehorn myself into their lives but now I'm there, I think they quite like it.'

'I'm really pleased about that,' said Imogen sincerely. 'Maybe I should have moved away sooner.' It was her turn to laugh.

Denise spun her wedding band around her finger. 'Don't say that. I'm not sure I would have got through these last few years without you.' She smiled at Imogen. 'I've missed you, I'm not going to lie. I didn't realise how much I looked forward to your visits. It wasn't just because you were James's wife – it was more than that. I'd come to regard you as more than a daughter-in-law, perhaps like a daughter and a friend.' She sighed. 'Sorry, I'm not trying to make you feel guilty. I'm just being honest.'

Imogen moved to sit beside the older woman on the sofa. She reached for her hand. 'Let's make the most of your visit, then.'

Denise patted Imogen's hand. 'Indeed. I'm only here for a couple of days. I'm travelling back on Friday.'

Imogen mulled this over. There was a possibility Denise and Laurent's visits might overlap. She wasn't sure how she felt about that and, more to the point, how Denise would. Not that there was anything going on now, but at the same time, Imogen wasn't up for an awkward meeting.

'Well, I want you to stay here, with me at the château,' said Imogen.

'I'd like that. Why don't you show me around?' suggested Denise.

Imogen was impressed, and a little amused, as Denise made a concerted effort to say something positive about the rooms as they walked around the château, despite her facial expressions sometimes giving away her real thoughts.

'And this is the main reception room,' said Imogen opening the double oak doors. 'Probably where they hosted parties once upon a time.'

'Gosh, it's still got the chandelier,' remarked Denise

walking into the room. 'I don't wish to sound negative, but you've really got your work cut out here, haven't you? Do you still think it's a good idea?'

'I do, actually,' replied Imogen, impressed Denise had made it that far without saying anything discouraging. 'I know it's going to take a long time and be a big financial commitment but I am happy here, Denise. I feel at home amongst all this and it's something I need to do as much as want to do.'

They walked out to the gardens and Imogen explained to Denise what she had planned for the outdoor space.

'It will be beautiful once it's done,' said Denise.

They were at the rear of the garden now. 'This is going to be the woodland area, I mentioned. I'm going to put the wild meadow garden all the way along that side leading up to the privet,' explained Imogen. 'And here… here I'm going to put the pond and bench under the tree. A place to think of James and his love for life, the outdoors and nature. I'm hoping to find someone to sculpt me three poppies to stand at the back of the pond – for James and the two babies.'

She looked across at Denise who had retrieved a hanky from her pocket and was dabbing at her eyes. 'That's a lovely thing to do,' she said softly.

'I'll never forget them or leave them behind,' said Imogen.

Denise lifted her face up to the sun and drew a deep breath. 'I know that. Now that I've had time to think about it properly. In fact, it was Tom who gave me a bit of a telling-off.'

'Tom?' Imogen couldn't quite contain her surprise.

'Yes. Tom – of all people,' said Denise with a laugh. 'I admit, I was having a bit of a drip and feeling awfully sorry for myself. Tom's not the most patient of people, unlike his father or brother. Anyway, he told me off and said I had no right to expect you to spend the rest of your life in mourning. Unlike me, who's had the best years of my life with Peter and James. He said James would be horrified at my behaviour and he was absolutely right.'

'Don't be so hard on yourself, Denise. James wouldn't have been horrified.'

'Maybe not but he would have been disappointed. So, basically, I've pulled myself together and stopped being so selfish. And here I am, offering the olive branch and hoping James… wherever he is… can forgive me. And you, of course.'

'And if there was anything to forgive, he absolutely would. And so would I.'

Denise smiled gratefully at Imogen and then slipped her arm through hers as they began to walk back towards the château. 'Now tell me, you may not have made many friends yet, but have you met anyone special?' She squeezed Imogen's arm, as if they were teenagers sharing their secret crushes with each other.

Imogen wasn't quite sure if Denise was ready for the answer and now there wasn't anything for her to tell. 'No, no one special,' she opted to reply.

'Hmm. So that little doodle on the notepad at the side of the sofa doesn't mean anything, then?' Denise gave a small laugh. 'The doodle that has the name Laurent surrounded by flowers and hearts.'

Imogen let out a groan. She'd totally forgotten about that. When he'd phoned her the other day, she did indeed doodle on the notepad. She hadn't realised she'd put hearts around his name. Oh, how embarrassing. She was a grown woman for goodness' sake. And now she could only confess to Denise. 'It wasn't anything serious,' she said. 'He's been advising me on the château. It was over before it even started. It was nothing.' She heard the break in her voice.

'Oh, dear. It doesn't sound like nothing.'

They continued in silence to the château and went in through the kitchen door, where Imogen made them both a hot drink. Denise placed herself at the kitchen table and Imogen sat opposite her.

'I didn't want to tell you because whatever it was, it's over,' said Imogen at last. 'I didn't want to hurt you.'

'I understand and I appreciate the thought,' replied Denise. 'The thing is, I came here to tell you I was sorry and I truly am, but I don't want you to think you have to keep things from me. I know I can be a stuck-up old cow at times but I don't think I'm totally unapproachable when it comes to friends – dear friends, at that.'

Unexpectedly, Imogen felt her resolve crumble and she held her head in her hands. She realised she'd missed Denise. Their regular chats and comfortable silences had become part of her life, a normality that had kept her sane during those early days of grief. Since moving to France, she'd had little to no contact with another woman, not someone she could sit and talk openly with. Talking or texting with her family didn't quite fill the gap of face-to-face contact with another woman.

She looked up at Denise. 'I've been very foolish and let myself get hurt.'

'You'd better tell me all about it.' Denise reached for her bag and produced a bottle of gin. 'I think we both deserve one of these.' She picked the cups up and tipped the contents down the sink, before rinsing them out and pouring a healthy dose of gin into each. 'I don't know where your glasses are, so we'll just have to rough it with the cups.'

Denise listened patiently as Imogen told her the whole sorry story, including her overnight trip to Paris, the conversation between Laurent and his father and her subsequent argument with Laurent.

'And that's where I am. Here. Kicking myself for being such an idiot and feeling like I've let James down.' Imogen swiped the tear that leaked from her eye. 'He'd be so cross at me.'

Denise took a deep breath. 'Right, firstly, you're not an idiot. Far from it. You're one of the most intelligent and kind-hearted women I've met. And I know that for a fact – James told me after the first day he met you. And he was right. So none of that nonsense.'

'I never knew that,' said Imogen.

'He loved you from day one,' said Denise softly and then more business-like: 'But tragically he's no longer with us and you, as we've established, have a life to live. What I'm about to say, I don't say lightly but I know it's right and you need to hear it.' She took a moment to compose herself. 'You've got to stop wondering what James would think of you, whether he'd approve, whether he'd tell you it was a good idea or a bad idea. You've got to stop deferring to him. He may be in your heart but he's not living your life with you.'

Imogen was rather stunned by this statement, especially coming from Denise. 'But I can't help it. I feel like he hasn't entirely left me. I'm scared to let him go.'

'I know, I really do. But all this moving to France and taking on this place, it may be a physical move but I worry you're not really moving on in your heart and mind. You're a young woman and you deserve happiness.' Denise gave a small smile. 'You don't want to end up like me. At my age, I can afford to indulge myself in grief.'

'I don't know,' began Imogen. 'I didn't realise that's what I was doing.'

'From what you've told me, you've run into a little blip with this Laurent chap and you've run away from it like a frightened fawn. Life and love aren't always easy – you've got to be brave. In the end, we only regret the chances we didn't take.' Imogen raised her eyebrows at Denise, surprised at this pearl of wisdom. Denise flapped her hand. 'I can't take any credit for that. I saw it on Facebook. One of those meme things.'

Imogen took a long sip of her drink before continuing the conversation. 'When I first met Laurent, I wasn't entirely sure about him. Call it intuition, but I always sensed he wasn't quite levelling with me. It bothered me to start with but then somewhere along the line, I began to trust him and believed he was genuine. I thought his feelings were too. I don't know how he can keep up a pretence for so long or be so good at it.'

'Maybe, just maybe, he didn't expect to develop any feelings for you. Maybe, he did actually start to fall for you. It's perfectly plausible.' Denise reached for the gin and made them both another drink. 'Did you give him a chance to explain?'

Imogen bit her lip. 'I didn't hang around for much of an explanation,' she finally confessed.

'That's a shame. You'll never know now, will you? There will always be a question mark over it and whether you made the right decision or not.' Denise sipped at her drink.

'Have you ever made a decision you've regretted?'

'Heaps of them, darling,' Denise replied without hesitation. 'If I were to do one of those things, where I write a letter of advice to my younger self, it would be to give people a chance to explain, find more empathy and understanding. No one is perfect.'

'Is it wrong to wish for perfection?'

'My turn to ask the question now. Have you ever done something you've regretted? Have you ever made a mistake? An error of judgement?'

'Well... yes, hasn't everyone?' replied Imogen, feeling defensive but also not missing the point Denise was making.

'And you don't consider yourself a bad person?' she continued. 'It sounds like Laurent was stuck between a rock and a hard place. As I'm fond of proverbs, I'll leave you with this one... those who live in glass houses, blah, blah, blah. I'm sure you know the rest.'

Imogen did of course know the rest and their conversation stayed with her all day. By the time she went to bed, she was pretty certain about what she needed to do.

THIRTY-FIVE
1944

Maman was indeed very cross with me for arriving late once again with the eggs and the women in the queue also let it be known if they had somewhere else to shop, then they would.

I offered sincere apologies to the women and to Maman. I hated to put her in this position. Max was right, we did need to meet somewhere different and at a better time.

All morning as I helped in the shop, I couldn't stop thinking about the Devereauxs and Max's words to trust no one. Surely I could trust the doctor? He'd been the one who had enlisted me in the first place. He didn't seem the sort of man who would secretly be working for the Germans – or did he? How did you actually know who you could trust?

As I was tidying the shelves at the end of the morning rush, it occurred to me that perhaps the doctor had recruited me to see if I would willingly help the resistance. He'd specifically told me not to tell anyone of my involvement and he would be my only point of contact – what if he was trying to flush out the resistance and those willing to stand against the Germans, so he could pass on their names to the Gestapo?

Maman moved out from behind the counter and went over to the shop door where she flicked the lock and turned the sign to *Fermé*. 'Now, tell me what is bothering you,' she said turning to face me. 'You need to tell me what is going on. You were late again coming back from the farm and you've been distracted all morning.'

'I'm sorry, Maman.' I dithered, considering how much I should say. 'There's going to be a spot check on the Devereaux farm,' I blurted out.

Maman pursed her lips, studying me. 'And you know this how?' I shifted on my feet but said nothing. Maman spoke again. 'If it helps you to decide what to tell me, then let me say this first. Whatever normal rules and expectations you think I may have, none of these apply at the moment. Not all the time we are at war and the Germans are occupying our country.'

I still couldn't meet Maman's gaze. 'It's complicated... No, that's not right. It's very straightforward and yet, feels so wrong.'

'Are we talking matters of your heart?'

'*Oui.*'

'So, there was some truth in what Christine Arnold said.' It was a statement rather than a question; one which I couldn't gauge her feelings about.

'Not then... but there is now.'

'I see.'

'He's a good man,' I began. 'He hates the war. He hates being here. He doesn't approve of what a lot of the soldiers are doing.'

'But he's a German soldier.'

'You said normal rules don't apply.'

'Normally, I would have no problem with you having a

relationship with a German. But as we have been invaded, then I cannot approve of what you are doing. He can't be trusted. You mustn't believe what he says; it will be lies. Once he has used you, got what he wants, he will be on to his next conquest. They treat women like meat.'

'He won't. He's not like that. You don't know him. He cares about me.' My voice rose an octave. I desperately wanted Maman to believe me. 'And I care about him.'

'You care about each other!' She gave a derisory laugh. 'He cares about getting what he wants.'

'He does not!'

Maman froze. She gaped at me for a moment. 'Have you...? You have, haven't you? You've had sex with a German soldier!'

'I'm a grown woman and I can do as I please.'

I thought for a moment Maman was going to burst as her face turned bright red and her eyes bulged with fury. And then, it was as if a pin had pricked a balloon and all the indignation and rage leaked away on the release of a long breath. Maman closed her eyes, bowed her head and wrung her hands together as if saying a silent prayer, before looking back up at me. 'Very well. I cannot stop you but I can tell you how dangerous this is. I am terrified I am going to be delivered with some awful news about you being arrested by the Nazis. I could not bear that.'

'*Maman*,' I sighed, rushing around the counter and hugging her. 'I promise, I will be very careful. Like I said, he is a good man. He's a teacher. He doesn't believe in what Hitler is doing but he cannot oppose it, otherwise he will be shot as a traitor.'

She cupped my face with her hand. 'I hope your trust is not misplaced, my darling child.'

'Now I must go and warn Monsieur Devereaux.'

Taking my bicycle I wheeled it out to the footpath and

then hoping I looked casual, I pedalled out the alleyway and onto the street. All the time on my guard, especially for any sign of Claus.

Once out of the village, I hastened to reach the farm. I wanted to give as much warning as possible. It wasn't just a case of the airmen getting away from the farm; they would have to be hidden somewhere else.

As I reached the doctor's house, I wondered again whether I should tell him, rather than take this on myself. What was I to say to M. Devereaux? He'd realise I was acting on behalf of the resistance or indeed part of the group. Would that put me more at risk? The doctor had told me not to tell anyone and I guessed that the fewer people who knew what I was doing then the safer I was so maybe I shouldn't tell M. Devereaux.

I swerved the bicycle into the doctor's driveway. Before I'd even leaned my bike against the wall, the doctor was coming out of the house.

'Is everything all right?' he asked. 'Is it your brother?'

I went to say no but caught the slight jerk of the head the doctor gave and saw him motion with his eyes back to the house.

'Er… yes, it is. It's my brother,' I said loudly, remaining by the wall so the doctor could come over to me.

'What is it?' asked the doctor in a hushed voice.

'You must warn Monsieur Devereaux – the Germans are going to raid the farm today just before dusk.'

The doctor's brow furrowed as he stroked his beard. 'Where did you hear this?'

'From a German soldier,' I said, reluctant to give Max's name.

'It might be a trap.'

I shook my head vehemently. 'He wouldn't lie to me.'

'Are you positive about that?'

'I wouldn't be here if I wasn't. If it was a trap, then I'd be giving myself up. I don't believe he would do that to me.'

'Very well. Go back home now. If anyone asks, you were here about your brother and I am to visit him tomorrow. And I will, just in case you are stopped.'

'Of course.' I hopped onto my bike and cycled back towards the village. My heart was beating hard but not from the exertion – more from the adrenalin that was racing through me. I was once again helping to resist the occupation. It may only be a small part, but it was an important one. I felt giddy with excitement. I threw my head back and laughed out loud.

THIRTY-SIX

2019

Imogen had slept on the sofa the night before, offering her bed up to Denise, who after some persuasion finally agreed.

Imogen had found a new sense of inner calm she hadn't experienced for a long time and, as she cleared away the breakfast dishes while Denise made them both a coffee, she attributed this to Denise and her kind words the day before.

To distract herself from thinking too much about Laurent, Imogen spent the following days weeding and tidying up the remembrance garden in the village. Denise proved a useful extra pair of hands and had been only too delighted to help. It was nice doing something together like this. Imogen realised that in all the time she'd been going to see Denise since James's death, they had hardly been anywhere or done anything together. The occasional shopping trip or coffee out, but never spending a significant amount of time doing anything tangible. Imogen had to admit, the thought of it had seemed heavy and weighed down with grief but here, in France, there was a different feeling. Maybe their chat had cleared some sort of unspoken barrier between them. Imogen wasn't quite sure but whatever had happened between them, it had certainly had a positive effect on their relationship.

Imogen looked at the memorial garden and the hard work they'd put in clearing the weeds and cutting back the overgrown planting. It had obviously once been very much loved but since Marcel had passed away, it must have become more and more neglected.

They were now at the stage where they could put the new plants in, which they'd collected from the garden centre that morning. Over the past few days, they'd attracted the attention of the villagers, some of whom had stopped to talk and ask what her plans were for the garden, some recommending what they'd like to see or what would work well and what to avoid, while others passed with a nod and a few words of encouragement.

On the whole it seemed the locals approved of what she was doing. There was, of course, Madame Petit from the restaurant where she and Laurent had first tried to have a meal. She had come over to the garden the day before and stood with her arms folded, scowling, as Imogen dead-headed a rose bush. Madame Petit had tutted and huffed several times as if trying to gain Imogen's attention, rather like a child, but Imogen chose to ignore her. She wasn't going to give the old woman the satisfaction of acknowledging her, let alone seeking her opinion on anything to do with the garden.

Today, however, the Frenchwoman wasn't going to allow Imogen to ignore her. She walked straight into the garden, letting the gate clank against the lock.

Imogen straightened herself up. '*Bonjour, madame,*' she said as neutrally as possible. Despite her own anger with Laurent, she wasn't ready to forgive Madame Petit for the appalling way she had treated them.

'I hope you're not going to make lots of changes. This

garden has been planted this way for many years. Marcel was very particular about it and we like it the way it was.'

'As you can see, it's very much in the original style,' replied Imogen. 'We've just added a few new plants to enhance what was already here and added a few where there were some gaps.'

'Marcel was an expert gardener,' continued the French-woman. 'He knew everything there was to know about plants.'

'Yes, I can see that.' Imogen sighed inwardly, aware her own knowledge and abilities were being called in to question. However, she refused to be drawn into a dual with Madame Petit.

Imogen wondered if that was all she'd come for and hoped the woman would return to her restaurant and leave her alone but Madame Petit didn't look in any hurry to go. The Frenchwoman cast her gaze around the garden and walked over to the stone monument, which carried the names of all the villagers killed during the war. She ran her fingers across one of the inscriptions but from the angle Imogen was standing, she couldn't read the lettering.

'My father,' said Madame Petit and for the first time Imogen heard a softness in the woman's voice.

'I'm sorry,' she replied gently.

Madame Petit dropped her hand and turned to Imogen. 'Where is Laurent Roussell? I haven't seen him for a few days.' As quick as the tone changed, it reverted to the brusqueness Imogen was used to from the older woman.

'He's in Paris, looking after his father,' replied Imogen and then immediately wondered whether she should have divulged any of Laurent's details.

Madame Petit tutted. 'You are best staying away from him.'

Imogen felt herself bristle at the unwelcome advice. 'That's really for me to decide.'

'Did he tell you about Elodie Bonnay?'

Really, this woman was a troublemaker. Imogen stood a little straighter. 'Yes, he did as a matter of fact.'

It was at that point, Denise came to stand beside Imogen. 'Is everything all right?' she asked and then to Madame Petit: '*Bonjour, madame.*'

'All OK,' replied Imogen. 'Just another local desperate to advise me what I should be doing.'

Madame Petit gave Denise the briefest of acknowledgements before returning her attention to Imogen. 'I don't think Laurent Roussell could have told you everything otherwise you wouldn't be standing here ready to defend him.'

'I don't think it's any of your business, actually.'

'Elodie Bonnay is my great-niece so I think it is my business.'

'A relationship between two young people ten years ago isn't anything to gossip about now.'

'Ha! He did not tell you everything. That is obvious.' She closed the gap between them, her shoes crunching on the gravel. 'Did he tell you Elodie was pregnant by him?'

He most certainly hadn't and Imogen knew she had been unable to disguise her surprise. 'Pregnant?' she repeated as if to confirm what she'd heard.

'Yes. That is what I said. He wanted her to have an abortion.'

'What?' Imogen felt sick at what she'd just heard. A termination? No. Not Laurent.

'He didn't want her to keep the child. Elodie was very upset. We all thought Laurent was better than that, but he proved to have no more morals than his grandmother. It's in his blood.'

'Wait, I have no idea what you're talking about but I don't think that's fair.'

'I tell you what is not fair,' snapped Madame Petit, 'Laurent Roussell getting Elodie pregnant and then when she refuses to get rid of it, him running away and leaving her to fend for herself. What sort of man does that?'

'But… but…' Imogen wanted to justify Laurent's actions, but no matter how hard she tried she couldn't think of a way to do so. Her heart pounded at the thought of what Laurent had done.

'There is no excuse for his behaviour. Now you might understand why he is not welcome here.' Madame Petit turned and began to walk away.

'Wait!' called Imogen intercepting her at the gate. 'The baby, what happened to the baby?'

The old woman's eyes narrowed and her lip curled almost in a snarl. 'Elodie was so overcome with distress when he left her that she miscarried the child.'

'Did Laurent know that?'

'He was told but he never contacted Elodie. Not even to ask if she was all right. The man has no morals.'

This time she didn't call Madame Petit back when she walked off. Imogen gripped the wrought-iron gate as she replayed the revelation.

Laurent Roussell was not the man she thought he was. She had been hoodwinked from the word go. No wonder the villagers hated him so much and she had been taken in by his charm. The shock made way for anger. What an utter fool she was. There certainly was no going back for them now. She wanted nothing whatsoever to do with him.

She wasn't sure what made her turn around and look back across the remembrance garden wall to the other side of the street, but as she did, she saw Elodie standing in the shade of the plane trees that lined the pavement. Imogen locked eyes with her contemporary. Had Elodie seen her great-aunt talking to her? Was there any way she knew what had been said? Just as Imogen decided to go over to speak to her, Elodie turned and walked quickly away, glancing back over her shoulder as she rounded the corner.

'What was that all about?' asked Denise. 'Gosh, I wish I spoke French.'

Imogen relayed the conversation to her. 'I can't believe he'd do something like that but, then again, he's lied to me before. Perhaps that's exactly what he is, a liar.'

'You need to speak to him,' said Denise. 'Rather than listen to tittle-tattle, it's Laurent you need to speak to.'

Imogen shook her head. 'I don't know if I want to. Not after that.'

THIRTY-SEVEN

1944

After warning the doctor about the Germans visiting the Devereaux farm, I was hesitant about cycling up to the farm to get the eggs that week or indeed delivering any provisions for Maman, but I knew I had to carry on as if everything was normal. If there was a sudden change in routine, I could be putting myself under suspicion and as a consequence endangering the whole resistance unit. It only took one person to break the chain.

Fortunately, my next two visits to the farm passed without incident. I wondered if M. Devereaux would say anything or give me a knowing look, but he carried on in his usual way. Even when I went in to see Madame Devereaux all she said was that the Germans had carried out a search of the farm but had gone away empty-handed. As I went to leave, she pointed towards the sideboard where three ripe red tomatoes were sitting.

'For your brother,' she said.

'Oh, I can't accept those,' I said, even though they looked delicious and my mouth was watering at the sight of them. I knew Maman would be able to make soup with them but even so, I had to refuse the offer.

Madame Devereaux put her finger to her lips. 'Shh. We must look after each other. Now take them. Don't make an old woman like me have to get up.'

As I cycled home, I wondered if I was reading too much into her comment but whether it did mean something or not, didn't really matter. I'd done my part in passing on the warning that the Germans were going to inspect the farm and I also had tomatoes for soup.

Pierre had been very unwell the past few days with what seemed like a relapse and Maman had been on the brink of sending for the doctor again, when this morning Pierre's fever broke and he had even managed to drink some water and take a few sips of soup. We were still being careful when we went into his room and keeping the window open, washing his bed sheets every other day after soaking them in the carbolic acid bath. My hands were dry and cracked from washing them so often but at least neither Maman nor myself had become ill.

Later that morning back at the shop, I was helping Maman serve the customers, when the door opened and in marched a German soldier. Everyone stopped talking and watched him come up to the counter and from his bag produce a package wrapped in white tissue paper and tied with a pink ribbon.

My eyes involuntarily widened at the sight.

He placed it on the counter with an envelope. 'Mademoiselle Varon? Simone Varon?'

'*Oui*,' I replied hesitantly knowing everyone in the shop was watching with intrigue and suspicion.

'From Herr Gossman. It is for the party on Friday evening.' The German soldier gave a swift nod of his head and marched back out of the shop.

I looked at the parcel and then up at the line of women who were craning their necks to see what had been delivered. The look of disgust was evident on every single one of their faces.

I gripped the edge of the counter and my stomach hardened into a nervous knot. It was Maman who took control.

She picked up the package. 'Take this upstairs,' she said to me.

One of the women muttered the word *whore*. I froze with the package in my hands.

'Who said that?' demanded Maman. 'If you want to say something at least be brave enough to say it out loud and not mutter it under your breath.' She glared at the women in the shop and for a few seconds there was silence but then one of the women in the queue stepped out of line. It was Monique's mother, Paulette Caron.

'Whore.' The word was clear and cut through the silence in the shop.

'How dare you,' began Maman and I could see her cheeks reddening with anger.

'Don't try to sound indignant,' said Paulette. 'Your daughter is up at the château every weekend, partying, dancing, eating, drinking and sleeping with *les Boches*.'

'No I am not!' I couldn't stop myself. I couldn't believe Monique's mother could be so cruel. She had always been warm and welcoming to me whenever I visited the house. How could she believe I was enjoying myself at the château? 'I am playing the flute because I have been ordered to, not because I want to and I am certainly not partying with them.'

'You're a liar, a whore and a coward,' spat Paulette. She strode over to the counter and reaching across snatched the package from my arms. She pulled off the ribbon and tore at the tissue paper.

Maman went to rush around the counter, but one of the other women slammed her hand down on the hatch blocking her way.

Paulette held up the dress that had been wrapped in the paper. It was black silk, with a low-cut neckline at the front and a long split up the side. A gold buckle sparkled at the waistline and gold clips pinched in the fabric at the shoulders.

One of the other women reached out to touch the fabric and then with a defiant look towards me and Maman, she spat on it. 'See how you look for your Nazi lover now.'

'Stop!' I implored.

'Stop,' mimicked Paulette and she yanked at the gold buckle, ripping it from the fabric before dropping the dress onto the floor, grinding it into the boards with her foot and then also spitting on it.

'Get out of my shop!' Maman shouted. 'Get out! Now!'

'You can't ban us,' said Paulette. 'You have to serve us.'

It was true. There had been an order by the general that no shop owner was allowed to refuse to serve a villager. There had been some trouble the year before where one of the cafés refused to serve a local man because he had been supporting the Germans by repairing their vehicles.

'We'll report you and then your shop will be closed down,' added the other woman who had spat on the dress.

I wanted Maman to still demand they left the shop, but I knew she couldn't and I felt her humiliation as silently she moved back to the till. Her head was held high and her rage now under control but I could tell there was a burning anger within her.

'Who's next?' she said and the customer who had blocked her at the counter moved to be served.

As soon as she did, I lifted up the counter and walked out into the shop, scooping up the dress and the buckle with as much poise and composure I could muster. I was not going to let those evil women reduce me to a crying mess.

'It should have been you shot in the village that day, not my daughter,' hissed Paulette and then for good measure added, 'Whore.'

I refused to look at Maman. I knew she couldn't defend me without getting reported by these… these bitches.

After we closed the shop for the day, Maman sponged down the dress and sewed the buckle back on.

'I wish I didn't have to go,' I complained as she zipped it up for me. I had to admit the dress looked even more beautiful now it was on and in any other circumstances I would have revelled in the luxury and expense but that night, I could find no joy from it.

'Now hurry along so you're not late,' said Maman, giving me one final inspection.

As I reached the end of the street, I saw Max waiting on the corner. My heart lifted at the sight of him but I was also aware the villagers might be watching and reporting back on my liaisons with the enemy.

Max must have seen the apprehension on my face. 'What's the matter?' he asked as I neared.

I carried on walking. 'Not here. I can't talk to you here.'

I heard his boots click on the path as he followed behind me, all the way down the hill, only stopping at the gates to the château where Max caught up with me. 'She's with me,' he said to the guard and escorted me up the drive. 'Do you want to tell me what's wrong?'

'I'm sorry. It's just some of the women in the village aren't very happy with me being here.'

'They think you're a collaborator?'

'Well, aren't I?' I asked, stopping and turning to look at him. 'I can't deny that accusation.'

'What else have you been accused of?'

I could see the indignation in his eyes, together with compassion, and I immediately felt guilty for taking my anger out on him. 'It doesn't matter what they've said. It's all lies anyway.'

'Don't go in yet,' he said. 'Come with me.'

'But I'll be late.'

'No, you won't. Anyway, they can wait and if there are any complaints, I'll deal with them.'

I didn't want to argue, I hadn't seen Max for several days and I had missed him, only being able to spend time with him in my dreams where there was no war and we could be together without any fear or reprisals.

We made our way around the corner of the château and under the privet, which was awash with wisteria and jasmine, the scent hanging on the still, warm air of the evening.

Max put his arm around me and kissed the top of my head as we walked along until we reached the middle of the privet where a wooden bench was situated. We sat down and Max took me in his arms, kissing me passionately. I just wanted to stay there forever and pretend the war around us was not happening.

Eventually Max broke from our kiss first. He looked a little nervous. 'What's wrong?' I asked.

'I have some bad news,' he said in a low voice, checking over his shoulder that no one was about.

I sat up straighter. 'Yes?'

'Your contact is not safe. He's under suspicion. The Gestapo is being called in to talk to him.' Max looked at me intently. 'You do know what that means, don't you? It means you are also not safe.'

My breath caught in my throat. 'Why do they suspect him?'

Max averted his gaze. 'I'm afraid that is my fault.'

'What?' I went to jump to my feet but Max pulled me back.

'It's not what you think,' he said urgently. 'The tip-off about the Devereaux farm. Apparently, he was there when Claus discussed it with the general. He'd been called to see the general and was in the adjoining office when Claus spoke about the airmen at the farm.'

'And they think he overheard and warned M. Devereaux?'

Max nodded. 'When it was me. I'm sorry.'

'Oh, Max. That is not your fault.' I wrapped my arms around him.

'I cannot warn him, for if I am seen talking to him, they will suspect me too and that could lead back to you also,' said Max. 'They are going to set a trap for him. They will give him false information and see if they can catch him out. You've got to warn him but you've also got to be careful. I will do everything I can to prevent them from suspecting you. I will tell them it's me if I have to.'

'No! Don't. I will warn the doctor. I will tell him tonight.'

'How?'

'I'll think of something.'

'He's been invited here tonight,' said Max. 'That's when they will give him the false information.'

'Don't worry about me. It will be all right,' I reassured Max. 'Now I'd better go. I don't want to be late.'

We got up and began to head back to the château. As we neared the end of the privet, a figure moved to stand in the middle of the path. With a sinking sensation in my stomach, I realised it was Claus and I went to move my hand from

Max's arm, but he squeezed his arm to his body so I couldn't and placed his free hand over mine.

'Ah, there you are,' said Claus. 'I'm sorry, but I didn't realise you two were…' He waved his finger between the two of us.

'Good evening, Claus,' said Max evenly, ignoring his comrade's comment.

Claus looked at his watch. 'You're going to be late.' He paused and took a step back, looking me up and down. 'Ah so you received the gift. It's a shame I didn't get to see it first.' He raised his eyebrows. 'Hurry along then – we can continue this conversation later.'

He went to put his hand on my shoulder but Max moved to discreetly shield me from his touch. 'I'll take Mademoiselle Varon indoors. Don't let us keep you from your guests.'

Claus frowned, decidedly unhappy at being outmanoeuvred by Max. 'Don't rush off again tonight,' he said tersely. 'Stay for the after-party. Shame Max won't be able to join us.'

'What do you mean?' asked Max frowning.

'The general wants you to report to him at *le maire's* office this evening.'

'I haven't been advised of this,' replied Max.

'You have now,' said Claus. 'And before you ask, no I don't know what he wants. Must be serious though.' He arched his eyebrows for a second time and then turned on his heel and strode back across the terrace to the main reception room.

'I don't like the sound of that,' said Max.

I wanted to beg Max not to leave me alone in the château with Claus and all his awful friends, but I could see Max was preoccupied, concerned with what the general wanted him for, so I didn't voice my fears.

I didn't play well that evening and made several

mistakes, which I was sure Max would have noticed but I hoped none of the guests had. Just as I was finishing, I looked over to the far side of the room where Max was standing. He gave me a slight nod before leaving to go to his appointment.

I had never felt more alone in a roomful of people than at that moment.

The guests politely applauded my performance and as soon as it was possible, without appearing rude, I left the stage and slid through the panelled door and down to the passageway.

No sooner had I reached the sanctuary of the dressing room, when there was a knock at the door and without waiting for me to reply, Jacques the doorman walked in.

'Water, as you requested,' he said coming over and placing a jug and glass on the table.

I was about to protest that I hadn't asked for any but caught the frown he gave me. 'Thank you,' I said.

He lowered his head so his mouth was next to my ear. 'Message from the doctor to repeat what you did last week. He is coming here tonight but has been called to an emergency and won't be here until later.' With that he moved away and left the room.

Again? I had to get the document again? I wasn't sure my nerves would hold out this evening. I rested my forehead in my hands for a moment, steeling myself to do the task I'd been instructed. I didn't have much time, I wasn't sure when Max would be back or if indeed Claus would come looking for me.

Taking my flute case with me, I slipped out of the dressing room and up the stairs.

In my haste, I didn't stop to check the landing as I reached the top of the stairs. To my horror, a guard was walking down the hallway.

'What are you doing?' he demanded. 'You're forbidden to be up here.'

'I'm… I'm meeting Oberleutnant Gossman,' I replied, hoping I sounded more confident than I felt.

The guard narrowed his eyes. 'Is he expecting you?'

'Of course.' The guard didn't look very convinced. 'And if you turn me away, I shall have to tell Oberleutnant Gossman and I don't think he will be very happy.' I could see the threat didn't sit too well with him. 'Look, he's left the door open for me.' I prayed Jacques had been up here and unlocked the door. I turned the handle and to my relief it opened. 'See.'

'Very well.' He moved to one side and I slipped into the room, taking a moment to rest against the back of the closed door so my pulse rate could slow.

The briefcase was where it had been the last two times and I quickly opened it, found the duplicated document and hid it in the secret compartment of my flute case.

I went over to the door, opening it just a fraction so I could check it was clear to leave.

To my horror Claus was walking along the hallway!

My heart hammered in my chest. If I was caught in the room now, I'd have to give a convincing argument for being there. What if he didn't believe me and searched the flute case? I looked around frantically trying to think of somewhere I could hide it and come back for it later. No, that was a ridiculous idea. How would I retrieve it? What if I couldn't get it later tonight?

Panic was setting in. I had mere seconds, if that, to do something.

It was then I spotted the chute. I'd seen this in the dressing room below. I raced over and yanked open the door and with only a moment's thought given to wondering how far it went down, I dropped the case.

I heard a bump and thud as it hit something below. I shut the door and then flung myself into the bedroom chair by the dressing table, crossing my legs and adjusting the dress so the split revealed rather a lot of flesh.

I didn't know what I was going to say or how far I'd have to go, but I didn't have time to think any further, as the door opened and in walked Claus.

He stopped in his tracks, staring at me for a few seconds, before speaking. 'Well, Mademoiselle Varon, I wasn't expecting to see you here. This is a nice surprise.' His voice was friendly but his eyes were full of suspicion as his gaze made a swift tour of the room. 'What are you doing in here?'

I went to speak but the words stuck in my throat. I gave a small cough. My palms were so sweaty, I was sure they would leave damp patches on the leather of the bedroom chair. 'I… I err…' I tried to look a little embarrassed but I was certain my eyes would give me away. I dropped my gaze to the floor.

In three strides Claus had crossed the room and was standing immediately in front of me. He yanked me to my feet. 'I asked you a question. What are you doing here?' His voice was harsh and it terrified me.

I had to pull myself together. I tried to think of a response but the panic was rising in me and I thought I was going to vomit. From somewhere in my foggy brain, I finally made myself speak. 'I wanted to surprise you,' I blurted out. I wanted to cry at what I was saying and what I was about to do but I couldn't falter now, not at this point. I thought of all the people who had paid the ultimate price and sacrificed themselves for the love of our homeland. I thought of Paulette in the shop earlier, wishing it was me and not Monique who had been shot.

I ran my finger playfully around the collar of Claus's

jacket, resting at the first button. 'I wanted to surprise you,' I repeated. Inwardly my whole body cringed at the thought. 'You don't mind, do you?'

A smirk stretched across Claus's face. 'What will Max say?'

I gave a small shrug and smiled coyly. 'Well, he's not here to say anything, is he? He shouldn't have left me.'

Claus's mouth formed a hungry leer. He pulled me towards him, kissing me hard, his tongue pushing my mouth open. I squirmed, trying to move away. And then suddenly he stopped and still holding my upper arm with one hand, he reached down and picked up the document case. 'You're not a very convincing actress,' he said and flung me onto the bed. 'Stay there.'

I scrambled backwards up to the headboard, trying to put as much distance between us as possible. My leg was shaking uncontrollably and I had to tuck it underneath to hide my nerves. He opened the document case and flicked through the papers.

'As I suspected,' he said, closing the lid slowly. 'What have you done with it?'

'Done with what?'

'Oh, come now, don't insult my intelligence.'

'I'm sorry, I don't know what you're talking about. Why don't you leave that for now?' A little voice in my head was on repeat telling me to hold my nerve. I adjusted the dress so more of my leg was revealed and I slipped my arms out of the straps. I swallowed several times, as Claus's eyes greedily lapped up the sight before them.

He put the case down on the dressing table and walked over to me, removing the belt from his jacket and unfastening the buttons.

'It's a shame really,' he said, as he flung his jacket on the end of the bed. 'I thought we could have a lot of fun together.'

'We still can,' I said.

'Oh, yes, I certainly will. You see, it's puzzled me for a couple of weeks now how the resistance was sabotaging certain trains. I thought it was a coincidence at first but it happened this week too.' He beckoned me with his hand and pulled me to my feet so I was standing right in front of him. 'I knew the information was being leaked and the only way it could be was from here when the documentation was left unattended. I'm so disappointed it was you.'

He pulled the pins from my hair so it tumbled down over my bare shoulders. He drew in a deep breath as he looked at me. I could feel the tears filling my eyes and I blinked them back.

'Don't be scared. I can make this easy for you,' he said, his hand combing through the ends of my hair. 'You know I would be quite within my rights to kill you now. Right here.'

All I could think about was how I had let the doctor down. How Maman would be devastated to learn of my death. Would I be arrested and tortured for days, weeks even?

'Before I decide what to do with you,' said Claus. 'I think we have unfinished business.'

'No.' I whispered and then said it again more loudly. 'No.' I wasn't going to let him do this to me, not now I had been found out. I was going to resist all the time there was a breath in my body.

'I don't think you're in any position to argue.'

Before I knew what was happening, Claus had pushed me back onto the bed and was straddling me.

'*Non! Non!*' I cried out, clawing at his face. I dug my fingers in and could feel the skin rucking up under my nails as I drew blood.

Claus yelled out, cursing in German and then without hesitation slapped me hard across the face, one way and then the other. The force and the pain nearly caused me to black out. He was ranting now in his native tongue and had me pinned down with one hand around my neck. I gasped for breath as my airways became more and more restricted. He was going to strangle me!

Then he was unfastening his trousers and pulling open my dress. I reached out to my side trying to find anything to grab hold of. My hand found the telephone on the bedside table.

I smashed the receiver into the side of his head. Again and again with such force it stopped Claus in his tracks. For a second he looked bewildered at me. His grip on my throat released and his hand went to the side of his head. Blood trickled from one nostril. He gave another bewildered look before swaying forwards, backwards and forwards again. Just as he was about to fall on me, I managed to push him to one side. He collapsed onto the bed and I wriggled my lower body out from under him before scrambling off the bed.

Gasping for breath and sobbing at the same time, I slumped back against the far wall, my eyes never leaving the prone body. There was absolutely no movement nor sound coming from Claus and I was certain I'd killed him.

THIRTY-EIGHT

2019

'Thank heavens for reliable French builders,' said Denise placing the two fresh cups of coffee on the table. 'It's pouring down out there.'

The rain had come in overnight and according to the weather forecast was set for the day. 'I'm glad they managed to weather in the roof,' said Imogen. 'They still need to actually tile it but they have been much more efficient than I expected. All the interior work structural-wise is done. New joists and flooring. They're going to make a new staircase. The servants' staircase at the back was wooden and didn't survive the fire.'

'Still think it's been worth it?' asked Denise.

Imogen smiled. 'Most days I do think it's worth it. Although, I'll admit, there are some days when I do wonder what I'm doing.'

'I think James would be very proud of you,' said Denise softly.

'Thank you. That means a lot.' Imogen sat down at the table. 'I also think he'd say it was indeed a crazy idea and perhaps you were right. But, I'm here now and much as I started out thinking I was doing this for me and James, I realise, I'm doing it for myself.'

'Now I've been here a few days, I've begun to understand your affection for the village and this château,' said Denise. 'It's a healing process. You're healing the château and healing your heart. And there's nothing wrong with that. Be kind to yourself, Imogen.'

Imogen thumbed the handle of her cup. 'There's plenty of things that need healing around here.'

'Maybe you can do that too.'

'I don't know. Not sure I'm the surgeon for the job.'

'You could try.' Imogen looked up at Denise with a blank expression, waiting for her to expand. 'Well, for a start you could find the flute and give it to Laurent. At least that way, he's got what he needs, what his grandmother wanted him to have. I know you're hurt by his deception, but maybe it came from a good place.'

'That's very charitable of you to think that.'

'I'm an expert at getting it wrong when the intention was otherwise.' Denise got up from her chair and took her cup over to the sink. 'Oh, hello, Kitty.' The cat had just strolled into the kitchen and Denise bent to give it an affectionate stroke behind her ears. 'I suppose you want some milk.'

As Denise fussed over the cat, Imogen considered their conversation. Yes, she was hurt and angry with Laurent but, and she couldn't ignore this, his motivation hadn't been to hurt her, he'd simply been trying to do something for his grandmother. To fulfil her dying wishes. He was motivated out of love and loyalty not driven by deceit or some sadistic pleasure in hurting anybody. What would she achieve by not letting him have the flute? Revenge wasn't on her agenda. As for what happened between him and Elodie, all she could do was put that to one side. It was far too close to her heart to look at objectively.

'OK,' she said standing up. 'Let's find this flute.'

Denise grinned back and rubbed her hands together. 'Excellent!'

~

Imogen hadn't fixed any lights up to the generator for the cellar, so armed with a torch each, she and Denise picked their way down the dusty stone steps and across to the pile of rubble occupying the corner.

'Laurent was adamant the flute was buried underneath all of this,' said Imogen.

'Perhaps you could ask the builders to help move the rubble,' said Denise.

'I was thinking about that, but I'm not sure if Laurent wants everyone to know about the flute. I have no idea what's so special about it but there's something important enough that his grandmother has sent him on this quest.'

'I suppose we'd better get stuck in then,' said Denise. She placed the torch on the floor and, already prepared with a pair of thick gloves, she began picking up the bricks and moving them to the other side of the cellar.

Imogen was slightly surprised by Denise's apparent enthusiasm. This was one of the last things she'd imagined her immaculately presented mother-in-law would be doing, but here she was, in the dusty, somewhat smelly, damp cellar of a sixteenth-century French château, shifting bricks!

It was backbreaking work and the decades-old dust now unsettled wasn't making it much fun either. In the end, Imogen had resorted to a couple of damp tea towels they could tie around their faces to cover their noses and mouths.

'We can stop if you want,' said Imogen after an hour of moving bricks.

'No, not at all,' replied Denise, her voice a little muffled through the tea towel.

The rubble was harder work, as they had to shovel it to one side, having nothing to put it into to get it out of the cellar. The thought of filling a bucket and then trying to get it up the steps and out into the garden, didn't inspire Imogen. Much as she liked getting stuck in, she knew what was beyond her and that would be a job for some muscly French builders.

Finally after another hour of shifting rubble and debris, their hard work was rewarded.

'Here! There's something here!' cried Imogen, as her shovel lifted a dusty and battered rectangular case from the rubble. 'Oh, wow, it's the case. It really is.'

Denise grabbed one of the torches and brought it over, shining it down on to the discovery. 'I was just beginning to think this was all for nothing,' she said.

Imogen wiped the top of the case with her hand and then opened one of the clips. The other clip, however, was rusted up and wouldn't budge. 'Let's go upstairs,' she said. 'Out of all this dust and have a proper look.'

Once up in the kitchen, free of makeshift dust masks and thankful for the fresh air coming in through the now open back door, Imogen and Denise eyed the case sitting on the table.

'Do you think you should let Laurent open it?' asked Denise.

'That would mean waiting until he got back from Paris,' replied Imogen. 'And what if I get his hopes up and there's nothing in there? If I look first, I can let him down gently.'

'That's very thoughtful of you.' Denise gave her a knowing smile, which Imogen chose to ignore. It was just the decent thing to do.

Taking a knife from the drawer, Imogen very carefully

slid it under the catch and with a bit of force and help from Denise to stop the case slipping, she managed to prise it open.

'OK, let's see what's so special about this flute,' said Imogen. She lifted the lid and they both peered in.

Considering the flute had been buried under all the rubble and debris for decades, it was in surprisingly good condition. The flute itself was tarnished and had black pitted marks over it, but the cloth it was sitting in was dry. There was a faint musty smell and a bit of the cloth in the lid had come away at the edges.

Imogen took the pieces of flute out and put them together. The head joint didn't quite fit on the main body due to the pitting on the metal but Imogen assumed with some cleaning and restoration that could easily be resolved.

Other than the flute, there was a folded piece of paper in the case. Carefully, Imogen opened out the brittle sheet.

'Music,' said Denise looking at it. She pointed to the title. '*Für immer*. That looks German.'

'I wish I could read music,' said Imogen. 'Do you think this is what Laurent's grandmother wanted him to find?'

'Well, I suppose without asking him, we won't know. It's seems an awful lot of trouble for a flute and a sheet of music.'

Imogen couldn't argue with that. 'The bit I can't understand,' she said, 'is what it's doing in the cellar? Why was it underneath all that rubble? And if Laurent's grandmother knew it was there, why didn't she get it back before?'

THIRTY-NINE

1944

I don't know how long I cowered up against the wall, looking at Claus's body. All I kept thinking over and over again was that he was dead. I hadn't intended to kill him. I had panicked and just wanted to stop him from attacking me.

I didn't hear the knock on the door at first but then it came louder and a voice called out. 'Claus? Claus? Are you there?'

It sounded like Max! Could it be Max or was it just a trick of my mind? I pushed myself further back into the wall. The handle turned and the door opened.

'Claus?'

It was Max. A small whimper emitted from my throat. Instantly, Max looked over and saw me. He took what seemed like minutes when it was only seconds, to take in the sight before him.

He closed the door, locking it behind him, before rushing over to me. 'Are you hurt?'

I shook my head but pointed towards Claus. 'I've killed him.'

Max helped me to my feet and sat me in the chair, before taking off his jacket and putting it around my shoulders as my whole body began to shake. 'I'm going to be sick.' I rushed through to the small bathroom adjoining the room and vomited into the toilet bowl.

It took all my energy to get to my feet again and splash cold water over my face.

Max appeared in the doorway. 'What happened?'

'He attacked me. I didn't mean to… I was scared…' I couldn't complete my sentences as the fear swamped me again.

Max held me in his arms, stroking my hair and rubbing my back. 'We need to get you out of here,' he said. 'Did anyone see you come up?'

'No. Yes! Oh, God, a soldier. One of the guards.'

Max rubbed at his chin agitatedly. 'Then they'll know you killed him. They'll come after you. Even if you disappear, they'll go for your mother and your brother.'

'Oh, no. I can't let them do that,' I cried. 'No. Just arrest me. Arrest me now. I'll confess and tell them everything. I don't care.'

'No! I won't let you do that,' said Max.

'But we have no choice.'

'No. Stop. Let me think.' He went out to the bedroom and looked over at Claus's body. I followed him out but avoided looking at his bludgeoned head and blood-splattered sheet. 'Right, this is what we do. I'm going to cause a distraction. You need to leave here immediately,' said Max. He took his jacket from me and hooked the straps of my dress back onto my shoulders, then smoothed down my hair. 'Be as discreet as you can. Just go downstairs and leave. Don't say goodbye to anyone or make a big scene. Understand?'

I nodded. 'But what about the doctor? I need to warn him.'

'Leave that to me.'

'What are you going to do?'

'It doesn't matter. I just need you to be away from here. Then if you're asked about this afterwards, you just say you left when everyone else did.'

'I don't understand.'

'You will soon enough.' He kissed me. 'Now, Simone, please go.'

I took one last look at Max, before fleeing from the room, treading as lightly as I could on the wooden staircase. I grabbed my coat from the dressing room and ran over to the shaft. I slid back the door, expecting to see the compartment where the food and linen was put to transport it between the floors, but it wasn't there. The shaft was empty. The compartment must be down at basement level. I peered into the depths of the shaft and could make out a shape that looked like the case, but there was no way I could reach it.

I thumped the wall in frustration as tears of anger filled my eyes.

If only I could get to the cellar but that would mean going into the kitchen where I'd be seen.

I'd have to leave it for today and ask Max to retrieve it for me tomorrow and hope I could still get the document to the doctor.

Right now, I had to get myself out of the château as Max had instructed.

I left the dressing room, avoiding eye contact with one of the waitresses who passed me in the corridor and forced myself to walk calmly across the hallway and out of the château.

As I reached the moat, I turned back to glance at the

building and wondered what Max was doing to cause a distraction.

I reached home and crept up to my bedroom, pausing at Maman's bedroom door to say goodnight to her. Up in my attic bedroom, I washed and got ready for bed. I was just about to climb under the sheets when I became aware of distant voices – too far away to hear what they were saying but there was an urgency to their shouts. It was then I noticed a strange orange glow seeping through the gaps in the shutters.

I opened the shutter a fraction. At first I couldn't work out what it was but as I pulled it open fully, I gasped at the sight.

The château was on fire!

My immediate thought was of Max and fear rushed through me as I imagined him trapped in the burning building. I wanted to run back to the château to find him, to make sure he was all right, but I stopped myself, remembering his words: that I was not to return under any circumstances.

All I could do was to stand and watch from my bedroom window, transfixed as the flames licked their way up the turret and thick smoke bellowed out to the backdrop of a full moon.

FORTY

2019

The builders had arrived back early Monday morning, not long after Imogen and Denise had woken up.

Paul, the foreman, knocked on the kitchen door and Imogen waved him in.

'We're going to start tiling the roof today,' he said. 'Hopefully, we will get it done before the next lot of rain is due at the end of the week. Are you going to be in the house today?'

'No, not for much longer. We're going to finish tidying up the memorial garden in the village,' replied Imogen, putting her rinsed-out cup on the drainer and drying her hands on the towel.

'Oh, yes, I heard you were doing that.'

'I expect you have,' said Imogen. 'It seems everyone knows everything around here.'

'That's what my mother always says. She's lived here all her life and what she doesn't know about Trédion, isn't worth knowing.'

'Oh, I didn't realise you were local,' said Imogen, trying to remember if Laurent had mentioned it and then automatically finding herself wondering if he'd purposely kept that from her too.

'I grew up here. That's how I know Laurent. We hung around together in the school holidays. I live near Vannes now but I've worked for Laurent before and he asked me if I'd do him a favour by working here,' replied Paul.

'And you weren't put off like the local builders?' asked Imogen.

Paul gave a shrug. 'Like I said to my mother, what happened in the past, is in the past. As long as I get paid, I don't let grudges and superstition trouble me. He's a good man, Laurent, despite what some say about him.'

It was the first time Imogen had heard anyone saying something positive about Laurent. She was intrigued that Paul appeared to know about the elusive past and seized the opportunity to question him some more. 'I know some of the older villagers have got a grudge against Laurent's family, or at least that what it seems, but what superstitions do you mean?'

'Oh, about this place being bad luck.' Paul looked from Imogen to Denise and back again. 'You do know the story, don't you?'

'No, I don't actually,' confessed Imogen. 'Every time I ask someone, it's like they suddenly have a bout of amnesia. Please don't tell me you're going to be affected in the same way.'

Paul rubbed at his chin. 'I'm surprised no one has told you.'

Imogen somehow managed to quell the desire to shake the information from the builder. 'So, what is the story?'

'*Alors*, the château is bad luck, or so they say. Everything was perfectly fine up until the Germans got their hands on it. There was this fire in 1944, as you know. And, of course, the whole west wing went up in flames.'

Imogen nodded while internally screaming. She knew all this! 'Yes, so what don't I know?'

'Two people died in the fire. I think they were German officers. I can't remember exactly. I know at least one of them was anyway. There was talk of it being started deliberately.' Paul hesitated but much to Imogen's relief decided to carry on. 'I don't know how, but Laurent's grandmother was involved in some way. Or she had some connection to the château and the Germans at least.'

'What happened to her?'

'I don't know. I'd have to ask my own grandmother. She was young then so only knows what she's been told. I'm surprised Laurent hasn't told you himself.'

'He doesn't like talking about it,' replied Imogen. 'Anyway, why was the château closed up all this time? Why wasn't it restored?'

'After the war, the house went back to the owner who was something of a recluse. They thought of the building as a memorial to what had happened to the village and those who were lost.'

'Oh, I see,' said Imogen, as a small pang of guilt for what she was doing ran through her. Was she being disrespectful to the dead? She didn't like to think so. 'I want to bring life and happiness back to the château. I don't want to erase what happened in its history, but I'm sure there are far more good times to focus on.'

'Yes. I've no doubt. And I hope that once the château has been fully restored, the villagers will see it that way too.'

'I'm sure they will,' piped up Denise. 'If anyone can transform it, then it's Imogen.'

Imogen smiled at Denise, appreciating her cheerleading efforts.

Paul gave a sigh. 'You just have to be patient; they can be very stuck in their ways here in rural Brittany. *Alors*, I must get on with the roof otherwise we'll never have it finished before the bad weather returns.'

'Don't be disheartened,' said Denise after Paul had left. 'Let's get that memorial garden finished and win a few brownie points with the locals.'

It didn't take Imogen and Denise long to finish tidying up the memorial garden and washing down the stone monument. Imogen arranged some flowers in a vase at the foot of the stone that she'd cut from her garden that morning. It was a mixture of hydrangea, wisteria, fuchsia, lavender and some greenery from the hedges.

'There, that looks better,' she said, standing back to admire their work. 'Thank you so much for all your help, Denise. I've really enjoyed you being here.'

Denise put her arm around Imogen's shoulders. 'And I have too. It's wonderful to see what you've done.'

'*We've* done,' corrected Imogen.

'Oh, I'm just the sweeper-upper.' She gave Imogen another hug. 'Now, haven't you got to interrogate a certain someone?' She held up her finger to stop Imogen's protests. 'I think you should at least talk to him. There are always two sides to a story and that old woman, Madame Petit, or whatever her name is, seems to be causing a lot of unnecessary trouble, if you ask me.'

'I don't know if it's a good idea.'

'What have you got to lose?' Denise took her arm away. 'Chin up and all that. Now's not the time to chicken out.' From her tote bag, Denise produced the flute case. 'Yes, I know, it was rather presumptuous of me, but strike while the iron's hot and all that. You did say he was due back yesterday, didn't you? And something about needing to get your bag.'

Imogen relented although wasn't entirely convinced it was the best idea. After making sure Denise could manage the few hand tools and cleaning products they'd brought with them that morning, Imogen headed across the road towards Laurent's apartment.

She found herself suddenly wishing she'd gone home and at least freshened up and changed her clothes, maybe even put a bit of lipstick on.

She stood outside the front of what used to be the shop but couldn't see a bell anywhere. She tried knocking on the door several times but there was no answer. She looked back over at Denise who was watching from the end of the street. Denise gestured with her hand to go around the back. There was an alleyway to her left and Imogen made her way down it to a side gate that led into a small courtyard at the rear of the shop. She clicked open the latch and approached the back door. A doorbell was attached to the doorframe and on a faded piece of paper, Imogen could just make out the name of Roussell.

She pressed the buzzer, resting on it for several seconds.

A few moments later, she heard Laurent's voice across the intercom system.

'You're going to break the buzzer if you carry on like that.'

'Are you going to let me in?' Her voice was rather more brittle than she intended but she could feel her nerves beginning to get to her.

'Come on up, but I warn you, I'm not dressed. I've just got out of the shower.'

Imogen didn't reply but opened the door cautiously and stepped inside. She was in a small room which, if she had her bearings right, was at the back of the shop. There was a door in front of her but it was closed and bolted at the top and bottom. To her left was a narrow wooden staircase and with a certain amount of caution, she made her way up the stairs.

She was taken aback to see Laurent still in his towel and did her level best to make sure she looked him in the eye and nowhere else.

'Can I have my bag, please?' It was the first thing she thought of to say, unsure how she was going to ask him about anything else.

'Your bag. Of course. It's in the bedroom. I'll just get it.'

'And while you're there, you might want to put some clothes on.'

'Might I?'

She walked over to the window. 'I'd prefer it if you did.'

Laurent returned a few minutes later with her bag and now fully dressed in jeans and T-shirt. 'There, I'm decent now.'

She turned to look at him. 'On the surface maybe so.' She wasn't quite sure why she'd said that. It was unnecessary and she could see her words had stung him.

'Imogen, please listen to me. I know I've said it before but I am truly sorry for not telling you the truth. I made a mistake. A huge mistake. I totally underestimated you and by the time I realised you were, in fact, someone who was genuine and who could be trusted, things had gone too far.' He held up his hand. 'Please, let me finish. I really care about you. Everything between us was real, well, it was for me anyway. None of my feelings were false. None of them were faked. I promise you that.'

Where did she go from there? She hadn't been expecting that but there were things she needed to ask him about. 'It's not just about that,' she said with a sigh.

Laurent frowned. 'What is it, then?'

'Madame Petit told me what happened. How Elodie was pregnant and you wanted her to terminate the pregnancy. How you left Elodie when she refused. You didn't stand by her and then she lost the baby anyway. And where were you – nowhere to be seen.' The thought of Elodie suffering a miscarriage resonated with Imogen so much, it was as if she was talking about herself.

'Wow,' said Laurent. 'She didn't hold back.'

'No, she didn't. It's a shame I had to hear it from her.'

'It wasn't as simple as that.'

'I knew you'd say that.' Imogen brushed away a stray tear that had decided to put in an unwelcome appearance. 'Don't forget, I've been there myself. I've been pregnant and suffered a miscarriage, two to be precise.' She hadn't planned to blurt that out again but she found herself continuing to talk. 'The second time I was four months pregnant and I was alone in a hospital bed, losing our child. So I know how that must have felt for Elodie. James wasn't with me but I know if he'd still been alive, there was no way on earth he would have left me to go through that on my own.' She didn't care she was properly crying now. The hurt had resurfaced and the pain was slashing at her heart. The anger was there too. And she blamed Laurent for it. His actions were making her relive that awful period of time. 'You obviously didn't care about either Elodie or your child.'

'That is not true!' he almost shouted the words. 'You have no idea how I felt.'

'How can you justify your actions? I can't forgive you that, even though it didn't happen to me; you abandoned a woman when she needed you most. And I don't want anything to do with a man like that. I am not putting myself in such a vulnerable position.'

'Imogen, please—' he began before she cut him off.

'Oh, I nearly forgot.' She pulled the flute from her tote

bag and dropped it onto the sofa. 'There's your flute. I hope you're happy now you've got what you wanted.'

She swiped up her luggage bag from where Laurent had left it and fled from the apartment, not caring if anyone saw her as she ran down the street sobbing. She just wanted to get back to the château and lock herself away.

FORTY-ONE

1944

I barely slept that night of the fire. How could I even contemplate going to bed and sleeping easy? Not only had I killed a man but I also could not stop worrying about Max.

As soon as I woke the next morning, I raced to the window to see the château. Smoke was still drifting in the air and the smell of burning timber had crept across the village, finding its way in through the closed doors and windows.

'What's that smell?' asked Pierre as I made sure he was settled on the sofa. He had made such an improvement in the past week. It was hard to believe he was the same boy. He was still pale and weak but the light was back in his eyes and I was so relieved.

'The château has been on fire all night,' I explained. 'Keep the windows closed. You should avoid breathing any of the dirty air in. We don't want you ill again.'

I pulled the blanket over him and gave him his book to look at, with promises of popping back later if I had any news of the fire, before heading downstairs.

Maman was already in the shop when I went down and had been briefed several times by different customers on what had happened. In fact, she was talking to Madame Picard who lived across the road from the château. She had her young son, Claude with her.

'Apparently, the whole of the west wing has been gutted,' Madame Picard was saying. 'It didn't reach the turret though, which is a relief.'

'Ah, Simone, there you are,' Maman said as I came to stand beside her.

'You weren't there last night, then?' asked Madame Picard.

'I was actually,' I replied, unsure whether Madame Picard disapproved or not. 'I left before the fire though.'

'Thank goodness,' said Maman.

'Was anybody hurt?' I asked. 'Did they say if anyone had been killed?'

Madame Picard gave me a curious look. 'A German officer, which is no loss but…' She hesitated.

'What?' I asked. 'But what?'

Maman put her arm around my shoulders. 'The doctor was there. He rescued someone from one of the rooms in the wing but he inhaled so much smoke, he collapsed soon after and, I'm afraid, he died.'

'The doctor! He's dead?' I could barely comprehend what Maman was saying. He must have arrived before I left. 'I don't understand. Why was he there? What was he doing at the château?' And then my thoughts were immediately of Max. 'Who did he rescue?'

It was Madame Picard who spoke first. 'A German officer. Why would he put his life in danger for *les Boches?*' Her face contorted into an expression of disgust. 'A good man's life has been wasted just so a bad one can be saved.'

I wanted to scream at her that they weren't all bad. Max wasn't! He was a good man. But I knew I couldn't defend him, not for my sake. I didn't care what the gossipy old women of Trédion thought about me, but I didn't want them to hold it against Maman.

'He was a good man,' said Maman. 'He will be greatly missed. We should go to see his wife to offer any help we can.'

'Christine Arnold is already with her,' replied Madame Picard. She gave me a glance as she spoke. 'Anyway, I need to go. Come along, Claude. Say goodbye.'

'*Au revoir, madame,*' said the little four-year-old. They held hands as they left the shop.

Maman turned to me. 'Before you even say anything, the answer's no,' she said. 'No, you can't go to the château and ask if your friend is all right.'

'But, Maman, how will I know? I must go.'

'No. You cannot. You will stay here and wait to find out. I don't want you going anywhere near there. They will be baying for blood and trying to blame someone. You left just before the fire started. Can't you see that makes you look suspicious?'

'But they don't know that. I could have been there and left when the building was being evacuated.'

'No. The answer is no. I forbid you to go.'

I was just about to argue and plead my case when the door opened and a German officer I didn't recognise came into the shop, flanked by two soldiers.

'Mademoiselle Varon?' He looked directly at me.

'*Oui.*' I nodded as fear ripped through me.

'You're to come with me immediately,' continued the officer. 'General Werner wants to speak to you.'

'General Werner? May I ask why he wants to speak to my daughter?' Maman asked.

'Don't ask questions,' came the swift and sharp reply. 'Hurry. Now.'

I hugged Maman and she held my face in her hands. I

could see the anguish in her eyes. '*Je t'aime*,' she whispered. '*Courage, ma chérie. Courage.*'

I was swiftly escorted from the shop and marched the short distance along the street to *le maire's* office where I was presented to General Werner.

'Mademoiselle Varon, thank you for coming,' said the general, making it sound like I'd accepted an invitation to dinner. 'Please, don't look so scared. Sit down.'

I slid into the chair in front of his desk and fought to keep my legs from shaking. '*Merci*,' I said feeling totally unprepared for whatever was about to happen.

'Before I begin, I must commend you on your performances the last few weeks at the château. You certainly have a talent.'

'*Merci*,' I said again.

'Of course, you must have heard by now about the fire at the château last night. Terrible. The whole of the west wing is beyond repair. Or repairs that we won't be doing at any rate. It was such a fierce fire, there was almost nothing left.'

'I'm sorry to hear that,' I ventured.

'Indeed. One of my men was killed in the fire. A fine officer, Oberleutnant Claus Gossman. I understand you knew him?'

'Yes. He asked me to perform at the château.'

'His body was found early this morning. Almost burned beyond recognition. We're assuming he became trapped in his room somehow and couldn't escape. Possibly hit by a burning beam or maybe he sustained the fatal head injury another way.' He fixed his gaze on me for a few seconds before continuing. 'Another of my officers has been badly injured. Suffered terrible burns. I believe you know him too. Oberleutnant Max Becker'

I swallowed and nodded. 'Yes. I do. I understand the

doctor was killed as well,' I said, trying to bide my time until I had a clearer idea of why I had been summoned here.

'Yes. That's most unfortunate. He saved Oberleutnant Becker.' The general rose to his feet and with his hands clasped behind his back, walked around the desk and perched on the edge in front of me. 'We're trying to establish exactly what happened. I've been informed by one of my men that you were seen going into Gossman's room shortly before the fire. Come now, don't be shy. Whatever you say to me, will go no further. Did you go into the room?'

'Yes. I did but he wasn't there so I left,' I answered as steady as I could, keeping eye contact with the general.

'Did Becker know you'd gone to see Gossman?'

'I don't think so.'

'You didn't tell him?'

I shook my head, not knowing if this was the right answer. I had an awful feeling I was walking blindly into a trap. The general, continued. 'How do you think he might have reacted?'

'I don't know.'

'Would he have been upset? Jealous?'

'I don't think so.'

The general got up from the edge of the desk and walked back around to his chair. 'Would you like to see Oberleutnant Becker?'

'Yes!' The word was out far too quickly and eagerly and I knew I had a made a mistake and yet I still couldn't see what the trap was.

The general smiled and pressed a button under his desk. Almost immediately the officer who had fetched me from the shop appeared in the room.

The general nodded at his officer who came over to me. 'Come with me, please.'

I rose, looking at the general, who gave a small raise of

his hand indicating I should leave. 'I'll talk to you again soon,' he said.

I was driven from *le maire's* office to the château where the smell of smoke and charred remains of the structure hung heavy in the air. I followed the officer into the building and was taken to a room at the back.

I gasped at the sight before me.

Lying on a makeshift bed, was Max. His hands were bandaged from his fingertips right up to his elbows. Another bandage was wrapped around his bare chest. One side of his neck was red raw from a burn, reaching up to the side of his face and his hair was singed. A nurse was dressing a wound on his jawline.

'Leave that,' ordered the officer and the nurse quickly obeyed. 'You have five minutes,' said the officer turning to me before following the nurse from the room.

As soon as the door was closed, I rushed over to Max. 'Oh God, Max. What happened?' I went to put my arms around him but didn't want to hurt him. Instead I pressed my face to his uninjured side. 'My darling.' I couldn't stop myself from crying. The smell of smoke and burnt flesh clung to him.

'I'm all right,' said Max, his voice husky, no doubt from the smoke inhalation. 'Are you all right? Have they done anything to you?'

I moved back so I could look at him. 'No. Nothing,' I said, feeling confused by his concern.

'Good.'

Talking was obviously a strain for him and my heart ached at the thought of the damage but I had to know what he'd done. 'What happened?'

He took a moment to swallow before he spoke. 'Started the fire in the bedroom… wanted to burn the evidence… it had to be an intense fire.' He winced and paused for a moment. 'I had to stay in the hall. Told them no one was in the bedroom and to raise the alarm. Had to go back inside to check. I got trapped.'

The guilt stabbed at my heart. I was responsible for this. If I hadn't fought Claus off, none of this would have happened. A tear trickled down my face. 'I'm so sorry,' I whispered.

Max moved his head from side to side. 'I should be sorry for not realising Claus... He tricked me... There was no meeting with the general... He wanted me out of the way.'

I cried silently, stroking Max's hair. 'I feel so responsible. You're badly injured and the doctor is dead. It's all because of what I did.' I was talking out loud to myself as I tried to rationalise what had happened.

Max coughed and took a moment to catch his breath. It was clearly painful even to speak. 'You mustn't blame yourself.'

I fought back my tears. 'I don't know how I'm going to live with myself.'

'You must,' he said with as much insistence as he could manage. 'Now, listen to me... I am to be charged with murder.'

'No!'

'Shh. Simone, please.' He moved one of his bandaged hands to rest against mine even though it caused him to wince in pain. 'You must stick to the story. You saw nothing... You went straight home after the fire. Do you understand? They will try to get you to say you were there so they can blame you for the fire, but you are not to say anything... Promise me.'

'But you can't take the blame for killing Claus,' I spoke frantically in hushed tones. 'I can't let you do that.'

'You must. There is no point both of us dying.'

'No, please,' I began to cry again.

'It's the only way… I am going to confess to the murder. Motivated by jealousy… I am also going to confess to the fire.' He paused and I could see the tears in his eyes but I could also see love. 'Let me do this for you. For myself… Please, Simone.'

'But I can't let you—'

'You can and you must. I cannot have your death on my conscience. You have so much to do with your life after this war is over.' He coughed and it was a moment before he could catch his breath again. 'Please, my darling, don't let this all be for nothing… Be brave. Do not cry otherwise they won't believe you. Promise me you will do this… Do this for me. Do this for us.'

Before I could protest any further, the door opened and the officer came back in. 'Time to go.'

I wanted to throw myself at Max and beg him not to do this. My gaze was fixed on his. I couldn't force myself to break away. The officer grabbed my arm and pulled me out of the room.

'Promise me,' Max mouthed.

I nodded, unable to speak as the door was closed behind me.

FORTY-TWO

2019

Imogen almost got herself run over as she fled across the road at the bottom of the hill. The driver leaned on the horn and shouted something out of the window at her but she didn't care. She raced across the bridge and up the gravel driveway. She had to get inside and shut herself away from the world before she broke down completely. She threw herself on to the sofa, burying her face in a cushion as uncontrollable sobs erupted.

She didn't just cry for the argument she'd had with Laurent, but she cried for the young Elodie given an awful ultimatum that no man had the right to demand of a woman. She cried for the Elodie left to deal with the consequences alone. The Elodie who then had to face a miscarriage alone. She also cried for herself and the loss of her unborn babies. The unfairness, the pain, the guilt. She felt it all as if it were yesterday.

At some point, Denise had crept into the room and sat on the edge of the sofa next to her, stroking Imogen's hair, rubbing her back and whispering soothing words.

It was the heavy knock on the main door that had her

sitting up. 'If it's Laurent, I don't want to see him,' she said to Denise.

Denise went to answer the door and returned a few moments later. 'There's someone here you need to speak to.'

'I said I don't want to talk to him.'

'It's not Laurent.' Denise stepped aside.

Imogen was shocked to see Elodie standing there. She jumped to her feet.

Elodie stepped into the room and looked Imogen up and down. 'God, you look awful,' she said in perfect English.

'Thanks,' muttered Imogen, grateful she was able to converse in English for a change. She wasn't sure she had the mental strength for French right now.

'I'll make you a cup of tea,' said Denise and then to the guest: 'Coffee?'

'No, thank you,' replied Elodie.

'Not for me either,' said Imogen. After Denise left the room, Imogen turned to Elodie. 'What can I do for you?' Imogen almost laughed at herself. How terribly English she sounded, as if she was some sort of receptionist.

'I need to talk to you… about Laurent.'

'Look, I don't know what you've come to say, but there's something you should know first. Today in the square when you saw me with Madame Petit, she told me what happened with you and Laurent. I'm sorry but she thought I should know. But most of all, I'm so sorry for what you went through.'

Elodie looked down at the floor and clenched her mouth tightly, before taking a deep breath. 'What my great-aunt told you may not have been the whole truth,' she said slowly.

Not the whole truth? Why did that not surprise Imogen? Was it because she was beginning to realise that far from being an innocent idyllic village, Trédion was turning out to be a hotbed of lies and secrets? 'Right, I think I'd better have that cup of tea and sit down,' replied Imogen.

'I'll have that coffee,' said Elodie.

A few minutes later the two women were sitting opposite each other at the kitchen table each with a hot drink courtesy of Denise who had now discreetly slipped out of the room.

Imogen was aware how scruffy she looked compared to Elodie, who was wearing stylish white blouse and smart red three-quarter-length trousers, her dark hair perfectly fashioned into a precision-cut bob, which gleamed like a highly polished piece of mahogany.

'You'll have to excuse me,' said Imogen. 'But I came straight from doing the memorial garden. I haven't had time to tidy myself up.' She pulled her hands into her lap to hide her dirty fingernails embedded with soil.

'I'm not here to judge you,' said Elodie. 'I'm here to speak to you as one woman to another.'

Imogen nodded, realising that whatever Elodie was about to tell her was going to be difficult for her. 'I'm won't be judging you either,' she said.

'As I'm sure you've been told, Laurent and I were in a relationship when we were much younger. I was eighteen and he was twenty. It was young love. It was never going to be the real thing but I found myself pregnant.'

Imogen knew this much of course. 'It must have been frightening for you.'

'Yes. It was,' Elodie looked down at her coffee cup. 'You see, the thing is… I mean… what I'm about to tell you, only three people know this – me, Laurent and one other.' She swallowed hard before continuing. 'Laurent and I broke up. He found out that I was actually seeing someone else behind his back.'

Imogen could feel her eyebrows shoot up so high they

were in danger of hitting her hairline. 'You were?' she asked, needing to clarify this point as her mind rushed ahead with what Elodie was going to say next.

'Yes. He was an older man. Married with a family. I thought he might leave his wife for me but he said he couldn't. You see, he was a teacher at the college.'

Imogen almost spat her tea out. 'At your college?'

'Yes, I was young and naïve. I thought it was true love. Anyway, it doesn't end there. I found out I was pregnant.'

There was still so much shame attached to Elodie's words and, as she hung her head, for a moment Imogen thought she was going to cry. Imogen reached across the table and squeezed the other woman's hand. 'It's OK. You don't have to tell me. I can guess what happened next.'

Elodie's head shot up. 'You can't. You see, it wasn't Laurent's child. It was the married man's. He didn't want me to keep it. He said he'd pay for me to go to a private clinic in Vannes. That no one would ever know.' This time the tears fell. She didn't flinch as they streaked down her face and puddled on the table. 'His wife was ill – she had severe post-natal depression after the birth of their second child. He said he couldn't leave her while the children were young.'

'He was worried about his children but not his unborn child?' Imogen heard herself almost spit the words out. 'Sorry, I didn't mean to speak out of turn.'

'But you are right,' said Elodie. 'I said I wouldn't have a termination. We were at… how do you say in English? Ah, yes, stalemate… *impasse.*'

'Did your parents know?'

'I had severe morning sickness and my mother guessed.'

'What did she say?' Imogen watched as Elodie wiped away her tears and straightened up in her seat. There was an inner strength that Imogen could relate to.

Elodie cleared her throat. 'She was horrified. She assumed it was Laurent's.'

'And you didn't tell them differently?'

Elodie shook her head. 'I couldn't. My lover, he begged me not to say anything. I would have done anything for him. You have to understand, I was deeply in love. Practically obsessed.'

'But what about Laurent? Weren't you in a relationship with him too?' Imogen couldn't help feeling indignant at the injustice unfolding in front of her.

'It was never a serious relationship. Not for me anyway.'

'And for Laurent?'

'He came back when he heard. He said he would stand by me. I told him it wasn't his child and I didn't want him. I only wanted the father of my child.'

Imogen rubbed her eyes with her fingertips. What a decent thing for a young twenty-year-old man to offer, even though he had no obligation whatsoever towards mother or child. Oh, how she had misjudged him. 'What happened after that?' she asked quietly.

'He stayed for a few days to try to convince me to change my mind but I was determined not to give in. After he left, I lost the baby.' Her bottom lip trembled and she fought to hold back renewed tears.

Imogen waited until she was sure Elodie had her emotions back under control. 'And your lover never had to admit to anything, you were absolved of all responsibility by your family and Laurent took all the blame, all the anger and all the criticism?' She couldn't hide the disbelief in her voice, even though she had said she wouldn't be judgemental, it was bloody difficult not to be, given all the facts.

'It was the easy way out, I know.'

'You let him take the blame because it was easier for you, not for him. It wasn't better for him. And he... he knew the truth and never once betrayed you. Wow.' Imogen wanted to scream in frustration. It said so much about Laurent, so much she hadn't known. And now she'd probably made a huge mistake. 'Why did you tell me? Why now have you decided to break the silence?'

'Because I'm about to get married and I don't want to take this secret into my married life. I've found someone I love and who loves me.' Her hand slid to her stomach.

Imogen blinked as she took in the ever so slightly rounded face of the woman opposite her. 'You're pregnant, aren't you?'

Elodie looked briefly surprised. 'You guessed.'

'How far?'

'Thirteen weeks. We're very happy and excited but I'm also terrified I'm going to lose this baby. I need to make things right.'

'So, you're telling me this for you, not for Laurent? You want atonement because it suits you now.' There was no way Imogen was going to even try to hide her indignation now. She was outraged on Laurent's behalf.

Elodie appeared taken aback by Imogen's outburst but she took it well. 'Yes. I won't pretend it's not but it's also because I know how much you mean to Laurent.'

It was now Imogen's turn to have the wind knocked from her sails. 'I think you might be reading too much into my relationship with him.'

'You forget, I know Laurent better than anyone else. I also know he is leaving Trédion. You should not let him go.'

'You're giving me advice about relationships.' Imogen gave a laugh. 'That's rich.'

'I'm not asking for forgiveness from you,' responded Elodie. 'You cannot judge me because you have not walked in my shoes but I am now trying to do right for both me, my

342

unborn child, my future husband and for Laurent.' She rose from her seat. 'I've done my bit. The rest is up to you.'

Imogen was too stunned to say anything. Elodie was right – she wasn't in a position to judge her and she'd done exactly what she didn't want. She jumped up from her seat and ran to the front door, catching up with Elodie on the doorstep. 'The father of the child you lost; does he still live in the village?'

Elodie met Imogen's steady gaze with one of equal strength. 'Does it matter?'

'I don't know. Probably not. I just want all the pieces of the puzzle.'

Elodie looked briefly away towards the end of the drive and to Claude's house beyond, before returning to look at Imogen. 'No, he doesn't live in Trédion, but his father does. I'm going home now to tell my mother and my aunt the truth. Most of the truth, that is. All they will be told is that it was a one-night stand at a party. They don't need to know who the father was, just who he wasn't.'

Imogen looked towards Claude's house once again, where a car was just pulling up and a middle-aged man and woman got out, along with two young children who Imogen assumed were their grandchildren. The little ones squealed in delight as Claude appeared at the gate holding his arms out wide to greet his son and his great-grandchildren.

'That's Claude's son. He brings his grandchildren to see Claude every week,' said Elodie. 'He used to be a teacher at the college but he's retired now. He's a good family man.'

Imogen looked back at Elodie with understanding. 'Thank you for telling me everything. I hope you find the happiness you are looking for.'

FORTY-THREE

1944

I went to the château several times over the coming weeks to ask about Max's well-being. I didn't know if he was being treated in the château or if he had been transferred to a hospital. I still had not been able to retrieve my flute. There was no one to ask and how could I explain what it was doing at the bottom of the chute?

Every time I went to see Max, I was told to come back another day. Finally, I could bear it no longer and in desperation I went to *le maire* and asked to see the general.

'Has he requested you to attend?' asked the frosty receptionist.

'No. He hasn't but it's imperative I speak to him.'

'You can't just turn up here and demand to speak to the general.'

At that moment fate was on my side, as the general himself came down the staircase.

'General Werner!' I called out.

He stopped and looked at me, trying to work out where he knew me from. The receptionist by now was on her feet and around the desk, blocking my way while profusely apologising to her superior.

'It's Simone Varon. I played the flute at the château.'

A look of recognition swept over his face. 'Ah, yes, Mademoiselle Varon.' He waved his assistant away. 'What is it you want? I don't take too kindly to being ambushed in my own office.'

I internally flinched at his ownership of the office. 'I'm trying to find out what happened to Max Becker. No one seems to know or if they do, they won't tell me.'

The general looked thoughtful for a moment and then muttered something to the officer who was with him. Then at me. 'Please come through here.' He showed me into a side room, where several women were seated at individual desks – in front of them a typewriter each. An older woman was sitting at a desk overseeing their work. She jumped to attention as the general came in, but he waved her back into her seat. He took me through to a further office beyond the typing room.

I waited nervously as the general took his time to be seated. He pushed his hands together, with his elbows resting on the arms of the chair. 'So, Oberleutnant Becker was charged with murder. He was transferred to a German hospital in Berlin but he never recovered from his injuries.'

The room swayed and my stomach clenched. I had to hold on to the arms of the chair to stop myself from doubling over in agony of the news. 'No,' I said quietly. 'No. No. No.'

'Mademoiselle, please.' The general's voice sounded far away as if he was in a different room. Then, without warning, he slammed his hand down on the desk so hard, I jumped with fright, bringing my focus back to the room. I willed myself not to cry.

'He didn't do it,' I said. 'Max didn't kill your officer…'

'SILENCE!' The general held up his hand. 'That's better. Now, Mademoiselle Varon, listen to me. Of course, Oberleutnant Becker didn't kill his comrade. Becker was one of my finest officers and I know, as well as you do, that he simply wouldn't do that. But, alas, he signed a confession and was adamant he was telling the truth.' Werner sighed and sat back in his chair. 'So, that leaves me with the possibility that perhaps it was you who killed my officer and then, of course, if that were true, I'd have to have you executed. Isn't that right?'

I swallowed hard. 'Yes,' I managed to eke the word out.

'But I've decided to give you a much worse punishment. I shall simply let your fellow countrymen deal with you. They, of course, think you're a collaborator and, no doubt, will hold you responsible for the death of the doctor. I expect in time they will get around to you. Until then, you will have to watch your step, always looking over your shoulder, as you will never know when the knives are out.'

With that, he left the room and the officer escorted me from the building.

My legs felt weak and my stomach churned as the pain and grief swamped me. I don't know how I made it back to the shop but as I bundled in through the door, I crumpled into a heap on the floor.

I spent the next few days in bed at Maman's insistence and I was happy to do so. I didn't want to eat, to talk, to get up, nor get dressed. I just wanted to bury my head under the blankets and hope the world would swallow me up. Despair racked my mind and burrowed itself bone-deep in my body. I didn't care if I died. In fact, death would have been most welcome.

I remember Maman coming in to see me regularly, encouraging me to at least drink some water and if it were not for her and the thought of causing her the same distress and grief I was suffering, then I would not have done what she said.

'Come on, Simone, you must drink and eat a little,' she encouraged on the fifth day. 'There is hope. The Allied troops have landed. I am sure it will only be a matter of time before we are liberated.'

'Are they winning?' I asked.

'The Americans and the British, they are fighting now as we speak. The Germans are trying to hold on but it is not possible. I know we will be freed. You must get your strength up. I need someone to celebrate with me.'

I wasn't sure if she was as convinced as she was making out, but I took heart from the notion. If the Germans retreated then everything that had happened would not be in vain.

That night I prayed for the first time in years that God would spare us and help the Allied forces to free Brittany very soon.

It was, in fact, another forty days before Brittany was liberated. The German troops had been ordered to defend all the major ports around the region and left very few protecting their positions in the interior. The Americans advanced through Brittany, accompanied by the FFI and met very little resistance until they reached the coast.

As the Allied troops drove through Trédion, the whole village came out to cheer and wave at them. Maman, Pierre, who was still recovering from his illness, and I rushed out onto the street to join in the celebrations. We hugged and kissed each other.

'I have prayed for this moment every day for the last five years,' cried Maman. Someone came along and caught Maman in an embrace and they danced and swirled around in an uncontrollable Viennese waltz. Maman threw her head back and laughed out loud, then her dance partner was off, catching hold of another woman and spinning her around.

I hugged Pierre and we laughed together to see Maman so very happy. It had been a long time since we'd seen such undiluted joy on her face.

The crowd was throwing flowers on to the passing vehicles and the American soldiers were cheering and waving back at everyone. Two of the young women in the village had climbed onto the back of a car and were catching the flowers as they were tossed into the air, then holding them aloft like a trophy, squealing in delight, before throwing them back to the crowd.

Amongst all the cheering and celebrations, I could hear an accordion playing and the sound of voices singing along. The bar was open and drinks were being handed out to anyone who wanted one.

Pierre held on to my arm and was tapping me. 'I don't feel very well,' he said, followed by a bout of coughing.

I felt guilty for encouraging him to come out onto the street. He had made such a good recovery recently, it was easy to forget how ill he had been. He tired very easily these days, having not regained all his strength. I secretly wondered if he would always be a little weak and fragile. 'I'll take you home,' I said.

Maman appeared at our side. 'You stay,' she said to me. 'Enjoy the party. I'll take Pierre in and come back in a minute.'

I carried on watching all the celebrations in the street. It was just the most joyous occasion I had ever witnessed in my whole life. Even though I don't think I had ever been happier, at the same time, I couldn't help thinking of Max and my heart broke a little more as I wished he was here with me.

Suddenly, I felt both my arms being grabbed. At first I thought it as another reveller, wanting to dance but as I looked from one side to the other, I realised the men weren't here to celebrate with me. They were wearing FFI armbands and each had a rifle hooked over their shoulder.

'Come with us,' one said. 'Whore.'

I tried to struggle free but they gripped me even harder. It was then Maman appeared back in the street and saw what was happening. She tried to push her way through the crowd towards me, but two more men stepped into her path, blocking her way.

'Maman!' I cried but it was no use.

'Shut up,' snapped the man on my right, the older of the two. 'Unless you want your mother to join you.'

The crowds parted and some of the locals began jeering at me, calling me a whore.

'Mattress for the *Boches*!' someone in the crowd shouted.

A woman rushed forwards and slapped me hard across my face. I had no way to defend myself. Without anyone to stop her, she did it again, this time with a closed fist.

The pain was horrendous and I felt the blood trickle down from my nose. As the men hauled me towards *le maire's* office, I was punched, slapped and spat on several more times.

On the steps to *le mairie*, four other women were already there. One was being held on a stool while a man used a pair of hand shears to shave off her hair.

I cried out, as I realised this was my fate, only to receive a slap and be told to shut up. I knew there was absolutely nothing I could do at this point. I had to accept what was about to happen. If the doctor was still alive, he would vouch for me that I was working for the resistance and these… these brutes, would have to let me go but instead there was no one to help me and I was to be treated as a collaborator.

The head shaving was not just humiliating but savage also. They yanked my head back and dug the shears in. The gathered crowd cheered as the first clump of my hair fell to the ground. When it was over, one of the women who seemed to be overseeing events along with the men, drew a swastika with red lipstick on our foreheads. I was powerless to do anything and could only wonder how a woman could do this to another woman.

If that wasn't bad enough, one of the men who had dragged me over, made us all line up and then systematically ripped our dresses from our shoulders, leaving us in tattered clothing with just our underwear to cover our breasts.

Our final humiliation was to be loaded up onto the back of an open truck and driven around the village like some sort of evil carnival.

When the ordeal was finally over, we were dumped outside the château. I ran as fast as I could down the road until I reached the alleyway that ran along the back of the shop.

Maman was waiting for me at the door. She held me in her arms for a long time as we both cried and cried until there were no more tears. Then she made a hot bath for me in the tub in front of the fire and gently washed my bruised and battered body as I sat in the water hugging my knees to my chest.

FORTY-FOUR

2019

Denise appeared at Imogen's side as they watched the figure of Elodie walk down the driveway. 'Are you OK?'

Imogen turned to Denise. 'I need to get hold of Laurent.' She rushed inside to grab her phone, followed by Denise. 'Laurent never told me the whole truth because he was still protecting Elodie. He's leaving Trédion, I need to speak to him.'

She found her phone in the kitchen and quickly called Laurent. It rang out and went to voicemail.

'Try again,' urged Denise. 'He just might not have been able to answer it in time.'

On the third attempt, Laurent picked up. '*Oui*, hello. Imogen?'

'Where are you?' Imogen could hear a radio playing in the background and was sure Laurent was driving.

'Is everything all right?' he asked, concern heavy in his voice.

'No. Yes. No. I mean, it could be.'

'Imogen you're not making any sense. Wait while I pull over.' The radio was switched off and the background noise of the car travelling abated. 'Now, tell me, are you all right? Has something happened?'

'I'm fine, nothing has happened to me but I need to speak to you… in person. Please?'

'In person?'

'Yes!'

'How soon?'

'Now?'

'OK. Where are you?'

'At the château.'

'I'll be there in twenty minutes.'

Imogen breathed a sigh of relief as the call ended. She turned to Denise who was hovering in the doorway. 'He's coming back.'

'Jolly good, that will give you just enough time to clean yourself up.'

'Shit!' Imogen suddenly remembered how untidy she looked. She raced past Denise and hurtled up the steps to the bathroom.

Fifteen minutes later, Imogen came back downstairs, washed, in clean clothes and her hair brushed. 'There, how do I look?'

'One minute,' said Denise, fishing in her handbag and retrieving a pale pink lipstick. 'Finishing touch and here, have a squirt of my perfume. It's Chanel Number 5 − very appropriate for a meeting with a Frenchman.'

Imogen hurriedly applied the lipstick and gave her wrists a quick spray. 'Oh, he's here,' she said, as his car pulled up on the driveway. Her stomach felt as if a dozen eels were wriggling around inside it.

Denise gave her a kiss on the cheek. With a '*Bon courage, my darling*,' she then left Imogen to speak to Laurent alone.

Imogen opened the door to Laurent, who looked slightly

guarded but at the same time, pleased to see her. 'Nice lipstick,' he said as they went into the living room.

Imogen squeezed her hands together to stop them trembling as she stood opposite him in the middle of the rug. 'I owe you an apology,' she began. 'I've made a mistake and totally misjudged you.'

'OK, apology accepted.' Still he sounded guarded and she couldn't blame him after her outburst earlier.

'Elodie came to see me,' she began. 'She told me the truth about the pregnancy.'

Laurent assessed her with his walnut-coloured eyes, the flecks of gold highlighted by the sun shining through the window. 'That was brave of her after all this time. She must have a good reason,' he said evenly.

'She said she wanted to unburden herself from the guilt, she wanted to unburden you too. She's getting married and wants to make amends. She wants things put right for you as much as herself.'

Laurent rubbed his forehead with his fingertips and exhaled deeply. 'That is more of a relief than I expected it to be.'

'You have done more than anyone would have expected. You have been beyond honourable and loyal.'

'It was easy to let them hate me more,' he said. 'It wasn't everyone, just Madame Petit and her group of gossips but they have lived here all their lives and people pay attention to the matriarchs of the village.'

'Well, hopefully, things will be different now.' Imogen paused. 'Elodie is not going to tell her family everything though.'

'No?'

'She is still going to protect the father of the child.'

Laurent's shoulders relaxed and he nodded as he considered this information. 'And I will too. There has been enough hate in this village.'

'I wish you'd told me but I understand now why you didn't. I'm sorry.'

Laurent nodded. 'Forgiven.'

She waited for him to say something else, but he broke eye contact and pushing his hands into his pockets walked over to the window. Imogen wanted to say more, to ask him not to leave but her nerve left her and she found herself asking about the flute. 'Have you worked out what was so important about the flute?'

'No,' confessed Laurent, turning to face her and sounding rather more business-like. 'I have looked at that flute and case and the sheet of music but I cannot see what my grandmother meant by it would reveal the truth.'

'And she actually said that?' asked Imogen, feeling completely flustered as she tried to focus on their rather polite conversation. How had it gone from personal to professional so soon?

'In the letter she left me. She said it would... you might as well read it yourself. I have it with me.'

Laurent reached into the back pocket of his jeans and pulled out his wallet, before removing a white envelope from inside and passing it to her.

Imogen unfolded the several sheets of paper.

Dear Laurent,

If you are reading this, then it is because my time in this world is up. Please don't grieve for me, for I have had a long and happy life, and I have not done anything I would not do again. Despite living through the occupation, life has been good to me and seen me through to old age, which so many other people of my generation were not able to because of the dreadful things that went on during those years.

I've never wanted to talk about what happened during the war as we were all driven to do things we would not otherwise have done.

After the war, I consider myself fortunate to have married your grandfather. He understood that not everything was as it appeared and he was good enough never to ask me questions despite the obvious hostility from some of the villagers.

As you know, after your grandfather died, I moved back to the apartment to care for my mother, Marianne Varon, and my brother, Pierre. I took your mother with me – she was only two years old. We all lived together in the apartment and I admit, it wasn't ideal, but we did what we had to do. Dear Pierre, he had been such a sickly child and ill health dogged him into his adult life. I was heartbroken when he passed away after another serious bout of pneumonia in the winter of 1964. His poor lungs had been very damaged from when he was ill during the war and had never fully recovered.

I carried on living at the apartment with my mother and your mother. We made a good trio, quite formidable. After your mother married your father and moved away, my own mother, Marianne, died and I was on my own but I didn't mind. I always looked forward to your visits and loved it when you were older and were able to come on your own. We did have fun, didn't we? I've never regretted anything that's happened, not for me personally, but I always resented the fact that your time in the village as a young man wasn't very happy due to the malicious gossips in Trédion.

I have to admit, I did think enough time had gone by to allow the wounds of the past to heal, but I was wrong and some were unwilling or unable to forgive, not least forget. This just made me more belligerent to them and it became almost a stalemate – a cold war.

That said, I cannot deny you have brought much light and happiness to some of my darkest days when my thoughts travel back to those who were not so lucky as I and during the years afterwards when I was shunned and often felt so lonely. You have been one of my greatest pleasures in life.

So, why am I telling you all this now, you may ask?

I accepted a long time ago that I would never win favour with some of the local people and I know you too have experienced this feeling of isolation and rejection. They were so ready to tarnish you with the same brush and that has played on my conscience for a long time. So much so, I cannot end my days knowing I have in some way added to your burden.

It is not for my own peace of mind that I am telling you all this, but so you can have peace at Trédion. Up until recently, I thought memories and talk of what happened here in the village would disappear like a receding tide once all my generation had died but I realise this is not the case. Prejudices, like stories, can be passed down the generations and, as I feared, those same assumptions held against me and what they believed I did, have blighted you. For that, I am truly sorry.

I have also become increasingly concerned that those who did brave things during the war have not been recognised and will never be acknowledged for their efforts. I do not include myself amongst that number, for I do not seek approval or thanks from anyone. I did what I did in the knowledge no one would ever know and I am happy to die that way but I have found my mind travelling back to a very dear friend of mine, Max Becker, a German Officer, who did not have the fortitude to survive the war. And it is for him, and you – two people I have loved the most in the world – that I want my story to be known.

So, my dearest grandchild, I need you to do one important thing for me. In the cellar of the château in Trédion, buried amongst the rubble is my flute. I abandoned it there at the time of the fire and because of the terrible things that happened in that place, I thought it best if it stayed buried forever. Now, though, I need you to find the flute.

Once you do, you will find the proof you need and you will know what to do with it.

I can only pray now that you are able to fulfil my dying wish and

I can rest in peace knowing the burden of those war years have been lifted from our family and Max Becker will be remembered for his kindness and bravery.

Bisous,
    Mémé

Imogen read the letter again. 'So, whatever your grandmother wants you to find out, basically, she has carried a secret around with her for all this time, something that will absolve her of all blame and also any blame attached to this German officer.'

'That's as far as I got,' agreed Laurent. 'She never spoke about Max Becker. I have no idea what she did during the war. This leads me to believe she was part of the resistance but in a secret capacity. I wish she had told me before she died. There are so many questions I want to ask her.'

'I think that's the point,' replied Imogen. 'She never wanted to be questioned about it. She just wants the record set straight, for your benefit rather than her own and for this German officer. She's not worried about her own reputation.'

'But I feel I have failed,' said Laurent. 'There is nothing in the case.'

'Do you think it's got lost at some point?'

'I don't see how if it's been in the cellar all this time. I'll let you have another look at it.'

He returned a few minutes later with the instrument and passed it over to Imogen. She flicked open the catches and took a moment to look at the flute, running her hand along it as it lay embedded in position. 'You've cleaned it,' she observed.

'Just some gentle cleaning. It was so tarnished before.'

'It's amazing to think this has gone untouched for all

those years. The last person to see this was your grandmother.'

'It's hard to comprehend,' agreed Laurent.

Imogen lifted the pieces from the velvet cloth they were nestled in and examined each section carefully. Laurent was right: there wasn't anything else there. Whatever Simone Varon had been referring to in her letter, it had long gone.

She replaced the pieces of flute and was just about to close the case, when she noticed a small section of the lining fabric in the lid wasn't sitting as flat as the rest.

'What is it?' asked Laurent peering over her shoulder.

'I'm not sure. Just noticed this edge here is folded over.' She poked at it with her finger. 'Look, it's loose.'

'Maybe it has just come unstuck.'

'No. I don't think so.' Imogen picked up a pencil from the side table she'd been using to sketch out part of the garden earlier that day and slid the point inside the fabric, moving it away from the case and then proceeded to untuck the rest of the edge until she was able to fold the fabric back.

'There's something there!' said Laurent in amazement.

There was a piece of paper folded in half, hidden between the lid and the lining. Carefully, so as not to tear the paper, Imogen removed it and handed the thin yellow sheet to Laurent.

'It's a timetable of some description.' He looked at it more closely. 'It looks like a train timetable and this here,' he pointed to a column, 'this must be what was on board.'

Imogen gripped Laurent's arm. 'You know what this is, don't you?'

Laurent shook his head. 'I'm not sure.'

'Look at the date: May 1944. That's just before the D-Day Landings. It's a copy of the trains the Germans were using to move personnel, arms and ammunition about. You know the resistance sabotaged railway lines and it wasn't just random targets; it was specific trains. Especially so in the run-up to D-Day. This would have been gold to the resistance and the Allied troops. Your grandmother must have been smuggling this information to them.'

Laurent looked shell-shocked as he took in what Imogen was relaying. 'So she wasn't a collaborator?'

'She was a resistance fighter. Your grandmother was brave and courageous but no one ever knew and she never told them.'

'All those years she lived here and the villagers continued to snub her because they thought she was a traitor to her country.' Laurent pinched the bridge of his nose.

'And look at this,' said Imogen excitedly as she skipped from Simone's letter to the piece of music. 'This music was written by Maximillian Karl Becker. Look at the name in your grandmother's letter. It has to be the same Max!'

Laurent looked even more shocked than he had before. 'He must have been helping her in some way.'

'You have to let *le maire* know,' said Imogen. 'The whole village has to know. Your grandmother should be honoured in some way. Then they will have to accept they were wrong and that means they can't hold it against you.'

'I'm not worried about myself,' said Laurent.

'I am though. I want you to be accepted here. I don't want you snubbed for things you haven't done. I want them to know you are a good man. It's what your grandmother wanted and, not only that, her story deserves to be told.'

'You sound like you want me to hang around?'

Imogen wasn't going to let the chance to make her feelings clear slip by this time. 'I do. I want that very much.'

Laurent nodded. 'I want that too. Very much.'

FORTY-FIVE

2019

Imogen made her way down to the end of the garden with her morning cup of tea to admire her and Laurent's handiwork where they had spent a backbreaking week of planting out the new orchard and digging out the pond in the wild garden.

The trees would take a few days to settle into their new spot, having been brought in from the local garden centre in Ploërmel. Today they would be filling up the pond and Imogen had a stack of plants waiting to be put into place. She took her phone from her pocket and snapped a few shots, before sending them to Denise with a message.

Imogen: Phase 2 completed! Should have it all finished by the time you next visit. x

Since Denise's first visit to the château, she and Imogen had kept in touch much more regularly and their relationship had moved on from two women grieving for the loss of a husband and son, to a deep and solid friendship born out of grief but grown out of love and respect. Not unlike her garden, reflected Imogen.

Her relationship with Denise wasn't the only one that

had developed for the better either. The past few months Laurent had split his time between Paris during the week and Trédion at weekends. It was their first tentative steps into their relationship and Imogen couldn't be happier how it was turning out. It had been nerve-racking initially but she had gradually found herself falling in love with Laurent and knew he felt the same way. It wasn't the rush of first love, not when they had been through so much in the past, but the gentle simmer of a mature and heartfelt love.

As she made her way back up the garden to the kitchen, she could see Laurent standing at the window with the phone to his ear. He winked at her as she came in and she rinsed out her cup while he finished his call.

'Thank you so much,' he was saying. 'That's fantastic news. I really appreciate it. Of course, we'd be delighted and honoured to attend. Thank you. *Au revoir.*'

'What was that all about?' asked Imogen as she looked at Laurent's rather bemused expression.

He turned to her and grinned before lifting her off her feet and spinning her around. Imogen laughed despite having no idea what was going on. 'That was *le maire* himself,' explained Laurent, as he brought Imogen back down on her feet, but still kept her in his arms.

'Bernard?' queried Imogen.

'Oh, yes, I forgot you two were on first-name terms now,' he teased.

'Just tell me, what did he say?'

Laurent's face grew serious. 'They are going to have my grandmother's name engraved on the memorial in the village.' His eyes shone with tears.

'Oh, Laurent, that is wonderful,' cried Imogen. 'The best news ever.'

'And he wants us to be there for the unveiling,' said Laurent.

Imogen hugged Laurent tightly. She was so pleased for him. It was as if the village was not only accepting Simone but Laurent too. It had been a gradual welcoming of a prodigal son throughout the village and even old Madame Petit acknowledged Laurent with a polite *bonjour* whenever she saw him and Imogen knew they had Elodie to thank for that.

The buzz of the recently installed doorbell sounded out and Imogen went off to answer it.

She returned carrying a box. 'It was the postman. It's for you. It's actually addressed to your grandmother's apartment, but he said he knew you'd be here.'

'Ah, as I've always said, everyone knows everything in this village,' said Laurent good-humouredly taking the package from her.

Laurent opened the parcel on the kitchen table. Inside was a sealed box file and an envelope on top. Laurent picked it up. 'That's my grandmother's handwriting.'

He took out the handwritten letter. Imogen waited patiently while he read it.

'What is it?' asked Imogen, noting the frown on Laurent's face.

He passed the letter over to her.

Dear Laurent,

If you're reading this then you've done what I asked and although I will not be able to thank you, please know that this was one of the most important things you could have ever done for me. I had to make certain you'd found the flute before I sent you this final letter, as without the flute and what you found, there would be no evidence to back up my story.

No doubt, you have far more questions than answers now and I feel it is only right that I tell you everything that happened during the war.

Inside the box you will find all the answers to your questions and answers to questions you didn't even know you had.

Thank you for everything you have done for me in life and in death.

Take care my darling.

Bisous,
  Mémé

Imogen put the letter on the counter and stood next to Laurent as they both eyed up the box file. 'I suppose you should open it,' she said.

'I suppose I should.'

Laurent took a knife from the block and sliced through the tape. He hesitated with his hands on the lid. 'What do you think it is?'

Imogen shrugged. 'Who can say where your grandmother is concerned,' she said with a smile. 'Perhaps another task.'

Laurent rolled his eyes. 'It had better not be.'

He lifted the lid to reveal a ream of A4 paper, held together by two wide elastic bands. Imogen read the top page.

Memoirs of Simone Varon:
For my dearest grandson, Laurent Roussell

Laurent lifted the wad of paper from the box and slipped off the elastic bands. He flicked through the papers. 'It's a manuscript.'

'Look at the date it starts: 1944,' said Imogen. 'Your grandmother must have got someone to type this up for her, maybe the *notaire*.'

Laurent flicked through the pages. 'My grandmother's story,' he said, looking in amazement at page after page of typing.

'This is so exciting,' said Imogen. 'All the secrets, all the mystery, all the questions we still have… This is going to answer them all. Your grandmother's story is finally going to be told.'

FORTY-SIX

2019

Imogen stood in front of the memorial stone, her arm linked with Laurent's, as they gazed at the new inscription.

'It's perfect,' said Imogen.

'I still can hardly believe it.' Laurent stepped forward and ran his finger across his grandmother's name. 'And I have you to thank for this.'

After he had received the memoirs from his grandmother, Laurent had been unsure what to do with them, but Imogen had been certain from the moment she'd finished reading them.

It had taken some gentle persuasion, but she had finally got Laurent to agree to taking them to Bernard Le Roux, *le maire*, to share all of Simone's story of the weeks leading up to D-Day and what she did so loyally and bravely for her country.

Today, there had been a small but poignant ceremony to commemorate the addition of Simone's name to the memorial stone and to Trédion's history.

'I know your grandmother was content for her part in the resistance to pass without acknowledgement,' said

Imogen. 'But I'm certain she would be secretly pleased her name has been added to the memorial.'

'I'm sure she would,' agreed Laurent.

'There is one thing that I've never quite understood,' said Imogen. 'Why did your grandmother stay in Trédion? What kept her here after everything that happened?'

'I guess after the war she had nowhere to go. She was only young and then she met my grandfather. He was a lot older than her but had known her for a long time. He came back from the war and took over the running of his family farm. My grandmother was given a job there and they fell in love.'

'The farm was here?' asked Imogen.

'A mile or so outside the village. When my grandfather died, the farm went to his brother. My grandmother, along with my mother who would have been about two years old, moved back to the apartment and helped run the shop. Her mother, Marianne, wouldn't have wanted to give up her livelihood. And again, where would she have gone?'

'I suppose the country was on its knees after the war. There just wasn't the opportunity to pack up and move, not without help from family,' said Imogen.

'Exactly.' He took Imogen's hand. 'I don't think my grandmother would have left anyway, even if she had the opportunity. She loved the village, despite it not loving her back. Plus she was bloody-minded and stubborn. She would have refused to be hounded out of the place she grew up in and went through so much for.'

'I'm glad the whole truth has finally come out,' said Imogen.

'I feel as if a line can now be drawn under everything that has happened, to my grandmother and to me. For the first time in many years, I feel welcomed in Trédion.'

'And you are,' said Imogen. She looked up at the gate of

the memorial garden. 'And so is someone else.' She nodded at the sight of Denise talking to Bernard Le Roux, or rather, giggling.

Laurent gave a small laugh. 'Is she flirting with *Monsieur Le Maire*?'

'I believe she is.' It was rather amusing to see Denise laughing with the mayor who was clearly very taken with her. His English, although a little broken, obviously wasn't a barrier for them.

Denise turned as they reached the gate. 'Oh, Imogen. I was just telling Bernard how lovely the ceremony was.'

'Yes, it was. Thank you again, Bernard,' said Imogen.

'It was my pleasure.' He shook hands with Laurent. 'I feel honoured to have read your grandmother's story. It makes me proud to be mayor of this village.' He thumped his heart with a clenched fist. 'And thank you for allowing your grandmother's memoirs to be displayed in the town hall.'

'Bernard and I were just going for a coffee,' said Denise.

'Oh, yes, would you care to join us?' *Le maire* looked at Imogen and Laurent.

'That's very kind of you, but we're going to take a look at the display,' replied Laurent.

They said their goodbyes, with Denise promising to see them back at the château later that evening. 'Good luck!' she called over her shoulder as she strolled away, her arm through the mayor's.

'Good luck?' Imogen looked at Laurent. 'What did she mean by that?'

Laurent cleared his throat. 'Ah, yes. Erm. Well, I happened to mention something to Denise the other day when you were out in the garden and, you know what she's like – she's taken it as a foregone conclusion.'

'What exactly?'

'I wanted to speak to you first and I was going to wait until all this fuss had died down a little bit but now it looks as if Denise has forced my hand.'

'About what?' Imogen wished Laurent would just tell her and his hesitancy was troubling her. It wasn't like him at all.

'You see, I was thinking about making my move to Trédion a permanent one,' he said at last. 'I would need to go the Paris office once a week, but other than that, I could work from home.'

'Oh, that's fabulous news!' said Imogen. 'Your grand-mother would be thrilled.'

'I was hoping maybe you would be as well.'

'Of course! I'm very happy for you.' She paused in her celebrations. He looked disappointed. Had she said some-thing wrong?

'Hmm, this isn't going quite as I planned.' Laurent looked at her intently. 'I'm trying to say… my move to Trédion is not the only thing I want to make permanent. I would like us to be more permanent too.'

'Us?'

'If you want to. If you feel you can, that is. I know James is a part of you, a part of your heart and always will be. Without him, you would not be you,' said Laurent earnestly. 'You would not be the woman I have fallen in love with.'

Imogen thought of James. The pain and grief that had always put in an appearance first were instead playing second fiddle to the love and comfort she now associated with his memory. For some time, Imogen had been aware of a gentle release as if James was letting her go.

She reached out and found Laurent's hand. 'I didn't think I'd ever love anyone again,' she said. 'I didn't think there was a single soul in the world who would match up to James and what we had. And I was right… but… that was the old me, the grieving Imogen Wren. You've shown me that it is possible not just to live again, but to love again, and the new me, loves you very much.'

The relief on Laurent's face was undisputed. 'Thank you for everything you have done,' whispered Laurent after they'd finished kissing.

'I'm not sure it was really down to me,' said Imogen, looking back at the newly engraved name on the memorial. She turned back to Laurent as a feeling of contentment and excitement at the future wrapped itself around her. 'Come on, we have one more thing to do.'

'We do?'

Imogen led the way across the road and into the main street, where she made Laurent wait outside the florist's shop while she nipped in and picked up a delicate bouquet of purple irises.

'I haven't got any in my garden otherwise I would have used them,' she explained to Laurent as he crossed the road alongside her.

'The French national flower,' said Laurent. 'Very pretty.'

They reached *le mairie*. 'I asked Bernard if it would be OK to leave these by the side of your grandmother's diary.'

She could see the gesture had touched Laurent and he visibly swallowed hard to keep his composure. 'Thank you.' He lifted her hand to his lips, before going inside.

On the left of the marbled reception area was a rectangular glass display cabinet where a bound copy of Simone Varon's memoirs was on display. Next to it was a photograph of Simone when she was about eighteen, standing beside a grand piano with her flute to her mouth. It was the photograph Laurent had found tucked inside the sheets of paper from his grandmother. There was a short passage about Simone outlining how she'd helped the resistance and on the other side was her flute, buffed and shining like it was brand new.

Imogen handed Laurent the bouquet of irises and he placed them reverently on top of the glass.

The memoirs were open on the first page, words Imogen knew by heart and which she felt were just as fitting today as they were then. They could all learn a lesson from Simone Varon, thought Imogen as she read them once again.

Trédion, April 1944

Papa always told us that to be brave doesn't mean you have no fear, it just means you can move forwards in spite of that fear.

ACKNOWLEDGMENTS

On the outskirts of a village in the Morbihan department of Brittany, there is a small monument on the side of the road, dedicated to four local men: Theophile Denoual, his son Henry Denoual, Yves Kouriou and Marcel Sene, who gave their lives in 1944 in the fight against the German occupation. I've passed that monument many times over the years and for a long time wondered about the men and the events leading up to their deaths. My original research didn't throw up much more than their names being listed as victims of German occupation but, in more recent years, the internet has revealed what happened to each of them. Whilst this book is in no way shape or form their story, the monument and the sacrifice by the people of France inspired me to write *All That We Have Lost*.

A lot of the research for this book came from a visit to the Musée de la Résistance Bretonne at Saint-Marcel, Brittany, where there is a wealth of information, personal testimonies, recreated street scenes and much more, giving an insight into what life was like during the occupation for the local residents and the important role the resistance played in the liberation of Brittany.

I would like to take the opportunity to thank Emily Ruston, who first saw this book when it was a very rough first draft several years ago and who gave me great feedback to shape it into a full-length novel.

Also, thank you to my editors, Hannah Smith and Hannah Todd, for their advice and support for this story, as well as all the team at Aria who work behind the scenes to get a book to publication.

As always, thank you to my agent, Hattie Grünewald, for being on the other end of an email or a phone call with much-appreciated words of wisdom and for making sure things run smoothly.

Finally, a HUGE thank you to all you wonderful readers and book bloggers. Without your support, I wouldn't be able to continue to bring these stories to you.

ABOUT THE AUTHOR

SUZANNE FORTIN also writes as Sue Fortin a *USA Today* and Amazon UK & USA best-selling author, with *The Girl Who Lied* and *Sister Sister* both reaching #1 in the Amazon UK Kindle chart in 2016 and 2017 respectively. Her books have sold over a million copies and translation rights for her novels have been sold worldwide. She was born in Hertfordshire but had a nomadic childhood, moving often with her family, before eventually settling in West Sussex where she now lives with her husband and family.

Find her online at www.suefortin.com

Hello from Aria

We hope you enjoyed this book! If you did, let us know, we'd love to hear from you.

We are Aria, a dynamic fiction imprint from award-winning publishers Head of Zeus. At heart, we're committed to publishing fantastic commercial fiction – from romance to sagas to historical fiction.

Visit us online and discover a community of like-minded fiction fans.

You can find us at:

www.ariafiction.com

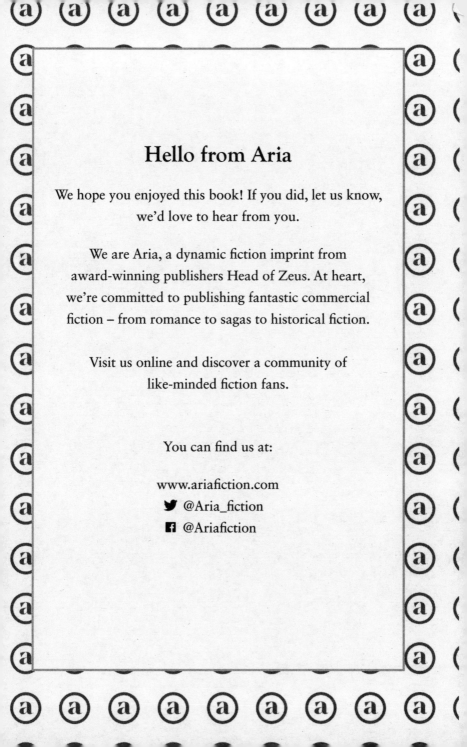 @Aria_fiction

 @Ariafiction